NO
MORE
GOOD

Also by Angela Winters

NEVER ENOUGH

VIEW PARK

Published by Kensington Publishing Corporation

NO MORE MORE GOOD

A VIEW PARK NOVEL

ANGELA WINTERS

Dafina Books

KENSINGTON PUBLISHING CORP.

www.kensingtonbooks.com

I want to dedicate this book to Harriet
for introducing me to the pen and pad.

1

"What is this, Daddy?" Six-year-old Daniel Chase was standing over something in the hallway of his uncle's penthouse condo in downtown L.A.

"What is what?" Thirty-year-old Michael Chase waited for Evan, Daniel's twin brother, to get inside before closing the door behind him.

"It's a bra!" Evan rushed to his brother, picking up the lacy pink lingerie for his father to see, his little brown hand waving it in the air.

Michael sighed, realizing it might be a mistake to bring his boys over to his brother's place. He should have known something this like would happen. He'd been warned last month when he walked in on Carter and a Brazilian model having very loud sex hanging halfway off the dining room table.

"Put that down," Michael ordered. "Just drop it."

"These are panties!" Evan was reaching for the matching bottoms just a few feet away. They were lying on top of a silk cocktail dress.

"Don't touch that." Michael took his son's arm.

"Mommy has these." Evan struggled to get away from his father. "Is Mommy here?"

"All mommies have these, stupid." Daniel rolled his eyes.

"Uncle Carter needs to do laundry." Michael cautiously led his boys down the hallway, praying that he wouldn't have to explain the birds and bees to them today. That really wasn't on the schedule.

"Where is he?" Daniel asked impatiently as soon as they were at the steps to the living room of the three-thousand-square-foot, three-bedroom penthouse condo.

"He's probably working in his office," Michael answered. "Working hard."

He led his boys to the living room sofa and reached for the remote control. "You boys stay here, do you understand?"

Evan was already looking antsy, eager to get out of his church clothes. They were both used to being able to run wild whenever they were here.

Michael found a suitable television station on the large plasma screen on the wall. "Just watch this and don't move."

"Why not?" Evan asked.

"Look at me," Michael ordered, waiting until both of them did so. Keeping stern eye contact, he said, "Because I said so. Do you understand?"

Daniel nodded, but Evan just shrugged, always the difficult one.

As Michael made his way to the master bedroom, passing scattered pieces of clothing along the way, he wasn't looking forward to the reason he was sent over here by their mother. He had to remind Carter to show up tonight at Chase Mansion, their parents' fifteen-thousand-square-foot estate in View Park, to celebrate in his honor. Carter hadn't been answering his phone for three days now, so Janet sent Michael to track him down.

This wasn't the first time in the last six months Carter had "disappeared." Ever since his fiancé, Avery Jackson, left him, Carter would leave for long periods of time. Avery not only left Carter, but left L.A. and didn't want to be found. He'd gone ballistic when he realized she had no intention of coming back.

He had become a Jekyll and Hyde, moving between two states of being. One was an obsessed psycho desperate to find Avery, who he swore on the Bible was the only love of his life, using the considerable means at his disposal whether legal or not. The other was a reckless drunk who didn't care about Avery, swore he was better off without her, and wanted to prove it by nailing every woman he could get his hands on.

And the bra and panties in the hallway suggested Carter had been doing just that. This was the Carter that their parents were concerned about, the one who could get the family in real trouble.

And trouble for this family meant more than it did for others. The Chase family was American black royalty. They were not part of the entertainment or sports worlds, which high society looked down on. Those people didn't belong to, nor were they invited into, the world the Chase family ran in. No, the Chases were a cut above that. Filthy rich was where the Chase family stood—or stood out depending on how you looked at it.

The family was led by Steven Chase, a man from humble beginnings who built his cosmetics company, Chase Beauty, into a multibillion-dollar corporation. He had become an American titan and used the family's billions to influence business and politics all the way to Capitol Hill. His money was invested in several industries, including real estate in some of the most exclusive areas in the western United States.

Meanwhile, his wife, Janet, brought social standing to the family as the daughter of high-society East Coast lawyers with a strong heritage and several generations of wealth and community leadership. From their gated palace in the mostly black, affluent suburb of View Park, she single-handedly took over L.A.'s society scene, black and white, and created an empire envied by even the best East Coast families. Together, no one could rival what they had created.

And although it was Steven's money, influence, and power that put out the fires his children started, it was Janet who was the architect of the Chase family image and publicity. With the recent family scandals still lingering, she couldn't allow Carter to throw the family into another one. Especially not one of a sexual nature, which of course is what Carter was known for. He not only slept with lots of women, but he also treated them badly when he was through. Word was starting to get around, and that can be dangerous.

Michael stood in the doorway to Carter's bedroom and observed the mess in front of him. He could only smile because Carter was such a neat freak, almost to the point of obsessive, and here he was, living like a frat boy complete with a naked woman sprawled facedown on the bed.

Carter Chase's light brown eyes flew open as he heard a loud bang. Had something just happened or was it the awful pounding in his head again?

"Wake up!" Michael yelled, closing the door behind him. "It's afternoon, boy."

Carter struggled to sit up on his bed with his hand pressing against his forehead. He felt like shit. "What the fuck are you doing here, man?"

His younger brother, dressed in a sharp gray suit, sat down on the bed looking at him with a smirk on his face. At least Carter thought it was a smirk. Things were a little blurry.

"You know I brought my boys here," Michael said. "You got her thong in the hallway. They don't need to see that."

"Don't come by uninvited, then." Carter cleared his throat.

Michael nodded to the naked, chocolate body next to Carter. "She is?"

Carter turned his head slowly, because that was all he could do to keep it from exploding. Nice ass, was all he could think of. "I don't know."

"That's smart." Michael was envious of his brother's wanton freedom. With his having been married seven years himself, things were a bit more complicated. "This is what Mom is talking about."

"Can you not mention her right now?" Carter asked. He leaned back against the headboard. "What day is it?"

"She's afraid you're going to get some strange girl pregnant."

"Like you did?" Carter asked, reminding Michael of how he had introduced his current wife to the family seven years ago.

"Touché." Michael made a fist and socked Carter in the arm.

"Stop." Carter pointed to the half-empty condom box on the dresser. "I'm not stupid."

"But you don't know her name."

"Her name doesn't matter," Carter said. "She's getting out of here as soon as she wakes up."

The woman made a sound as if she'd heard Carter, but didn't move. It wouldn't matter to him if she sat up and started a scene. She was just some hot chick who had offered to buy him a drink at Level Three Nightclub. They moved on to one of the club's infamous beds with the curtains closed. Less than twenty minutes later, he took her home. In these matters, he preferred to go to the woman's place, so he could leave as soon as he was done, but this one had a kid and a mother at home and . . . well, a very nice ass.

"Mom sent you here?" Carter asked.

"No one has been able to reach you for days. I thought you'd gone off to chase after Avery again."

Carter felt his temperature boil at the mention of her name. "She's not in Tampa."

"Last month it was Atlanta."

"It was never Atlanta!" Carter swung around on the bed, feeling the room move around him. "I told you she was never in Atlanta. Her stupid sister used to go to school there, so I—"

"Hey!" Michael stood up. "Don't yell at me. I don't give a shit where Avery is. And last week you said you didn't either."

"I didn't," Carter lied. "I don't. She can be in hell for all I care."

"Who do you think you're talking to?" Michael asked. "I've seen you break down and all . . . this. Like it's not all about her."

"So you're my therapist now?"

Michael turned away from his brother, not willing to get caught up in this argument again. There was no talking to him when it came to his precious Avery. Instead he walked over to the full-length mirror and checked himself out, something he never tired of doing. He smiled at his fine, dark features. Everyone said he looked like Sidney Poitier at his most handsome, but Michael knew he looked much better than that.

"What about Sunday?" Michael asked.

Carter didn't feel like facing the family. He was tired of having to put on that perfect front that was such a lie. His life was a mess and he had embraced that. He didn't appreciate his mother making him act as if everything was okay.

After finding out Carter paid a woman to have sex with her fiancé, Alex, in order to win her away from him, Avery left him. Despite everything he had done—the millions it had cost him to hide his mistake and all he promised never to do again—she handed him his engagement ring and walked away. Carter was devastated, but never considered giving up. He had come to love Avery, the middle-class girl next door, more than he knew he was capable of loving a woman. She was different from him, but she quickly became the only thing that mattered in his life. So there was no doubt in his mind he would win her back. It would take some time and a lot of work, but he would get her back. After all, he was Carter Chase and what woman could resist him?

Then Avery disappeared. Actually, she ran away with her family's help, and Carter hadn't been able to find her. It seemed impossible, considering he had the power of the Chase name and all its money and connections. If only her father hadn't been chief of police of View Park and her brother a detective, he would have been able to impose himself on them more. They were keeping an eye on everything he did in trying to find Avery, waiting for the chance to catch him breaking the law. He'd even gotten a call from the FBI after a bug was found in Nikki Jackson's car. They couldn't trace it to him, but they all knew he'd had it done. It was driving him crazy.

He'd begun trying to find her immediately, his only distractions being the law firm he ran and the commitment he'd made to his father to look after Chase Beauty while his parents were away for his mother's rehab treatment. He had everyone she knew traced and bugged. He put a flag on Avery's Social Security number and credit cards, but her family found out and he was blocked out after only one week. He tried to get the police involved, but Avery's father convinced them that she wasn't missing and of course they sided with him. They were getting in contact with Avery some way that satisfied Missing Persons enough.

Even Carter's deep connections as one of the hottest up-and-coming lawyers in L.A. couldn't help him.

After a few months, he gave up and decided he didn't care. It was all a lie, but he knew it would drive him crazy if he didn't at least try to convince himself he didn't want her anymore. He called off all but one of the ten private investigators he had on retainer but still remained focused on the Jackson family. The Jacksons knew he was following them and they were able to elude him at every step. Still, whenever they left L.A., Carter had someone on them, searching for Avery. The last trip had been to Tampa, Florida, followed by a rental car driven to St. Petersburg, which was where Avery's mother, Nikki, disappeared before showing up in Charlotte, where she caught a plane back home to L.A. Carter had sent his P.I. to Charlotte two days ago.

"You're coming to the celebration whether you want to or not. It's for you."

"My birthday was last month," Carter said.

"It's not for your birthday, asshole. You better come, you bastard!"

"Stop yelling." Carter covered his ears.

"Stop being such a—"

"She might be in Charlotte," Carter said.

Michael sighed, feeling pity for the brother he had always looked up to. Carter had never been this sick over a woman. "You don't have time for another trip."

"I'm not going until my P.I. comes back with proof."

"What about the board?" Michael asked.

Carter made a grumbling sound. "That's what the party is about, right?"

Michael couldn't believe this. "You're going to be made a member of the board of directors Wednesday, Carter. That's a big deal."

"I know," Carter said. "I'll be there."

"Do you have any idea how important this is to Dad?"

"Of course I do. It's important to me too."

The idea that he would be made a member of Chase Beauty's board was still odd to Carter, considering that when he made the choice to start his own law firm instead of going to work for

Daddy, Steven had all but promised him he'd never be on the board. It had been a major bone of contention between him and his father and their relationship, which had always been on edge. It had been better some times than others, but never recovered from that decision to do his own thing years ago.

"Nothing is important to you anymore," Michael said, concealing his envy.

Michael was always a little on edge when Carter and their father started getting close again, even though he knew it never lasted. Still, this one-millionth make-up was lasting longer than usual and Michael felt left out. He was the favorite son and that position meant more than anything in the world to him. Chase Beauty was going to be his, and Carter's so-called invasion didn't make him happy. Michael had always been fine with Carter as the company's legal firm on retainer. He enjoyed working with him almost as much as he enjoyed working with his father. But this was more, much more. He loved his brother without question, but couldn't ignore that he felt uneasy about his formally joining the company.

"You better straighten up," Michael ordered. "Avery is gone. Stop being such a pussy and get over it."

Carter stood up from the bed and faced his brother head-on. Both a little over six feet, they met eye to eye. Even though his head was spinning, Carter stayed steady. "Back off."

Michael didn't blink. "You lost her, but you keep this up, you'll lose everything."

Carter smiled, because at that moment, he believed Michael, but he really didn't care.

"I need you to tell me what you mean when you say . . . complete renovation." Marcus Abbott, interior designer to the fabulously wealthy, made a quotation marks gesture around his last two words. "I mean, this pool is only two years old. It has all the state of the art technology, so—"

"It's ugly," Kimberly Chase answered with a pout. "That's what I mean."

The pool wasn't the only thing Kimberly hated about the new house. Actually, the house was beautiful. Nestled in the ultralux

Hollywood Hills, the gated, Tuscan-inspired villa was six thousand square feet with four bedrooms, sixteen-foot-high ceilings, and opulent furnishings purchased by a world-famous designer from every end of the globe. It had everything Kimberly wanted: oversized French doors, large windows for ample sunlight, precision-cut inlaid imported marble, custom wood floors, an enormous gourmet kitchen, a dramatic rotunda entryway with an Italian Renaissance–styled garden and a four-car garage.

There was one problem; it was a consolation prize.

It was a rushed choice made so because of a plan gone horribly wrong. Under any other circumstance, it might have been her dream home and it wasn't as if she hadn't tried to make it so. They had been living in the house for four months now and Kimberly was miserable. She believed if she could change everything, it might make her happy. She was starting with the pool, expecting to spend much of the upcoming summer out back.

"This whole area looks like it's from the eighties." Kimberly's Jimmy Choo heels clacked against the stone-paved ground surrounding the house's backyard pool as she walked the length of it. "Plus, it's . . . it's a square."

Marcus nodded with an upturned nose. "I can't imagine what the designer was thinking. This beautiful house and then this pool? Must have been designed by a straight man."

"Even a child would have been more creative," Kimberly said, hands on hips. "I want it to be beautiful and luxurious."

"Speaking of children." Marcus looked around. "Where are those little hell-raising munchkins of yours?"

"At church."

Kimberly had known Marcus for a while through friends he had decorated for, but hadn't really spent time with him until she moved into her new home. The few times they'd been together, he was getting increasingly personal with his questions. He was fabulous with a capital F and reminded her of the best parts of her life as a model in New York. The life she'd had before she met and married Michael Chase and entered the world of unreasonable expectations and unheard-of snobbery. Besides, she needed a friend. She was all alone now.

"They are with my husband," she finished.

He looked down at his watch, the only thing shinier than the silver-sequined top he was wearing. "They must love them some Jesus to still be there at this hour."

Kimberly looked down at her watch too. It was getting late in the afternoon. She didn't want to worry because he had the boys, but Michael was so unpredictable of late. Not really of late. He'd been this way for the last six months. Ever since the incident they never talked about, the one where he blamed her for almost killing his mother, Janet, even though she was never really near death.

Although she had fantasized about the death of the woman who had treated her like trash from the first moment she met her, Kimberly never really intended for Janet to end up in the hospital. No one would have been good enough for her precious Prince Michael, but certainly not a piece of nothing from nowhere with no family, education, or social status who showed up pregnant and completely oblivious. And Janet had reminded her of that every day; made much easier by the fact that Michael insisted they live at Chase Mansion.

Kimberly had had her fill. The emotional, verbal, psychological torture was too much to take and this was saying something considering the childhood she had had. Growing up poor with an alcoholic mother, an absent and mostly in-jail father, and a gang-banging brother who was shot to death in the alley behind a strip club, Kimberly had withstood a lot. She had run away and been pimped out at fifteen. After two years on the streets, she found her way into modeling, realizing that her exceptional beauty could be good for more than a cheap blow job.

Michael had accepted her past because he loved her so much, but he warned her that his family wouldn't, and when he found out she was pregnant, he told her they would have to get married because of who he was. He would also have to erase her past. Kimberly should have known what she was getting into when a man as incredible as Michael was too scared to tell his parents the truth.

But she wasn't the only one with a secret. Janet had one, a much smaller one, but to a woman obsessed with perfection who presented herself as the paragon of virtue, a small secret could be bigger than a bomb. Kimberly thought she could bring Janet's French ex-lover, Paul Devereaux, back to L.A. to reveal, and hopefully rekindle, the affair they had while Janet was engaged to Steven, while threatening to expose the abortion Janet had as a result of the lurid summer getaway in Paris.

And it was working. Steven had walked in on Janet kissing Paul and he'd left her. Janet was falling apart and Kimberly had her where she wanted her. She just hadn't counted on the old hag being so much of a drug addict that she was taking uppers and downers together. One bad drug interaction, washed down with a bottle of champagne, led to a trip to the hospital and Kimberly's plan went down the tubes.

Being the genius she was, Janet spun everything in her favor. Instead of being the lying, deceitful bitch she truly was, she became the victim of her regretful past dredged up by the evil, low-class daughter-in-law who showed her true ghetto character and almost killed the matriarch of the untouchable Chase family. She played it beautifully.

At her lowest, Kimberly feared losing Michael. He turned colder than the Arctic to her; shut her off, threatened to divorce her, take the boys away, and make her pay. Ultimately, things settled down and Kimberly could once again count on his love for her, their incredible sexual chemistry, and their boys to keep them together.

But nothing had been the same since.

"Gavea, baby," Marcus said. "That's what you . . . Kimberly?"

Kimberly broke from her trance. "I'm sorry, what?"

Marcus walked over to her as if he were a runway model. It was the way he walked everywhere. "You gonna break that phone you keep squeezing it so hard."

Kimberly looked at the phone in her hand. "Michael should have been home by now."

Marcus made a smacking sound with his lips as he rolled his eyes. "Who is he with, baby girl?"

"No," Kimberly was quick to say. "He's not with a woman. He has the boys with him."

"Are you sure?" Marcus asked, looking her up and down. "You don't look so sure."

She wasn't anymore. Michael was a young, rich, handsome man with a penchant for wrongdoing and Kimberly understood what that meant. Before Janet's incident, she thought he might have been unfaithful to her, pretty sure of it, but he gave no indication. He was loving, always attentive, and came home at night. Their sex life was still mind-blowing, but she wasn't a fool. However, without any proof, Kimberly refused to live with worry.

But since they had been forced to leave Chase Mansion and find a place of their own, it was as if Michael no longer felt the need to appear above suspicion. She realized it was living in the same house with the father he worshipped and constantly sought to impress that made Michael want to be the perfect husband. Since leaving, he spent more time away from home than ever and felt less and less need to explain himself about it.

"He's probably just at the mansion," Kimberly said. She pressed the speed dial for Michael's cell phone. "Don't try to get me riled up. I know my husband. You don't."

"True," Marcus said, flipping his head back so his shoulder-length braids would fling in the air. "However, my living is made working with women like you."

"Women like me?" Kimberly hung up as soon as she got his voice mail.

"Wives of rich men," he answered. "I know your looks, Mrs. Chase."

"You're being too forward," Kimberly admonished, phone at her side. "Now get back to pool talk."

After rolling his eyes, Marcus said, "I was suggesting Gavea Stone tile to replace . . . whatever this crunchy mess is we are standing on. It will complement the desert-tan concrete and cultured stone along the edges."

"Sounds good." Kimberly's mind wasn't at all on the pool. Michael was never without his cell phone.

She was a complete outsider now, although she always had been. Upon showing up in View Park, Kimberly was made aware she didn't belong in the world of the upper crust, but she had Michael on her side and she had the only Chase babies. Michael's sister Leigh was kind and of course Carter was cool because he was so close to Michael, but that was it. Steven acted as if she wasn't even there most of the time and Haley treated her as if she'd never seen her before.

She had grown used to that, but even that was all over now. Everyone in the Chase family hated her, even the angelic Leigh, despite being herself a victim of Janet's obsessive control her entire life. Carter, being as close as he was to Michael, was polite, but no longer friendly. The only friend she really had was Carter's fiancée, Avery, who had left town.

She was never invited to family events anymore, just Michael and the twins. She missed Leigh's and Carter's birthdays, Steven and Janet's anniversary party, several charity events held at the mansion, and other special occasions she had enjoyed in the past.

Michael never suggested she come or offered to stand up for her in case anyone gave her a hard time. And in order to get back in his father's good graces to make up for what his wife had done, he spent more time than ever at work and at Chase Mansion. It was as if he still lived there.

"We also need to resurface the pool with a quartz finish," Marcus said, seeming almost giddy over his own idea. "It will be brilliant, Kimberly. You'll be entertaining your ass off out here."

Kimberly laughed. "Entertaining who? No one ever comes over here."

Marcus frowned, confused. "Do you want to get personal or not?"

"I don't . . . . Just ignore me."

"It's hard to, Ms. Head-to-toe-Gucci-looking fierce, but if it's the family thing, no matter. You still have the husband, the money, and the munchkins."

And she would fight to the death to keep it all. "Do whatever you want. Just make it beautiful. It's March now. I want it ready by the time it gets warm."

"Let me get some samples for the furniture out here. I'm thinking azul and coral."

As Marcus cat-walked away, Kimberly hurried to press the speed dial for Chase Mansion before she could change her mind. She knew it was stupid to call that house, but she wanted to make sure Michael hadn't left the children there and gone running off with . . . whatever.

"Hello, Kimberly." Janet Chase felt a sliver of delight run through her the second she saw the caller ID.

Kimberly felt sick to her stomach at the sound of her mother-in-law's voice. "Is Michael there?"

"Always consistent with the manners," Janet said. "I'm doing well, thank you. Of course that isn't what you want to hear. And how are you?"

Janet didn't need an answer to that question. She knew Kimberly was miserable and nothing made her happier. Six months ago, she had let old emotions encourage her to let her guard down and Kimberly took advantage. She had faltered and could have done irreparable damage to the family's reputation and her marriage. But she recovered as Janet Chase always did. In the end, she got her husband back and got rid of her prescription drug addiction. No, she couldn't sink into the gutter like Kimberly, but she was a better woman, and the better woman always won.

Kimberly was not a Chase by blood, but she had forgotten that. She would always be secondary, expendable. The family was on Janet's side and Kimberly was a foregone conclusion. Yes, it was disappointing that Michael hadn't left her, but Janet could see that eventuality with every passing day. She was hearing and seeing things, and she could clearly tell that Kimberly's hold on Michael was dwindling. And with a little help from her, their marriage was soon to follow suit.

"Is he there or not?" Kimberly asked.

Janet took her time as she admonished the flower delivery person to place this week's set of roses on top of the grand piano in the great room. "He must not be answering his cell."

"Janet, I swear if you don't—"

"You're not in a position to make threats, little girl." Janet waited for the hired help to leave the room. "It isn't my fault he won't take your calls."

"Janet!" Kimberly was ready to hang up, just imagining the smirk on Janet's face.

"He left here hours ago," Janet answered. "And if you want to know more, ask him."

"Where did he say he was going?" Kimberly asked. "Are the boys with him?"

"Yes, they are. His entire family is with him. At least everyone that counts."

"That was a little weak even for you," Kimberly said. "Not feeling very creative today, I guess. Well, drug addicts can't be fresh every day."

Janet smiled as her husband appeared in the archway from the foyer. Steven Chase looked handsome as usual, having changed out of his church suit and into a pair of khaki pants and a white polo.

"Anything else, dear?" she asked.

"Yes." Kimberly winked at Marcus, who had just returned. "Go to hell, bitch!"

"Likewise." Janet slowly hung up the phone even though Kimberly had hung up before she could even respond.

"Who was that?" Steven asked as he approached.

"The catering company calling about tonight."

"Are we still on?"

"Of course." Janet met her husband halfway and wrapped her arms around him. Leaning up to kiss him, she took a second to bask in his power and presence.

He looked much younger than fifty-four, despite the white temples. His dark skin only made his strong face more powerful and his lean body more masculine. She never tired of looking at him.

They had recently celebrated their thirty-first anniversary with a lavish party at the Peninsula Hotel, followed by a two-week Mediterranean cruise on the Queen Mary 2. The romance that had been missing from their lives was rekindled and Janet never felt more confident about their marriage or her family's unity.

She couldn't have said the same thing six months ago. Her oldest daughter had cut her out of her life, her youngest daughter had threatened to do the same, and Steven had walked in on her kissing another man. For the first time in their life together, he had walked out on her. Janet had been ready to do whatever it took to get him back, while fighting off all the gold-digging hounds ready to steal him away, but her hospitalization made it all unnecessary. Thinking he would lose her, Steven realized how much he loved her and hadn't left her side since. He even joined her for a month as she recovered in South Africa to work on their issues.

Kimberly had failed and Janet was stronger than ever. It was all just a matter of time.

"I know I'm 'sposed to use the condoms, but . . ."

Despite her own heavy heart, twenty-seven-year-old Leigh Chase placed her hand on the shoulder of the fifteen-year-old-girl, sitting on the edge of the patient's bed. "Sonia, it's going to be okay."

"My mom wouldn't let me take birth control pills," Sonia said, before smacking the gum that was making her mouth purple. She was tugging at one of her braids with one hand, while wiping her tears with the other. "Even though you talked to her, Dr. Chase, she said no."

"Did you go to the clinic I referred you to?" Leigh asked, her mind trying to figure out how she could save this baby. "They can give you the pills."

Leigh didn't like encouraging young women to go against their parents' wishes, but Sonia wasn't just any young woman. Last year, her nineteen-year-old boyfriend had given her HIV. Her father didn't exist and her mother seemed merely annoyed at the inconvenience of knowing.

Sonia shrugged her shoulders and looked down at the floor. "I was getting around to it, but I wasn't really doing anything. You know, because of the HIV."

"Your HIV status isn't the only reason why you decided it was good to abstain from sex right now." Leigh reached for her clipboard, taking notes on all the medication Sonia would need. Expensive medication.

"Things just happen," Sonia said. "You know how it is when you're partying and—"

"Who is the father of your baby?" Leigh tried to check her

own frustration. The last thing the child needed now was another person yelling at her.

She remembered the names Sonia's mother called her when she finally came down to the Hope Clinic for Leigh to explain what HIV meant for Sonia. A whore, a slut, a dyke were some of the nicer names. Sonia looked as if she'd heard them all, only a few steps from not giving a damn about herself anyway.

Leigh started Hope Clinic in South Central L.A. for children with HIV and AIDS after returning from a year in Africa with the peace corps. She wanted to make a difference and some days she did. Most days were like this one, where all the explanations and offers fell on deaf ears. No lessons learned. Now there was a baby coming and Leigh desperately needed Sonia to care.

"I'm not . . . sure." Sonia held her hand to her bare stomach. "But I'm keeping it. Unless you tell me I shouldn't."

"That has to be your decision," Leigh said. "If you go to the family planning center, they can explain this to you."

"They'll just tell me to get rid of it," Sonia said with a dismissive tone. "But you're honest, Dr. Chase. You'll tell me the truth."

"I'll tell you the facts." Leigh smiled, taking a seat across from the table. "First, you have to tell whoever this guy is that you are HIV-positive."

Sonia shook her head vigorously. "He would kill me. He hasn't even called me since that night. No way in hell . . ."

"Tell me who he is and I'll have the clinic track him down and send him a note." Leigh saw Sonia's continued reluctance. "I won't use your name. I'll just tell him it's come to our attention that one of your partners has the virus and he should be checked. Sonia, it's your obligation."

"Fine!" She folded her arms across her chest and pouted, reminding the world that she was still just a baby herself. "I gotta ask around. I don't know who he is exactly, but I know who he runs with. I just need to know . . . is my baby gonna die?"

"It doesn't have to," Leigh said. "But that's up to you."

"I think I want it," she said uncertainly. "I mean, it's not what I wanted, but . . . it's mine, right? I can have it and I can love it like a real mom should."

"Babies need more than love," Leigh said. "Especially right now. That baby needs a whole lot more than your love."

Sonia's worried expression was trying to change to a smile. "I just think I want it. So what do I have to do?"

"There are a lot of advances in medicine today." Leigh handed Sonia a brochure on HIV and pregnancy. "If we do this right, there is a less than two percent chance your baby will be HIV-positive."

Sonia's eyes widened and her lips formed an unbelieving smile. "Are you . . . really?"

Leigh nodded. "There is a combination of medications you'll have to start taking immediately. You might have to deliver via C-section and—"

"What is that? C-section?"

"It's when the doctor takes the baby out of your uterus through a surgical procedure instead of a regular, vaginal birth." Leigh could see Sonia wasn't too excited about this. "But that's for later and it might not be necessary. What's most important is that you will have to take these drugs several times a day for the duration of the pregnancy."

"I do that now," Sonia said, encouraged. "When do we get started?"

Leigh sighed, not certain that Sonia really understood the seriousness of her situation. With such a chaotic, unstable life, she was not a good candidate for success. But Leigh wasn't going to give up on her or the baby.

"Dr. Chase." The silhouette of Hope Clinic's receptionist, Joanne West, could be seen outside the curtains to the room. "Call on line two for you. They said it's urgent."

"I'll be there in a second." Leigh stood up. "Sonia, take some time to read this brochure. When I come back, we'll talk about the new regimen you'll have to follow."

"Cool." Sonia was already placing her iPod earphones in her ears as she leaned back and started reading.

Leigh picked up the first phone she could find and pressed line two. "This is Dr. Chase."

"Dr. Leigh Chase?" the male voice asked.

"Yes, who is this?"

"Dr. Chase, I'm a big fan of yours, but more importantly, so is my client."

"Who am I speaking to?" Leigh asked impatiently.

"My name is James Monroe."

Leigh could tell from his pause that she was supposed to know him. At least in his mind she was. She didn't respond.

"I get it," he said, laughing. "You're too busy saving lives to know about Hollywood. I'm an agent with CCM. I have many A-list clients, one of which is Lyndon Prior."

Even though she didn't care about Hollywood, Leigh knew who Lyndon Prior was; everyone did. He was one of the hottest young actors in Hollywood. His last two movies, one an action-adventure, the other a romantic comedy, both busted the box office. He was considered the only really versatile actor of his generation. He was twenty-seven, blond with blue eyes, handsome, and six feet tall: a moviemaker's dream.

"I'm very busy," Leigh said. "What can I do for you, Mr. Monroe?"

"Leigh, I want to—"

"It's Dr. Chase."

"I'm sorry." He laughed nervously. "Dr. Chase, I want to give you the chance to meet Lyndon Prior."

"I'm not really interested in meeting him," Leigh said. "Now if you'll excuse me . . ."

"Are you serious?"

"Why would I want to?" she asked.

"This could be a great opportunity for you, Doctor."

"Unless he's going to roll up his sleeves and help me tend to my patients, I sincerely doubt that."

"That's exactly what he wants to do," James answered, his tone finally turning serious. "Lyndon read an article about the incredible things your clinic is doing."

"The *L.A. Times* article," Leigh said. It was supposed to be great publicity for the clinic and she agreed to the interview hoping it would get more donations. "Tell him I said thanks and—"

"You can tell him yourself. He wants to study you."

"You're not making any sense." Leigh nodded to one of the nurses' aides waving her over. "I have to . . ."

"He's just got a new role playing a clinic doctor, doing exactly what you do. He needs to study someone and he picked you after reading that article."

Leigh could tell from his tone James thought she should be eternally grateful to be selected. "No, thanks."

"No, thanks?"

"You heard me," Leigh answered. "What I do down here is serious stuff. I don't have time to accommodate spoiled actors who think spending a day with a pair of gloves makes them a medical expert. Tell him to rent a DVD."

Leigh hung up before she could get a response and started for the nurse.

"Leigh, come here." Dr. Alicia Spender was waving her over.

Alicia was one of her founding partners. The other, Richard Powell, was now dead. Leigh had fallen in love with Richard, and he'd made a huge mistake by falling in love with her. She hadn't the heart to warn him that getting involved with the Chase family almost always spelled disaster. That disaster was a man named Leo Bridges, whom her mother was desperately trying to set Leigh up with at the same time she was dating Richard. Leo turned out to be a complete psycho who believed he was in love with Leigh despite no encouragement on her part. His jealousy got so out of control, he shot and killed Richard before turning the gun on himself right in front of Leigh. It was later found out that he had a carefully hidden history of psychotic behavior.

It was more than a year ago and she still had nightmares.

"What's wrong?" Leigh asked, noting the worried expression on Alicia's face.

"We need some money," Alicia said, showing her a bill from the equipment manufacturer.

Leigh nodded. "We need more of a lot of things. One of my patients is pregnant. I've already committed my trust fund limit."

Until she turned thirty, Leigh was only allowed to withdraw two hundred thousand dollars a year from her trust fund, an amount raised from one hundred thousand after she turned twenty-five. It was her parents' way of making sure their children didn't blow away their future and become lazy. Leigh had given all that she could. Even though she was again at Chase Mansion and living off her parents, she couldn't beg for everything.

"I'm petitioning for more state funding," Leigh said. "I know we'll hear from them soon."

"I don't like the rules that come along with state funding," Alicia said. "We need private funding. Can you talk to your mother again?"

"The Chase Foundation sponsors more than seventy-five charities and causes, Alicia." Leigh didn't want to ask for more money. Since opening less than two years ago, her mother had put together four social events just for the Hope Clinic, more than any other organization the foundation sponsored. "They can't show me any more favoritism."

"Yes, they can. You're their daughter. That's what favoritism is all about."

"I'll think of something," Leigh said. "I always do."

2

"**B**aby!" Michael was admiring himself in the bathroom mirror. Everything was perfect as usual. Everything except . . . "Kimberly!"

"Stop yelling," Kimberly said as she appeared in the doorway. "I'm right here."

"I need another . . ." Michael stopped the second he noticed what she was wearing.

Kimberly was impossible not to notice. She was tall, thin but curvy, and ridiculously beautiful. She was the kind of woman that both men and women couldn't stop staring at. That wasn't the problem right now. Right now she was supposed to be in the same pair of shorts and T-shirt she had on when Michael stepped into the shower. Now she had on a lavender cocktail dress and as hot as she looked, Michael wasn't getting a good feeling.

"What's this?"

"I'm coming with you." She walked over to him with two Stefano Ricci ties in hand. "You want the purple or the blue?"

"Kimberly."

"I say be conservative and go with the blue," she offered. "It's how Carter would dress."

He took the tie, offering her the one he had taken off. "You can't come."

"I can come," she said, feeling the bite of pain from his actually saying that. "And I am. I'm your wife and I'm a Chase."

"Tonight is for Carter." Michael felt a little angry that she would challenge him this way. He thought they had an understanding. "You'll be a distraction."

"I'm always a distraction," she answered. "I'm gorgeous. You used to like to show that off."

"I still do," Michael said. "Just not at the mansion."

"There will be enough nonfamily there to keep me busy." Kimberly had made up her mind earlier that day. She couldn't take the isolation anymore. She wanted back in. "I have a right to be there."

"You have a right?" He turned away from her, putting his tie on. "Don't get me started."

Maybe he was wrong, but Michael didn't care. Although he still loved her, Kimberly's reckless choices had put him in a horrible position and he was doing what he had to do. He couldn't let her mess things up again.

"You need me there," she insisted. "And I've been punished enough."

"I'm not punishing you," he said, although it was a lie. He couldn't leave her because he loved her too much, but deep down inside, a part of him still wanted her to pay for the position she had put him in.

"Oh, please." Kimberly let out a bitter laugh. "You punish me by shutting down, turning your back to me. You control everything I do. You don't want me going anywhere or doing anything. I'm completely isolated, Michael. It's driving me crazy. If you love me at all, you'll stop—"

"Are you questioning whether or not I love you?" Michael couldn't believe the nerve of her. "You almost single-handedly destroyed my parents' marriage, my mother's life, and my position at Chase Beauty. I should have left you."

"Don't say that," Kimberly pleaded. "You know how hurtful that is."

Michael couldn't ignore the pain in his heart at the look on her face. God, he still loved her so much. "I'm sorry, baby. I didn't mean that."

She rushed into his open arms, tears already streaming down her face. When she felt him embrace her, she went limp against his strength. He was so strong; smelled so good. She loved him more than made any sense. "I just want to be your wife again."

"You are my wife," Michael said. "I love you, baby."

"Then why do you keep leaving me behind?" she asked. "I want to come tonight and I want you to want me there."

"Mommy's coming?"

They both turned to see Evan standing in the doorway to the bathroom. The second he saw his mother's tears, he became upset. "What's wrong, Mommy?"

Kimberly turned away, wiping her eyes. Her boys had seen her cry too many times these past six months.

"Nothing's wrong," Michael said. "It's good crying, little man. Where's your brother?"

"He's watching TV." Evan didn't seem satisfied; he never was. "Mommy, are you coming with us to Uncle Carter's party?"

Kimberly looked at Michael, who nodded to his son.

"Yes," Michael said. "Mommy's coming with us."

"Yeah!" Evan made a fist in the air as Kimberly turned around with a big smile. "I'm so happy. Mommy never comes anymore."

"Go watch TV with Daniel," Michael ordered. "Mommy and Daddy will be down in a little bit."

Kimberly walked to the door and closed it, turning back to her husband. "Thank you, Michael."

Michael went to her, trying to field his own emotions. No matter what apprehension he felt about her coming, he knew he was happy she would be there. "It won't be nice."

"I know." She closed her eyes as his hand gently came to her cheek. "I'll behave."

"It's not you I'm worried about." His father would give him hell and he supposed his mother and youngest sister, Haley, just for the hell of it, would try to murder her.

"Don't worry about anything," Kimberly said. "I just want to be there for you."

"This night isn't about me."

"That's why I need to be there." Kimberly opened her eyes, looking into his dark, mysterious orbs. "I know you're feeling conflicted. It's okay. With me, you don't have to pretend. You don't have to feel what everyone else thinks you should."

She was right and that was why he needed her. Even his worst thoughts she held to her heart. When his father told him that he'd be spending a month in South Africa with their mom, Michael wasn't surprised that he was being put in charge. He was, however, more than surprised when he was told that Carter would help him. Not just because Carter didn't work at Chase Beauty, but because Carter wasn't supposed to be speaking to their father after Steven fired Avery from her job as head of the beauty salon chain, Chase Expressions.

Janet's "incident" changed everything. The family came together and Carter swallowed his animosity toward Steven for their mother's sake. Steven had warned Michael that Carter would eventually come to Chase Beauty and used it as a threat to keep Michael in line. This was why Michael felt threatened by his brother and best friend getting a taste. Maybe he would want more, and at a time when Michael was no one's favorite considering what Kimberly had done, Carter's presence at Chase Beauty could be nothing but a threat.

The month went by quickly and when Steven returned, much to his dismay, Carter went away without a fight. He was too preoccupied with finding Avery and had his own company to run. He seemed almost grateful to be done with the tour of duty and go back to having Chase Beauty as a client and nothing more. Michael watched with growing anxiety as the father who was pushing away from him went to great lengths to keep Carter involved. Steven knew Carter loved power just as much as any man who'd had a taste of it, and the decision to have him join the board of directors was just enough to lure him back in.

"I love Carter," Michael said flatly.

"I know you do," Kimberly said. "But, baby, it's okay not to be so happy for yourself. It won't make a difference. Chase Beauty is yours. Steven is yours."

The touch of her lips on his made him hungry and he grabbed her by the waist. Kissing her hard and deep, Michael felt himself light on fire. After all this time, she still had this effect on him. No matter how he felt about her, even when he hated her, he always wanted her.

Kimberly let out a gasp as Michael pushed her against the wall and began rubbing his hands furiously up and down her body. She moved her hips against him, pulling at his shirt. She loved the sweet insanity that his hands on her could bring.

"Baby," he grunted as he ripped the dress down the middle and grabbed her bare breast. Her skin was soft as silk and her nipples were already hard. He had to have her now.

As they slid to the floor, the need she felt for him wasn't explainable. Neither was the satisfaction in knowing his need was the same.

"You really want to do this?" Charlie Jackson, View Park's forty-seven-year-old chief of police, asked his son, Sean.

"Yes, sir, I do." Twenty-six-year-old police detective Sean Jackson walked side by side with his father across the street in Baldwin Hills.

They hadn't done this in a while, hanging out and talking in peace, but things were better between them than they had been in a long time. They had always been a close family, but bad choices, particularly Sean's involvement with Haley Chase, had caused some rifts in the past year. Of late, things were getting back to normal.

"So, what do you think?" Sean asked as soon as they were back on the sidewalk.

Over dinner, Sean had shared his latest decision. He was going back to college. Although he'd graduated first in his class at the police academy and was the youngest officer to make detective in Los Angeles County history, Sean wanted a future in the district attorney's office and that meant he needed a law degree. First, he had to finish his bachelor's degree, which he had started off and on part-time over the past four years.

"What do you mean what do I think?" Charlie couldn't remember being so proud. He needed good news, not having had much of it in a while. "I think it's great. I just . . . It's going to take a long time."

"I'm going to work through college," Sean said. "I only have about a year and a half to get my bachelor's if UCLA will accept all the credits I've earned so far. Then I'm going to go to law school full-time, so I can get out in three years."

"You're going to make Homicide soon." Charlie said.

"We don't know that." Homicide was every detective's dream. Sean would love to get Homicide while finishing school, but he didn't think it was possible. "Besides, if that happens, I'll deal with it. Do you think Mom will be happy?"

Charlie made a loud sigh. "Not much makes her happy these days, but I think this is definitely going to do that."

"I know she misses Avery, but—" Sean stopped as his father grabbed his arm. Turning to him, he could see that Charlie was alarmed. He followed his gaze and saw what was happening.

About a hundred yards away, two teenaged boys were hovering on the driver's side of a sterling silver Mercedes coupe.

"Stay here," Charlie said as he reached for his concealed weapon.

"Yeah, right." With his hand on his own gun, Sean followed his father as they scurried to the left behind a blue minivan.

"You go around." Charlie gestured to the next aisle of cars in the expansive parking lot. "I'll take them head-on."

"I will," Sean protested.

"Boy, don't get into this with me." Charlie pointed. "Now go."

Sean reluctantly did what he was told. It had been a long time since his father had been on the streets, so he wasn't settled about this at all. Going around the next aisle, he could come up behind the boys and crowd them in.

"Oh my God!"

As he turned behind a large SUV, he ran into a petite, curly-haired woman carrying a small baby who set eyes on the large gun in his hand.

"I'm a cop," Sean said, reaching for the badge on the necklace underneath his shirt. "Just go now."

"What's going on?" It wasn't so much a question as it was a demand. Her tone held a hint of assumed authority as if he was obligated to answer to her.

"Just go!" Sean started for the next car.

The popping sound seemed to vibrate around the parking lot

and Sean felt his adrenaline kick into supercharge. He rushed around the SUV, knowing he was completely exposing himself. When he saw the two boys running off, he acted on instinct.

He yelled for them to freeze while he raised his gun and planted himself in the middle of the aisle. "Stop now!"

One of the boys, dressed in a Lakers jersey and jeans, turned and shot indiscriminately. Sean fired his gun low as he lunged for the protection of the nearest vehicle. Another shot rang out just as he raised his head.

After a second, Sean jumped from behind the car and intended to go after them, but not before checking on his father. He let out a whimper as he saw the man he thought was made of steel lying flat on his back, clutching his stomach.

"Dad!" Sean put his gun in the holster, kneeling at his father's side. "Oh my God."

"I'm . . . okay," Charlie said, feeling the warm blood ooze between his fingers.

"Jesus!" Sean stumbled for his cell as he dialed 9-1-1. This couldn't be happening. "Dad, press harder."

Sean placed his hand over his father's, but the blood wouldn't stop flowing. When someone came on the line, he identified himself as an officer and gave his badge number and location. "I have an officer down! Shots fired! Chief Jackson has been shot! Get here now!"

Sean felt his chest beginning to cave in and fear taking over. Taking off his shirt, he quickly balled it up and added it to the pressure against the wound. This couldn't be happening. "Dad, please stay with me. Think of Mom, Dad. Please, think of Mom."

Carlos, the evening security guard for Hope Clinic, opened the door for Leigh as she stepped outside. A very intimidating man in stature and size, he was actually one of the kindest, most gentle people Leigh had ever met. He always had a smile for her, but tonight's seemed exceptionally warm.

"What's making you so happy?" Leigh asked.

"It's nice to see you make an early night of it for once, Dr. Chase." He nodded to the dress she had changed into just five minutes ago. "A date?"

"I wish," Leigh answered. "It's a family thing."

"Whatever the case," he said, "it's nice to see you get out of here before it's dark out."

Leigh didn't have any life outside of Hope Clinic, and that had been what she needed for a long time. But now she thought she might be ready to look for more. Just how was a single sister to go about that these days? "I do what I . . ."

Any white person would stand out in this neighborhood, but the man who stepped in front of Carlos and Leigh as he walked her to her car would stand out anywhere.

"Dr. Chase?" he asked, looking at Leigh with a charming smile highlighted by a dimple in both cheeks.

"Who are you?" Carlos stood in front of Leigh speaking in that tone that would make even a serial killer think twice.

Lyndon halted, clearly intimidated. "I, uh, I'm not a criminal or anything, dude. I'm an actor. Don't you recognize me?"

"No," Carlos answered. "Now get the hell away from—"

"Lyndon Prior?" Leigh peeked out from behind Carlos.

Lyndon smiled again, seeming to relax. "She recognizes me."

Carlos turned back to Leigh, who nodded her approval. He lowered his arm, letting her step beside him, but still not in front of him.

"I don't recognize you," Leigh said. He actually looked much better than any picture she had seen him in. "Your agent called me earlier today."

Lyndon nodded with a Tom Cruise–type cocky grin. "I have to apologize for James. He lives in Hollywood and thinks everyone else does or wants to."

"I don't," Leigh said. "Let's go, Carlos."

"Wait." Lyndon took a step closer, but jumped two steps back as Carlos held his hand up to him. "Dude, I'm not—"

"I'm not your dude! The doctor has someplace to be."

"I get it." Lyndon turned to Leigh. "Dr. Chase, if you'll just give me a minute."

"That's all I have," Leigh said, taking Carlos's arm. They started toward her car, which was parked right in front of the clinic. "I'm not interested in your offer."

"I just want to follow you," Lyndon said. "I won't get in your way."

"You will." Leigh turned to him as they reached the sidewalk. "The work at the clinic is very serious and important. I won't let it be used for your entertainment."

"You've got it all wrong," Lyndon said. "This is a very serious movie."

"Mr. Prior, I—"

"Doctor, just hear me out."

There were those damn dimples again. Leigh found them hard to resist. He was pretty hot. "I have someplace I need to be."

"This character I'm playing is a rich kid who went to medical school to get chicks and make money. He doesn't give a shit . . . I mean, he doesn't care about people. Then his parents die. He finds out that, before he can inherit their millions, he has to run the community clinic named in his grandfather's honor in the roughest part of Oakland for a year."

Leigh frowned, pressing her lips together. "That sounds stupid. Like a . . . I don't know. Like an Adam Sandler movie or something."

"It's not," Lyndon said. "His life is changed while he works there. He comes to understand the real purpose for getting into medicine, the value of working your ass off even when you get nothing for it. He comes to understand people and realizes the inequity in health care for the impoverished and the working poor. He connects with people he once considered invisible."

"That actually sounds kind of good," Carlos said as he nodded his head. "You put a couple of car chase scenes in there and I'd go see it."

Leigh couldn't hold back her laughter, but despite the satisfied look on Lyndon's face, he was about to get something he probably never got: turned down. "I'm sorry, Mr. Prior—"

"Lyndon," he corrected, his smile fading.

"Lyndon, I'm sorry." Leigh stepped around to the driver's side and opened the door. "There are plenty of clinic doctors who would love to help you get into their minds. I'm not one of them. Good night, Carlos. Good luck, Lyndon."

As she drove away, Leigh glanced up at her rearview mirror and he was standing in the street looking as confident and comfortable as if this were his block. She hadn't seen any bodyguards or entourage. Maybe they were too chicken to come down to this neighborhood. Lyndon Prior was either brave or just crazy; and considering what world he lived in, Leigh assumed it was the latter.

Everyone wanted an invite to Chase Mansion in View Park. It was why they always slowed down when driving by the gated estate. Its exclusiveness only made it more appealing, intriguing. Money alone wasn't enough to get invited to one of the many charitable events Janet held there every year. Where and how you made the money and what you did with it made all the difference in the world.

Once you were invited, the black iron gates would open and you would drive up to the circular, black driveway in front of the redbrick and white-columned house. A valet would park your car somewhere along the front gardens or in the multicar garage that kept the family's luxury sedans, sports cars, and SUVs. The treat wasn't seeing what was inside the place, which seemed more likely to fit in Hollywood Hills or Bel Air. Everyone had seen the house, which was previously two large houses torn apart to make one gigantic home, in countless magazines featuring its seven bedrooms, nine baths, exercise room, game room, media room, library, and more. They had also seen the two-thousand-square-foot guest house beyond the pool, party area, and court out back.

What they were eager for was the feel of being inside the home themselves, seeing the ornate, elegant decorations with their own eyes. Nothing was garish and glowing like you would find in the house of the newly rich eager to prove they had money. You had to have taste and class to understand the value of the art, furnishings, marble, and glass Janet selected.

They wanted to see the pictures of the family spending time at their many homes across the world: Italy, London, Maui, the Hamptons. They wanted to see the countless awards and tokens of recognition for their charitable mastery, educational achievements, and business prowess. They wanted to see how one family could collect the accolades a dozen couldn't achieve together.

Most of all, they wanted to witness the family in action, see them in person inside their own home. Was it anything like they imagined? Although the tabloids always found a way to get the Chase family inside their folds, there was still an unattainable mystery about them that made people—even those considered to be in their own circle—curious.

Only a small group of fifty people were invited to tonight's event, which was supposed to be a family occasion. However, Janet always found a way to turn a party into a chance to raise money for a good cause and elevate the family's name. Since tonight's party was celebrating Carter, everyone invited was encouraged, emphasis on the word *encouraged*, to make a donation to Carter's favorite charity, the Legal Aid Foundation of Los Angeles, of which he was on the board as well.

Steven stole a kiss from his wife while he had her. He knew how precious it was to get ahold of Janet while she was entertaining at their home. Both she and Maya, the family maid, worked nonstop to insure everything was perfect and everyone couldn't be happier.

"Don't mess up my makeup." Janet pushed against his chest even though she enjoyed every bit of his attention. "Have you spoken to Congressman Wornton yet? He's come just to talk to you."

"What about your lecture earlier saying this evening wasn't about me?"

"You know what I meant." From where they were in the great room, Janet could tell someone had just come in. Everyone's attention had turned to the foyer. "Maybe that's Leigh."

"Where is Carter?" Steven asked.

Janet pointed to their eldest, leaning against the wall talking to a beautiful young woman. "Engaging in his favorite new hobby, flirting with every pretty girl he meets."

Steven grinned. "You prefer he stand there staring like someone just tore his guts out. I'm glad that phase is over."

Janet had invited the young woman to meet Michael. "He'll be so happy when he sees your present."

"For what that thing cost," Steven said, "he better jump up and down and kiss me."

Janet laughed. "That would be the day. Just be happy you're both getting along."

Steven grumbled as he turned toward the foyer. "Oh, shit."

Janet's head swung around just as Michael and Kimberly entered the foyer, the twins circling them. "What the . . ."

"This will be interesting." Steven was disappointed. This would only upset Janet, and when Janet was upset, nothing went well. "I'll talk to him."

"No." Janet grabbed him before he could get away. "Just ignore her. I'm sure she's hoping to start something."

"Whatever you say." Steven headed for the first waiter he could find with a drink.

"I need a drink," Kimberly said, leaning into her husband. "Now."

"There's Maya!" Evan pointed to the maid who had practically raised them, and he and his brother rushed to her open arms.

"You gonna leave me too?" Kimberly asked.

Michael shrugged his shoulders. "You can't expect me to hold your hand all night. I'm gonna go holler at Carter. Grab a glass from a waiter."

"I don't want wine," she said. "I want a drink."

Michael shook his head. "The last thing you need is to get drunk. Take it easy, Kimberly."

As he walked away, Kimberly knew Michael was right. She was in enemy territory and she needed to keep a clear head. She had to be smart, and that started with finding out where Janet was and keeping as far away from her as possible.

"Oh, hell," Kimberly said to herself as she grabbed a glass of wine off a passing tray as Janet made her way to her.

"Crashing the party, are you, dear?" Janet could only imagine what seduction the little tramp had pulled off to get Michael to agree to this.

"I was invited by my husband."

Janet's head fell back as she laughed out loud. "I'm sure you coaxed the invite out of him between the sheets. I don't blame you. You must have heard of all the single, available, much more socially desirable women I invited here to meet him."

"You don't scare me," Kimberly said.

"Yes, I do." Janet leaned into her, making it seem to anyone looking that they were sharing a friendly secret. Janet always placed appearances first. "You see that one he's talking to now?"

Kimberly followed Janet's directing finger and saw Michael, standing next to Carter, speaking to a young, beautiful, caramel-skinned woman with long auburn hair that flew in the air as she flipped her head back and laughed.

"She's interested in Carter," Kimberly said, if only to reassure herself.

"Every single woman is interested in both of them and you know it." Janet placed her hands on her pleasing hips. "Kathryn Tibbin will be graduating from the Darden School of Business, one of the top MBA programs in the world, in a couple of months. She and Michael will have so much in common. Steven is eager to hire her for our finance department."

"You're wasting your time," Kimberly said. "Michael has forgiven me. Our marriage is fine."

"Of course it is," Janet said. "But even if Kathryn isn't the one, Julia Hall over there will be perfect for him. They've already met. This is the third event I've invited her to, and she and Michael get along great. She comes from a wonderful family in Dallas. So suit—"

"Stop it." Kimberly could feel her nails digging into her palms. "No matter what you say, Janet, I am here. You see, I've already won. Because I'm here and there isn't a damn thing you can do about it."

"Mrs. Chase." The photographer, hired often by the family for events, knelt down a few feet from them. "The *L.A. Times* wants a pic."

Both women smiled for the picture as if everything was perfect. Years of being a Chase had taught them both to smile even if the world was falling apart.

"Enjoy it all while you can, dear," Janet said with a pasted smile. "You're on a thin line and you'll slip up again. And that will be it for Michael. You are on your way out."

"You trying to steal my thunder?"

Leigh turned away from the group of women she was talking with to see her younger sister, Haley Chase, standing behind her. "Hey, schoolgirl. How's it going?"

"Don't call me that." Haley turned her button nose up. "What are you wearing?"

Leigh always felt like she might as well be wearing a potato sack when she was standing next to her soon to be twenty-four-year-old sister, the cinnamon-colored siren.

While Leigh was always described as very cute and pretty in a sweet kind of way, Haley was the fiery beauty. While Leigh was always seen as the gentle, softhearted feminine one men wanted to love and take care of, Haley was the sexy, difficult temptress that men wanted to kill and die for.

"You can't insult my dress this time," Leigh said. "It's yours. I stole it out of your closet this morning."

Haley's mouth flew open as she looked Leigh over again. "That is mine! I can't believe you managed to make a Dolce and Gabbana look like off-the-rack for spring. Only you, Leigh."

"I was actually in the middle of an adult conversation," Leigh said. "Something I know you want nothing of, so . . ."

"Why were you late?" Haley asked. "I'm the one that gets to show up late."

"Don't you have homework to do?"

Leigh loved teasing Haley about being in graduate school at UCLA. She had fought going back to school, but their mother guilted her into it and their father used his control over her trust fund to keep her there. It required unfamiliar discipline for the reckless debutante who only wanted to shop, vacation, and party.

"I pay people to do my homework," Haley said. "Poor, smart students are in abundance on that campus."

"Taking the path of least resistance," Leigh said. "The pride of the Chase family."

"I've been behaving, haven't I?"

That was mostly true. Haley had done her best to stay under the radar. After last year's sordid, masochistic affair with club manager, illegal-casino owner, and wanna-be pimp Chris Reman, Haley wanted to take a break from trouble. She had almost been killed twice in less than a year, once by Chris and once by a drug dealer named Rudio whom she saw kill someone. Being a college student and getting into regular college student trouble suited her fine for now. Just for now.

Leigh put her hands on her hips with an unbelieving grin. "Really? I thought I heard Mom on the phone asking someone not to kick you out of that school."

"That was an empty threat," Haley said. "So I slept with one professor. He's a visiting and they don't count. Besides, Daddy donated a hundred and fifty thousand to that damn school last year. I'm not going anywhere."

"For now."

Haley smiled. "Until then, being the last Chase to show up at family parties is still my thing."

"Stop being childish." Leigh leaned against the back of the sofa, waving to a family friend she needed to hit up for a donation to the clinic. "I was unexpectedly delayed. You would be interested in why."

"I doubt it."

"Does the name Lyndon Prior ring a bell?" Leigh smiled as Haley's eyes widened.

"What about him?" Haley asked. Lyndon was currently one of the top actors on her he-can-get-it list.

"He came by the clinic. He wants to shadow me for a film he's doing. He's playing a clinic doctor."

"Sounds boring. When can I meet him?"

"I said no." Leigh winced when Haley socked her in the arm.

"You can't have said no," Haley said. "Not even someone as dense as you would turn down that sweet piece of ass."

"Okay, first, ewww. Second, I run a serious clinic for people with serious health concerns. I'm not going to have actors and agents running around studying on how to keep it real."

"For someone so smart, you're such an idiot." Haley shook her head. "You're always complaining about needing money for the clinic. You could've used him for publicity."

Leigh paused, wondering if she had been too hasty. "I'm not taking advice from someone who thinks charity is showing up for a party with a check written by her daddy."

"Remember that next time you run out of penicillin to treat your little herpes-ridden—"

"What are you two talking about?" Janet asked, arriving just in time to be disgusted.

"Leigh's dying clinic."

"It's not—"

"Well, enough about that." Janet took each of them by the arm. "Come into the garage. It's time for Carter's gift and it's family only."

"You're just jealous," Carter said as Michael pushed him past the kitchen and into the mudroom. "You saw me getting her number and you're hating on me."

"Please." Michael stood at the door that led to the garage. "If I wanted her number, I could have gotten it."

"Not with Kimberly watching your ass like you owe her money." Carter stuffed his hands in the pockets of his pleated Ralph Laurens. "Now, what did you have to drag me out here to tell me? Hurry up so I can get back to my new best friend."

"It's in—" As Michael put his hand on the door, a voice on the other side interrupted his plan.

"This is not fair!"

"Damn, Haley," Michael said.

Carter laughed. "Step aside, little boy."

Michael opened the door to the garage full of the family's cars, and Carter stepped inside. His first inclination, upon seeing his family standing in front of him, was to be defensive. In the last six months he had been trapped into more than one intervention with his parents, who warned him of his reckless behavior. Was this another one?

"This sucks!" Haley said, her arms folded across her chest. "I'm the one with a birthday coming up."

Michael pushed Carter closer to the family.

"What is going . . ." Carter saw the smiles on his parents' faces and Leigh's while Haley stood a few feet away, pouting. This wasn't an intervention.

"Congratulations, son." With a proud nod, Steven stepped aside and revealed the surprise.

As his mother and sisters stepped away, Carter couldn't believe his eyes. He opened his mouth but couldn't find words as Michael slapped him on the back and called him a lucky bastard.

"Are you serious?" Carter asked, approaching the car. "You cannot be serious."

Steven smiled as Janet squeezed his hand in hers. "Michael said it's what you talk about all the time."

The Maybach 62 was on the top of the list of Carter's cars to buy. After seeing the ultraluxury vehicle at a show, he had become obsessed with it. The price tag of four hundred thousand dollars usually would have been insignificant, but after having paid $2.5 million to Lisette McDaniel in a failed attempt to keep her from telling Avery, he had to put a handle on his frivolous spending for a while.

"I . . . I . . ." Carter walked along the side of the sparkling black sedan, touching the detailed trim. "I can't believe this. What did you . . . ?" Carter looked at his father, searching for the right words. "I can't believe this."

Haley sighed impatiently. "I'm very unimpressed."

"Wait until you look inside," Carter said.

"You'll need to give me a ride in this right now," she ordered, "or my thumbs-down stands."

"Congratulations, Carter." Leigh took his arm and reached up to kiss his cheek. "You, at a loss for words? What kind of lawyer are you?"

Carter smiled, grabbing Leigh and kissing her on the forehead. "I'm the kind that can't believe this."

"Neither can I," Michael said. "Pretty generous."

"You got the Range Rover when you were appointed to the board," Janet said. If he got rid of that whore he was married to, she'd buy him two Maybachs. "And you love that, right?"

Carter approached his father, feeling a genuine happiness for the first time in the longest. "Thanks, Dad. I can't thank you enough."

Steven opened his arms and when Carter reached out to hug him, Janet felt her eyes begin to tear up. It had been years since she'd seen them hug each other.

Steven patted his son on the back and leaned away. "You want to thank me? Be a good member of the board. Be a part of Chase Beauty."

"I guess I can't refuse that," Carter said.

Michael turned away from the scene, pretending to be more interested in the car. He hated himself for being so envious. It was all a little too close for his taste. He wished Kimberly was here. He needed her now.

"This is really convenient," Haley said, sidling up to Carter. "Considering you wrapped your Mercedes around a tree."

"Haley." Janet gave her daughter a warning stare. "We aren't going there."

"Going where?" she asked. "So he got in a drunken rage over his girlfriend leaving him. He got out of it with barely a scratch."

"What is she talking about?" Leigh asked. "I thought you said you got hit by a truck running a red light. Mom said—"

"I did," Carter said, not interested in reliving the moment. "As far as anyone is concerned."

"As far as he remembers." Michael opened the driver's-side door. He got a glimpse at the center console. The car was really amazing.

"I don't want to talk about that," Janet said. The accident happened just after she and Steven had returned from South Africa. Carter was a mess and she still wasn't sure he hadn't done it on purpose.

Haley wrapped her arms around Carter's waist and dragged behind him to the car. "Please take me on the first ride. Please, please . . ."

"All right, hot stuff," Carter said, laughing. "Get in."

Haley jumped and yelled as she ran around to the other side.

"You can't go now," Janet said. "We have a party, remember? It's for you."

"Just a quick ride, please?" Haley slid into the driver's-side seat, which was smoother and softer than any seat she'd ever been in. Even though the car wasn't sexy, it was luxurious.

"Don't touch anything," Carter ordered.

Haley shrugged. "You should have asked for a convertible."

"You can't even get out," Janet said. "The driveway is blocked with cars."

"Make them move," Haley ordered.

"Later, Princess," Carter said as he leaned into the car.

Just then, the garage door opened and everyone turned to see

Kimberly standing in the doorway. The look on her face made Michael rush to her.

"What is it? What's wrong?" he asked, thinking of his boys.

"It's on the news," Kimberly said. "Chief Jackson has been shot."

There was a silence as everyone in the room looked at Kimberly as if she would say she was joking in a second even though they knew she wouldn't.

"Chief Jackson?" Janet asked. "Is he . . ."

"He's in the hospital is all the news would say." Kimberly's hand went to her stomach. "Shot twice in the stomach by some kids trying to steal a car."

"Oh my God." Leigh turned to her father. "If everyone has seen it, I . . . I guess we should send them home."

"Let's go." Janet took Leigh's hand and they headed for the party.

As Steven watched Michael comfort his wife, he wondered if he should care more. He didn't want Charlie Jackson dead, but he wasn't going to pretend to be emotional about the man who once tried to pin an attempted murder charge on Carter and an assault charge on Haley.

"Carter?" Steven was a little uneasy about the look on his son's face. Mostly because something odd was there that he couldn't figure out.

Carter turned to his father.

"You okay?" Steven asked. He had been going to marry the man's daughter once.

With every sense inside him on high alert, Carter felt adrenaline kick in. He didn't know what to do or what to think. Instead, the only thing he thought to do was slowly run his fingers along the edges of the door to his new car.

Two gifts in one day, he thought as his head cleared.

"I'm fine," Carter finally said.

"Of course he's fine." Haley got out of the car with a devilish smirk on her face. "His girlfriend is coming back."

Carter looked at his baby sister and met her smile with one of his own.

3

As she lay on the beach in Saint-Tropez, Avery's eyes were closed and her trashy novel had already fallen to the side of her lounge chair. She was half asleep, the sun slowly darkening her smooth brown complexion. But suddenly something was blocking the sun and when she opened her eyes and saw who it was, she smiled and felt her body temperature heat up.

"Where have you been?" she asked, swinging her legs to the side of the chair so he could sit down.

"Getting some ice," Carter answered. From around his back he exposed a sterling silver ice bucket with a glass of seven-hundred-and-fifty-dollar Bollinger Blanc de Noir champagne inside. "Thirsty?"

"Yes." She leaned forward and grabbed hold of the top of his linen pants, the only thing he was wearing. "But not for champagne."

Carter had that wicked smile on his face that drove her insane. "Maybe I should just throw this ice on you to cool you down."

"Don't you dare."

His mouth was on hers in a second and Avery felt the warm breeze whizzing around them as their bodies lifted into the air.

His kiss was like flying and made her tingle from head to toe. Her torch was lit when she felt his tongue flirt with her own and she wanted him again as if she'd hadn't had him in years.

"Avery," he whispered as he lowered his mouth to the cleavage between her large breasts. "I love you so much."

As his mouth teased her left nipple, Avery felt her entire body shiver from the anticipation. It was always like this with Carter. Damn him, she thought. The man just owned her body and he knew it. She would let him do anything and still want more.

Just as she reached behind her back to undo her bikini, Carter suddenly pushed away with an angry expression on his face. "What is that?"

She followed his eyes to her stomach, her very pregnant stomach, and became very, very nervous. "It's nothing. I just ate too much."

She went to kiss him again, but he pulled away. "You're a liar, Avery. You're pregnant, aren't you?"

Avery turned away from him. "I didn't want to tell you."

"Why not? Don't I have a right to know? It's my baby!"

The anger in his voice made her turn back to him and she leaped in fear as suddenly the entire family was behind him. Steven, Janet, Michael, Haley, and Leigh all stared at her with eyes so angry they were red.

"This is my baby!" Avery's hands went defensively to her stomach as she backed up.

"No," Carter said. "It's mine and I want it."

"We want it," Janet said with a voice sounding more like a snake's hiss. "It's a Chase. It belongs to us."

"You can't have my baby," Avery yelled.

"If I can't have you," Carter said, "I will take the baby. I won't end up with nothing."

"We'll get the baby," Steven said as he put a hand on Carter's shoulder. "The courts will give us the baby. We'll buy the judge."

Carter's frown quickly turned to a smile. "That's right. You're a liar. You left me because I kept secrets from you and that's exactly what you're doing to me. No secret is worse than this."

"No," was all Avery could repeat over and over again as the family took one step closer, then another and . . .

Avery's eyes shot open in a panic, her entire body tense and shaking. She looked around, trying to get ahold of herself. Yes, it was just a dream. It was the same dream she'd had last week and the week before that.

All twenty-seven-year-old Avery Jackson wanted was to spend a calm Monday morning sitting in the window seat of her second-floor apartment catching up on her magazines, but she'd made the mistake of dozing off.

She took a deep breath to relieve some of the tension inside her. It was just a dream. She reached for the magazine that had fallen out of her hands as she slept and opened it back up. The irony of what she saw frightened her and she couldn't turn away from it. Maybe she shouldn't have chosen *Upscale* magazine, considering the odds of coming across a picture like this.

God help her, all she could think of was how handsome he was and then how that little part of her that still missed him really, really missed him. It was the part that she told no one about, not even her mother.

CHASE FOUNDATION SPONSORS SMALL BUSINESS SYMPOSIUM was the headline. The article was about yet another good cause the family would support: paying for top consulting firm services to minority-owned small businesses that opened shop in underprivileged areas around the country. The picture was of Janet Chase, in all her glamorous wonder, speaking at a podium with Steven standing behind her and Carter and Michael standing next to him.

Carter always stood out, even next to a man as powerful as Steven Chase and one as good looking and vibrant as Michael. All the Chase men had a way of lighting up a room, but for Avery, no one shone brighter than Carter. He had that familiar smirk on his face, the smirk of a man who had life going his way as far back as he could remember.

Part of her wanted him miserable because of the stress he was causing her family. The way he had acted toward them since she'd left only solidified her belief that she had made the right choice in leaving.

Turning the page, Avery smiled at the next two pictures. One was of Leigh and Haley looking like the beautiful princesses they both were, the other of Michael again with the twins. She missed those boys much more than she expected to. She missed Kimberly and Leigh.

"Stop it," she ordered herself, closing the magazine.

She couldn't let herself dwell on her life with Carter. Because no matter how much she thought of the secrets, deceptions, and lies, ultimately she would remember the things that made her happy and she would want that life back. She had this amazing, powerful man who blinded her with a beautiful lifestyle, charm, addictive affection, and incredible sex. The cherry on top was the best of everything, a way of living she had never imagined she would have. The sheen and gloss of endless money, influence, and power was all wonderful and tantalizing. It was all a seduction and she had paid a high price for letting it get to her.

As she looked out the window, watching the backpack-laden students rush to campus for their morning class, Avery found peace and joy in her life now. She hadn't expected to be happy when she moved to the small close-knit college community in Coral Gables, Florida. She was going to stay with her second cousin, Alissa, while she figured out how to keep away from Carter until the baby was born. She needed the time to get her head straight before that Chase family tried to get their hands on her baby.

As if on cue, the baby kicked and Avery's hand went instinctively to her stomach. Although not always comfortable, the baby's kicking always elated her.

"You trying to start something?" she asked the little love of her life. "It's a little early for all that nonsense, so keep it down."

Another kick and Avery laughed. This little one was defiant from the start. She was going to have her hands full with him or her. She was going to have her hands full with Carter as well. Because even though something had happened only a few weeks after arriving in Florida that changed the course of everything, ultimately she would have to deal with Carter and the Chase family. She only hoped she was up to it.

The phone, which she had taken with her to the window, startled her when it rang. She had caught herself again thinking of Carter, which seemed to be happening more and more frequently. Avery felt a tightening in her chest at the sight of the number on caller ID. She blinked, certain she was just imagining it because of her homesickness, but she wasn't.

"Are you gonna get that?" the voice from the back bedroom yelled. "I'm getting dressed! I'm already late."

"Yeah." Avery slowly brought the phone to her ear and pressed the button. "H . . . hello?"

"Avery? Avery, is that you?"

Avery immediately recognized the voice as that of her twenty-year-old baby sister. "Taylor, what's wrong with you? You know you aren't supposed to call me from home."

"Forget that, Avery. It's an emergency."

A sense of dread swept over her. "What is it? What happened?"

"It's Daddy," Taylor said. "Daddy's been shot and it's really bad."

Avery gasped, almost dropping the phone. "What happened?"

"He and Sean were . . . These guys were stealing a car and . . . they shot him and he's all hooked up to tubes. It's not good, Avery."

As Taylor began sobbing uncontrollably, Avery felt her stomach tightening. "Are you with Mama?"

"She's talking to . . . to the doctor. She's gonna lose it any second now."

"Okay," Avery said calmly for Taylor's sake. "It's going to be okay. You stay with Mama and tell her I'm coming."

"Please hurry, Avery. I don't know if he'll make it."

"He'll make it, baby," Avery assured before hanging the phone up. "Anthony!"

Six feet tall and a smooth raisin brown, Professor Anthony Harper rushed into the living room with a half-buttoned shirt on and pants unzipped. Anthony was the "thing that had happened" to Avery only a few weeks after arriving in Coral Gables and he changed the course of everything. He had saved her, and Avery loved him for it.

"What is it?" He looked ready for anything, like most men with expecting wives. "What's wrong?"

"We have to go home." Avery was trying to keep from panicking. It wasn't good for the baby. "It's Daddy. He's been shot."

"Jesus!" Anthony's hands went to his head as he stared in disbelief. His plainly handsome face made that squinting look like it did whenever he was upset. "Is he . . ."

"He's in the hospital and it doesn't look good." Avery wiped the tears from her cheeks. "Mom will just die . . . She . . . I have to be there."

"I'll call Dean Sims." Anthony started back toward the hallway, but quickly turned around. "Avery?"

Avery looked at her husband, a man with a kind heart, understanding beyond words. "I'll go pack."

"Wait." He rushed to her, helping her up. "What about . . ."

Avery sighed, looking into his eyes. He usually got angry when the subject of Carter came up, but now he seemed concerned. "We'll have to deal with that later. Daddy is more important."

"I'm prepared to do this," he said confidently. "Are you?"

Avery swallowed hard, trying not to think of all the lies. "I can try."

"We have to think of what's best for the baby," he said. "What you need to focus on right now."

Avery nodded. She couldn't imagine dealing with Carter, her father, and trying to stay healthy for the baby in these last crucial months all at the same time.

"I'll call Dr. Kanata. Everything should be in place."

As she started down the hallway, Avery turned to see Anthony on the phone, dialing in everything that needed to be confirmed. This web of lies was Anthony's idea in case Carter found Avery. She was reluctant at first, but as she came to care for Anthony, her resistance weakened. She told herself she was going along with it because she felt she owed him for all he had done for her. But now that she was happy and could see a life without battling the Chase family over her baby, she wanted Anthony's idea to work just as much as he did. She just didn't think it would.

Avery knew Carter and she wasn't sure Anthony fully understood what he was up against no matter how much she tried to explain it to him. He'd never met people like the Chases. He was a college statistics professor who had lived a quiet, calm life for thirty-six years. She wondered if he would want anything to do with her after the truth about what he had gotten himself into really hit him.

Kimberly was glued to the local news station as the reporter gave an update on Chief Jackson's condition. Since being shot yesterday, he had been placed in ICU, had two operations, and was still in very critical condition. All she could think of was Avery, wondering where the girl was and when she would come back. She missed her and although she knew it would mean Carter would probably go nuts, Kimberly wanted Avery back. She had never felt so lonely.

"I'm off." Marisol, Kimberly's maid, stood in the doorway to the living room in a pair of three-hundred-dollar jeans and an A&F T-shirt Kimberly had given her. "Do you want your mail or should I leave it on Mr. Michael's desk?"

Kimberly held her hand out as she kept her eyes on the television. They were showing the throngs of police officers congregating outside the hospital. "I need you to pick the boys up from school."

"That's where I'm going." Marisol sighed, rolling her eyes. "Here."

"Thanks." Kimberly took the mail. "What did Michael say he wanted for dinner tonight?"

"No dinner for him," Marisol said.

This got Kimberly's attention as she swung around. "Why not?"

"I ask him." She shrugged. "He said he won't be home. Has a meeting or something. I'll make dinner for you and the boys."

Furious, Kimberly shot up from the sofa. "Where did he say he was going for dinner?"

"What do I know?" she asked, and rushed out of the room.

Kimberly reached for her ever-present cell phone and dialed Michael. When it went to voice mail, she wanted to scream. How could he not take her call? This had to stop. The neglect and disregard, except in order to control, were driving her crazy. Another business dinner without her? What happened to wanting to show off his gorgeous wife to partners and clients?

Kimberly tossed the phone on the sofa and sifted through the mail. Bills, catalogs, invitations, and magazines. At the bottom of the pile, she saw a large, flat envelope addressed to her. Kimberly dumped the rest of the mail and opened the envelope. What slid out was a newspaper cutout picture of her dressed up for a formal benefit of some kind. It was a little unusual. She and Michael had agreed that she would stay out of the limelight, not wanting to take any chances with her past coming back. For that reason, Kimberly was rarely seen in newspapers or magazines in the early years, but as time went on, good fortune allowed them to relax. She no longer bore any resemblance to that fifteen-year-old girl.

She tried to remember when this photo was taken, as whoever had sent it cut off the caption. From the dress, a Versace, it had to be last fall. Opening the envelope a bit more, Kimberly noticed a small piece of paper stuck to the edges. Reaching in, she pulled it out and read it.

You clean up well, Paige

Kimberly gasped, dropping the envelope to the floor. Another picture slid halfway out and with shaky fingers, she reached down to pick it up. As she looked at the photo, her knees went weak and she dropped to the floor.

It was her all right, only her from about ten years ago. With seventeen-year-old eyes mixing innocence with damage, she was sitting at a bar stool, her tongue in the process of licking her upper lip while staring into the camera. There was a can of beer in one hand and the other was squeezing her right breast. There were too-drunk, half-naked people in the background. She remembered the girl, but couldn't place her name.

Kimberly ran to the half bath outside the foyer and threw up as fear swept over her, crippling fear. Paige was the name she used when she was a teenaged prostitute in Detroit. It had finally happened. Someone had recognized her, and the world she had come to live and love was about to fall apart. At the worst possible time.

She thought of her boys and sobbed uncontrollably. She thought of Janet and what she would do when she found out and threw up again. Most of all, she thought of Michael and was scared to death. He had gone through painstaking efforts to make her past disappear, telling her that she didn't want to know the details of what he'd done. She didn't. She was glad for the chance to pretend that world never existed.

What would happen to him if the family found out he had married a whore? Right now only Carter knew and Kimberly trusted his bond with Michael. Beyond the family, what would happen if this got public? Would Michael stay with her? Not after everything she had done, already jeopardizing his status within the family. Then the boys; what about the boys?

"No." Kimberly lifted herself from the floor and stumbled back to the family room.

She picked up the envelope to see who it was from, but there was no return address. There was nothing on the slip of paper but one line. Whoever it was didn't want her to know who they were. At least, not yet.

She tried to compose herself, tried to get her mind around what this could mean. It could mean a disaster worse than death. Or she could fix it. She could fix it herself and Michael would never have to know. Just as he did when he thought he had erased her past, Kimberly would do whatever it took and make sure it was really erased this time. She wouldn't let whoever this was destroy her life, destroy everything.

Leigh thanked Maya for the fruit plate she offered before digging in.

"You're certainly hungry," Janet acknowledged, sitting across from her at the kitchen table.

Leigh nodded, swallowing the pineapple before speaking. "I missed dinner last night. Working late at the clinic."

Despite the security, paid for by Chase Beauty, Janet didn't like Leigh working late at the clinic at all. "You're supposed to close at nine, but you never do."

"We don't like turning people away." Leigh reached for the

copy of the *L.A. Times* already worked through by her father. She noticed her mother's angry stare. "Don't look at me like that. We're never open one second without security."

"Maya would have made you something if you were hungry."

"I'm not waking her up late at night. She works hard enough. I can get something out of the fridge myself. I was just too tired."

"With the twins gone, Maya has more free time than any of us."

"Still," Leigh protested.

"Well, you have to find some free time, Leigh. I haven't heard the piano in days."

"I practiced yesterday," Leigh said. "You can't hear it all the way from your bedroom. It's like a mile."

Janet sipped her coffee. "The benefit is only a month away. You have to be sharp."

Leigh focused on the paper, trying to ignore her mother's pushing. She had agreed to play the piano, which she had learned as a child, as part of a benefit the Chase Foundation was holding for music programs at L.A.'s public schools. She had been a little rusty, with all her time spent at the clinic, but felt confident she could pull it off.

"Are you bringing anyone?" Janet asked.

Leigh shook her head. "And don't start with me."

Janet wouldn't do that. She had interfered with Leigh's love life hundreds of times, but the last time almost got her daughter killed. Janet would always have to live with the fact that she was the one who introduced Leigh to Leo Bridges and guilted her into dating him.

Her mistake had cost too many too much, including Leigh cutting Janet out of her life. It was the impetus to her prescription drug dependency. It was such an ugly, difficult time, made worse by Kimberly's scheming. Fortunately, Leigh had forgiven her and moved back home, but Janet knew there was now a line that, if crossed again, there would be no forgiveness for.

Turning the page, Leigh was drawn to the picture of Sean Jackson with his arms around his mother, Nikki, leading her out of the hospital. "What's the latest on Chief Jackson?"

"Nothing new," Janet said thoughtfully.

"Should we do something?" Leigh asked. "I mean, they were almost family."

"It's complicated," Janet said. "Besides, what would we do? Raise money? I don't know if that family would take money from us. Not after the way Carter has behaved."

"I thought he was over that . . . crazy period." Leigh had been out of touch of late, but she knew enough to know that Carter hadn't taken Avery's leaving him well. "He seems to be dating again."

"Dating isn't really the right word for what's he doing," Janet said. "But at least he isn't stalking the Jacksons anymore."

"Avery should be coming back," Leigh said. "What do you think will happen?"

Janet was very worried, but ultimately she knew what she wanted to happen. "Maybe it will be good. It's been six months. She should be over her anger. If this means anything, it will show her what really matters."

Leigh wasn't sure what her mother was getting at. "You don't think they'll get back together, do you?"

"Why not?" Janet asked.

Avery was an unlikely choice for her son because Janet had wanted both Michael and Carter to marry someone from the family's social circles. A young woman, well educated with social standing, professional, with a family that had history and substance. But Avery was a wonderful person and Janet couldn't help but warm to her from the second she met her. It would be a lot of work making Avery suitable for the world the Chases lived in, but Janet always thought she would be worth it. She had an inborn sense of class and character. She held herself better than many of the best-bred young society women these days and she loved Carter to death. At least she had.

"I don't think that will happen," Leigh said. "And if Carter goes back to wrapping his car around trees . . ."

"Don't talk about that," Janet said.

"I guess he'll just get away with it. He is a Chase."

Janet put her cup down, staring at the one child who had never really come to grips with her last name. "Would you rather your brother, a lawyer, get a DUI?"

Leigh sighed. "No, but . . . I don't know. It's just if he gets away with it, what's to keep him from doing it again? He could have killed himself or someone else."

"That's enough, Leigh." Janet tried to shake off the suspicion she'd had that it hadn't really been an accident.

"You have to do this!" Haley said as she rushed into the kitchen, still dressed in her pajamas. She plopped the inch-thick script titled BEDPANS & BILLIONAIRES, in front of Leigh on the table.

"When is your class?" Janet looked at her watch.

"Ten." Haley reached for what was left of her mother's croissant and stuffed it in her mouth. "But I'm not going. I have someone taking notes."

"I want you to go," Janet said. "What is that?"

"How did you get this?" Leigh was flipping through the script, peppered with notes in the margins. "Is this . . . Is this Lyndon's script?"

Haley nodded. "It's the movie he wants to shadow you for. It's full of morals and all those everyone-has-value ideals. Complete lies, but you love that crap."

"Someone want to explain this to me?" Janet asked.

Leigh filled her mother in on Lyndon's request, before closing the pages of the script and looking up at Haley. "How did you get this?"

"A courier dropped it off for you yesterday," Haley answered. "Maya! Where is she? I'm hungry."

"You're getting dressed, Haley." Janet gestured for her youngest to leave, but she didn't move. "I'm serious, Haley. You're going to class."

Haley's hands clenched into fists as she groaned out loud. "Leave me alone."

"What were you doing with it?" Leigh asked.

"I was reading it."

"It was addressed to me, so you stole it?"

Haley just shrugged. "I want to meet him. So you have to do it."

"I thought you were seeing someone," Janet said, wondering if

Steven had yet done the background check on Haley's latest diversion. "One of your classmates."

"I'm not married to him," Haley answered.

"Hollywood is nothing to get involved with," Janet said. "Not for us."

Leigh nodded in agreement. "It's more trouble than it's worth. I have to get to the clinic."

As she stood up, with Haley quickly taking her place, Janet noticed that Leigh still had the script in her hand. "You can leave that. Maya will toss it for you. Or should we send it back?"

Leigh looked down at the script. "No, I'll . . . I'd like to read it actually, just to see. Even if I don't want him following me around, I might be able to give him some pointers."

Janet painted a smile on her face, but she had a bad feeling about this. Who was Lyndon Prior anyway?

Michael was in the middle of signing off on yet another expense for the marketing group when his father grabbed him by the arm and pulled.

"Hey," Michael protested. "I actually need this arm, you know."

"Where is he?" Steven asked, ready to explode. The board was convening and there was no sign of Carter.

Michael reached down and grabbed his phone from the clip. "I can call him again, but he isn't picking up."

"Did you send—"

"Yes, I have all the little minions out looking for him. He's not in his office or the condo." Michael looked down at his watch. "Patricia says he'll be here."

"This meeting starts in ten minutes," Steven said. Why . . . How could he do this? "This board put their faith in me by voting Carter in."

"Like they had a choice," Michael said. "It's your company. I'll just say he was in a car accident or one of his clients was arrested."

"Is this funny to you?" Steven asked in that tone that quickly erased the smirk from Michael's face. "I gave you the responsibility of finding him. If he doesn't show up, I'll blame you."

"Well, that certainly seems fair," Michael said sarcastically before turning away from his father's threatening glare.

Michael was always jealous of Carter's ability to stand up to their father. No one won against Steven, but Carter came the closest to making him crazy and Michael didn't have the guts. He worshipped the man and feared him too much.

Carter's absence assured Michael that Steven would know that he could only count on him to put Chase Beauty first. In that sense, this worked in his favor. On the other hand, where in the hell was he? As defiant as Carter was, even he knew that you could only push their father so far before hell came down on you. He had a feeling he knew what was keeping him, and Michael feared that his brother was about to make a bad situation much, much worse.

Carter was across the street from the hospital parking lot and could barely see the entrance. He saw nothing but uniformed cops and assumed the other men and women were probably detectives. Then there was all the equipment from the news stations blocking his view. He couldn't go anywhere else. This was the main entrance and the only entrance visible from the street.

He was annoyed by the ringing of his cell phone lying on the passenger seat of his car. It was Michael's ring tone again. He knew he was late, but he couldn't help it. He had to . . .

"Hey." Matt Tustin, a longtime private investigator for the family, seemed to come from nowhere to the driver's-side window. He was a bland, invisible type of man, which made his job as a P.I. all the easier.

"Where in the hell have you been?" Carter asked.

"You see that hospital, man? There are cops everywhere."

"I thought you were in with the cops," Carter said. "It would be no problem getting past them were your exact words."

"Do you want the pictures or not?" Matt said.

It was Matt that Carter called the second he realized Avery had run away. He was willing to do anything to find her, but Matt had proved just as useless as the other investigators.

"Give them to me." Carter held out one hand, offering an envelope with cash in the other.

"This wasn't easy. I hope you know."

"I don't care." Carter opened the envelope and the first photo he pulled out was of Avery sitting in a chair next to the hospital bed.

Carter felt something odd come over him at the sight of her. It was more than relief, but God, how he missed her. She was beautiful even though her eyes were red and she looked tired. She wasn't looking at her father, but at someone standing next to her, who wasn't visible in the picture. She looked as if she needed help, needed a strong arm around her. She needed him.

How could she leave him? Carter had torn himself apart trying to figure out how he could have been so mistaken about her love for him. He'd felt it so strong himself; maybe it was that and his arrogance that believed no woman would ever leave him. He had gotten over himself as to how much of a catch he knew he was. He was marrying Avery, so what he meant to other women didn't matter anymore.

He had held on to the belief that no matter how awful what he'd done was, she would come back. She had promised to love him, take care of him, and be his forever. He needed her and yes, had made mistakes to make her his, but had done nothing but try to make her happy since the day she became his. He deserved better than what she had done to him: leaving as if what they had shared meant nothing. They had almost died together that night of the explosion at her salon.

He ached for her as he touched the photo. All those nights he drank himself to sleep or tried to forget her by being inside another woman had done nothing to dampen the love he felt for Avery. Seeing her picture made him think he could be complete again. If he could just see her, touch her, hold her, maybe he could let go of the anger he felt all the time.

Carter turned back to the hospital, trying to control the emotions taking him over. She was his and he had to have her back. There was no better time than now considering the pain she was in. She needed him. He opened the car door, prepared to face whatever barriers the family had set up to keep him out, but as he looked back at the picture, something caught his eye.

There was something . . .

"No." He brought the picture closer.

He had to be seeing things. It was the angle or maybe a reflection off the light. Anything other than what it looked like, because it looked like a wedding band on her left middle finger. It was. A simple gold band clearly visible as she held her hand out over her father's chest.

It couldn't be.

Carter was transfixed as he tried to convince himself he was making a mistake, but he knew he wasn't. He looked around, unsure of what to do, think, or feel. He needed something . . . he had to . . . his mind was a mess. His insides were in pieces and still he told himself that there was an explanation. There had to be.

He closed the car door, deciding against a confrontation right now. He was too mixed up. He needed more information before going forward. As he drove off, Carter felt rage growing inside him. This meant nothing, he told himself. He was still going to get Avery back and nothing and no one was going to stand in his way.

Private Investigator Neil Owen held the envelope away as he studied it. He was shaking his head and Kimberly assumed that wasn't good news.

"There's no way to know where it came from," he said in his monotone, disaffected voice, "except that it was mailed out of a post office in Pasadena."

"Maybe that post office has video cameras?" Kimberly sat across from him, squeezing the Prada purse on her lap tighter and tighter.

She knew she probably shouldn't be here. It was Neil who helped her track down Paul Devereaux and bring him to L.A. to tear Janet and Steven apart. She had promised Michael she would never go to a private investigator behind his back again, but all bets and promises were off now.

"Possibly." Neil placed the envelope on his desk. "Wanna tell me what was in it?"

"No," Kimberly said. "I just need to find out who sent it. I think they want to blackmail me."

"Did they say they wanted money?" Neil asked, looking as if his sixty years had caught up with him, which wouldn't be hard considering he had spent a considerable part of his life on secret missions for the CIA.

"There were pictures inside." Both of which Kimberly burned as soon as she got her head back on straight. "I'm sure they want money."

"Then they'll tell you that," Neil said. "My advice is to stay calm, keep a low profile, and wait."

Kimberly leaned forward. "I can't wait. This could . . . this could destroy everything. You have to do something!"

"Video is out of the question. This post office is probably huge and the person mostly likely picked a busy time when he couldn't be singled out. If I could, by some miracle, get access to video from the date on the postmark, you would have to look at it. I can't recognize who I don't know."

"Try and get it anyway," Kimberly said. "I'll look at all of them. I don't care. What else can you do? What about prints?"

"On this?" He pointed to the envelope. "Not a chance. I used gloves, but you didn't. Neither did your maid or the myriads of other people who could have touched this in between."

"Damn it!"

"Now, whatever was inside is another story." Neil leaned back in his chair. "If only you and the blackmailer touched it, then . . ."

"It's burned."

Neil nodded as if he understood. "Then like I said, you wait. If it's money they want, they'll give you a chance to give it to them."

Kimberly thought of the ordeal with Carter and Lisette McDaniel, which the entire family found out about after Avery left him. Carter had paid Lisette once, but she came back for more. He'd had to pay her again. When he tried to get it back, Steven made him give it up. He considered it suitable punishment.

"They'll come back for more," Kimberly said. "It won't stop."

"Unless you make it stop," Neil said.

Kimberly understood what he meant. "I'm willing to do anything."

"I can help you make sure this person doesn't want to come back for more," Neil said, "but I can't help you make it impossible for them to come back for more. You'll have to go elsewhere for that."

Kimberly wondered if she had the guts to get rid of someone. If she was still in the world she'd been in when she was a hooker, yes, she would have done it. She had wanted to kill just about every man she met in those days. But things were different now. She thought of her sons and what made her a good mother. She thought of lowering herself to be the person that Janet always told her she knew she was.

"What is it?" Neil asked as Kimberly's hand went to her chest.

"I just thought of my mother-in-law again."

"That bad?" Neil laughed. "Mine gives me heartburn too."

You'll slip up again were her words. Kimberly remembered them clearly. *You'll slip up again and that will be it for Michael.*

"I'll do whatever it takes to make this go away."

4

As the waiter led her to the table, Leigh could feel people staring at her. They were wondering if she was somebody. Most realized that she wasn't and quickly lost interest, but a few stares lingered. They were probably people who had seen her picture in the papers because of her family. It all made her very uncomfortable.

"Is there a private table somewhere?" Leigh asked the hostess.

The hostess, who had short, sandy blond hair with blue highlights, turned around and laughed. "Yeah, right."

"No," Leigh said. "I'm serious. I feel exposed."

"That's why people come to the Ivy, sweetheart. To be exposed."

"I don't come here," Leigh said.

"You're here, aren't you?" She stopped at a table in the corner with a view of the front porch packed with people, many of whom Leigh recognized immediately from some movie or television show. "The food is great, but no one actually comes here to eat."

Leigh mumbled that this wasn't her choice as she sat down. What was Lyndon up to? She had called him on the number he left on the script and agreed to meet him to share her feedback. Was he trying to turn it into some publicity stunt?

She felt her beeper vibrating and reached down to check it. It was her mother, not the clinic. Just as she reached for her phone she saw Lyndon walking toward her and forgot all about her mother.

Patiently taking him in, she noticed again that he was everything that was said about him: tall, fit, and ridiculously handsome. He played the rugged, but not too rugged, part well. White linen pants and a beige shirt that hung on him as if it was made just for him, a fresh tan finishing the look perfectly.

"Sorry I'm late," he said as he took a seat next to her.

Leigh figured he was probably always late. That was what his type did, make an entrance. "It's all right. I—"

"What can I get you, Mr. Prior?" The hostess leaned forward, showing her recently purchased bosoms. "You like a Mojito, right?"

"Sure," he said, turning to Leigh. "You want one?"

"It's only noon," Leigh said.

Lyndon frowned as if he regretted asking. "You know what? Why not just bring a water with lemon?"

"Two," Leigh added.

The hostess nodded and walked away.

"Thanks for meeting me . . ." Lyndon smiled, showing white shiny teeth. "You look great, Dr. Chase."

Leigh couldn't believe it. She was blushing. "Thanks. I enjoyed your script."

"It's not mine," he said. "The writer is a guy name Deke Minton. This is more or less his real life story. It's a little exaggerated for Hollywood, but he's actually a doctor in Philadelphia."

"He wrote this?" Leigh thought she would like to meet Deke Minton one day.

"With some help." Lyndon took the menu from Leigh just as she reached for it. "Please, get the crab cakes. I promise you, you'll love them."

"Okay." Leigh wasn't sure if he was being controlling or gentlemanly.

As Lyndon ordered two servings of softshell crab, she took a second to look around and realized that everyone was staring at them, or at least at him. There were a lot of celebrities here and she assumed all the noncelebrities were writers, directors, agents, and more.

"I guess you're okay with being the center of attention," Leigh said, once the hostess took their orders and left. "You have to be."

Lyndon shrugged, leaning back in his seat. "You know all of this is fleeting. You have to enjoy it while you can. Being humble won't make me rich."

"You're already rich," she said. "You made fifteen million your last two pictures."

"That's chicken feed." Lyndon pointed to the script Leigh placed on the table. "I'm getting more for that."

"I don't need to know this," Leigh said. "It's rude to ask about money."

"In this business," Lyndon said, "it's rude not to ask. But you know all about money, don't you?"

Leigh shifted in her seat. "About your . . . this script. You mentioned exaggerations?"

"The writer embellished a bit. You know, for effect. But mostly it's true. What did you think? I'm eager to hear your opinion."

Leigh wasn't sure if he was being genuine, but she offered her ideas anyway. He seemed to listen and even asked the waitress who brought their lunches for her pen so he could take notes on the back of the script. Leigh's suggestions were all mostly superficial but all the little things that can add up to a lot.

"This is good stuff," Lyndon said as he put his pen down. "I'll talk to the director about it."

"You don't have to," Leigh said. "It's just small stuff you could do in the role without even telling anyone."

"It'll make it look more authentic." He nodded, seeming satisfied with his choice. "Dr. Chase, I—"

"Call me Leigh." She covered her mouth, filled with crab cakes.

Lyndon smiled. "Cool, but I want you to know I really care about this role. I know what you think of me."

"I haven't said anything."

"You don't have to," Lyndon said. "People always make assumptions based on what they think they know about me, have read about me. Like I'm sure people do with you all the time."

Before she could protest, she realized he was right. Because she was Leigh Chase, people assumed a lot. "I didn't mean to offend you."

"You didn't." He shrugged, leaning back. "I did some research on you after I read that article. I know about your family, so I figured you might understand."

"Understand?"

"That it's just . . . you know how it is when people don't believe you're genuine because you have money or fame. They think everything is trivial to you, just for kicks. Like you couldn't possibly understand anything other than your own circumstances."

"They assume you think the world revolves around you," Leigh said.

"It's like, yeah, I am lucky and I'm not going to pretend I'm not." Lyndon was talking excitedly, all of a sudden unable to sit still. "But that doesn't mean I can't be genuine. I still work hard at my job."

"But unless you're struggling to pay your bills," Leigh said, "you can't be a real person."

Their eyes caught and Leigh felt a spark rush through her. This was silly. There was no way she was actually interested in him. She was starstruck and starved for male attention. He was a professional flirt, always working whoever he was with. That's all this was. Besides, he was probably handling a dozen women right now and her parents would kill her if she dated an actor, a white actor at that.

"You want the truth?" Leigh asked.

"Let me brace myself," Lyndon said, placing his fork down.

"The ending sort of bothered me," she said. "I mean, he goes through all these horrible things, but it's somehow tied to his lack of real commitment to the job. In the end, he realizes he loves this, it matters, and everything seems to work out. That's not reality."

"You aren't happy because of the clinic?"

"You're reading me wrong," Leigh corrected. "We're dealing with a deadly disease here, and at a clinic like this, the people who come in have so many other problems. It's dangerous, it's ugly, and it's heartbreaking even when you're committed. Most of the time, things don't work out no matter how hard you try. Most days don't have a happy ending."

"But you wouldn't want to see that movie, would you?" Lyndon asked. "I mean, I get it. I know that the reality is different, but a movie has to have a happy ending or at least one that makes people not want to slit their wrists when they leave."

Leigh laughed at her own heaviness. "Sorry, I guess I was getting a little preachy."

"I don't mind," he said in a low, soft voice. "You do it well, Dr. . . . Leigh."

"You can stop working me, Lyndon. You've already gotten what you want. You can come to the clinic."

Lyndon laughed. "You think I'm working you?"

"Aren't you?" She raised an eyebrow.

"Actually I am," he answered, "but I really enjoy it, so can I keep it up a little while longer?"

She rolled her eyes, thinking this was probably a big mistake.

When she heard the bedroom door open, Kimberly looked at the clock on the nightstand. It was three in the morning. *This son of a bitch!*

"Where have you been?" she asked, sitting up.

"I was with Carter." Michael had crossed his fingers she was asleep, but he was really too drunk to care that she would be angry right now.

"You drove in that condition?"

"No." He closed the door to the master bathroom behind him, hoping she would get the message, but she was right behind him. "Kimberly, just go to bed. I'll be there in a minute."

"How can you not call me?" she asked. "How can you not pick up your cell phone?"

"I told you I was going to go by Carter's." He splashed some water on his face before trying to get out of his clothes.

"Where did you go?" she asked, although she wanted to ask *who did you see?* She thought together with the alcohol, she smelled perfume. "What were you doing?"

"We went out to the club for some drinks." His shirt off, Michael started on his pants. "Can you get my shorts?"

She reached up behind the door and tossed the shorts at him. "Were there women there?"

Michael laughed. "At the club? Um . . . yeah. What the hell kind of question is that?"

"You know what kind of question it is, Michael. Carter can't do anything these days but fuck whatever he finds. So what were you doing?"

Michael's grin faded as he looked at her. "You need to change your direction right now, Kimberly."

He sort of remembered making out with a woman near the bathroom, but couldn't recall her name. He probably never asked. She had red hair and he liked redheads. They kissed for a few minutes, but as soon as he heard footsteps around the corner, he stopped.

So what if he cheated? He was only a man and he'd done it only a few times. Those women meant nothing more than a one-night stand. No matter what, he loved Kimberly, and none of those women could make him feel the way she did. He wasn't a perfect husband, but he was discreet.

"Or what?" Kimberly asked.

"I couldn't leave him," Michael said. "He's a mess."

"He's thirty-one years old! He doesn't need a babysitter."

Michael slid into his boxers. "Avery's back."

Kimberly paused at the news. "I knew she'd come . . . Did Carter talk to her?"

He shook his head. "No, you have to talk to her."

Kimberly's hand went to her hips. "Why? What are you up to?"

"She had a wedding ring on her finger."

"No." Kimberly would never believe Avery was married. "She wouldn't get over Carter that fast."

"She hated him, remember? She left."

"She never hated him," Kimberly said.

"He saw it. She had a wedding band on and you have to find

out what that's about." Michael approached her, trying not to sound so drunk. "You're still her friend."

Kimberly backed away. "Don't try to talk me into this. You and Carter have already played too many games with her. I won't help you play anymore."

Kimberly was surprised by the sudden anger that took over her husband's face.

"Are you going to help me or not?" he asked.

"How does this help you?"

"Help Carter, I mean."

She nodded reluctantly. "You have to stop doing this."

"Doing what?"

"Staying out all night with him," she said. "You're not single. You're my husband."

"But I'm not your child," he said. "So don't tell what I can and can't do."

"You don't seem to have any problem doing that with me."

With a sharp angry tone, he said, "I don't need any more problems from you, Kimberly. I've had enough to last a lifetime. Do you understand me?"

Kimberly immediately thought of the pictures, and her heart sank. She didn't answer him. She just turned and went back to bed. She couldn't get to sleep for hours, thinking of who had sent her the pictures and what they wanted. Her life as Kimberly Chase, Janet notwithstanding, had been like a fairy tale up until the incident six months ago. And even as difficult as things were now, she could never have imagined being this lucky.

She'd almost forgotten about those two years that seemed to last a decade at the time. Two years of selling herself for food, being beaten and degraded for a roof to sleep under. Meeting Michael made it all go away. But she would never really be able to forget and she was afraid that whoever was behind this wasn't just after money. They wanted to drag her back down into the gutter, the gutter where Janet had always told her she belonged.

"Cancel it," Carter snapped into his Bluetooth as he parked his car surprisingly close to the Jackson home.

Surprisingly, because he had just driven by the house and witnessed the police presence around it, it seemed unlikely he would get this close. He hadn't expected to find an open space only three homes down the road.

"I can't keep canceling your appointments, Carter." Patricia, his assistant who was usually calm even under the worst circumstances, sounded irritated. "When will you be in today?"

"I'll be in by three," he said, even though he didn't think he would. "Clear everything until three."

The office hadn't been on his mind at all since he'd seen the picture of Avery. He'd tried to drink that ring on her finger out of his head, but it hadn't worked. He couldn't wait for Kimberly to get to Avery, as Michael suggested. He'd already waited six months and he wasn't going to wait one more.

Carter had to squint to believe his eyes. Perfect timing couldn't describe it as he saw a silver Honda drive past him with Avery in the passenger's seat. She was looking down, but he knew it was her. He caught a quick glimpse of the man driving the car and already felt his anger rising.

The car pulled up to the house, blocking the driveway from the street, and Carter picked up his pace. He watched as Avery's hand reached up and slid a few runaway strands of her hair behind her ear. He was always touched by the beauty of simplicity only she could pull off.

"Avery." He waited for her to look up before he stopped. He wanted to take in every bit of her seeing him. Her beautiful, smooth chocolate skin was glowing. Her large, innocent eyes, button nose, and full lips all made up that face he had come to adore.

When she saw him, Avery felt as if the wind whipped through her, taking her breath with it as it left. She blinked, thinking she was hallucinating. She wasn't. It was Carter in the flesh, and the first thought in her mind was . . . God, she still loved him. Her heart ached for him just at the sight and she hated herself for it.

His light brown eyes were piercing and her instinct, her heart saw his pain and wanted to reach out to him, comfort him, but Avery knew she had to keep her emotions in check. She looked ahead as Anthony, who had already gotten out of the car, was coming around the side. This was her husband and this was the man she loved now. This was . . .

Oh no, she thought. She was going to have to get out.

Seeing her like this, Carter was hit again by how much he missed every bit of her, and he wanted to, needed to hold her. He took a few more steps before noticing there was a world around them. And in that world, a man was walking in his direction.

"Can I help you?" Anthony asked, rushing to stand between Carter and the car.

Carter looked the man up and down with disdain, taking notice of the ring on his wedding finger. He was an older, safe-looking man, the kind that someone would expect to be a teacher. He was raisin brown with forgettable features, wire-rimmed glasses, and about ten extra pounds.

Carter wanted to blast him with his fists right away, but knew he couldn't do that. Not in front of Avery at least. He knew how she felt about violence. Besides, this was about him and Avery. This little man didn't matter and would soon be out of the picture.

"No, you can't." Carter stared him down. He would make him blink and the stage would be set. It was all just paperwork after that.

"You're not welcome here," Anthony offered.

Carter continued to stare without answering until Anthony blinked. Carter's lips casually slipped into a victorious smile because he believed Anthony was smart enough to know what he'd just done.

"So you know who I am?" Carter asked calmly.

"Who you are isn't important," Anthony said.

"Then you don't know who I am," Carter answered with a smirk.

"Who I am is . . ." Anthony looked back as Avery began opening the door. "Honey, no."

Carter cringed inside at the sound of that man calling Avery honey. He looked forward to the first chance he would get to beat the crap out of him. "What's wrong, buddy? She's not afraid. Are you?"

"I'm not afraid of you, you son of a bitch." Anthony took a step forward, but stopped as Carter did the same. "You stay away from my wife."

Before he could catch himself, Carter blinked and he knew the other man noticed. Just the sound of someone, anyone other than him, calling Avery his wife hit him in the gut like a sledgehammer.

"Please stop." Avery took a deep breath, looking at both men, who seemed ready to pounce. Carter wasn't going to leave. To avoid getting out would only work against them. She had to appear to have nothing to hide.

Anthony turned around and helped Avery out of the car. Carter, at first distracted by the sight of him touching Avery, was completely blown away when her full belly came into sight.

What the . . .

When he looked at her face, Avery was turned away from him, whispering something to Anthony, who was shaking his head defiantly. Carter looked back at her belly and it was as if a bolt of lightning had struck twice. She was pregnant.

"Av-ery." Her name came out broken because Carter didn't have a mind to keep up any pretense.

"Hold on." Avery held up her hand to Carter.

She wasn't sure she was strong enough for this, dealing with her emotions, her physical state, her attraction to him, and her concern for her husband. It was all too much, but she couldn't have expected it to happen any other way.

"Please, Anthony." She squeezed his hand, looking up at him. "I'm begging you."

"No." Anthony shut the car door, turning from Avery to Carter. "I'm staying right here."

"What the hell is this?" Carter asked. "You're—"

"I'm pregnant," Avery said, hopeful he would act like a jerk so she could keep her wits together. This tortured baby boy look only made her weak.

"It's not yours," Anthony insisted.

Carter looked at him as if he were an annoying child. "Fuck you."

"Carter!" Avery stepped forward, still holding Anthony's hand. "Anthony is my husband. Don't talk to him like that."

Carter laughed because he couldn't think of any other way to respond. "What bullshit is this, Avery? You run away and then . . . you come back with . . . I want an explanation. I deserve an—"

"You don't deserve anything!" Anthony yelled.

"Please." Avery squeezed Anthony's hand more firmly as Carter's frown tightened. He would start a fight, she knew that much. "Anthony, for me."

"He's a bully, baby. Just like you said. He'll only push you around if I—"

"I'm not asking you," Avery said. "Let me talk to him. We've discussed this."

Anthony huffed as if he could drop to the floor in a tantrum any second. He looked at Carter, who was still staring at Avery's belly. Turning back to her, he sighed. "I'll stand at the door. I won't go inside without you."

"Okay." Avery smiled, raising her hand to his chest as she leaned forward.

Carter's hands clenched into fists at his sides at seeing Anthony kiss Avery, his Avery, on the lips. He wasn't having this. Whatever the hell was going on, this wasn't going to continue.

As Anthony walked away, he continued to look back and Avery put on her best face. She wanted him to think she had everything under control, but she couldn't fool him that easily. It didn't matter. She couldn't avoid it any longer. So, taking a deep breath, she turned back to Carter, reminding herself that stress was bad for the baby—her baby.

Carter took another step toward her, his hand reaching out.

"No." Avery stepped back. "Don't touch me, Carter."

He stopped, the all too familiar pain rippling through his body at her rejection. How could she not miss him? How could she not want to hold him? He felt he was about to explode just being this close to her after all this time.

"Baby." His voice was weak in a way only she had heard before. "Where have you been? Why did you leave me?"

Avery hadn't expected the storm of emotion that whipped up inside her in response to the desperation in his voice. After everything he had done to her, to her family, how could she still love him? "You know why I left."

"You didn't have to disappear," he said. "You didn't have to—"

"I did," she said. "And from the way you've acted with my family, I was right to."

"I wouldn't have done that if you hadn't left," Carter said. "You could have just told me—"

"You wouldn't have left me alone," she said. "You know that, so let's skip this part."

"The baby." He looked at her belly and this time the shock he'd been feeling was leaving slight room for excitement. "That's my baby. That's why you left?"

"No, Carter." Avery felt sick now that the lie had started. She would never get away with it, and there was a part of her that knew she didn't really want to be the kind of woman that would get away with this. But for Anthony, she would try. "This is not your baby. I got pregnant after—"

"It is," Carter insisted, because he refused to accept anything else. "It's mine and you married some man to—"

"That is not some man." Avery briefly glanced at Anthony, who was staring from the porch. "Anthony is my husband, I love him and this is his baby."

"Bullshit." Carter swallowed the pain in her words. "You love me, Avery. I know you wouldn't—"

"It's not yours," she said. "I knew you'd think it was, but I'm only five months pregnant. It's impossible."

"What in the hell are you doing here?" Sean stormed over to his sister and Carter with a warning glare on his boyish face. As he waved over one of the officers standing on the inside of the garage, Sean said, "Haven't you caused my family enough pain? My father is in the hospital and you—"

"I just want to talk to you." Carter, ignoring the boy, focused on Avery, who was visibly shaken by the escalation of events. "Avery, you disappeared and I have to know—"

"Not now," Avery said. "I need to focus on my father."

"I know," Carter said. "But we have to—"

She didn't like that he kept looking at her stomach, but he was off his guard enough that she could control him. She had to use that to her advantage. "I'll talk to you later, but you'll have to go now."

"When?" Carter asked as the cop approached.

"This man is leaving," Sean said.

"Stop." Avery stopped the officer from approaching Carter. "He can leave on his own, right?"

Carter didn't know what to say or think. It wasn't in his nature to take orders or do anything he didn't want to do. He didn't want to walk away from Avery; he had just found her again after what seemed like much more than six months. He was so close to touching her, holding her. "When can I see you again?"

"I'll call you next week," she said, almost wanting to sigh at the fact that he didn't protest.

He ran his hand across his mouth with a tortured frown on his face. "Don't . . . please, Avery, don't . . ."

"I won't leave." Her voice caught in her throat as she saw the fear in his eyes. Carter Chase was afraid and that was something she had only seen when she told him it was over. "I'm not leaving."

As she turned and headed for the house, Carter looked away. He didn't want to see her walk to that man; see him touch her and think of what that meant.

Anthony wrapped his arms around Avery as they entered the house, and she knew she was in trouble because she desperately wanted to look back. She had thought loving Anthony was enough, but was it? She wanted to run to her mother and ask her how it was possible to still care for Carter as much as her heart told her she did. But she couldn't. Her mother had too much to deal with and Avery had to handle Carter on her own.

Carter headed back for his car, but didn't drive off for another half hour. He was shaken, confused, happy, angry, and afraid of what it all meant. He had gotten used to being at a disadvantage when it came to Avery long ago, but this scared him.

Everything inside him told him that the baby was his. It had to be. He didn't want to imagine Avery ever having sex with any other man, but he wasn't a fool. He could see that as a possibility over the course of six months, considering how angry she was at

him when she left. But he couldn't imagine her marrying one
and having his baby. She couldn't, wouldn't do that.

That was his baby and she was his woman.

"Don't look at me like that," Alicia said as she sat next to
Leigh in the back office of the clinic. "You're the one who didn't
want a signature stamp."

"That's so impersonal." Leigh signed the final thank-you note.
"Besides, Mother said it's a breach of etiquette and she knows
this game better than anyone."

"She would know," Alicia agreed.

"These people donate tens of thousands of dollars to the
clinic." Leigh handed Alicia the stack of cards. "The least they
can get in return is a real, signed thank-you note."

"All most of them want is the receipt for tax purposes." Alicia
grabbed the stack with one hand and a box of envelopes with the
other. "I'll get them out."

"Wait." Leigh looked down at her watch. "I can probably help
you with that."

"Your movie star is coming in five minutes."

Lyndon was due at eight that morning, a time Leigh gave him
to call his bluff. Movie stars don't show up anywhere at eight in
the morning. She was a little surprised he immediately agreed
without even a hint at negotiating a later time. It was five minutes
to eight now, and she had a feeling she would be waiting a while.

"Trust me," Leigh said. "I have time to help you."

"Then you should get out there." Alicia nodded to the clinic.
"It's already starting to stack up."

The clinic wasn't big enough for separate rooms, so they did
as best they could with partitions and spacing. It was important
to Leigh that her patients have the privacy that everyone deserved, even if they didn't have health insurance.

Partitions with a blue sash flipped over the top meant someone had been checked in and was waiting to be seen, but it wasn't
an emergency. Red sashes meant emergency, and not seeing any
of those, Leigh headed for the first blue sash she could find.
First would be toward the front. She wasn't expecting what she
saw as soon as she entered.

"Hello, I'm Dr. . . . ."

The patient sitting on the end of the bed was a young Hispanic boy not much older than thirteen, who was laughing so hard he looked as if he would fall over. His source of entertainment was none other than Lyndon Prior.

"Hey." Laughing, Lyndon slapped the young boy on the back. "Now straighten up. The doctor's here."

The boy was waving his hands in an apology, seeming unable to stop laughing. "I'm . . . I'm . . . I'm sorry. I just . . . This dude is so cool."

Leigh didn't crack a smile. If Lyndon thought this was how it was going to go, he could just turn tail and leave now. She reached for the clipboard. "You must be . . . Dusty?"

The boy cleared his throat, trying to sit up straight. He was wearing a Michael Jordan T-shirt over a pair of raggedy blue jean shorts. "That's my name."

"No last name?" Leigh asked, doing a quick survey of the board. She knew Lyndon was staring at her, but she wouldn't look at him. This wasn't a game.

"My name is Dusty," the boy answered, his expression finally serious. "The lady at the home said I didn't have to . . ."

"You don't," Leigh answered, looking up at him with a smile. She could see he was uncertain. "If you say your name is Dusty, then that's what it is. Are you here alone?"

He nodded, looking over at Lyndon. "But I wish I had told some of the boys at the home, 'cause they won't believe me. I need, like, a picture, or something. Lyndon Prior!"

Lyndon laughed with a shrug, but the second Leigh turned to him, he looked away.

"I'm gonna make you a deal," Lyndon said. "This is real serious business, so if you don't tell anyone I'm here, I'll sign a picture for you. I have a ton in my car and I—"

"You will not," Leigh interrupted.

Lyndon's eyes widened. "I thought I would just—"

"It don't matter," Dusty said, looking despondent. "I can't tell nobody I was here. I don't want them to know what's wrong with me."

Leigh could see from the board that the boy had been selling himself to men for money and hadn't been feeling well. She skimmed his symptoms. "Well, Dusty, my name is Dr. Chase. It's nice to meet you."

He smiled shyly.

"I'm gonna help you find out what's going on. Mr. Prior here is —"

"Studying for a role," Dusty said. "He told me already."

Leigh shot an angry glance in Lyndon's direction. She had specifically told him not to talk to the patients without a doctor present. "Well, he doesn't have to be here. Only if it's okay with you."

Dusty looked at Lyndon with an expression that said the excitement was over and reality was setting in. He lowered his head. "I . . . I don't think I . . ."

"It's all right," Leigh said. She nodded for Lyndon to leave. He frowned before turning and leaving behind the partition.

"I'm sorry," Dusty said. "I just . . . He's such a cool guy. He'd think I was a . . ."

"Don't apologize," Leigh said. "It's okay. You know you can tell me anything and it will stay between me and you."

Dusty nodded, what was left of the little boy in him coming through. "I don't feel so good."

Leigh was distracted by the loud voices she heard somewhere out front, but that wasn't uncommon in the clinic. "Tell me how you've been feeling, Dusty."

"Well, I . . ." Dusty looked past the partition, even though it wasn't possible to see anything. "What's going on out there? Is Lyndon Prior in trouble?"

The voices got louder and suddenly there was a scream. Leigh couldn't ignore it any longer.

"Please wait here and don't leave," she ordered. "I will be back as soon as I figure this out."

Leigh was down the hallway and into the lobby in a second. She saw a security guard and one of the volunteer doctors holding down a teenaged girl who was screaming and cursing obscenities at another girl being held down by Alicia and . . . Lyndon.

"Lyndon." Leigh approached, trying to figure out the scene. "You can't get involved. I told you not to touch—"

"They were fighting," Lyndon said.

Carlos stormed inside, quickly surveying the scene. He turned to his coworker. "Take her outside."

With one of the girls gone, the girl Alicia and Lyndon had ahold of started to calm down. She was dressed like a prostitute and was probably in her teens although she looked as if she was in her late twenties. Her wig had fallen off, revealing multicolored, unkempt hair, and her dark face was covered with running black eyeliner.

Carlos pushed Lyndon out of the way and took hold of the girl, ordering her to calm down. As Alicia stepped away, Carlos directed the girl to the closest chair, which she fell into with quiet sobs.

"What is going on?" Leigh asked.

"That girl stuck her!" Lyndon pointed to the door. "She stuck her with a needle from—"

"What are you doing?" Leigh grabbed Lyndon by the arm. "Were you questioning her?"

"She told me," Lyndon said. "I didn't—"

"It's true." The girl looked up, wiping her tears with the back of her hands. "That bitch stuck me!"

"What's your name?" Leigh asked.

The girl opened her mouth, but stopped herself. She looked up at Carlos and shifted in her seat. "Um . . . Lucy. My name is Lucy."

"Lucy," Leigh said. "Where did she stick you?"

Lucy pointed to a spot on her upper arm. With her gloves on, Leigh reached down to examine it and there was definitely a puncture.

"Can you take her to the back room, Carlos?" Leigh asked. "Red sash and stay with her."

"Let's go." Carlos led her away.

"Is she going to be arrested?" Lyndon asked.

"Who do you think you are?" Leigh grabbed him by the arm and pulled him away from everyone else.

"I'm just trying to help," Lyndon said.

"I told you not to do anything. Did you actually listen to any of the rules I laid out for you?"

"Yes, but . . ." He looked around. "Rules don't really work in a place like this, right? I mean, you should have seen those girls. They were gonna kill each other. You can't let her get away with sticking her with a needle. If that's HIV-positive, that's attempted murder isn't it?"

"I should have known better." Leigh was shaking her head. "This will never work. You're gonna have to leave."

"Wait." Lyndon held up a cautioning hand. "Leigh, I . . . I'm just trying to—"

"Help," she said. "I told you not to do that. You're not a doctor, a nurse, or a psych. You are just here to observe when the patients allow it. You can't sign autographs, interfere with my care or any of the patients."

"Is this some kind of legal thing?" he asked. "Because I have my own insurance if something happens—"

"Enough." Leigh held up her hand to stop him. "You should leave, Lyndon."

Lyndon sighed, his demeanor calming a little. "Look, I'm sorry. I got a little excited. The atmosphere is so charged, I couldn't—"

"You think this is charged?" Leigh asked. "This is a slow morning, Lyndon. If you can't keep control of yourself under these conditions, you're not ready for this clinic."

Lyndon nodded. "I can. I just . . . I get excited about things and I get ahead of myself. I can behave, Dr. Chase. If you give me one more chance."

Leigh hated that he was offering her puppy dog eyes and it was working. "You stay in the background, say nothing and do nothing unless I tell you to. One more interference, and I'll throw your ass out with my own bare hands."

Kimberly was losing patience with the security guard. "Would you just tell them who I am and—"

"You think 'cause you're a Chase, they'll see you?" The guard held a sarcastic grin on his haggard face.

"No." Kimberly placed her hands on her hips. "I think because I'm a Chase I can get you fired if you don't go in there and tell them I'm out here. Avery Jackson is my best friend."

The guard pressed his lips together, looking as if he had to put forth an effort to contain himself. He turned to the other guard, standing ten feet away. "Make sure she stays here. I'll be right back."

Kimberly had been trying everything to get in touch with Avery, but the family was very protected. She hadn't been able to catch them at their home, and the ICU at the hospital was heavily guarded. Kimberly had no intention of telling Avery what was going on in her life, but she knew she would feel better just seeing her friend. Avery's homey sensibilities had a way of calming Kimberly down.

As she waited, Kimberly checked her cell phone again. She was under constant stress since receiving the pictures and she wasn't so sure how much longer she could just wait as Neil had told her to. She couldn't eat, couldn't sleep, and everywhere she went, she felt as if . . .

Her eyes caught the young woman looking right at her before she quickly turned away and headed for the water fountain. Kimberly knew she was paranoid, but the girl . . . looked familiar. And why was she looking at her?

She was letting herself go crazy, right? Kimberly was used to people staring at her. She was tall, leggy with glowing, smooth dark brown skin, almond-shaped eyes, eyelashes a mile long, and full, seductive lips. Her ebony hair fell past her shoulders in sexy tendrils and her clothes, always expensive, hung off her like butter, showing a thin, curvy figure most women would die for.

But this girl, caramel colored and looking in her late teens, stood out. She looked hastily put together with khaki shorts that were too short to be decent and a cheap pink T-shirt with a glitter rose in the middle. Something told Kimberly she didn't belong here. Waiting for the girl to finish at the water fountain, she expected her to look again.

But she didn't; she didn't look back at all. After her last sip, she stood up straight and stared at the wall in front of her for almost five full seconds before turning her back to Kimberly and walking away.

"Sorry."

Kimberly's breath caught as she turned back to the security guard who had returned.

"They said no." He seemed extremely satisfied to bring her the bad news.

"Did you tell them it was—"

"Kimberly Chase, yes." He shrugged. "They said no one but immediate family. The woman you want, Avery, said you might be able to catch her in about an hour when they plan on having lunch in the café across the street."

"I don't . . ." It hit Kimberly like a blow to the chest. The café! That was where she had seen the girl with the pink shirt before! Even in that split second that they made eye contact, Kimberly knew it was the same girl she'd caught staring at her earlier that morning in the coffee shop about five blocks from the hospital. She was willing to accept that she was paranoid then, but not now.

But she was gone!

"Did you see that woman?" Kimberly asked the nurse at the service desk. "She was standing right there at the fountain. Shorts and a pink tee . . ."

"I think she left." The nurse pointed down the hallway that led to the exit.

Kimberly ran as fast as she could. She felt her heart beating out of control as she burst out the side doors of the hospital, looking everywhere for the girl.

There she was!

Across the street, the girl rushed past traffic to a white Chevy Impala. She turned back, catching Kimberly's pursuit, and seemed visibly agitated. Hastily, she opened the driver's-side rear door and jumped in the car just before it sped off.

Kimberly couldn't see who was driving; the windows were too dark and there was too much traffic going both ways to catch the full plate. She saw an L84, but that was it. She hoped Neil could do something with that.

"Are you okay?" An elderly woman approached Kimberly, who was leaning against the bus stop stall, trying to catch her breath.

Kimberly nodded, feeling as if she could throw up. "Thank you, yes."

"You don't need to be running in those shoes." The woman pointed to Kimberly's three-and-a-half-inch-heeled Yves Saint Laurent sling-backs. "It's too risky."

Kimberly had to smile at the woman's last words. Did she have any idea what a real risk was? She'd never been on the receiving end of Janet Chase's desire for revenge.

5

"Hey, you," Carter said the second he stepped inside Chase Mansion. "Stop, I know you hear me. I've been looking for you."

Haley turned around, rolling her eyes. "You've been looking? You've got some nerve. Everyone has been looking for you. Well, not me 'cause I don't give a—"

"Come here," Carter ordered. "Have you been in my car?"

"Who have you been talking to?" Haley asked, trying to think up a good lie.

"Have you been in the car or not?" Carter asked.

"I haven't driven it." She smiled, tilting her head to the side. She could tell just from looking at him, Carter wasn't on his game. She could push if she wanted to, but she wasn't in the mood.

"But you've been sitting in it?" Carter asked.

"Why do you still have it here?" she asked. "Isn't there a tree out there waiting for you to wrap that little baby around it?"

"Stay out of my damn car," Carter warned. "Where's Dad?"

"They're in the great room," she answered. "I was just escaping, but now that you're here, I think I'll go back. Haven't seen Daddy rip you a new one in a while."

She bumped him with her hip as she hurried ahead of him.

With pleasure she announced him before he entered and sat next to Michael to watch the fireworks.

"Get over here!" Steven yelled out the second he saw Carter. "Who in the hell do you think you are?"

"Steven." Janet reached for her husband's arm and squeezed. "Don't start this. It's too late in the evening for—"

Steven was too angry to listen. He'd been trying to track this boy down all week, ever since he was a no-show at the board meeting. "Where have you been?"

"I'd like to know that too," Michael said.

Carter kissed his mother on the cheek as she reached out to him. She was always trying to make up for Steven's harshness. "Dad, I'm sorry."

"You're sorry?" Steven laughed. "Do you actually believe sorry is gonna cut it for disappearing like that? Do you have any idea what the board thinks now that you haven't shown up?"

"I will call each and every member of the board and apologize."

"This isn't etiquette class!" Steven shook his head, unable to find the right words to express his anger. "You can't send flowers and a kindly worded letter to these people. I look like a fool. The board had faith in me and you've—"

"I know, Dad!" Carter appeared exasperated. "I do realize the importance of this position and I—"

"The way you've disregarded everything," Steven said, "I might as well have given that seat to Haley."

Michael leaned into his little sister. "Dad just insulted you in case you didn't get that."

"You can all kiss my ass," Haley answered back. Obviously she got it loud and clear.

Janet stepped between her son and husband. "Steven, you know how upset he was to find out that Avery is married."

"Avery's married?" Haley asked, so glad she had stayed. "When did this happen?"

Carter's eyes darted to Michael, who shrugged.

"I had to tell them," Michael said. "Trust me, you needed the sympathy. Dad was gonna kill you."

"I still will," Steven said. "I don't care if she's married. You run a business, Carter. You know better than to let your personal problems interfere with your obligations. Your priority is this family!"

"I know," Carter admitted. He was ashamed, but was too obsessed with the image of Avery's belly to concentrate. "I just—"

"Why don't you take the car back, Daddy?" Haley asked.

"Weren't you leaving?" Janet asked her.

"She's pregnant." Carter watched as everyone, even Steven, looked at him stunned. "Avery is pregnant."

"Oh my . . ." Janet's hand went to her chest. This was some news. "What—"

Michael shot up from the sofa. "Why didn't you tell me?"

"I just found out today." Carter ran a frustrated hand over his head. "I talked to her today."

"What did she say?" Janet asked. "Is everything okay? Is she . . . How—"

"Wait a second," Haley interjected. "She's married, so what difference—"

"It's mine," Carter said. "It's not . . . his."

Janet gasped, wanting to laugh from her joy. "Oh, this is . . . I hope it's a girl. I'll finally have a granddaughter. Steven?"

Steven didn't know what to think. "How do you know it's yours?"

Michael searched his feelings. He was happy, but . . . he always knew he wouldn't have the only grandchildren forever.

"She's big," Carter said.

"How big?" Janet asked.

"Not like . . ." Carter made a gesture trying to define her size. "But she's obviously pregnant."

"Did she say it's yours or not?" Steven's words were more of a statement than a question.

"I know it's mine," Carter said.

"You don't know for sure?" Michael asked. "You had to ask, right?"

Carter sighed. "She said . . . she said it wasn't."

Steven slammed his glass of scotch on the bar. "That's it. I've had it with him and that girl."

Carter watched as his father started to leave, and something inside him hurt even more. He felt his desperation begin to yell through the exterior, and without any thought, he called to his father.

Steven turned because the sound of his son's injured voice urged him to, and when he did, the look on Carter's face jolted him. He was really scared and Steven's anger immediately disappeared. Sometimes he forgot the kid was only thirty-one. He walked back to his boy, standing before him as Janet reached out and held Carter's hand.

"She said it wasn't," Carter said, "but . . . I saw the look in her eyes. She's a horrible liar. That is my baby, but she's married and she's saying that . . . ."

Steven kept eye contact with his son. "First, we find out the truth."

"No woman is gonna deny a millionaire's baby unless it's true," Haley said. "She'd want the money."

"Avery's not like that," Carter said.

"Everyone's like that," Haley answered back.

"I'll call her," Janet said. "Avery and I got along very well. She won't lie to me. She's an honest girl and I'll—"

"No," Steven said. "None of us can challenge her. She'll feel ganged up on and she'll just entrench herself further into her lie if that's what it is." He looked at Haley with a deadly expression. "You especially stay away from her."

"I don't even give a damn," Haley said, angry for always being singled out by her father.

"We might be able to use her," Janet said. "Avery's sister goes to UCLA now. Haley can befriend her and—"

"Listen to yourself," Carter said. "No one's going to buy that Haley wants to be anyone's friend."

Janet smiled, nodding. "You seem to still have your sense of humor."

Carter tried to smile, but he didn't have it in him. "I'm trying to think, but seeing her again, all the feelings I had rushing back made it hard. Coming face-to-face with this guy who—"

"You haven't been a nun these last six months," Haley added.

"I didn't expect her to be celibate," Carter said. "But married? Avery takes that too seriously. She wouldn't just—"

"He's not important," Michael said. "He can be dealt with."

Carter nodded. "I know, but that was before. . . . Now that she's pregnant, I have too much more to consider."

"What are you thinking about?" Janet asked. "With her husband, I mean. Are you planning something?"

"No," Steven said. "Leave him out of this for now."

"I can't," Carter said. "She's mine and he—"

"She's not yours," Steven corrected. "You can get her back if you want her, but right now she is not yours. Get that through your head."

"There are records," Michael said. "Now that she's back, we can trace her and find out where they live. We'll get the records and find out how far along she is."

"She can't find out," Carter said. "I can't risk her running away again."

"So you made it," Leigh said as she reached Lyndon, who was waiting at the clinic's front door for her.

Lyndon didn't seem so sure. "If you say so."

"You picked a good day to start." They walked outside. "It was pretty slow."

"This was slow?" Lyndon asked. "Tell me you're joking. Even with the kid that had the gun?"

"It was a toy gun." Leigh typed in the security code.

"Don't play me, Leigh. The look on your face when he lifted his shirt and you saw it tucked in his pants gave you away. You were scared."

"You learn to conquer your fear if you're going to work in a place like this."

"I got it, dude." Lyndon was gesturing for Carlos to leave, but he wouldn't. "I'm walking her, okay?"

Carlos looked at Leigh, who nodded her approval. "Good night, Carlos."

"Thank you, Dr. Chase." His voice naturally sounded as if it had a microphone attached to it.

"He's still watching us," Lyndon said, glancing back.

"That's his job per my father's instructions."

"He wanted you to be afraid," Lyndon said.

Leigh looked at him, confused.

"The kid." Lyndon snapped his fingers. "What was his name?"

"Dondre," she offered, intrigued by his statement. "What do you mean?"

"They test you, right? They want to know that you'll still help them even when you realize they aren't, in their own opinion, good like you."

"Where most of them come from, you prove yourself through violence, either enduring it or acting it out."

"So how do you do it?" Lyndon asked. " 'Cause I'll be honest with you, I was ready to wet my pants. An eleven-year-old with a gun and it was still a slow day? How do you . . ."

"Conquer my fear?"

A loud horn sounded as a black Mercedes drove up alongside Leigh's car just as she and Lyndon approached. The roof opened and a beautiful blonde jumped up.

"Lyndon!"

"Your ride?" Leigh asked.

"Hey, Polly!" Lyndon turned back to her. "Yeah. My agent said my insurance company won't let me drive the Porsche down here."

"He doesn't like the neighborhood," Leigh said.

Lyndon shrugged. "It's kind of hard to get a car service to come down here too."

Leigh laughed at the idea that Lyndon was still kind of confused as to why. "Well, at least you've got her."

"Her?" Lyndon waved a dismissive hand. "What I've got is her boyfriend, Jack. He's my boy and we're . . . Hey, come with us."

"Where?" Leigh asked. "And . . . no."

"We're going to grab a bite at Koi and have a few drinks. I'll make sure you get home."

"That's not my thing."

"What's not your thing?" Lyndon asked. "Having a good time? Don't you think you've earned it?"

"I'm not into the Hollywood scene."

Lyndon threw his hands in the air. "Oh, here we go with the

stereotyping again. I thought we were past that. Besides, it's not Hollywood. It would just be the four of us. I haven't seen you eat since you had a BLT around noon."

Leigh was starving, but . . . this was just not her world. "Thanks, but—"

"I want to hear about how you do it." Lyndon's charm and good-time grin were gone as he looked earnestly into her eyes. "How you conquer the fear."

Carlos cleared his throat as he approached the car. "Is everything okay, Dr. Chase?"

Leigh nodded. "Thanks, Carlos. I'm going for dinner with Lyndon. I'll come back later for my car."

With a delighted, boyish smile, Lyndon rushed to the car and opened the backseat. As Leigh stepped inside, she only hoped she wouldn't regret this.

This was simply not doable, Kimberly thought as she grabbed Evan with her free hand. She had three bags in the other and could only pray that Daniel would behave.

"Boy, I'm not gonna tell you again to stay right next to me." She eyed him sternly, but he was already pouting.

"I want some ice cream now!" He stomped his foot, but didn't pull away from her.

"You won't get anything if you keep acting up," Kimberly warned. "I'm gonna tell your father."

That seemed to have some effect as Evan lowered his head. She let go of his hand to test him and he stayed at her side. She was thankful the boys had a healthy fear of Michael. Kimberly just didn't know how women did this on their own. Without Michael to back her up, getting these kids to obey would be impossible most times.

She should have known better than to think she could manage both of them on a shopping trip to Rodeo Drive, but Kimberly was letting her fear get the best of her. Last night, she had seen Michael tumbling around with the boys in their bedroom. He was trying to make them tired so they would go to bed without complaint, but the scene touched her so deeply. Her family was everything and Michael was the glue to it all. She couldn't lose him and she would die if she lost her boys.

So much so that she kept them out of school so she could be with them today. She hadn't been able to get rid of the image of the girl in the pink shirt. She hadn't been able to sleep at all and knew the only thing that would keep her sane were the two little things that mattered most.

Then the crew came to work on the pool and to keep the boys out of their way, Kimberly decided to take them shopping. Only seven-year-old boys did not grasp the beauty of Rodeo Drive, and store owners weren't too crazy about active kids next to their glass jewelry cases and designer silk dresses.

"Paige?"

Kimberly turned around before it even registered that someone was calling her by that name. When she saw the girl again, this time in a blue jean jumper and a ponytail, Kimberly realized what she had done and the bags dropped out of her hand to the ground.

Kimberly opened her mouth, but no words came out. She didn't know this girl. How did she know that name?

"This is for you," the girl said with a saccharine smile as she handed a stunned Kimberly an envelope. "You gonna take it or not?"

"Who are you?" Kimberly asked, her voice barely audible. She felt her entire body trembling.

"I'm a friend of a friend." The girl shook the envelope, making a smacking sound with the gum in her mouth. "You'll want to take this."

"I don't want anything from you."

"Yours?" The girl looked from Daniel to Evan. "They're cute. I'm sure you'll want to take this so they don't end up remembering this moment."

She was warning her and Kimberly got her point immediately. She was going to do something if she didn't take the envelope. She was ambushed while with her boys so she couldn't make a scene; so she couldn't follow the girl without dragging her boys along or leaving them. She couldn't do anything but take the envelope and pray that they didn't mention a word of this to Michael.

"See you 'round, Paige." The girl waved to the twins before turning around and walking away.

"Who is that?" Daniel asked. "Why she call you that?"

The girl never looked back. She knew she wasn't being followed. She turned the corner, her finger twirling the gum sticking out of her mouth.

"I don't like her," Evan said. "She called you the wrong name. She looks stupid."

"Don't say that," Kimberly admonished as she opened the envelope. "That's not nice."

"How would you even know?" Daniel asked.

"Grandma says . . ." Evan paused, trying to remember. "Anyone who chews gum looks stupid."

Paige—
It's time we meet. Bistro 45—Pasadena at noon tomorrow.

Kimberly held the letter to her chest as she begged herself to stay standing.

"Looks stupid," Daniel said. "Not is stupid. It's different."

"Same difference," Evan argued.

Kimberly looked down at her boys as they argued over something they didn't even understand. They were the most beautiful things in this world to her. They were the only purity in her life and the thought of losing them, even tearing them between their parents, wasn't an option. She had the strength to see this through and she would do whatever it took.

As she picked the shopping bags from Gucci and Christian Dior and Valentino, Kimberly tried to remember where Michael kept the handgun. If she was willing to do whatever it took, she'd better start getting ready.

Carter wouldn't let jealousy cloud his mind as he watched the two of them together. He had too much to do to let this little man mess him up. Anthony Harper was collateral damage, not the target. He had to remind himself of this as he watched Avery wrap her arms around him outside their hotel.

Carter was at least grateful they had decided to stay at a hotel instead of the Jacksons' house. There was too much activity over there, too many restrictions. Here, at a small inn just a few miles away, he could have Avery to himself.

After his father calmed him down, Carter called Matt Tustin with what he had, which was a license plate on a rental car. Matt worked fast. Anthony Harper was a stats professor at the University of Miami in Coral Gables. Tustin told him he had gotten his hands on Anthony's information and traced his credit card to this hotel. Earlier that morning, he had called with the room number for Mr. and Mrs. Anthony Harper.

He had also traced a credit card charge to Delta Airlines for a trip from LAX to Miami International Airport, leaving this morning and returning at the end of the week. He was going back to teach and Avery was staying behind. This was good news.

Carter's hands gripped the steering wheel so tight it hurt as he watched Avery lean up and kiss Anthony like a loving wife. He wanted to kill him now, but told himself to control his rage. He was angry at so much: at Avery for leaving, at himself for hurting her, and at her family for helping her stay away so Anthony could get to her. But if he let his anger make his decisions, he would lose her forever.

He reassured himself by believing that whatever a sham of a marriage this was, it could never have the passion they had shared. From the first moment he saw her, the attraction was intense even though they hated each other. The stolen glances, the electricity-charged touches, and the kisses that made him forget how to think could never be duplicated with another man.

When they had had sex for the first time, Carter didn't give a damn about what horrible things he'd done to get her in his bed. He just wanted her more than anything and would deal with the consequences later. He hadn't expected to fall in love, but thinking back on the kind of woman Avery was, he knew there was nothing else that could have happened. Avery was the kind of woman men who didn't want to get married said they would marry if they ever found because they were confident no such woman existed. Every day, the simplicity of her perfection made him want more. When he realized he would be willing to change his life just to make her smile, everything else came naturally.

And the sex was incredible, especially when they were fighting. They would always lose control and make each other crazy. Just a touch, a brush of the shoulders as they passed would bring a sense of urgency from within Carter that consumed him.

Despite the women he tried to drown himself in over the past six months to forget her, to get back at her, none of them could compare to sex with Avery. And Carter would never believe she could have that with another man, especially not a hometown teacher from the middle of nowhere.

As Anthony's cab drove off, Carter was unnerved by the fact that Avery stayed in the hotel driveway watching until the cab was out of sight. He didn't like the affection implied in such an action, but that was Avery, completely devoted. That is, unless you screwed her over, of course.

Finally, she turned and headed back for the hotel and Carter started his car. Once in front, he placed the car in park and handed the keys to the valet.

"Don't park this in the garage," he ordered, pointing to the only empty spot inside the hotel driveway.

The valet smiled wide as he saw the hundred-dollar bill Carter had wrapped around the key. "Yes, sir."

"Is there anything I can help you with?" another young bellboy asked as he opened the door to the hotel.

"No," Carter answered, moving with quick, powerful strides. "I already know what I want."

When she heard someone knocking on the door, Avery immediately glanced down at her watch. For once in her life could Taylor actually be early? Taylor had been unexpectedly reliable throughout this ordeal and maybe she was really maturing. At twenty, she had a ways to go, but Avery couldn't thank her enough for being there for their mother while she was gone.

Nothing was harder on Avery than being away from her mother, her best friend.

She was only half dressed, but that was fine. Visiting hours at the hospital didn't start for another hour anyway.

"You're ear . . ." Avery was shocked to see Carter standing there. He looked angry and confused, but still . . . he looked good. The man didn't know how not to.

"Morning, Avery." Carter had one-tenth of a second to enjoy the smile on her beautiful face before it disappeared upon seeing him.

She had taken off the shirt she'd been wearing outside, exposing a skimpy white tank. Her breasts were much larger and her belly stuck out from underneath the edges of the top. Her chocolate skin was glowing and begged to be touched. Carter felt the desire he had missed and he wanted her bad.

As his eyes lowered to her chest, Avery felt a rush of heat rip through her, and her body began to tingle all over. This was so wrong, but she couldn't stop it. Her hormones were already making her libido go crazy. Afraid he would see the reaction he was causing, she turned away from him and rushed to the bed to grab her bathrobe.

Carter closed the door behind him, looking around. He didn't want to look at the bed, only able to think of Avery lying in it with another man. "We need to talk."

"Go home, Carter." Avery took a deep breath before tying the bathrobe belt tight and turning around. "My husband will—"

"He's on his way to the airport," Carter said. He grabbed a cheap-looking chair from the desk against the wall and sat down. "He'll be in Florida all week. Sit down, Avery. I want to talk to you."

"Damn it!" Avery's hands clenched into fists as she once again felt helpless against him. "You have no right to do this, to pry into people's lives without their consent."

"I have every right," Carter said. "You won't tell me the truth. You run away from—"

"Shut up." Avery didn't want to hear this. She wouldn't let him make her feel guilty. "You drove me away and you know it."

Carter hated this cold side of Avery because he knew that she only brought it out when she was angry beyond consolation. It was all she seemed to have for him toward the end. "I'm sorry."

"No, you're not." She sat down on the edge of the bed, facing him. What else did he know? "I have to go see my father, so—"

"Is he okay?" Carter asked. "Is he going to be?"

Avery felt the emotion welling inside her. "They aren't sure. He's out of ICU, but he's still critical. He's already had three surgeries, I can't . . ."

As she lowered her face into her hands, Carter rushed to her side. Next to her, he wrapped his arms around her, but she pushed away. "Avery, please."

"Don't." She stood up, afraid of the feelings his being so close stirred within her. She loved Anthony. She loved her husband. "Don't touch me."

"I can help you. I can get the best doctors from anywhere in the world to come and—"

"No." Avery leaned against the dresser, feeling angrier by the minute. "Don't try to buy me through my father."

"You want the best for him." Carter knew it was wrong to use her father to manipulate her, but he couldn't care about that. "His policeman's health insurance can't afford that."

"Please," Avery begged because she wanted him to help. No matter what the consequences and strings attached, she wanted anything for her father and she knew that the Chase family had access to the best.

She had seen it firsthand while with Carter. The best of everything was the standard, and the highest quality was the least of what was expected. It was the way one could live when money was no object and influence got things done. She had no doubt that one call from a Chase could have the best doctor from anywhere in the world at the hospital within a day.

"Don't talk to me about my father," she said. "I can't handle it right now. If you care at all for me, don't."

"If I care at all?" Carter was stung by her words. How could she say that? "Okay, I won't talk about your father, but I will talk about that baby. I want to know—"

"It's not yours." Avery placed her hand protectively on her stomach.

"How can you prove that?" Carter asked.

"I don't have to."

"Yes, you do!" Carter stood up. "You can't just show up pregnant and . . . I don't know how far along you are, but—"

"I told you. Five months. This baby belongs to Anthony, so just stay out of it."

"You know me better," Carter said, sounding like his father.

Yes, she did and that was why she had to stick with her lie. She could deal with him later down the line, but right now she didn't have the strength. Her family needed all of her strength now, and the baby.

"When I left you, I was very upset." She returned to the bed and gestured for him to sit away from her when it looked as if he was going to join her. "I was an emotional mess. I came to stay with a cousin in Florida and I made a lot of bad choices."

Carter knew what was coming and he cringed at the thought. "You slept around?"

"No," she cried. "I just . . . I was babysitting to make money and one of the kids was Anthony's nephew. I met him and he was very . . . kind."

"So you fucked him." Carter gripped the edges of the chair. "I can take that, but I don't want to hear about a romance. Spare me those fake details."

"Either you shut up or I'll call security and have you removed. Better yet, I'll call the cops. They hate you and no one is in a mood to see the chief's family messed with right now."

When she realized he was sufficiently obedient, she continued. "Anthony was the only person who I could feel safe telling the truth to and not having it get back to you."

"He took advantage of you!" Carter shot up from the chair and began pacing the room. "He took advantage of your emotional state and slept with you."

"You mean something like what you did?" Avery asked, looking up. "Like when I came to you after I found out that Alex had cheated on me? I was drunk and an emotional mess. You slept with me that night. You mean that kind of advantage?"

Carter couldn't believe she was bringing that up. If she was intent on playing in the past, then so could he. "I tried to resist you, Avery. If you can remember that night, you wouldn't take no for an answer. I couldn't fight it. The chemistry between us is . . . we're both powerless against it."

Her lips parted a bit and she turned away. Carter smiled, knowing he still had that effect on her. She might be able to pretend she didn't love him, but he wouldn't let her pretend she didn't want him.

"Anthony did not take advantage of me," Avery said. "We bonded immediately."

"You want me to believe that you got over me that quick?" Carter asked. "After everything we shared?"

"I don't need to be over you to have sex with someone." Avery saw him cringe and she felt awful.

The truth was she hadn't slept with Anthony until three months after meeting him. He had known the truth about everything, and the morning after they'd made love, he proposed to her.

"I found out I was pregnant a little while after that."

"So it could still be mine," Carter said. "It was only a few weeks—"

"Carter, I got my period the week after I left you." Avery couldn't believe how easy it had become for her to lie. She wanted to believe it was to defend her baby, but maybe she was just a liar. "This baby is Anthony's."

Carter felt a sense of emptiness inside. She couldn't be having this man's child. "If you're lying to me, I'll find out eventually."

"Exactly," she answered. "So why would I?"

Would she try to fight a blood test once the baby was born? What consequence would lying now have in a custody battle? Avery felt a headache coming on just thinking about where her lies were leading her. What chance did she have whether she told the truth or not? If she could convince him that the baby wasn't his, he might not want to test her after it was born. That's what the medical records were for.

Carter knew Avery wasn't a liar, but he felt like she was lying to him. He knew her heart and just couldn't believe . . . Maybe he just wasn't willing to believe that she would be, could be pregnant with someone else's baby. She was supposed to be his wife, the mother of his children.

"So you married him because you were pregnant," Carter said, searching his heart for what mattered and what didn't. "I can understand that."

"I love him," Avery said, grateful to be able to tell the truth about something.

Carter gritted his teeth. "Look at me, Avery."

She slowly turned her head, promising herself this was the truth. She could do it. "Carter, I love—"

"You can't," he said, holding her eyes with his as he sat down next to her on the bed. "I was awful, baby. I know I deceived you, manipulated you. I lied to you to cover it up and made you think you were crazy to suspect me. I know I messed everything up, but I also know that you love me."

"Not anymore." The words came out more like a whisper and Avery was frightened. When he called her "baby," something weakened inside her. "I'm married now and that's all that matters."

"What's between us has never been that simple," Carter said. "The way we met, the way we've been together, and the way things ended when—"

"We ended," she corrected. "Things didn't end, Carter. We ended."

"He can't possibly make you as happy as I did," Carter said.

Avery swallowed hard as he leaned in closer. "He can't ever make me as miserable as you did either."

Carter stopped, feeling that one deep. "Is that what you want? Someone you only care about enough so they can't hurt you? You can't be happy with that. You can't be happy without this."

Her eyes closed as his hand gently touched her cheek. She could smell his clean, fresh scent and it always did something to her. Just a touch and it all came rushing back; how his hands controlled her body, how when he caressed her, she so easily surrendered her will to his desire.

The knock on the door jolted them both and Avery shot up from the bed. She looked at Carter, who looked up at her, and was horrified by what she'd done, what she'd almost allowed to happen.

Carter slowly stood, never taking his eyes from hers. "You can't fight this."

Avery couldn't respond. She walked past him toward the door. Looking in the peephole this time, she could see it was her sister.

Avery turned back to Carter. "I love my husband and I would never betray him."

"Bullshit," Carter said with a sneer. "If it wasn't for whoever is on the other side of that door, that robe you're wearing would be on the floor right now. And that, unlike anything you've said today, is the truth."

As he started toward her, Avery opened the door wide, revealing Taylor, who looked stunned. Carter stopped, angry but still satisfied that he had proved his point. Avery still wanted him and it didn't matter that she would fight him. When there was conflict between them it only heightened their desire, their sexual chemistry. This all worked in his favor and he would have her back before the professor could return.

"Hello, Taylor," Carter said as he passed. "Give your father my family's best."

Avery closed the door behind him and turned to her little sister, who looked both stunned and amused. She didn't say a word, only stood there with her arms folded across her chest.

"Don't say anything," Avery warned. "You will *not* mention this to Mom or anyone. Do you understand?"

Taylor rolled her eyes and tossed her purse on the bed. "Hurry up and get ready so we can get out of here."

Leigh was a patient person; she had to be as a doctor. Especially as a trained pediatrician. Dealing with difficult children required patience above all. This was why she never lost her smile as seven-year-old Keisha Gibson squirmed and complained. However, her mother, Paula, was losing patience fast.

"Stop it!" Paula, a heavyset woman in her early thirties, grabbed her daughter by the arms and shook her once as they sat together on the patient's chair.

Leigh was getting nervous. Paula was under a lot of stress. Her husband was dead and both of their families had abandoned her. She was dealing with her own illness and had just lost her job. She was easily irritated and Leigh needed to find a free psychologist she could go to for help.

"It's okay, Ms. Gibson," Leigh said. "It's a pretty big needle, Keisha. I can understand why you don't want me to stick you, but I promise it won't hurt but a little bit and it'll be really, really quick."

"No!" Keisha pushed away from her mother. "No more shots!"

Leigh had endless compassion for the girl. Born with HIV, contracted from her mother, who had gotten it from her boyfriend, Keisha had been dealt many bad blows. Recently, she had come down with a bad cold that turned into the flu, and her immune system wasn't prepared for it. Leigh had been doing a lot of poking and sticking while trying to get Keisha back on track.

"I need to check your blood to make sure you're doing better," Leigh said. "We've talked about this."

"She looks good to me."

Leigh turned to Lyndon, who was sitting in the corner of the room with a smile on his face that she wanted to slap off. How dare he? "Yes, but we need to check."

"Leave her alone." Without getting up, Lyndon slid his chair to the bed. "She's just a baby. Babies can't take shots."

Leigh was ready to ask Lyndon to leave until . . .

"I'm not a baby!" Keisha protested vehemently.

"Yes, you are." Lyndon rubbed his chin, looking Keisha over. "You look like a—"

"I'm a big girl!" She held up both hands. "I'm seven!"

"You can't be," Lyndon said, shaking his head. "Seven-year-olds are big girls who take their shots."

"Yeah, but . . ." Keisha looked from Leigh to Lyndon and then back at her mother.

"I'm sorry." Leigh acted as if she was going to put the needle away. "I guess we'll have to wait until you become a big girl to—"

"I am a . . ." With a pouting of her lips, the little nutmeg-brown beauty stuck her arm out. "I'm almost eight."

"Hey." Lyndon gestured for her attention. "Look at me."

"What for?" Keisha asked.

"Look at my face," Lyndon said. "Have you ever seen any face this good looking in your life?"

Keisha laughed although she looked a little confused.

"I mean, am I not the cutest guy on the planet?" Lyndon offered a profile, running his fingers through his blond locks.

"Say yes," Paula whispered into her daughter's ear.

"I don't know." Keisha shrugged. "You're white."

Lyndon's mouth opened wide in shock. "Are you sure?"

Keisha blinked as Leigh stuck the needle in, but kept her stride. "Of course I'm sure."

"Does that matter?" Lyndon asked.

Keisha bit her lower lip with a thoughtful frown on her little face. "No, it's not 'sposed to."

"So, tell me . . ."

"Yes!" Keisha rolled her eyes, laughing. "You're very cute."

"There we go," Leigh said as she pulled the needle out. "All done."

When she looked down at Lyndon, who was pinching Keisha's nose, Leigh couldn't contain her own smile.

Last night had been interesting to say the least. Leigh hadn't cared much for Jack or Polly, finding them both a little obnoxious and immature. But Lyndon turned out to be great company. He was charming, but never put it on too thick. Leigh could tell he was tired, but his set didn't sleep so he tried to pretend he wasn't.

They talked a lot about the patients they had seen that day, the clinic, and what Leigh wanted it to become. She talked about the worst moments she'd had there, leaving out the time Leo shot and killed Richard and then himself. She stuck to the patients and how she grew courage and strength with every frightening experience.

He was listening. Leigh had only been on three dates since Richard died and not one of them actually listened. They asked her all types of questions and nodded their heads when she spoke, but they never really listened. Then again, last night hadn't really been a date.

"It's not too late, you know." Leigh slipped off her latex gloves and dropped them in the garbage. They were alone now that Keisha and Paula were gone.

"For what?" Lyndon swung around in the swivel chair.

"Medical school. You can certainly afford it and I think you have a knack."

"That's called being a show-off, Leigh." He stopped turning and looked at her. "I could never do what you do."

"Something we have in common," she said. "I could never act. I'm too self-conscious."

"You would be great on-screen," he said. "You have a look that . . . You're, like, very sweet, but also sexy, and that's a combo that people love."

Leigh turned away from him, hiding her flirtatious smile. "What about being able to act?"

"What's acting?" Lyndon stood up and walked over to her. He leaned against the counter she was working on. "I don't know how to act and I've made millions."

"Well, I'm a very good doctor and I've made nothing," Leigh joked.

She could tell he was staring at her as she tried to focus on preparing Keisha's blood sample. Talk about self-conscious. She had already spent too much time thinking about him since last night. She never wore makeup to the clinic, but had put on lipstick this morning. It was all ridiculous and she was embarrassed for herself.

"Will you have dinner with me?"

Leigh almost dropped the vial of blood in her hand as she looked at him. "What?"

"Dinner," Lyndon said. "Last night was great, but I'd like to be alone with you."

"What do you mean?" Leigh tried to filter the stereotypes of promiscuous sex and meaningless relationships so pervasive in young Hollywood.

Lyndon frowned, not seeming sure of her question. "I don't . . . I mean, I think we could talk better without Jack screaming in my ear."

"Oh." Leigh turned to him with a heavy sigh. "I don't think that's a good idea."

Lyndon looked deflated. "Didn't you have a good time? I thought—"

"Oh yes, I did. I just . . ." She stepped away, wishing someone would interrupt them, anything to get out of this. "This is supposed to be a professional relationship."

"I'd like a chance to change that." He was at her side again.

Leigh felt a flutter in her belly at the assertiveness of his movement. It compelled her to look at him, and the serious look on his face made her want to . . .

"No," she said. "Lyndon, you don't know who I am. I'm not like Jack or Polly. I'm not like some fan you might meet at the Ivy. I'm not—"

"Don't you think I know that?" he asked. "Why do you think I'm asking you out?"

"Because you're curious," she said.

Lyndon nodded, rolling his eyes. "You think I'm the white boy looking to see what a little brown sugar tastes like."

Leigh shrugged. "Every white boy decides that chocolate is his flavor of the month at one point."

"Leigh." He smiled seductively. "I've tasted brown sugar, so there is no fascination here. This isn't an experimental discovery mission. I'm just a guy who likes a girl and wants to impress her by spending money and seeming important."

Leigh pressed her lips together to keep from laughing, but she couldn't hide the smile. The victorious grin on his face told her she shouldn't bother to protest. She was going to dinner with Lyndon Prior.

Kimberly handed Michael a glass of Macallan whiskey, but he didn't even look at her when he thanked her. Since coming home he'd been in a world all his own, and it bothered her that he didn't want to share with her. They used to share everything. Well, not everything, but almost. After her encounter on Rodeo Drive earlier that day, Kimberly needed comfort even though she couldn't tell him why. But Michael offered her nothing more than a kiss before retreating to his office.

"You sure you don't want any dinner?" she asked. "I can make you a plate and bring it—"

"I'm not hungry." Michael's eyes stayed focused on the computer screen. He had to read the supplier projections for the third time, because he couldn't seem to take anything in.

Standing behind him, Kimberly reached down and touched his shoulders. He didn't shrug her away as she began to massage them. She needed to be close to him, to touch him and know that he was hers forever.

"Baby, I wish you would—"

"Kimberly," Michael said. "I'm very busy."

"If you talk to me, you know you'll feel better." She knelt down and kissed him on the neck. "You always do."

Michael closed his eyes, loving the touch of her lips on him. He hated himself for being angry at nothing. "Have you spoken to Avery yet?"

"I haven't been able to get to her," Kimberly said. "She kind of invited me to lunch, but I couldn't make it."

"I thought you were going to find out what was going on with that husband of hers."

Kimberly had too many things on her mind to worry about Carter's jealousy. "I will, honey. I'll call the house again tonight."

"She's not at the house," Michael said. "She's staying at some hotel nearby. Her last name is Harper."

"If you know so much, why do you need me?"

"Just talk to her, baby." Michael put his hand over Kimberly's and squeezed.

"I know you love your brother, but you can't let his jealousy ruin your—"

"It's not about that," Michael said. "It's stupid. Just—"

"What is it?" She grabbed the back of the chair and turned it around, positing herself on Michael's lap. "I won't go away until you tell me."

"Avery's pregnant."

Kimberly almost fell on the floor. "How . . . Carter must be devastated."

"He thinks it's his."

"Why would he . . ." Kimberly's mind skipped several steps to the conclusion, the one that mattered. "Are you afraid?"

"I'm happy for him if it's his."

"So what's the problem?"

"Last night at the house." Michael replayed the scene in his mind, watching his father place his hand on Carter's shoulder and walk him away from the rest of the family. What were they talking about? "Carter kind of lost it and Dad . . . I don't think I've ever seen Dad be that . . . It was like they were closer than they've ever been."

"He'd do it for you." Kimberly caressed his arm. "You can't expect to have all of Steven's affection. There are three other children."

Michael frowned. "I never said I did."

"Don't get mad at me," Kimberly said. "I'm not the cause . . ." From the look on his face, Kimberly realized that he did blame her; he still blamed her.

"Where you going?" As she stood up, Michael reached out to her, but she pushed away from him. "What did I say?"

"This is my fault, right?" Kimberly felt herself already near tears because of this and so much more. "Steven is closer to Carter because of what I did. You get punished for it."

Michael refused to feel sorry for her. Her scheming had almost killed his mother and it did hurt his standing with his father. "Don't bring that up, Kimberly. It won't end the way you want. You aren't the victim. You did a horrible thing and our entire family paid the price, not just me."

"How long are you going to punish me for my mistakes?" Kimberly asked. "How long before everything isn't my fault anymore?"

"Damn it, Kimberly!" Michael shot up from the chair and slammed his hand against the bookcase, making her jump away. "I'm trying, okay? I'm doing the best I can. I love you and I'm here. But this hurts. I can still feel something between me and him and—"

"What about me and you?" Kimberly asked. "Our relationship is supposed to be more important. He's your father, but I'm your wife. Nothing means more than you and me."

She was right, but it didn't make a difference. He lived and breathed his father's opinion of and affection for him, with the latter being almost impossible to come by. But he loved his wife. She was the mother of his children and he didn't enjoy hurting her.

He stepped toward her and she leaned into his chest. She wanted to disappear inside him. "I'm sorry, Michael. I'm so sorry."

"I know." Michael caressed her back. "It's not you. It's me and I'm just scared. I'm scared that something is slipping away with him and I'm afraid if I make one more mistake, it'll do me in."

Kimberly shivered at the eerie resemblance his words had to Janet's the night of Carter's party. She had to find that gun before she left the house tomorrow.

6

As they walked up the steps to the massive front doors of Chase Mansion, Leigh was curious about Lyndon's expression.

"Your house is bigger than this," she said. "Isn't it?"

"I think so," he answered. "I just didn't know houses this size were out this way."

"You expected me to live in Bel Air or Malibu?"

He nodded. "Or someplace where other filthy-rich people live."

"Most rich people do," she said. "View Park used to be like black Hollywood in the day, but the stars are all in the Hills. Now, just old-fashioned honest money lives here."

Lyndon had a smirk on his face. "You saying my millions aren't honest?"

She shrugged with a coy smile. "All I'm saying is that View Park stays under the radar and that's the way we like it."

"I'm moving in next week," Lyndon said defiantly. And I'm telling all my movie star friends, especially the white ones."

"Stop it." Leigh slapped him on the arm. "My father will disown me if he knows I started this."

Just before Leigh reached for the door, Lyndon took a step closer to her, making her hesitate. "I had a great time tonight, Leigh."

Dinner at a hidden-away Turkish restaurant and a walk along the beach. There were some stares, but none of the drama that Leigh had been so anxious about. It was actually a simple, romantic night and she couldn't remember the last time she'd had that.

"I'll see you tomorrow." She placed one hand on the doorknob, feeling the anticipation creeping inside her.

Lyndon frowned. "Is that my brush-off?"

"I don't know what you're talking about."

"I know a brush-off when I get one and—"

"Yeah, like you ever get a brush-off."

Lyndon tilted his head in a cocky gesture. "It's been a while, but—"

"Get your arrogant butt back in there." She pointed to the Porsche in the driveway. "And I will see you tomorrow."

"I won't be in tomorrow," he said.

Leigh blinked, taken off guard. "Why . . . why not?"

"I have some publicity thing I have to do." He seemed uninterested in his own words. "The DVD for my last movie is coming out and I have to film some promo reels."

"Okay." She hesitated. "Well, I'll see you when I see—"

"I love it." Lyndon laughed with boyish pleasure. "You just made my night, Dr. Chase."

"What?" Leigh was too self-conscious for the level of their relationship.

"You're upset that I won't be there tomorrow," he said proudly. "You're going to miss me."

Leigh rolled her eyes. "You just love yourself, don't you? If you must know, I'm actually glad you're not coming."

"Oh, really?" he asked sarcastically.

"Yes, really." She was searching for the words, knowing she was going to trip over them anyway. "I could use the break of having to watch after you. I'll get more done if I don't have to—"

His lips came to hers in a second and Leigh was surprised by the surge of energy that lifted through her. As his mouth pressed a little harder, she heard herself let out a little sigh and her tense body relaxed. Her stomach felt a pull at its core, and a tinge of excitement wrapped around her.

This was a problem, a voice inside told her. Common sense that she had relied on her entire life said she couldn't be into this man, but her body said she definitely, most definitely was. And as her arms rose around his neck, pulling him closer, Leigh said to hell with playing it safe. What girl would turn down a chance with Lyndon Prior? She would deal with the drama. How bad could it be?

Kimberly had already thrown up in the bathroom of Bistro 45 and was afraid she would again. She was scared to death, but tried her best to look cool and collected. She looked devastating in her St. John Couture vanilla/black dress. Michael always told her when you dress like you don't have to take crap from anyone, people are disinclined to give you any. So she'd done her best Janet Chase impression with the outfit and had her hair and makeup as intimidating and unattainable as possible. Whoever she would be dealing with had to know that she was not Paige anymore.

She still had the gun in her purse and it was loaded. No, she didn't have the guts to do anything yet, but she needed to get used to the reality if that's what it was going to lead to. She was in public now, so it was out of the question to act on her impulse, but having it on her gave her just enough confidence to keep from falling to the ground.

She kept praying and begging that this was just about money, but something told her she wouldn't be that lucky. She'd been lucky for too long and life required that her luck run out at the worst possible time it could: when everything else was going wrong.

Kimberly's hand went to her queasy stomach as she looked around the restaurant. She didn't recognize anyone. She was looking for the girl, but didn't expect her to show up. She would stick out like a sore thumb in this type of place. Besides, she was just a kid and didn't appear capable of being the brains of any operation. No, Kimberly was waiting for the girl's boss.

She gasped loud enough for the couple at the next table to turn and look, but she didn't notice them. What she'd seen was a woman, a regal-looking black woman in a Christian Dior white silk pantsuit, pass by the door. She looked like . . . Kimberly was paralyzed with fear.

Could Janet be behind this? She had tried desperately to search into Kimberly's past the moment Michael introduced her to the family, but Michael had spent his time prior to this erasing that past. When Kimberly asked why it was so important he did all this before his parents knew who she was, he only answered, "Because of my mother."

Kimberly's world of invisible, absent, and wandering people had served their purpose, and Janet gave up looking into her past. It wasn't as if she could prevent the wedding, and once Kimberly was a Chase, it was more likely Janet would want the past to stay where it was for appearances' sake.

But that was before last September and the incident that had revived Janet's obsession with destroying Kimberly. She promised revenge. Had she somehow found out that—

"Hello, Paige."

Kimberly jumped, almost falling out of her seat. She had been so preoccupied with the door, waiting for Janet to walk in, she hadn't noticed the man who had come up behind her. When she looked up at him, she was certain she would die in that moment.

Kimberly blinked, feeling all breath escape her. Her hand went to her pounding heart as her mouth opened to no words. This was going to be the end of her life, the absolute end. As David Harris sat down across from her, she asked herself if this was real or an apparition.

Her hand fell limply to her lap as she screamed inside. He smiled at her, with that greedy face of his. Nothing had changed from the day she'd first seen him. She had been waiting at the bus stop for nothing in particular. She'd been a runaway for two months and was out of money or places to stay. It was raining for the third night in a row and she was freezing. Kimberly remembered it now as clearly as if it were the day before.

"Hello, little girl," he'd said. "Aren't you as pretty as a rose?"

That was how it began. That night he offered her food and a bed in a nice, cheap hotel in exchange for sex. Two weeks later, he pimped her out to a friend of his. Then another and . . . Kimberly needed to throw up again, but she couldn't move.

David was in his early forties and looked as if he'd ridden every bit of those years rough. He was thinner than usual, on the shorter side with saddle-brown skin, large eyes surrounded by even larger dark circles around them. His skin was dry and lips had grown dark from smoking weed all his life.

"Aren't you gonna say hello, Paige?"

Kimberly dug her nails into her palms to keep from crying. She would not give him this satisfaction. She fought with everything she had to not feel like that fifteen-year-old girl again.

"My name . . . is Kimberly." She sighed from the exhaustion of just managing four words.

"Yes, that's right." David's smile was ear to ear. "Used to be Kimberly Hill, but now it's Kimberly Chase. Damn, girl, you look good."

"I know." She hoped she seemed tough. She certainly didn't feel it.

David's smile faded. "You always were conceited, but you had a right to it. You are one exceptionally beautiful bitch."

Kimberly needed a drink of water, but she couldn't even muster the strength to lift her hand to the glass in front of her. She kept it on her purse where the gun was. She would kill him. She'd thought Michael had.

"Bet you never thought you'd see me again." David brushed away an invisible strand of dust on his silk shirt. "Thought I was dead, huh?"

"Didn't care either way." Kimberly remembered those first few months after she'd run away from David and Detroit. She'd been kept up nights wondering if David was coming after her to kill her as he'd always promised he would if she ever left him.

She was seventeen, and a modeling agent she'd met at a bar with some girlfriends offered to take her to New York to be his little kept thing. He was going to make her a model. That was what David had promised as well, but this one had a business card, a Web site, and a wedding ring, so she took the chance that he wasn't a pimp and it paid off.

"That's not right, Paige." He waved the waiter over. "After all I did for you. I took care of you and made you into a woman."

"You're a pig," she said. "You're an animal. I was fifteen."

"You weren't no virgin," he said. "You took to it too well."

"I don't owe you anything."

Kimberly took the moment the waiter came for David's order to try to compose herself. She would have to kill him. There was no other choice. *Now get over it and get on with it.* He was nobody, only important in his own mind. No one would miss him.

"Aren't you curious about where I been these last seven years?" David asked as soon as the waiter was gone. He leaned forward with that threatening left bushy eyebrow raised.

"No." Kimberly finally gripped the glass of water and took a drink. Her hands shook only a little. "You haven't been on my mind since the day I left Detroit ten years ago."

David leaned back, nodding as if this was what he'd expected. "You can't lie to me, Paige. I'm your daddy, and you—"

"You're not . . ." Kimberly checked herself, realizing that her voice was getting too high. "You're no one to me and my name is Kimberly Chase."

"You better watch your attitude with me," he warned.

"You think you still own me? I'm not that little girl anymore, David. I'm a woman, my own woman, and there isn't shit you can do about it."

David looked around the place with an approving grin before returning his attention to her. "You're still a ho. You just got a different pimp."

The waiter brought their drinks and Kimberly couldn't bear to make eye contact with him because she wasn't sure if he'd heard David or not. She couldn't be seen with him. Someone would know it was she who killed him.

"Back to me," David said. "I was hurt when you left, Paige. Your ass made me a lot of money. But I bounce back. There are always younger, prettier girls than the next. I was going about my business for a couple of years, then guess what?"

Kimberly couldn't stand this anymore. "David, what do you want?"

"Guess," he ordered. His hands were clenched in fists on top of the table.

Kimberly looked down at her glass. Why was she still afraid of him?

"Some motherfucker calls me and tells me I need to come out to L.A. for a player's ball. That I've made a name for myself in the Midwest and I need to flaunt that shit." He laughed bitterly for a moment. "I was, like, fuck it at first, but he kept calling. Offered to fly me out there first class and let me stay at the Peninsula, whatever that was. It sounded tight, so I come out there, brought a couple of my best hos with me. I'm ready to get my play on in my pimp suite, but next thing I know, some niggas jump me and knock me out. I wake up, but I'm not in L.A. anymore."

Kimberly shrugged as if he was boring her, but he wasn't.

"I'm in motherfuckin' Mexico!" David slammed his fist on the table.

Kimberly looked around nervously. Several people were staring at them now.

"But that's not all," David said. "I was in a whorehouse with ten kilos of cocaine and you know who woke me up?"

"The Mexican police." Kimberly had to hand it to Michael. He'd known what he was doing.

"Five minutes later I'm sentenced to forty years in a Mexican prison." David straightened up, clearing his throat. "But someone, whoever it was that set me up, thought I was nobody. They thought I would rot forever in that prison, but they were wrong."

Kimberly gripped the edges of the table. "Just tell me what you want."

"Oh, I will," he said. "But you gotta hear my story. You see, about a year ago we got a new guard. He's an Ese with family in Chicago. I convinced him I could get him there with ten thousand dollars if he could get me out of Mexico."

"Not too smart," Kimberly said. "You're only a hop, skip, and a jump from Mexico. You should be in Canada if you want—"

"Thanks for your concern about my freedom." He waved his hand dismissively. "But when I got out, the first thing I did was set my operation back up so I can make that money. Then I got down to business, finding out who tried to take my life away. It wasn't easy. It took me more than a year and a lot of money. Tracing cell phone calls, airline tickets, hotel rooms. The more brick walls I came against, the harder I wanted to fight. Made me broke, but I wouldn't give up."

Kimberly imagined Michael's mistakes had been because of his youth or maybe the P.I. he hired to handle this hadn't been the best. He'd told her that he couldn't use anyone the family had used before because he couldn't risk its getting back to his parents.

"I understand why he did it." David's tone was solemn and reserved. "When I finally got the name Michael Chase, I was wondering why in the hell would this rich bougie brother want to ruin my life?"

"You want money," Kimberly said. "Give me a number and get the hell out."

"I ain't going nowhere, bitch." The words seethed from his lips. "You will listen to me!"

"Okay." Kimberly gestured for him to keep his voice down. She couldn't kill him today. Too many people would remember seeing them together. Maybe tomorrow.

"He had to keep his embarrassment quiet." He looked her up and down. "You got yourself an impressive catch, but you always had it going on. Sisters are always using the baby trap and come up empty. You're all too stupid to realize that the baby trap only makes a brother want to get as far away as possible. But you did it. When did you tell him who you really were? After the wedding night?"

"He always knew who I was," Kimberly said. "He loved me anyway and I didn't have to lie or trap anyone."

"No," he said. "You just had to get rid of me."

"David, I—"

"Do you know what it's like to be in a Mexican prison?"

Kimberly couldn't believe his nerve. "I know what it's like to be pimped out at fifteen. You can't possibly expect me to pity you after everything you put me through."

"I didn't do nothing to you!" David stood up.

Kimberly gripped the edges of the table. Her head was pounding and the world around her starting to float into a haze. What was about to happen? Where was Michael? She needed her husband right now.

When he stopped just before reaching her, David leaned down and Kimberly winced, bracing herself.

"You don't have to pity me, bitch. But you will pay me. And money isn't going to be enough." Standing up straight, he placed a hand gently on her shoulder.

Kimberly let out a whimper but she didn't move away. She couldn't move away.

"I'll be in touch, Paige."

Kimberly was numb as she sat there, for how long she wasn't sure. She remembered Michael's words when she asked about David. *"You don't want to know,"* he'd said, *"but he won't ever be a problem for us."*

She hadn't asked for more explanation because in her heart, she had hoped he was dead. It would be justice for all the little girls he had damaged. Death was what he still deserved and it was going to be what he got.

Avery's heart was torn to shreds at the sight of her mother entering the hospital courtyard. Nikki Jackson, well known for looking much younger than her age, looked all of forty-eight and then some right now. Her long braids were pulled back, revealing a tired, emotionally drained face.

"Hey, baby," Nikki joined her daughter on the stone bench and kissed her on the forehead. "He's still sleeping, so I thought I would join you."

Avery had come to the courtyard to get some exercise. She was trying very hard to keep to a healthy weight during her pregnancy so she wouldn't have a hard time losing after the baby was born. She had walked for about twenty minutes and was tired. She hadn't been taking as good care of herself as she should have, but it was hard considering everything that was going on.

"The doctor said he's doing better." Avery placed her hand over her mother's, which was flat on her lap. "He's so strong."

Nikki nodded. "I know God will answer my prayers. Have you heard anything about the case?"

"Mom."

"I can handle it whatever it is."

"They caught the boy that Sean shot. He was at a hospital in Oakland."

"He got that far?" Nikki asked, even though she didn't know why it would matter. "He's going to be okay?"

"The shot didn't kill him, but he didn't get proper care soon enough. He had a bad infection. They had to amputate the leg. They don't know if he'll survive. Plus, now that the cops know . . ."

"Charlie would never want them to seek revenge."

"You know what Sean said. That kid is not safe. Neither is the one they're still looking for."

"I'm going to issue a statement on Charlie's behalf," Nikki said. "He would want them to keep this clean. We'll get those boys the right way."

"I hope so."

As she felt more tears coming on, Nikki reached into her pockets for some tissue, but couldn't find any. She reached for Avery's purse, which was lying at her feet.

"What do you need?" Avery asked.

"A tissue." Just as she stuck her hand inside, Avery reached for the purse.

"I'll get it for . . ." Avery sighed as she saw her mother grab the cream-colored slip of paper. "I can explain, Mom."

Nikki read the script on the invitation and felt a dull pain in the pit of her stomach. "Why would she do this?"

"Janet wants to see me." Avery retrieved the invitation to Haley's upcoming birthday party. "We were close."

"You don't doubt that Carter is behind this, do you?"

"I can't tell," Avery said. "The whole family is . . . I'm not going, so what does it matter?"

"It matters," Nikki said. "He didn't buy your story. That family isn't going to give up."

Avery had to tell her mother about Carter's visit to the hotel after Taylor blabbed. She wouldn't have been able to keep it from her anyway. They were so close that her mother could read her every thought and emotion.

"I'm handling it," Avery said.

"At what cost?" Nikki asked. "This was why you went away. Because you knew you couldn't deal with that crazy family and take care of yourself and the baby all at the same time."

"My baby is fine." Avery placed her hand on her belly. "Carter, I'll just . . . I'll deal with him."

"Like you did this morning? You almost kissed him, Avery."

"Mom, please." Avery didn't want to relive the moment. Not because it made her angry, but because it made her want him. "I love Anthony and I would never betray him."

"I know you wouldn't." Nikki rubbed her back reassuringly. "I'm just afraid you'll want to. You said yourself the passion that existed between you and Carter isn't there with Anthony."

"It's been difficult." Avery feared Anthony would never make her feel the way Carter had in bed even though she wanted to believe it was the pregnancy getting in the way. "But we are going to make this . . ."

Still holding Avery's purse on her lap, Nikki reached into her side pocket and picked up the cell phone. She checked it first. "Good, it's Anthony."

"Anthony?"

"How are you, baby?"

Avery already felt better just from the sound of his voice. "I just wish you were here."

"I'll be back tomorrow. How is Charlie?"

Avery updated him on Charlie's status, becoming emotional as she spoke.

"You should know," Anthony said before an awkward pause. "Um, baby, I think someone broke into the apartment."

Avery felt her chest tightening. "How do you know?"

"Nothing is out of place," he said. "It just feels different than it did yesterday. Like everything has been . . . touched. The doctor's office has probably been broken into too."

"Or the computers hacked."

"But everything is good," Anthony said. "I know we can rely on Dr. Kanata."

Dr. Kanata offered to do this as a favor to Anthony. Because of missing paperwork, he was about to be deported to Japan. Anthony not only helped him stay, but had been able to expedite the entry of his wife and daughter to America using friends he had gone to school with at Georgetown University who were now in ICE (Immigration and Customs Enforcement).

"I hope you're right." Avery couldn't stand this. It was wrong and just couldn't, wouldn't work. But it was too late. She owed Anthony.

They said their good-byes and Avery gave the phone back to her mother. "You don't have to worry about me falling for Carter again. He'll never change."

Kimberly had never seen Neil at a loss for words, but he was mum over the news of David's coming to town.

"It's that bad?" Kimberly asked as she sat across from him in his office.

Neil's brows rose as if he wanted to say something but couldn't think of the right words.

Kimberly hated telling him, but she couldn't keep this to herself. She had been a walking zombie since David reappeared in her life two days ago. She needed help and Neil was the only person she could think of.

"Your husband should have come to me," Neil said. "He left too many ways to trace this back to him."

"Do you think David will go to the police and try to get Michael in trouble?"

Neil took a second to laugh. "Men like Mr. Harris don't go to the police for anything."

"He wants revenge," Kimberly said. "Money isn't going to be enough. He said so himself."

"Would it be enough for you?" Neil asked.

Kimberly frowned. "Are you passing judgment on me? I just told you what this man—"

"I'm not." Neil held up a hand to stop her. "Mr. Chase did exactly what I would have done in his situation. The man is scum and I'd be happy to have him roughed up for you."

"But . . ." Kimberly could sense his hesitation.

"I don't think that will help. He's a determined son of a bitch."

"David is from the streets of Detroit," Kimberly said. "An ass-kicking won't do."

"What I had in mind wasn't just an ass-kicking, Mrs. Chase."

Neil leaned forward. "I mean to really hurt him if that's what you want."

"But you won't kill him," she said.

Neil shook his head. "I don't do that."

"I don't think there is any other choice." Kimberly had never taken the gun out of her purse. Next time she would do it. Next time. "He's going to ruin my life and I have a feeling that will just be for starters."

"I can give you a few names."

"I can't risk anyone else getting involved," Kimberly said. "I've already told you too much."

"I will forget this conversation as soon as it's over." He pointed to the stack of cash Kimberly had placed on the table after walking in and swearing his secrecy. "But if you think you can do it . . ."

"Why wouldn't I be able to?" Kimberly asked defensively. "I've never hated anyone as much as I hate David."

"Do you hate him?" Neil asked. "You should, but from my perspective, what I saw as you explained this entire situation doesn't equate to hate."

Kimberly was incredulous. "You can't be implying . . ."

"He took you in at fifteen," Neil said. "Yes, he turned you out, but he also took care of you. He was the father you never really had, wasn't he?"

"The father from hell," Kimberly said.

"For a kid, that is better than no father. Mrs. Chase, I think Mr. Harris has a hold on you that you haven't gotten over. It's how he paralyzed you, controlled you. Let's face it. You're a far cry from a teenaged hooker, but he brought you back there, didn't he?"

Kimberly lowered her head, ashamed. "I tried my best to stand up to him. I was just too scared."

"I've seen this before," he said matter-of-factly. "The man is the instigator of some of the most traumatizing years of your life, but he was also your only protector and provider during that time."

"You don't know what you're talking about," Kimberly said. "I can kill him. When the time comes, all I have to do is think of what this could do to my family and I'll get the strength I need."

"Let's just find out what he wants." Neil didn't appear at all convinced. "If it's not doable, then you can make your decision. Meanwhile, I will track him down and find out where he is and what avenues of attack you have."

Kimberly nodded, gripping her purse with both hands to keep them from shaking. She realized that she had come to Neil hoping he would take care of this for her because she wasn't sure she could. Neil was right. Something very sick inside her was still endeared to David, and as painful as it was, Kimberly couldn't ignore it. She didn't think she could kill him, but would have to find someone who could.

"Don't start with me," Janet said as she dragged her husband down the hallway from his office and toward the foyer. "You've been in that office all day."

"I've got an empire to run." Steven smiled as his wife turned back to him. "Yes, I said empire. I don't have time for birthday parties for overgrown children."

"It's just a get-together," Janet said. "She's having her own party at some club. I just thought it would be nice. She's been behaving herself lately and . . ."

"Does the name Professor Cook mean anything to you?" Steven remembered the phone call from the dean when the news broke of Haley's latest ill-advised affair.

"That was last semester." Janet stopped as they reached the foyer. "Besides, the family is here."

"Why do I have to suffer through all these family events you're so obsessed with lately?" Steven asked. "Just for you to stick it to Kimberly?"

"What are you talking about?" Janet knew he'd caught on, but she would play innocent to the end.

"You find every excuse you can to have a family event just so Michael and the boys can come and Kimberly is left behind." Steven pulled his wife to him. "Give it up, Janet. He isn't leaving her. He would have done it by now."

"That has nothing to do with me." Janet leaned up and kissed him on the nose. "Now everyone is out back and I—"

They both turned as the front doors opened and Leigh

stepped inside. Janet started for her but was halted by the sight of the person who entered right behind her. He was a handsome, young, tall white man and looked vaguely familiar. Janet blinked at the sight of Leigh's hand entwined with his. She looked back at Steven, who had apparently seen the same thing.

What in the hell was this? Steven asked himself.

Leigh was adept at reading beyond her parents' perfectly orchestrated expressions, but she was certain Lyndon couldn't tell the difference. "Mom, Dad. I want you to meet Lyndon Prior."

Janet suddenly remembered, but was still confused. "You're the actor?"

"Yes, ma'am." Lyndon smiled politely and held his hand out to Janet. "It's very nice to meet you. You have a lovely home."

Janet shook his hand, looking back at Steven. "Steven, Lyndon is an actor. He—"

"I know who he is," Steven said. "I thought you were trailing Leigh at the clinic? What are you doing here?"

"Dad." Leigh sent her father a warning look. "Lyndon is here as my date."

"Hello, sir." Lyndon held his hand out.

Steven took his good time accepting the man's hand but was impressed with the firmness of his shake. He must think he was really something. "Do you think that's a good idea? Wasn't the intent to keep things professional? That's what your mother said."

"I never said that," Janet protested. "Welcome to our home, Lyndon. I hope you'll enjoy yourself. Since the weather is exceptionally nice for March, everyone is out by the pool. Leigh can show you the way."

"Thanks." Lyndon nodded, seeming less confident than a few moments ago.

Leigh kissed her mother on the cheek before starting off with Lyndon. When they were a few feet away, she squeezed his hand tight.

"That went well," she said.

"Are you serious?" he asked. "Your father is not cool with the white boy."

"Trust me," Leigh assured him. "Considering how it could have gone, that went well."

"Am I going to be the only white person here?" he asked.

Leigh stopped, turning to him. "You're not white, Lyndon. You're a movie star."

"Is that supposed to be funny?" Lyndon still looked worried.

"You're a famous superstar," she said. "You don't have the option of being uncomfortable."

She looked back at her parents, who were both staring at them from the foyer. She could only imagine what they were saying.

"Kiss me," she ordered to his surprise.

"No way." Lyndon was turning his head to see if Steven and Janet were still behind them, but Leigh placed her hand on his cheek, turning his head back to her.

"Kiss me," she repeated, leaning in.

Lyndon sighed as if he was being asked to do something awful, but he kissed her. When they separated, he winced. "I'll be getting kicked out in ten seconds."

"No," Leigh said. "Now that they've seen that, they'll leave you alone. My parents are a lot of things, but they aren't stupid. They know what trouble messing in my love life will bring them."

"Did you know about this?" Steven asked.

Janet rubbed his back reassuringly. "I had no idea, but it doesn't matter."

Steven turned to her. "Are you serious? He's white and an actor. That's something Haley would do."

"You're overreacting." Janet watched Leigh kiss Lyndon briefly on the lips. She got the message. "Now, that was something Haley would do."

"I'm not putting up with this," Steven said. "She's a doctor, a Chase. We did not put our blood, sweat, and tears into that girl so she could marry some—"

"No one is getting married," Janet said. "It's just a date. Leigh would never get serious with an actor. They're all too superficial for her. She's just fascinated and probably has a big crush. He's very handsome."

Steven watched as Leigh and Lyndon disappeared down the hallway. "You better make sure that's all it is."

"There is no way I'm meddling in her private life again. I've learned my lesson."

The front door opened again and this time it was Carter. Janet rushed to him and wrapped her arms around him. She'd been constantly worried about him lately.

"I didn't think you'd come," she said.

"I wouldn't miss Haley's birthday party for the world," Carter answered sarcastically. "It's not at all weird for parents to still throw birthday parties for their twenty-four-year-old like she was ten."

"You can leave the smart-ass comments at the door," Janet said.

"Mom, you know why I'm here."

Janet turned to Steven, whose expression darkened. "You mean . . . Do we know?"

Steven nodded. "Let's go into my office. Janet, go get Michael."

In his father's office, decorated in dark cherry wood, hunter green, and white marble with walls of dark rose, Carter looked at the records Steven gave him, reading them over a third time. He was moving through his emotions with as much control as he could muster, but couldn't hide his anger.

"Say something, dear." Janet was at his side, her hand on his arm. "I know you're upset, but . . ."

"No." Carter closed the folder and tossed it on his father's desk. "I'm not upset. How can we even be sure these are accurate?"

Steven looked at Michael, who shrugged as if dealing with this was above his head. It was up to him to convince his son of the truth. "Those are copies of the actual medical records from the doctor's office. They coincide with the records on the computer. They also coincide with the papers found in Avery's house regarding her medical care. She's only five months pregnant."

"Doctors can be off," Carter said, despite his knowing otherwise.

"Not a whole month," Janet said. "Oh, baby, I know how you feel. I was hoping . . ."

"You don't know how I feel." Carter pulled away from her, isolating himself from the rest of his family as they all stared at him. "Don't feel sorry for me either. I'm gonna be fine."

"All your mother is saying," Steven said, "is that we were all excited about a chance to add another person to our family, but it wasn't meant to be. You know it's for the best, don't you?"

Carter laughed bitterly. "Do I know it's for the best that Avery is having another man's child?"

"Get over that girl now." Steven held his hand out to Janet. "She's married, she's pregnant, and she has other family problems to deal with. It's over."

Carter didn't respond as his parents walked past him, not even to his mother as she brushed his arm briefly with her hand. "Say happy birthday to your sister before you leave," she whispered before leaving.

Michael shot up from the French Victorian leather chaise and clapped his hands together. "That does it, man. You and me are gonna go out and get drunk."

"No." Carter reached out and grabbed the folder again. "There's something—"

"Stop it." Michael was just as fed up as Steven now. He was patient with Carter because he understood how much he loved Avery, but this was enough. "Once you get your hands on the prettiest girl at the club, you'll forget all about her."

"You didn't see her," Carter said. "I know Avery and I saw her eyes, the way her lip trembles a little when she's trying to lie."

"You can't trust anything," Michael said. "She's under too much stress. All you can rely on are the facts. The facts say that it's ole boy's kid she's carrying. Besides, why would he have married her if she was pregnant with another man's baby?"

"Because she's Avery," Carter said. "Because she's incredible, beautiful, smart, sexy, strong, and vulnerable. Because her heart is so open no man could help but fall into it."

"You're scaring me, man." Michael didn't know if Carter had been reading romance novels or watching the Lifetime Network, but he didn't like the sound of this.

"It doesn't matter. This isn't what I wanted to hear, but I'm not going to let something like another man's child get in the way of being with her."

Michael was clueless to Carter's obsession with Avery. Yes, she was pretty and had curves in all the right places, but she was too girl-next-door, boring and holier than thou. Carter always went for a more natural look than Michael's desire for glamour and exceptional beauty, but he could have any woman he wanted. That he still pined for this woman, even after she deserted him and came back pregnant and married, made him wonder even more.

Michael raised his hands in the air. "I don't know what to tell you, bro. So she might have possessed him with the magic that is Avery if she had to, but she didn't. It's right in front of you. The baby might not be his, but it isn't yours."

"Avery doesn't sleep around," Carter said.

"That's what they all say." Michael watched as Carter's expression darkened. They rarely came to blows, but the last two times they had, it had been because of Avery. "Don't blame me for this. You're the one that can't accept it's over."

"It's not." Carter straightened up and took a deep breath. "If Taylor hadn't interrupted at that hotel, something would have happened."

"She's vulnerable right now," Michael said. "Her hormones are all messed up and her daddy's half dead in the hospital. You want to take advantage of that? What did that get you the last time?"

"It got me her," Carter answered.

Michael couldn't believe what he was saying. "You really need a drink."

"What I need," Carter said, "is my woman back and I'll do whatever it takes."

"She's married," Michael yelled.

"So are you," Carter said. "That doesn't keep you from—"

"Whoa!" Michael held up his hands. "This isn't about me. Besides, Avery is not me. She wouldn't cheat and she sure as hell wouldn't leave."

"She obviously married him because she was pregnant," Carter said. "She was trying to do the right thing. That can be undone."

"Except for the baby," Michael said. "You can't undo that she's carrying his baby."

"Oh, really?" Carter feigned a dumfounded expression. "That's right, I forgot. Thanks for reminding me."

"Go ahead and be a smart-ass," Michael said.

Carter ripped the folder in two before tossing it in the garbage. "This doesn't mean anything. Like I said, no real man would let a baby get in the way of a woman like Avery. Why would I?"

7

On her way to the dressing room in the back of Fred Segal's in West Hollywood, Kimberly was stopped in her tracks when David suddenly appeared in her way. He laughed as she gasped, half the clothes in her arms falling to the floor in front of her. She hated that she so obviously showed the effect he had on her, but Kimberly knew there was no way to avoid this. In the past week, her every waking and very few sleeping moments had been consumed with her life in Detroit, a life dominated by David Harris.

"How you doing, Paige?" He leaned against the wall. He was trying to blend in with his country club polo and khaki pants outfit, but it wasn't working. "You're looking good as usual."

When she could gather herself together, Kimberly knelt down and picked up the stray clothing. The last thing she needed was more attention. She was well known in this store. If anyone saw her with David and he showed up dead . . .

"I asked you a question." He seemed amused as he watched her stumble with the clothes.

"What do you want?" she asked.

"I'm just amazed at how well you got it, girl. A ho from Detroit living among royalty." He looked around the store. "You saw your cash cow and went after it."

"It wasn't like that," Kimberly said, disgusted that she found the need to explain this to him.

"It's a compliment," he answered. "You didn't go after any brother, 'cause most of them don't give a damn about a bitch having their baby. You went after the one who was so high up, he didn't have the social option of having a baby mama."

Kimberly couldn't stand this. "This has to end, David."

"It ends when I say it ends," he said angrily before returning his expression to normal. "Did you blackmail him? What did the prenup say? I know there was one. You're pretty but you're dumb as a rock, so you couldn't have outsmarted him there. You get nothing if he dumps you, right?"

"Michael will never . . ."

David pointed his finger at her. "Don't lie to me. You can't lie to your daddy, Paige."

Kimberly was frozen as he walked to within inches of her. Everything about him was the same, even his cheap cologne. Even though she towered over him by four inches, she could feel herself getting smaller with every second.

"All I have to do is make one phone call to a variety of media outlets and then what?"

Kimberly didn't, couldn't respond.

" 'Cause I know you think your man loves you, but this family is not like any other rich family with skeletons in their closets." David reached out and touched a strand of her hair, flipping it with his fingers. "They are like fucking Kennedys or something. A ho in the family won't go over well. He'll have no choice but to act like he didn't know. You lied and betrayed him and you won't just be cut off. You'll have to pay."

Kimberly swallowed hard. "You think that because you don't know what it means to be a real man. You don't know what real love is."

David laughed. "Is that what you think you have? Bitch, please. I've been watching you for weeks, baby. Your man is never home. You know where he is? Where he goes? I do, Paige.

He runs the streets with his brother and acts like he's a single playa playa."

"Shut up!" Kimberly bit her lower lip just to keep the tears at bay.

"Did you know he liked redheads?" David asked.

"Shut up!" Kimberly surprised herself with the anger in her voice. Yes, she did know he liked redheads. He always had.

"It's okay, baby." David placed a comforting hand on her shoulder and squeezed. "It happens to the best of them. How does the saying go? Show me a beautiful woman and I'll show you a man that tired of sleeping with her."

Kimberly pushed away from him, wishing she could shoot him right there. "What do you want from me?"

"You had no right to leave me," he said.

"I had every right," she countered. "And I didn't leave. I escaped."

"There is no escape," David said. "You see, even now, look at you. Trembling like that luscious little child you were when I found you. You're still mine. You'll always be mine and even a rich motherfucker like Michael Chase can't take that away."

"Can I help you, Mrs. Chase?" Simone, the perky blonde who always tended to Kimberly, approached looking cautiously at David.

Kimberly turned away from her, not wanting her to see the state she was in. "I'm fine, Simone. Thanks."

David leaned in with a whisper and said, "One million. That's the price, Paige."

Kimberly rushed into the dressing room the second David walked away. She tossed the clothes on the floor and fell to the floor with them. She had to cover her mouth to stifle the sounds of her crying.

One million dollars. There was no way she could get that amount without Michael finding out. What in the hell was she going to do?

Leigh was skeptical and Lyndon apparently deciphered that from her expression.

"I swear," he said, hands in the air. "I did this."

Leigh placed her hands on her hips, her expression remaining. "I won't care that you didn't. I think it's all beautiful."

Lyndon bit his lower lip, seeming to contemplate a confession. "I did most of it. Let's say, eighty percent."

"And yet I'm a hundred percent impressed," Leigh said

She was impressed with Lyndon's house in Hollywood Hills. Far from giant, it was a mansion, but still modest by the standards of this neighborhood.

Leigh hadn't expected to see such detailed design inside the house. She had an image in her mind of what a young, good-time, bachelor pad would look like. Lots of red or black, leather everything, and plenty of large-screen televisions. Lyndon's place had much more class and style, but still looked like a home; a place where people actually lived.

After a tour, he slid the glass doors open and led her to the stone patio and the S-shaped swimming pool. It looked like every Ralph Lauren ad Leigh had ever seen.

"I picked out all the furniture you see here." He guided her to the fully stocked bar and began pouring drinks.

"This definitely looks like you," Leigh said.

"Meaning?" He put the bottle down and turned to her.

"It's adventurous," she said. "A little less . . . predictable."

"I'm taking that as a compliment." He reached out and wrapped his hands around her waist, pulling her to him.

Leigh didn't wait for him to kiss her, making the move first herself. When their lips touched, she felt a tingling sensation chased down with full-flared heat. Was she really kissing Lyndon Prior? Was that why she liked it so much? She wasn't sure, but she did like it and she wanted more. She hadn't suffered through a Brazilian bikini wax for nothing.

When he whispered her name and pulled her even closer, Leigh knew this wasn't about his being famous. His lips lowered to her chin before focusing their hunger on her neck. She let out a quiet sigh just from the relief of feeling good. It had been so long and she missed it.

Her arms wrapped around him and her hands squeezed at

the back of his shoulders. She wondered for a second if it was too soon, too easy, but she really wanted him and with the Brazilian and all, she was feeling . . .

"Getting busy!"

Leigh jumped as she opened her eyes and saw three men standing only a few feet away. They all stood there with immature smirks on their faces. She recognized one as Jack.

Lyndon turned around. "Dude, not cool. Where did you come from?"

"Lock the door for once, jackass." Jack approached, socking Lyndon in the belly before stumbling to the bar.

Already angry that the mood had been destroyed, Leigh wasn't happy to see that Jack was either high or drunk to add to it.

"You remember Jack." Lyndon wrapped his arm around Leigh's waist possessively.

"Hey, babe!" Jack said without turning around.

Leigh smiled politely, turning to the other two men, who were sizing her up and making her feel uncomfortable.

"This is Jeff Sloan and Nick Gagan." Lyndon pointed to each guy as he introduced them. "Guys, this is Leigh Chase."

Jeff, a textbook California surfer dude, pink-painted shell necklace and all, waved a polite hello before joining Jack at the bar. But Nick stepped to within inches of Leigh, making her want to back away.

"Aren't you pretty?" he said as he leaned into her. "Lyndon always gets the pretty ones."

"Back up." Lyndon pushed Nick back a few steps, but Nick frowned as if he didn't appreciate the interference.

He held his hand out to Leigh. "Ms. Chase, right?"

Leigh could tell right away he was high. His eyes were bloodshot red and his pupils were dilated. His hand was unsteady. "Actually it's Dr. Chase and you don't look so good. Are you okay?"

He frowned again, not seeming to like anything anyone had to say to him. "I'm always okay, baby."

Lyndon cleared his throat.

"Sorry." Nick offered a lazy smile. "Dr. Chase."

"You can call me Leigh," she said, even though she really didn't want him to. Leigh tried not to be a judgmental person. She couldn't be a good doctor if she was. But something told her she was never going to like this guy.

"You can call me anything you want." Nick winked at her as he ran his hands through his thick black hair.

"Watch it!" Jack yelled as he and Jeff bumped into each other and a glass hit the floor, shattering into pieces.

Lyndon quickly moved Leigh away from the glass before going to clean it all up. He was cursing Jack, pushing him away while Jeff reached down to try to help him clean up. Leigh watched as Jack stumbled back, laughing as if this was the funniest thing he'd seen in years. She thought to go after him, before he fell into the pool, but a shiver down the back of her spine made her turn back to Nick.

With a tilted head, he was staring at her chest either so preoccupied he didn't realize she was noticing or too much of a jerk to care. Leigh suddenly felt naked even though she was well covered up.

She placed her hands on her hips and glared at him. Taking his own sweet time, he finally looked up at her face. There was no hint of shame or embarrassment. In fact, Leigh noticed a slight grin before he walked over to Jack and pushed him into the pool before jumping in after him.

"Lyndon."

Lyndon turned around quickly, seeming to sense the level of irritation in Leigh's voice. "What's wrong?"

"Nothing," she said. "I just think I need to get going. I have to be at the clinic in two hours."

Lyndon looked down at his watch. "I thought I was going to drive and we'd both—"

"I need to stop at home and take care of a few things." Leigh was already walking away.

Lyndon traced behind her, ignoring the guys calling his name. When they were inside the house, he reached out, turning her around to him. "What's wrong, Leigh? Is it Jack? He's just a—"

"He's drunk or high and it's barely noon," Leigh said. "And what about Nick? He's high too, isn't he?"

"This is not the way I wanted you to meet my friends."

"I'm sorry if you think I'm being judgmental, but I'm trained to notice these things and—"

"It's the weekend," Lyndon said. "So he smokes a joint or two. He's an okay guy."

Leigh wondered if Lyndon was being naive or lying. "His behavior isn't indicative of marijuana."

"Great. Now you think we're all drug-addicted degenerates. Leigh, this is not who I am."

"I wasn't judging you," Leigh said.

"I know Nick has a problem. I'm trying to help him, but it's not easy. He's my boy, you know. We've been running since before I was anyone. So now I'm supposed to drop him because he could be embarrassing to me?"

Leigh got the feeling Lyndon had been warned about Nick more than a few times before. "Of course not. But you've got to get him help before embarrassing you is the nicest thing he could do."

She watched as he nodded, seeming reluctant to make eye contact with her. She was touched by his humility. "I think I can help you."

"How?"

"I have connections and I can get a list of facilities that are really good and very anonymous. If you're willing to pay a lot of money."

"Anything," Lyndon said.

He finally looked up and the honesty in his eyes warmed her. She smiled and in the next second, they were kissing like mad.

"I knew I could make you laugh," said Nina Calloway.

For ten years, Nina was the receptionist/clerk/bookkeeper and anything else one could think of for her to do at Hue, Nikki Jackson's art gallery in Baldwin Hills.

Avery and Taylor had been helping out at the shop while Nikki spent most of her time at the hospital and Nina was doing everything she could to cheer them up. After several failed attempts, showing Avery the newest piece by a sculptor featuring rabbits on a life raft did the trick. It was titled *Self-control*.

"It's silly," Avery said. "How could I not laugh?"

"One Jackson sister down." Nina air-fisted a gesture of victory. "One to go."

Avery stopped laughing as she felt her baby kick again. Maybe she or he was upset that Avery waked him up.

"I'm sorry," Avery said, as she rubbed her belly. "I'll try to keep it down."

"It's a shame, isn't it?" Janet wasn't so sure what to make of Avery's expression when she saw her. Fear? Surprise? A little of both maybe. "They just take over your life with no apologies."

"What's the matter, dear?" Janet looked down at Avery's hands covering her belly. "You look as if you're afraid I'll try to take her."

"What is that supposed to mean?" Although she removed her hands immediately, Avery didn't appreciate the joke.

Janet found a bench across from an abstract painting and sat down. "Bad choice of words. I apologize. Come sit, dear."

"What are you doing here?" Avery stayed right where she was.

Janet surveyed the gallery. "I've never been here. I don't really come around this part of town. It's actually quite lovely. Maybe I could hold an opening here. You know, for your father or something."

"My father doesn't need money," Avery said. "The police association is doing everything for him."

"How is Chief Jackson?"

"As good as can be expected," Avery answered, still waiting for the shoe to drop. "He's going to make it."

"Of course he is," Janet said. "He's a strong man and has the most wonderful support. I hope this isn't putting too much stress on you in your condition."

"I'm fine," Avery said too quickly to sound natural.

Janet couldn't take her eyes off Avery's belly, trying to accept the truth. "You know, I carried very small with Carter."

Hadn't Janet been in on stealing her medical records? She had to be, so what was this about? "I know where you're going, Janet. This is not—"

"I know," Janet said. "I guess it's wishful thinking on my part. Most women are very small their first baby. You look wonderful, by the way."

"Thank you," Avery said. "I'm sorry I couldn't come to Haley's birthday party."

"Of course it's probably best you didn't. I just hope that your relationship with Carter doesn't mean I can never see you."

"That all depends on how Carter behaves, Janet."

Janet smiled. "You know he's changed, Avery."

"I'm married, Janet."

"Were we only friends because you were with my son?" Janet asked, showing just the right emotion to pull Avery in.

"No." Avery joined her on the bench, feeling guilty for being so cold. This, even though she knew Janet Chase wouldn't consider her worth knowing if it hadn't been for Carter's interest in her. "But you have to understand, I have too much on my plate right now to . . ."

"Deal with my crazy family," Janet said. "Don't worry, Avery. I know why you ran away. Carter broke your heart and he wasn't going to leave you alone. Chase men don't understand no. They think everything they want is theirs just because they want it. Carter is so competitive. He always has to win."

"I needed a break from my life," Avery said. "I know what I did wasn't the most mature way to handle things, but I just needed to get away."

"You just turned him around so much," Janet said. "And not on purpose, I know. Just being yourself you challenged him more than any woman ever had. You made him crazy."

Avery didn't want to hear this. Carter had given her this line before. He wanted her to believe his love for her was somehow to blame for the crazy things he'd done.

"We would have been celebrating a wedding in June instead of . . ." Janet lowered her head to her hands as they lay flat on her lap. "It would have been so wonderful."

Avery was wringing her hands together now, anything to keep from touching Janet. Part of her feared that if she did touch her, Janet's emotions might spread. "It wasn't meant to be."

Janet turned to her. "But it would have been great, wouldn't it? You two loved each other so much. You would have been so good for our family. You're like Leigh in that sense, Avery. Your life with Carter would have been—"

"Please." Avery stood up, turning away. The emotion had come so quickly it frightened her. "Janet, please stop."

Janet knew what she was doing was wrong, but she had to do what was best for her children and her family. The only thing that was going to get Carter back in line was having Avery back in his life. And there was just a part of her, the mother inside her, that didn't believe the medical records.

"I'm sorry, dear." Janet stood up. "I should leave. I just hope you'll consider seeing me sometime. Carter doesn't have to be involved. He doesn't even have to know."

Janet was gone for less than a minute before Anthony showed up. When his hands took a gentle hold of her arms, she jumped before looking up at him. In her heart, she thought herself the worst person in the world because she had expected to see Carter. Maybe even wanted to see him?

"I saw her leaving," Anthony said. "What did she say? Did she threaten you?"

"No." Avery couldn't tell him she was crying because it hurt to think of all she lost with Carter. "She just . . ."

Anthony's understanding of her situation was so beyond what Avery could have expected in any man. She could tell he was strong and gentle from the moment she met him, but hadn't thought once of anything more. Carter still owned her heart even if she was determined to stay away from him. But Anthony was persistent and found a way into her good graces. He talked to fill up her silence, listened when she felt the urge to talk about anything, and most of all, he made her laugh and forget.

He was intelligent and aware of the world. He filled a room up with energy when he talked about the satisfaction he got from teaching. He reminded her of the values she was brought up on. He reminded her of the beauty of a simple, but meaningful life.

When she found herself caring for him, Avery wanted to push away. She hadn't thought she could bother to care for anyone but her baby. Besides, it was so soon and she had made that mistake with Carter. But Anthony wouldn't budge. Not even after she told him the truth. He only seemed to be more understanding, more patient.

He offered her security and stability at a time when she needed it the most. He offered her love knowing that she couldn't offer it back yet. He offered her warmth in his arms and satisfied the urges her pregnant hormones had. No, he wasn't the most exciting man in the world, mind-blowing in the way that Carter was, but he was safe and he was good. That's what she needed.

And he didn't deserve to be told, after all he'd done for her, that she was still aching over her lost love with Carter.

"It's nothing." Avery wiped her tears. "You know how emotional I get these days. I'm just so glad you're here."

Anthony smiled that now familiar smile that reassured her he would always be there to hold her in his arms. "Let's go back to the hotel, baby. You need some rest."

Kimberly rushed past the host toward the table he was leading her to. "Don't you dare," she said to Avery, who was trying to stand up. They hugged each other tight and kissed on the cheeks. This was the only joy Kimberly had experienced in weeks.

"Look at you!" Kimberly took the seat across from her. "You look . . ."

"Big," Avery said, laughing.

She had been a little apprehensive about meeting Kimberly after such an emotional encounter with Janet, but forgot why the second she saw her. The two had grown so close in such a short time and Avery missed her more than anyone in the Chase family; anyone except Carter of course.

Usually blindingly gorgeous, Kimberly looked a little tired and somewhat older than her twenty-seven years. Something had changed since the last time they'd seen each other more than six months ago. She was still one of the most beautiful women Avery had ever seen, but she wasn't her fabulous self right now.

"Not really," Kimberly said after a quick study. "You're carrying just in the stomach. Good for you."

"Mama says that I'll blow up over the next few months." Avery didn't want to think of being gigantically pregnant during a hot L.A. summer.

"If you're six months along and haven't—"

"Five," Avery corrected quickly, her smile fading.

Kimberly caught herself, remembering Michael's update. "Sorry. I forgot. Congratulations on your family. You're a lucky girl. Most women can't find a good man to take them to dinner. You get three who want to marry you in consecutive years."

"That's not something I'm proud of," Avery said. "But Anthony and I are very happy and we're excited about the baby."

"Boy or girl?"

Avery shrugged. "I'm hoping for a girl, though. I think Anthony would like a boy."

"They all want boys, but when they hold that little angel in their arms, they melt like butter." Kimberly quickly told the waiter her drink order and he was gone.

As Avery was glancing down at the menu, Kimberly stole a real look at her. She looked more than just pregnant. She looked tired and unhappy. Kimberly had no understanding of the kind of father-daughter love Avery shared with Charlie Jackson, but she imagined there was probably no soothing her right now.

"I'll just get the big salad," Avery said. Placing the menu down, she looked up and noticed Kimberly was staring at her with an odd look on her face. Paranoia made her think she was here to spy, but Avery tried to quell that thought. "What is it?"

"Are you . . . happy, Avery?"

Avery swallowed hard, but kept her head up. "Considering the circumstances."

"I mean in your marriage. You don't seem to me to be the type that would get married so soon after . . ."

"Actually, my history says I'm exactly the type." Avery looked out the window. "I jumped into Carter too soon and then . . . But Anthony is different than Alex or Carter."

"In a good way, I assume."

"Of course. What do you think I meant?" From Kimberly's expression, Avery realized she sounded defensive. "I mean, yes. He is the one I married."

"I just remembered you being so in love with Carter. You know, it's like . . . he's Carter Chase. You said that most men just pale in comparison to . . ."

"Anthony doesn't," Avery said. "He's a great guy and . . .

Carter broke my heart, so it wasn't as if I was looking for some-one like him."

"But you had to run away to get over him?" Kimberly asked.

The waiter came and took their lunch orders.

"I mean," she continued, "all the talk about how great the sex was, the trips, the jewelry, everything you loved. That doesn't seem like the kind of thing a girl moves on from in one month."

"It wasn't that simple," Avery said.

"Then tell me how complicated it was." Kimberly noticed Avery's skeptical expression. "No, I'm not here to tell Carter any-thing. He wanted me to, but . . ."

"What did he say?" Avery leaned forward.

"He just wants to know all about that husband of yours. You can imagine how he feels about him."

"I thought he knew everything already. He found out the Chase way."

Kimberly sighed. "Ah, yeah, the Chase family and private in-vestigators. It isn't so odd, you know. They just do what other rich people do."

"I learned that the hard way," Avery said. "When you go back home, tell him to stay away from me and my husband."

"Avery, he's had it so bad," Kimberly said. "You don't even know. The women and the drinking."

"I don't want to hear this, Kimberly."

"He sleeps with anything he can get his hands on. We're talk-ing Carter here, a man who is the snobbiest of the snobs. He used to be so selective. Most women don't even touch his radar, but these last six months, all you have to have is a vagina and a pretty face. And most of the time, the flavor of the day bears such an uncanny resemblance to you, it kind of freaks me out."

"Kimberly," Avery begged. "Can we talk about something other than Carter?"

"It's just crazy the way the two of you have handled getting over each other. You get married to the first guy you meet and he sleeps with every woman he can."

Avery was about to threaten to leave if she didn't stop, but she didn't have Kimberly's attention anymore. Kimberly had turned several shades lighter upon seeing something or someone who had just come in the front door. Avery strained to see who it was, but only saw the hostess guiding a young girl to the bar. The girl looked a little out of place for this type of restaurant, but otherwise harmless.

That was before she turned around and made direct eye contact with Kimberly. She hadn't hesitated or looked anywhere else, and the expression on her face was cold and comical at the same time. Something was very wrong.

"Who is that?" Avery asked.

Turning away, Kimberly suddenly felt ill as she reached for her drink. She couldn't escape this torment for even one hour.

"Kimberly?" Avery noticed how shaky Kimberly's hands were as she brought the glass of wine to her lips. "What's going on?"

Kimberly wished she could tell Avery the truth, but it wasn't possible. As much as she hoped to reconnect with her friend, she knew she was completely alone.

Avery slid her chair around the circular table until she was right next to Kimberly. "Who is that girl and why are you so upset?"

"She's no one," Kimberly said. She was digging her nails into her palms to keep from completely losing it. She had to come up with a lie fast. "She's just some woman I think Michael has . . ."

"Oh no." Avery looked at the girl again, who was flirting with the bartender. "Are you sure?"

"You don't know how it's been since you left, Avery. Everything has changed. Michael doesn't love me like he used to."

"You're going through a rough time," Avery said. "What you did was wrong. He was very angry and you know how much he values Steven's approval. But he's still your husband."

"I didn't know Steven was the reason he was being a good husband."

Avery felt the added guilt of having deserted Kimberly to face the family alone when it was Kimberly's warnings that made Avery aware that going against any Chase was a losing battle.

"He was never the perfect husband, but all this time . . . it was all show for Steven. Since we left that house, he comes home whenever he wants to. He leaves me behind to go show off for Daddy. I'm going to lose him."

Avery didn't believe in sticking with an unfaithful man. It was why she left Alex and why she would leave any man who cheated on her. But she wasn't naive enough not to know this wasn't the truth for every woman.

"Have you confronted him about . . . her?"

Kimberly shook her head. "She doesn't mean anything. It's everything else. My life is so . . . I can't make up for what I've done. Janet wouldn't let me if I tried. Everyone hates me and if I mess up one more time, he'll leave me, Avery. You have to help me. You have to."

"What can I do?" The last thing Avery needed was to get more involved with the Chase family, but seeing the desperation in Kimberly's eyes gave her no choice. She could say that she hoped she wouldn't regret it, but Avery knew better. She would totally regret it.

"So did I deliver?" Lyndon asked, leaning forward.

Leigh knew it was wrong, but she had to laugh. She could see his face contort into some form of embarrassment and uncertainty and it was interesting to her. This great movie star with an ego to match was way too eager.

He'd invited her to his house for dinner and she agreed only if he would promise to make it himself and not cater it. There was a long pause over the phone and Leigh got the impression he'd already had the caterer of choice in mind. Eventually he agreed and promised she would enjoy herself.

Over steak carpaccio with red wine risotto and asparagus, they talked about his upcoming projects, the ruthless world of agents and producers, her year in Africa working with HIV/AIDS patients, her life of cotillions and charity balls, a house he'd just purchased in London only two blocks from Sean Combs's house and anything else they could think of.

They ate in the dining room, where Lyndon admitted to have eaten in only twice in the year and a half he'd been living in the house. Throughout the evening, he kept asking if everything tasted okay, was she happy, did she need more wine or more anything else?

Finally, Leigh placed her hand over his on the table and said, "Lyndon, please stop. I'm having a great time."

He slid his chair toward hers so their knees were touching. "It's been a long time since . . . I'm used to showing off. You know, the money, the cars, VIP seats at the hottest restaurant or club. A quick trip to Fiji or the hottest caterers with the most exotic menus for a quiet dinner is how I impress women."

"There's no such thing as a quick trip to Fiji," Leigh said, smiling. "But I get your point. Trust me, just you is more than enough to make an evening."

"Money doesn't impress you," he said. "You've had it all your life. Fame too."

"The fame part I'm not crazy about. I didn't want it."

"But you handle it well." He leaned back. "This is L.A. There is no shortage of heiresses floating around acting nuts. They're all the same, but you . . . you're really something. You carry yourself with class and it's so natural, not forced."

"Years of etiquette training," Leigh said, unable to hide how flattered she was. "My mother comes from several generations of 'ladies.' I was reading Emily Post at age nine."

"Emily Post?" Lyndon stood up, holding his hand out to her. "I'm sure Mrs. Chase is thrilled to see you dating me, an actor."

Leigh let him lift her up and the strength with which he did it made her tingle inside. Every girl loved to feel feminine against a man's strength. He led her into the living room, which she had already told him was her favorite room in the house.

"I already told you," Leigh said. "She knows better than to mess with my love life."

He turned back to her with eager eyes. "Am I part of your love life?"

Leigh pushed him away as he leaned in. "Don't get ahead of yourself."

He fell back on the plush sofa and patted the seat next to him. "Okay, but what about King Chase? I'm sure he's said something."

"Why did you call him that?" she asked.

He shrugged. "I don't know. That's just the impression I get of him. Am I right?"

"That's what my brothers call him. I guess he has that effect on men."

"He's pretty intimidating."

Snuggling up next to him, Leigh patted his thigh. "I know he can come on strong, but that's what daddies do. Trust me. I would only be afraid if he was nice to you."

"I'm sure you don't want to talk about it," Lyndon said, "but I know about Richard Powell. The tabloids speculated that your parents played a part in—"

"Lyndon." Leigh turned to him. "You're right. I don't want to talk about it."

"Those damn tabloids are always lying anyway," he said after a short pause. "I just want you to know I understand. I've had crazy women stalking me. One tried to climb my gate and she slipped. One of the sharp daggers cut her and I came home to see her lying in blood and . . ."

Leigh watched as Lyndon turned away, visibly shaken by his own words. She placed her hand tenderly on his chest. "Did she die?"

"Almost," he answered. "She would have bled to death if . . . She ended up trying to sue me by saying the type of gate I have was dangerous."

"Dangerous to people who might be stalking you."

"Not according to her. She said she believed I wanted her to come over. We had a secret relationship and I asked her to come to my house. I was supposed to have left the gate open."

"Wow." Leigh tried to wipe away the images of Richard dying in her arms while parts of Leo's brain were splattered on the walkway in front of her. "Some people are just sick and they don't . . . they don't understand."

Lyndon smiled, looking as if he was about to laugh. "Leigh, you are something else."

Leigh turned his face to hers with her hand. "Why do I get the feeling you're about to make fun of me?"

"I just don't understand how someone can have the heart that you do after such an ugly thing happened. Honestly, are you for real?"

She placed her hand gently on his thigh and leaned forward. "Does that feel real?"

That playful expression Lyndon had on his face most of the time quickly faded and Leigh was instantly excited by the look of passion that took over. She was really doing this. She was seducing Lyndon Prior!

Lyndon's lips met hers halfway and Leigh was pleased by the softness of his kiss. It was hungry, but cautious and it only made her want him more. Her hands went against his chest and he leaned in closer and she felt the muscle beneath the thin shirt.

They separated and Lyndon looked into her eyes. "Do you know what you're doing?"

"What do I look like to you?" Leigh asked. "A virgin?"

"No, Leigh. But I don't just want to kiss you." His hand came to her waist and squeezed.

"What do you want?" she asked coyly.

"You know what I want," he answered. "I just . . ."

Lyndon gasped as Leigh ripped at the front of his shirt, pulling it apart.

"I think we've talked enough," she said.

In a second, he was all over her, but it wasn't sloppy and it wasn't greedy. It had been so long since Leigh had sex that she expected some hesitation, but there was none. The way he touched her face, stroked her breast, gently tugged at her hair quickly wiped away any doubt. He rubbed her in just the right place and in just the right way: not too soft, but not too hard.

When she realized that Lyndon knew what he was doing, Leigh just let him take over. From the way he positioned himself on top of her, removed her shirt, and then her bra, she could tell he liked to be in charge and she let him. She let him remove every inch of her clothing all while leaving slow, wet kisses all over her body.

As his mouth warmed her neck, he took her hand and directed it to his groin. When she took hold of him, he was already getting hard and as she gently stroked him, he groaned his pleasure when she reached the pace he liked.

Leigh's noises were getting louder with every touch and her body was moving on its own as his hands deliberately traveled from the middle of her thighs, parting her legs. Her arms were around his neck and her fingers pulled at his hair as he rubbed his fingers against her. She let out a loud whimper as two fingers slowly entered her. Leigh's head went back as he moved his hand in and out of her while he continued to rub her outside with his thumb.

Leigh was losing control of everything. She fell back on the sofa, her eyes closed, as Lyndon concentrated on what he was doing. He pressed his other hand gently against her pelvis as the pace of his fingers picked up. He wasn't just trying to make her feel good. He was going for her G-spot and he knew exactly where it was.

It was only seconds before Leigh's entire body contracted and she screamed in pleasure. When she opened her eyes, Lyndon was looking down at her with a proud smile on his face. "What?" he asked. "Did you think that was it?"

He leaned across her and picked up his jeans, which had been discarded on the floor next to the sofa. He reached into his back pocket and pulled out a condom. "I'm nowhere near done, Doctor. This is about to get good."

8

"Carter, there's someone here to see you."

Sitting at his desk, Carter looked up from the *Wall Street Journal* in his hands and eyed the phone on his desk. Patricia, his assistant, always warned him fifteen, ten, and five minutes before an appointment arrived. And she always said the name. He didn't need to check his BlackBerry to know he had no appointment scheduled.

"Send them in," he responded as he tossed the paper on his desk and positioned his chair to face the door.

When Anthony entered with a threatening scowl on his face, Carter was a little surprised, but he didn't show it. He kept stone-faced as the man who had stolen his family approached. There was no need to prove anything. This was his domain and Anthony had come to him first as he had planned. Now he could tell Avery that Anthony started this and he wouldn't be lying.

"I'm here to tell you to stop," Anthony said as he stood just at the edge of the desk.

Carter let a smile flirt at the edges of his lips. "I was just reading the paper. Does that offend you?"

"You know what I mean," he said. "You sent my wife flowers this morning."

Carter's smile went flat at the mention of this man referring to Avery as his wife. It angered him that Anthony, no matter how much less of a man, was the winner here. Not only did he have Avery, but he was her husband and she was carrying his child. Carter wanted to explode just thinking about it.

"Yes, the flowers. You didn't like them? They weren't really for you, but . . ."

"She's made her feelings clear. She wants nothing to do with you."

"Those were over her father." Carter leaned back in his chair.

"Bullshit. You sent them to our hotel room and the note didn't mention—"

"You read it?" Carter asked. "It was addressed to Avery. That's not polite."

"You son of a—"

"You weren't supposed to be there." Carter enjoyed making him angry. "I intended for them to be delivered after eight a.m. You should have been on your way to the airport. You know, for your Monday trip back to the little school you work at."

Anthony shook his head. "Don't think you can get me riled up with that. So you spend your money spying on people. It's pretty sad actually."

"I wouldn't expect you to get angry at that," Carter said. "If you weren't angry about me spending time in your hotel room last week, why would you care if I sent flowers?"

Carter felt a wicked sense of satisfaction at the look on Anthony's face. The man would lose at poker every time. As he expected, Avery hadn't told her husband about his visit to the hotel room and while debating whether or not Carter was telling the truth, he appeared enraged at the possibility that he was.

Anthony took a few seconds longer than he should have, but recovered. "I know who you are."

"You've said that before," Carter said, "but I don't believe you do."

"I do and it doesn't matter, because this is my family."

Carter controlled his rage to assess Anthony's knowledge of his upper hand here, his temporary upper hand. He wasn't as simple as he seemed, but he still wasn't going to keep Avery. Carter had already decided.

"You had your chance," Anthony continued. "And you blew it."

Carter gripped the armrests of his thick mahogany leather chair. "Do you actually think you can win against me?"

"I don't need to. I have everything I want already."

"No," Carter corrected him. "You were able to take advantage of a situation without me around. Things are different now. You're smart enough to sense that. Scared?"

"Scared of what, brother? Avery told me everything. You turned her against you by being yourself, and all your money and power can't change who you are. I should thank you. The way you lied to her, manipulated her, and acted like such an ass with her family while she was gone only cemented her disdain for you."

"And you conveniently swooped in to heal her wounds." Carter was distinctly hurt at the thought of Avery sharing details of their relationship with Anthony. "You're a rebound, Anthony, and the rebound guy never lasts long. She got pregnant by accident, so you got lucky. She's an old-fashioned girl, but even that won't save you."

"I don't need to be saved." He hesitated, seeming suddenly very impatient. "Like I said. Stay away from my wife."

As soon as Anthony closed the door behind him, Carter slammed his fist on the desk and shot up from his chair. How much had Avery told him? How intimate the details? He was fuming and there was a voice inside him that said give it up. Just let her go. Why did he want her anyway? If she really loved him she would have stayed and worked it out. She wouldn't have run away and made him crazy. She wouldn't have slept with another man so soon and certainly wouldn't have married him. She was no longer the Avery he'd fallen in love with. How could she be?

But after only a few minutes, Carter's rage subsided. This was all a waste of time and he knew it. He loved this woman and there wasn't going to be any getting past this. Despite all the pitfalls he'd made for himself, the year they were together was the best of his life. He hadn't felt complete since she'd been gone and he wouldn't again until he got her back.

He was going to have to take it up a notch.

* * *

Kimberly almost tripped over herself when she stepped out of the Beverly Hills Chase Expressions salon and found David leaning against a parking meter with an extremely pleased smile on his face.

He didn't move and Kimberly knew this was his way. His hos came to him, not the other way around. She'd been told that too many times to count. As she composed herself and walked over to him, she felt her stomach turning to mush and prayed that no one would notice or remember they had seen her here.

"You can't do this," she said. Looking around, she put her sunglasses on even though she doubted it would do any good. "You know the tabloids have people with cameras and cell phones all over Beverly Hills. Someone will take my—"

"This is to teach you a lesson," David said, his expression darkening. "Do you think I won't walk up to your front steps?"

"I didn't—"

"You've been locking yourself in that little palace of yours to avoid me," he said. "If you want to play that game, I'll walk up to your fucking steps."

"Don't you dare come to my home." If it wasn't for fear of Michael finding out, Kimberly almost wished David would come to her house. Maybe then she could, she would find the strength to kill him.

"You got my money?" he asked.

"I don't carry that around with me." Kimberly turned her back to the salon as another patron walked out. These women knew who she was and someone would say something. They were catty, gossipy, and eager to get their hands on her husband. "Can we please just go—"

"We'll stay right here," he said. "This is your punishment for trying to avoid me. You know better than to disobey me, girl."

Kimberly wanted to smack that superior grin off his face. He was nothing, a nobody piece-of-shit pimp from Detroit, and he thought he was a god. "I can give you a quarter of a million now, but the rest will take time."

"That family has billions!" He looked around as if hoping that someone had heard him.

She gestured for him to quiet down. "I'm not married to Steven Chase. I'm married to Michael."

"I don't care if you were married to the family dog, you stupid cow. I want the money."

"That's all I can—" Kimberly jumped with a gasp as David started for her. He was faking, but the smile on his face said he was satisfied with the effect.

"You know what I can do if you don't give me my money," he said. "It wasn't that long ago, Paige."

Kimberly couldn't control herself and began to cry. She stumbled to the nearest support, which was a street sign, and leaned against it to keep from falling to the ground. It was as if the past ten years had disappeared in that second. When he'd fronted, his arms raised at his sides, she remembered the consequences of crossing him and she was scared. It was as if she wasn't a member of one of the richest, most powerful black families in the country, but a helpless girl with nowhere to turn.

"It's okay, baby." David approached her, placing a hand on her shoulder. With his finger, he touched her chin, lifting her face to him. "I know it's been a while. You've forgotten your place, so I can be forgiving."

Kimberly slapped his hand away, leaning back. She could tell from his reaction that this made him angry. "I'm not your little whore anymore. I don't need your forgiveness."

"Fine," he said. "No more forgiveness. No more patience. Paige, your time is up. I want the money."

"I can only—"

He shoved a piece of paper in her hand. "Bring it to this hotel room by three on Friday. If you don't, I'll be calling every local radio and television station to introduce myself. I have plenty more pictures of you, of us. Don't test me, Paige. You should know better."

Leigh stepped outside the clinic salty as she saw Lyndon drive up in his most recent purchase, a convertible Maserati Spyder, with Jack and Nick sitting in the back. Now that they had slept together, things were different between them and Leigh liked that. It had been a long time since she felt safe to care about someone; give herself to someone. Lyndon was exciting, smarter than he liked to give the impression he was, funny, and could throw down pretty well in the bedroom. The gossip was true about that.

But these friends of his were pure Hollywood and Leigh didn't like them one bit. And she especially didn't like Nick, who was already focused on her breasts the second she reached the car.

Slipping inside, she met Lyndon halfway and he gave her a sweet kiss that made her feel good after a hard day at the clinic.

"Good stuff," he said. "How was today?"

"Take a guess." She looked back, wondering if Lyndon had talked to either of them about the rehab centers she had scooped him on. "Hi."

Jack bid an enthusiastic hello while Nick merely nodded, but never took his eyes off her.

"I know I've been MIA for a while," Lyndon said as he slid back into traffic and sped away. "But this DVD work is killing me."

"The clinic isn't going anywhere," she said, wishing she had something to tie her hair up with. It was flying all over the place and Lyndon was driving really fast. "At least I get to see you when—"

Leigh caught her breath, her hand coming to her chest as Lyndon sped through a red light and Jack yelled his approval.

"What was that?" she asked.

Lyndon looked at her and winked. "There was no one there."

"Not the point," Leigh said. She didn't want to nag, so she let it go.

"Don't worry," Lyndon yelled above the traffic. "I'm dumping these bums in Hollywood before we go downtown."

Leigh wouldn't say it, but was very glad to hear it. "Where are we going?"

"It's a surprise!" He looked at her with that sparkling smile.

"Lyndon," Leigh pleaded. "Watch the road. You're driving too—"

She screamed as he swerved into the next lane, cutting off a black SUV. Jack yelled again, this time in an incomprehensible holler.

"Do you know where you are?" she asked. "You don't cut people off in this neighborhood unless you want to start something."

"Don't worry." Lyndon pressed on the gas to make a yellow light. "I have protection."

"What does that . . ." She suddenly realized what it meant. "You have a gun in this car?"

"I always have a gun." Lyndon swerved onto the highway, picking up the pace. "I have a permit, Leigh. You know who I am. I have to—"

"Slow down!" Leigh grabbed the dashboard as if it could brace her. She turned to Lyndon, who was smiling as if he thought this was a game.

"Gun it!" Jack yelled. "You drive like my grandma, asshole."

"Like a bat out of hell!" Lyndon yelled back and sped up even more.

"Lyndon!" Leigh looked back at Jack, who threw both arms in the air as if he were on a roller coaster. She looked at Nick, who was just staring at her without any expression on his face. "I'm serious!"

When Lyndon looked at her this time, Leigh saw something different. His eyes weren't just excited; they were jumping out of his eye sockets. Something was wrong and she was scared.

"Please, Lyndon." With one hand, she reached out and squeezed his thigh. "I don't like this. I'm scared."

"I'm a great driver." Lyndon sped around a few cars, jumping in and out of lanes. "This is a flawless machine. She knows how to handle the road."

"Lyndon, I—"

"You're distracting him!" Jack yelled. "Gun it! Gun it!"

"Shut up!" Leigh yelled as she eyed Jack. He seemed unsure what to make of it and his arms fell to his sides. "You're going to get us—"

The sudden fear on Jack's face made her turn just in time to see the truck that was heading straight for them. She screamed, her eyes slamming shut. The guys were screaming now too as tires screeched and the car turned in circles until it rammed right into the concrete median. Leigh heard a popping sound and felt something hit her face before everything went black.

* * *

Avery didn't like being in the hospital courtyard by herself. She hadn't noticed she was actually alone until a young, teary-eyed mother and her very noisy baby left. The kid made enough noise for several children, but once they were gone, Avery realized she was all alone and it depressed her. So when the door opened to the courtyard, she expected to be relieved to have some distraction. She was anything but.

"Hey, baby." As he walked to her, Carter's heart softened at how vulnerable and small she looked sitting on a stone gray bench by herself. Her hand was on her belly again and it only made him think of how good a mother she'd be.

The gall of this man calling her baby, but Avery didn't take the bait. "What are you doing here?"

She didn't bother to tell him not to sit down next to her, because she knew he would anyway.

"Always asking silly questions," he said as he turned to face her.

"Always talking down to me when I do," she retorted.

He looked at her sweet face, a little fuller than usual. "Still keeping me in line, huh? In that way only you can. I miss that attitude."

"How did you find me?" She couldn't keep herself from looking at him. He was so fine and being this close made her remember how much she enjoyed talking to him.

"I flirted with the nurses," he said. "You doing okay?"

"I come out here to think," she said. "To get away, you know. It can get kind of intense in there."

"He's doing better, right? You know my offer—"

"Carter," she interrupted, "if you really want to do something for me, stay away."

"You sound like Anthony," Carter said.

"You mean my husband?" She eyed him as he blinked. It hurt him to hear her say that and Avery didn't feel good about it as she'd expected to. "He came by to see you, I guess."

"Did he run back to you with his tail between his legs?"

"No," she said firmly. "My husband is not afraid of you. I didn't want him to go because I knew that was what you wanted. I know how you play your games, Carter."

"I thought he'd be on his way to school by then."

"Either way," Avery said, "you shouldn't have sent the flowers."

"It was perfectly innocent to—"

"Nothing you do is innocent, Carter. And if you really intended for them to be for my father, you would have sent them to the hospital or my mother's house."

"Again sounding just like Anthony." Carter laughed. "Where is our elderly teacher today?"

"He's not elderly." Avery knew she was playing into his game, but it wasn't as if he would leave if she didn't. "He's only thirty-six and he's a professor. You won't get anywhere with this, Carter. Anthony is above your games."

"If he's so great, why doesn't he practice safe sex?"

Avery was too relieved at the idea that Carter believed the baby was Anthony's to think of a comeback for that.

"But then again," Carter continued, "we all make mistakes. Some of us get dumped and deserted and others get a wife."

"If you want me to feel guilty about leaving," Avery said, "I do. It was immature and cowardly. Are you satisfied?"

"I'm never satisfied," Carter answered. "You know that about me. I always want more. I always have to win. That's why you left me, right? Even though my mother was in the hospital and—"

"Enough. That's all in the past, Carter." Avery felt herself getting choked up just thinking about that horrible night in his apartment when she gave him his ring back.

"It will never be the past," Carter insisted. "Nothing with you and me is in the past. It's always with us. It has been since the first day we met. I wanted to strangle you and you wanted to run me over with a truck, but we both knew."

"No." She turned to him, feeling anger at his arrogance. "When I met you, I loved Alex. Do you remember him? He was my fiancé and you set him up to be seduced by that British whore. The same one you tried to make me think I was crazy when I told you I recognized her."

"Avery . . ."

"Maybe you remember that?" she asked. "You told me—"

"Don't you think I've paid the price for that?" Carter was angry, even though he had no right to be.

"I think you paid about two and a half million dollars for it," she answered. "That was what you paid her to go away so you could marry me under a veil of secrecy and lies."

Carter rolled his eyes. "Don't forget the quarter of a million bucks Michael and I paid her to sleep with Alex in the first place."

Avery didn't think before she slapped him in the face. "You think this is funny?"

Carter was rubbing his cheek, trying not to smile. "Avery, you know what happens to me when you slap me. I get very turned on and so do you."

It was wrong, but she did remember and suddenly her senses came alive. She was in danger, wanting something she could never have again.

"My point is . . . My point . . ." She slid away from him as his closeness seemed to overcome her.

He reveled in his effect on her. "Your point is that you want me to suffer forever for my mistakes."

"No, I . . ." She clenched her hands in fists. "Jesus, you make me so . . ."

"You talking to Jesus or you talking to me?" he asked.

His arrogance infuriated her. Avery pressed her lips together, refusing to let him make her laugh. "Just leave, Carter."

Carter didn't move. "You're the big churchgoer, right? Always coming back on Sunday talking about, *Carter, I wish you had come today. The sermon was so good. Pastor Milton talked about forgiveness and understanding.*"

"What difference would forgiving you make?" she asked. "You wouldn't learn from it or change your ways. You are who you are."

"And if you really loved me, you would have accepted me for that."

Avery gasped at the accusation. "How could you say that?"

Carter regretted his words as soon as he saw her eyes begin to water. "Avery, I . . ."

"I loved you with everything I had." Her words caught in her throat as the emotion threatened to overwhelm her. "I ignored so much because I wanted to spend my life making you happy. I would have given anything to—"

She slapped his hands away as he reached for her, but Carter didn't give up. "Baby, I'm sorry."

"I'm not your—" The baby kicked so hard, Avery gasped as she reached out and grabbed hold of Carter's arm.

"What is it?" Carter asked anxiously. "What's wrong?"

"The baby." Avery let go, trying to steady herself. "She doesn't like it when I yell."

Carter sighed in relief. "Who does she think she is?"

Avery let out a quick laugh. "I've told her she better be glad she's in there or I'd give her a spanking for all the carrying on she does."

"Please." Carter made a smacking sound with his lips. "You're going to be such a pushover. You'll spoil her rotten."

"I will not." She smiled. "Okay, so maybe I won't spank her, but I will be firm and—"

"Is she doing it again?" Carter asked. When Avery nodded, he said, "She's a little brat, already."

When his hand came to her stomach, Avery wanted to push it away. She wanted to tell him to stop, but she couldn't. All she could do was look at him and watch while he reacted to their baby running a marathon under her belly.

"Wow." Carter wasn't sure if this was wonderful or just very weird. Her stomach was moving, rolling around like a snake. Then the rolling turned into one bump and then another. "She's trying to get out."

He hadn't intended for their hands to touch, but when they did, Carter looked up and caught Avery's eyes in his own. His hand instinctively went over hers, and the touch of her soft skin made him weak.

Avery was suddenly taken into a fantasy world, one where she had never left Carter and she was sitting with her husband as they both touched the belly that held their baby. In that one second, she felt happier than she ever imagined she could. This was all she wanted, what she'd imagined and hoped her life would be.

He took her lips in his own, and the touch sent a blaze ripping through her entire body. The familiar command of his mouth sent her mind to a wicked distraction and she only wanted more.

His lips were demanding her surrender and she wanted to give in to his demand. This was just like her dreams, her dreams on the beach in Saint-Tropez when . . .

A kiss was never enough for Carter when it came to Avery. Just a second and all the electricity between them came rushing back. The urgency that tasting her eager mouth created inside him was strong, he couldn't control it. But then . . .

"No," a breathless Avery managed as she pushed away. "Carter, no . . ."

"Please, baby." Carter didn't care about anything but touching her, tasting her, having her back in his life. "I miss you so much."

"I'm married." She pushed again. "I won't do this."

"You can't help yourself." He reached for her as she started to stand, but she pushed his hands away again. "You'll never be able to. Neither of us will."

Just then, Avery saw her mother standing only a few feet away and she was speechless. She couldn't remember ever feeling so ashamed.

When Carter turned to see the hateful stare Nikki Jackson held for him, he looked away. Standing up, he turned to Avery, who was already in tears, and he felt like a monster. But he wasn't. All he wanted was to be with the woman he loved.

"You can leave anytime." Nikki's voice was as cold as her expression. If she had the strength, she would hit him.

Carter didn't make eye contact with Nikki. He wanted to say something; he was stubborn enough that it angered him to be dismissed, but he kept quiet. There was nothing to say, so he left. He couldn't be greedy. He would have to be happy with the kiss and wait for his next chance.

"You're going back to Coral Gables," Nikki said as she approached her daughter. "And I don't want to hear another word."

"I'm not going anywhere," Avery protested. "I'm sorry for what just happened, but—"

"You kissed him, Avery. You came close last time. This time you actually did it. Next time—"

"Mom, please." Avery's hands fell to her sides as she looked at her mother with all the helplessness of a child. "I don't know what just happened, but I can stop it."

Nikki, who felt she had used up all the emotion she had for the day, still had enough left to feel compassion for her child. "I know what just happened. The man that pushes all your buttons, the father of that baby you're carrying, has a hold on you that is stronger than your will is right now."

"I would never cheat on Anthony."

"So you kissed him because you wanted to?" Nikki asked, waiting for Avery's response. "Exactly. You'll do what you have no intention of doing with Carter because he brings it out in you."

"I'll just stay away from him," Avery said.

"He won't stay away from you." Nikki sighed helplessly. "Baby, I can't do this. I can't worry about you too."

"Don't worry about me, then. I can take care of myself."

Nikki fell to the bench, lowering her head. "I'm exhausted and I can't spare anything."

"I'm not leaving." Avery joined her. "No matter what you say, I won't . . . not until at least Daddy is better."

"That boy is going to destroy your life," Nikki warned. "You know he will."

"He believes the baby is Anthony's."

"I'm not talking about the baby," Nikki said. "That will be nightmare enough when it comes to that. I'm talking about your marriage. How can you protect your marriage from Carter Chase?"

Avery didn't answer because she didn't know. She wanted to believe she had the moral fiber to handle the situation, but that was out the window now that she'd kissed Carter. As usual, her mother was right. Carter wasn't going to stop. He was a Chase and they never stopped until they got what they wanted. And as her finger unconsciously went to her lips, Avery closed her eyes and prayed that she had strength she wasn't yet aware of.

"There has to be more money!" Kimberly was already losing her patience as she paced the backyard with the Bluetooth in her ear.

"Mrs. Chase, of course there is more money. I just can't—"

"Don't tell me you can't," she ordered. "It's my money and I need more."

She was trying desperately to find the million to give to David. She had taken everything she had from her credit cards, checking account, savings account, and hidden stashes. She had sold stock Michael had given to her as gifts over the years. She had taken cash out of the safe in the bedroom floor. She had even sold some of her jewelry, but being who she was Kimberly had to stay under the radar. She was stuck at half a million dollars, and with only one day left, was beyond panic.

"This is a joint account," the banker said. "You've already—"

"Do you know what a joint account is?" she asked. "It belongs to both of us, so why are you questioning me? You've never had a problem before."

She was now trying to pull funds from another of the many accounts in the diversified portfolio of Michael and Kimberly Chase. She knew there was at least three million in this one because she was already pulling from it for pool renovation. After this, she planned on raiding the online trading account that Michael liked to play around with for his own entertainment. She wasn't sure what was in there, but there was something.

There was money everywhere. She might even have a chance of getting into Michael's trust fund, which he never touched. He invested it all and paid little attention to it. If worse came to worst, she would have to dig into the twins' trust, but she cringed at the thought of doing that.

"But it's beyond your limit, Mrs. Chase. There is a three-hundred-thousand-dollar maximum withdrawal per year. You've already withdrawn one hundred and thirty thousand for decorations and renovations of your home and it's only March. I can give you the other one hundred and seventy, but nothing more than that."

"That's bullshit," Kimberly said. "I've taken out more than three hundred thousand before—"

"Yes, that was before," he interrupted. "Your purchase of the house last year caused Mr. Chase to move money around. This account is 2.5 million dollars smaller than it was just six months ago. There are minimums to maintain and that requires—"

"Fine." Kimberly didn't want to hear any more. "Wire my savings account the rest today."

She hung up before he could respond. As Marisol brought a glass of Chardonnay to her table, Kimberly searched her iPhone for the number to the bank that held the trust funds for all four Chase children and the two grandchildren. It took her longer than it should have, but she felt confident once she reached the family's personal banker at the firm. He seemed eager to please and once she read off the passwords, security codes, and numbers, he was more than happy to give her two hundred thousand until they ran into a glitch.

"What do you mean you can't approve that amount?"

He cleared his throat. "This account has been flagged."

Kimberly froze, afraid to know what this meant. "Explain everything and don't mess around."

"Your husband has requested that any withdrawal be cleared with him first."

"Are you saying I have to get permission from him to withdraw from this account?" Kimberly asked. "You mean at a certain limit, right?"

"No, Mrs. Chase. Any amount. It's okay. These are pretty normal. All I have to do is complete the request and contact Mr. Chase at—"

"No," Kimberly said. "I'll handle this myself."

Kimberly hung up wondering why in the world Michael would do this. Did he know something? Did he suspect something? Was he up to something? She looked at the glass of wine on the table in front of her.

"Marisol!" She was going to need something much stronger.

Leigh was in her office, rubbing her sore shoulder, when James Monroe walked in without knocking. She had met him only once when he interrupted a dinner at Nobu in Beverly Hills with Lyndon.

She didn't want to see him, and his rudeness only made that more so. It had been two days since the accident and she was still sore all over. The bump on her forehead wouldn't go away for a long time and her new bangs were barely covering it. None of that really mattered. She was just angry and trying hard to forget everything by throwing herself into the clinic.

"Dr. Chase." James helped himself to a chair along the wall and pulled it to the desk. "You look great. How you feeling?"

Leigh just stared at him, not interested in his Hollywood kiss-up act. She knew why he was here.

"I know you're angry," James said in a conciliatory tone. "You have every right to be. That's why I'm here."

"Lyndon sent you?" she asked. She hadn't returned any of his calls these past two days.

James nodded with an opposing finger in the air. "But I'm really here for more than Lyndon. Well, for something that is bigger than Lyndon."

"I'm not ready to talk to him," she said.

"He's fine, by the way."

"I know he is." Thank God for seat belts and air bags or they could all be dead. Leigh hadn't left the hospital without finding out that everyone was okay. She hadn't had time to check herself because she was too busy keeping her mother from having a fit.

"Everyone is fine," James said. "The car is pretty totaled, but that's nothing. Lyndon is very, very sorry. He just gets around those guys and they're in college all over again."

"He could have killed us all." Leigh shivered at the thought of seeing that truck coming straight for them.

"But he didn't," James said. "That's why there doesn't need to be a big . . .you know, thing about it."

Leigh knew exactly what James was getting at and it was nauseatingly familiar. "I'm not going to lie to the police for him."

"The police aren't going to come to see you," James said. "I've taken care of that. Well, the studio has."

"How nice for your client."

"My client is your boyfriend."

"I wouldn't say that," Leigh said. "You're thinking about the bottom line, I get that. This could bring bad publicity, but—"

"There is no but, Dr. Chase." James's expression became very serious. "We have the DVD coming out. The new movie will be out at Christmas."

Leigh leaned forward, wincing at the pain it caused her. "Do you care about him at all?"

"Of course I do." James appeared genuinely offended.

"Then what are you going to do about it?"

"I can't make him pick better friends, Doctor."

Leigh wondered if he really believed that was all it was or if he was hiding something. There was no truth to him. "He was on something, James."

His eyes widened for a second before he broke out in laughter. "Oh God, no. Doctor, no, he wasn't on anything. Lyndon doesn't do drugs and he wasn't drinking."

"Did the police do a Breathalyzer?"

He nodded. "He wasn't drunk. He just had a little extra testosterone."

Leigh wanted to believe him, but she remembered Lyndon's eyes. "It's not impossible to believe considering Jack is always drunk and Nick is on something. I don't know what, but I think—"

"Nick is a mess, but Lyndon . . ." James shook his head. "I wish he would get Nick out of his life. The guy is no good, but he won't desert his friends. That doesn't mean he condones it and he sure as hell doesn't take drugs. He knows there is just too much to lose."

"I wonder," Leigh said. "I referred him to some clinics that might be able to help Nick, but he hasn't done anything."

"That was my fault. I told him not to. I appreciate that you want to help him, but he can't be a part of that. He can't be in contact of any kind to a rehab that the press could pick up. Saying it's for a friend is the biggest lie out there."

"These places serve the very rich and they are extremely confidential."

"Have you read the gossip blogs these days?" James was shaking his head. "Right now it'll mean that he's on drugs too. I won't let him do it. There's too much to lose. That's the final word on that."

That wasn't the final word for Leigh, and if Lyndon ever wanted to see her again he would have to convince her he understood that his life, and the life of his friends, meant more than money in his wallet.

9

Avery took a deep breath before she started for Janet. As she walked through the lounge of the ornate, exclusive country club, one of a few the Chase family belonged to, she had to check herself. She remembered how nice it was to stop by the club after church on Sundays. Carter, who never came to church with her, would be waiting for her. The rest of the family was there, the twins playing in their crisp, clean little church suits. They would have drinks and brunch with impeccable service and Avery never saw anyone lift a finger to pay a bill. It was all going to some fantasy account that Steven probably never even checked for accuracy.

She wasn't wrong to miss that life, but she had to get over it. She was determined to get over it for the sake of her marriage and her baby. This was the only reason she had agreed to meet Janet at the club this morning. Janet had left a message for her at the hotel saying that Carter was acting erratic and she was afraid that he would try to hurt himself again.

Again? Avery panicked when she heard that word. Had Carter tried to hurt himself? That didn't sound at all like him. She knew she probably shouldn't have, but she called Janet to find out what she meant. That was when Janet told her of the "Mercedes wrapped around the tree" story. While everyone insisted it was a reckless accident, Janet feared it was more than that. She didn't want to go back to those days and asked Avery what to do.

"Help him get over any idea that we'll be together again," was Avery's answer. After a moment of silence and a long sigh, Janet agreed and asked Avery to meet with her to figure out how to convince Carter of what was good for him.

After they greeted each other with a hug, Avery sat down across from her. She ordered a glass of lemonade from the waiter and settled into the comfortable chairs overlooking the outdoor deck.

"You look lovely, dear." Janet leaned back comfortably, smoothing out the fabric of her charcoal-gray D&G slacks. "You've been able to maintain grace in the way you carry yourself. Some women wobble all over or stomp around like buffalo."

"I've got a few months left."

"Do you plan to have the baby here or in Miami?" Janet asked. "That's where you live now, right?"

This family wasn't afraid to let you know they knew all your business. "I would like to have it in Miami, but after another month, I won't be able to fly."

"Maybe it's for the best," Janet said. "You'll want your mother around when the baby comes and I doubt she'll be able to leave L.A. any time soon."

"You're right."

"I guess that was why I found it so odd that you left." Janet smiled politely as the waiter brought the lemonade. "You and Nikki were so close. I couldn't imagine you would leave."

"I didn't feel I had a choice," Avery replied. "Which is why we're having this talk."

Janet's smile faded. "I'm not proud of the way my son has behaved. Not from the beginning. When I found out what he'd done with that awful Lisette, I couldn't believe it. Not Carter."

Join the club, Avery thought but wouldn't dare say.

"I told him to just be patient and wait for you to come back." Janet sighed. "But I had to go away. The kids were telling Steven what Carter was up to, but he kept it from me during that time. When we came back, I tried, but I couldn't get through to him. When I heard about that accident, Avery, I almost fainted."

Avery felt her chest tightening just at the mention of it. No matter what was lost between her and Carter, she didn't want him hurt. "I appreciate your trying."

"I take it you've seen Kimberly." Janet purposefully kept a blank expression.

Avery nodded. "I don't want to get into it with either of you."

"That's fine." Janet took a sip of her tonic water. "It's not your job. You're not a part of this family anymore, regrettably."

"And that's not going to change, Janet. I need you to convince Carter of that."

"I thought once Carter accepted that you are married and having a family with someone else, he would stop behaving so recklessly, but he hasn't. Things are very strained between him and Steven again."

"After everything they've done to try and be close." Avery regretted her part in coming between Steven and Carter. "I should have quit working at Chase Beauty when Steven asked me to."

"They've had a million fights since that. The funny thing is they grew closer after we'd returned from South Africa." Janet smiled proudly. "They were doing it for me. But Carter's obsession with you and all the trouble it was causing with the police department ruined that."

"Is Carter in trouble?" Avery asked.

"Not any trouble we can't get him out of so far," Janet said. "He's a lawyer, so he knows what he's doing. If your father and brother hadn't been cops, he might have gone too far, but they've kept him within the law. Well, mostly."

"You know Carter better than anyone, Janet. How can you get him focused on other things?"

"Correction, dear. Michael knows him better than anyone. But I do know that both he and Steven are trying to get Carter more involved at Chase Beauty now that he's on the board. It will be a useful distraction."

Avery smiled, warmed at the idea that Carter was on the board. He'd wanted that for a long time.

"I've asked for his help with some of my charities, but he's been very wishy-washy of late. It's so unlike him. The disappearing acts. The women. Carter has always . . . done what he wanted, but never lost sight of everything else that mattered."

"Janet." Avery set her glass down. "I don't want to hear about the women."

"Well, I do."

Avery turned in disbelief at seeing Carter leaning against the wall only a few feet from them with a smug, cocky grin on his face.

"What do you know about all the women, Mother?" Carter asked in a nonchalant tone.

Avery swung around to Janet, ready to curse her for the setup. But she could tell from the look on Janet's face that she hadn't expected to see Carter either.

"Do you find yourself charming?" Janet asked, her eyes narrowing.

"I must be." Carter approached the women. "Like you said . . . all those women."

"What are you doing here?" Just seeing him made Avery think of the last kiss they had shared. Damn him!

"My ears were burning." He frowned at Avery. Who did she think she was? He didn't appreciate this shit one bit.

"You're stalking me now?" Janet asked. "Your own mother. That's a new low."

"You need to sharpen your skills of deception, Mother." He leaned against her chair. "You told Dad you were meeting Avery here. All I had to do was ask."

Janet rolled her eyes, looking away. "I'm sorry, Avery. I didn't know . . . If I thought Steven would tell him, I wouldn't have said anything."

"Dad is only trying to help." Carter's tone emphasized his disappointment. "I thought you were too. Until now."

"I am," Janet said.

"I'm leaving." Avery stood up awkwardly. "This was a waste of time. Carter doesn't care about what's good for him. He just cares about what he wants."

"At least I don't pretend I don't want what I clearly do like some people." Carter waved away the approaching waiter, never taking his eyes off Avery.

"I know what I want," Avery asserted. "That's why I'm here."

"To plot against me behind my back?"

"Carter, that isn't—"

"No, Janet." Avery stepped forward, always finding strength when met with his maddening audacity. "He came here for the truth, so don't hide it from him. Yes, we were figuring out how to get you off my back. Are you glad you asked?"

"I didn't ask," Carter corrected. "In putting this plot together, did you mention our kiss to my dear, concerned mother?"

Avery gritted her teeth in anger. She couldn't look at Janet, only imagining her response to that. "That's it. I'm out of here."

She turned to leave, walking as fast as she could with an extra twenty pounds on her belly. She could hear his footsteps behind her and he finally caught up just as they reached the lobby. Grabbing her by the arm, he turned her around to face her with that forceful anger that always excited her.

"Let me go." She tried to pull away, but his grip was too strong.

"Come with me." He didn't wait for a response, leading her to a secluded hallway near the bathrooms.

"This has to stop, Carter." She freed herself, but he blocked her way when she tried to leave.

"You are so full of shit," Carter said. "You forget how well I know you."

"You forget that it doesn't matter what you know anymore."

"Fine." Carter pressed his lips together with a tempered frown. "What I know doesn't matter? Then let's talk about what you know. Does that matter?"

"Not to you apparently. If it did, you'd leave me alone."

"You know that you still want me." He spoke just above a whisper. "You know that you married that man based on some antiquated idea of morality. You don't love him as much as you love me and you never will."

Her hands clenched into fists as she resisted the urge to hit him. "You are the most arrogant asshole on the face of this planet. Do you actually believe you're that incredible that you can't be gotten over? That no woman can love again after having loved you?"

Carter leaned back, folding his arms over his chest. *Hell yeah*, was what he wanted to say. "That kiss we shared is the answer to that question."

"That kiss was you taking advantage of me in a very emotional situation."

Carter threw his arms in the air. "Oh, here we go with the victim's defense. You have got to be the most taken-advantage-of person on the face of this planet, Avery. You're so helpless against everyone, especially that damn insolent, overbearing Carter. It's always easy to blame me, right? That way you never have to admit you did exactly what you wanted and what you would have done no matter what emotional state you were in."

"If I did exactly what I wanted, I would slap you across the face right now."

"Do it," he taunted, stepping so close to her they were only inches apart. He felt his temperature already hiking up. "You know what's gonna happen next and you can always blame it on me . . . again."

Avery felt him press against her belly, and the match it lit inside her made her step back. "I wouldn't give you the satisfaction."

"You wouldn't give yourself the satisfaction," he corrected. "Because you're all about suffering, aren't you? You feel superior to everyone because you deny yourself what you want. And every now and then you give in, but it's never your fault, so you still stay clean and pious."

Avery hated the fact that he was making sense. He did know her so well. "Maybe I should be more like you, indulging in everything I want no matter what the consequence or who it hurts. As long as I get what I want, what else matters?"

"I will not apologize for who I am," Carter assured her. "I'm done apologizing for doing what I have to do to get what I want. I'm just gonna get it. And what I want is you, Avery."

"I don't want you!" Avery turned to leave, but he took her by the arm and turned her back to him.

When she looked into his eyes, the passion mixed with anger

she saw ignited her entire body. She was lit up in a second and nothing would stop what was coming next. When it came to passion, Carter's nature was not slow and tender. His lips took hers in a demanding, hungry gesture that jolted her heart and made her pulse pound out of control.

The attraction between them was so potent that just a taste of his mouth sent waves of ecstasy through Avery's veins. She kissed him back, melting into him while she felt a dizzying current around her. His tongue explored, teased, and demanded a response that she was all too eager to give.

Carter could feel Avery giving herself to the passion of his kiss. That hot ache, with both fury and lust, that only she could bring was growing, building inside him. As her hands slipped up his arms, bringing him closer, he was conscious of every spot where her flesh touched his. Her soft lips, the sweet taste of her mouth, and that silky, tender skin ushered a slow descent into madness. He needed, wanted her closer than her belly would allow.

Avery let out an impassioned sigh as she felt him swing her body around. When he brought her back to him, she could feel his heart thudding wildly behind her own and his hardness pressing against her. Her senses were spinning out of control as his mouth touched her neck, each kiss imploring more and more. His hand came to her breast, caressing her until her entire body was trembling.

She moaned, leaning her head back against him while raising her hands to hold him. There was nothing that pleased Carter more than seducing Avery. The pull of coaxing her toward giving in to desire and laying all her vulnerability out there was overwhelming for him.

Instinctively, as if they had never parted, Avery's body molded to his. She arched her butt and moved her hips from left to right, feeling him get harder and harder. The sounds of desire were getting louder and threatened to make her crazy. Then his hand lowered, touching her stomach, and that last wisp of sanity brought Avery back to reality.

What was she doing? How could she do this to Anthony, to herself?

"Please, Carter." With an aching she couldn't bear, Avery was left only to beg for mercy. "Please."

"I know, baby." Carter's lips went to her ear and bit her tenderly. He would take her now if he could get away with it. "Let's go home. I can—"

She took his hands and moved them away from her. Taking a step forward, she said, "I'm not your baby and that place is not my home anymore. God, Carter, I'm pleading with you."

Recovering from the initial shock of her rejection, the symbolism of her back still turned to him made Carter unable to hide his anger. "You want mercy I can't give you. I'm not like you, baby. I can't sacrifice what I need to breathe, to drink because it doesn't fit nicely with everything else. I'm not going to."

When he turned her around, he was ready to kiss her again, but was taken aback by the look on her face. She was crying, tears staining both of her red cheeks. It was confusing, insulting, and infuriating and Carter didn't know what to say. He leaned away, looking down at her as if she were an injured bird.

"Are you happy?" Avery asked, feeling the guilt and shame eating away at her with every second. The lies and deception made her so far from pious. "You've proven your point. I'm still attracted to you. I still catch on fire every time you touch me. But I love my husb—"

"I don't want to hear it," Carter snapped. "You use him as some kind of shield to—"

"He isn't a shield, Carter." This time, Avery grabbed his arms and squeezed tight. She needed him to understand. "He's my husband and I'm married to him. No matter what I feel for you, I can't be this person."

"What person is that?" he asked. "The person that knows where her heart is, who her man really is? Your body gives you away, Avery. This is what you want. I'm what you want."

Her arms dropped to her sides as she sighed. "You're right. You are what I want. And if you keep this up, I'll give in to my desires. Eventually, I couldn't avoid it, but then what? I'll be an adulterer, a liar, a cheat. I already hate myself for kissing you, for wanting more. I won't blame you for my choice this time, but

I'm begging you to help me not become something I can't bear to be."

Carter groaned as he ran his hand over his face. "You want me to deny what we have? Pretend that we aren't meant for each other because . . ."

"Because I'm begging you to." Avery placed her hand on his chest, looking into his eyes. She could only pray she was reaching him. "I can't be someone I despise. You think you'd be happy because you had me, but you wouldn't like me like that. You wouldn't like the person I know I'll become after I cross that line I can't return from."

"I would love you no matter what," Carter said.

"But I'd hate you."

Carter swallowed hard, but held firm. Did that even matter? If he had her, what else mattered?

"And I'd hate myself more," she added. "Can you say you love me and live with that?"

Carter stepped away, hating himself for feeling pity. How could he be considering this? After everything he'd done to get her back. "I can't let you go, Avery."

"You have to. No matter what happened, I'm married to Anthony and . . . we're making a family. If you have any decency in you—"

"God, Avery, don't do—"

"—and I know you do," she continued, "you'll respect that."

He stared into her watery eyes and could see that she meant this. After all this, she still wanted to reject him. His anger spurred his stubborn spirit. "I don't have to respect anything that takes you away from me."

Avery lowered her head, unable and unwilling to fight anymore. "Then you'll do whatever you have to do. I've done all I can. I just want to be a good wife and mother. I just want to be a daughter my father can be proud . . ."

When she broke into sobs, Carter wanted to reach out to her, but he didn't; he couldn't. She was right. He could have her if he wanted to and he did. If he persisted, she would give in to him. But even if he succeeded in getting her to leave Anthony, she would hate herself because of the reason why. Cheating wasn't something she could stand. He had used that truth to his advantage when he'd wanted her before, and this was why he didn't have her now.

She would never forgive him for putting his own desire ahead of everything that mattered to her. He would eventually lose her all over again. No, this wasn't the way.

"Don't cry, Avery." Carter's hands felt like two-ton weights at his sides. He didn't trust himself to touch her again. Reason could only go so far. "You've won."

"Everything is a game to you, Carter." She was sickened by his attitude. "No one wins here."

"I guess you're right. I don't get what I want and neither do you. Anthony doesn't get what he wants because you want me. But we can all drown our sorrow in the reward of doing what's right."

She resented his sarcasm. "I know you're angry, but you have to see—"

"Don't," he said. "You keep your Bible and your virtues to yourself. I'm not doing this out of respect for the sanctity of marriage, a marriage that never should have happened. I'm doing this because I have some self-respect left and I'd like to keep it."

"I'm sorry." She stepped closer to him, but he moved away. His face was dark and somber and he was shutting off as he usually did when things got beyond him.

Without saying good-bye, Carter started to leave, but after a few steps, he stopped without turning around. "You're going to regret this, Avery. No matter what you do or how hard you try, you'll never love him like you love me. You'll never want him for any reason more than the fact that you should. But when you realize that, it'll be too late. Good-bye."

Avery stood in the hallway for another fifteen minutes, leaning against the wall for support. She tried to pull herself together, but was having a hard time. She was supposed to be relieved, but she felt broken inside. Carter had given up on her and that was supposed to be all she wanted. She was free now to focus on her baby, her father, and her marriage without the temptation and the frustration. So why did she feel trapped? Why did she feel so afraid? Why did she feel like she'd just lost everything?

He'd been feeling a little horny since watching that full-figured waitress sashay by him about ten times during lunch, so Michael was happy to hear Kimberly had stopped by the office just after he got back. He jumped up from his chair to greet her, planning to lock the door and get to it right away. But from the salty look on her face, Michael knew he wasn't getting anything.

"What did I do now?" he asked as she slammed the door behind him. "That's great, Kimberly. Very classy."

"You think I give a shit what those people out there think of me?" Kimberly was at her wits' end and wasn't about to concern herself with gossipy office help.

"You should." He returned to his chair.

"What's the matter?" she asked. "Do they all gossip about what I did to the precious, darling Janet Chase?"

Michael eyed her intently, not wanting to get into that. "I'm busy, baby."

"By baby, do you mean equal spouse?" She sat down with a sarcastic smirk to match her tone. "Or baby as in child?"

Michael frowned, trying to think of what he'd done, what he'd forgotten. "Can we skip the drama?"

"Because I think maybe I've called you Daddy so often, you've begun to think you're actually my father."

Michael leaned back in his chair and tugged at his chin. "I would never think I could replace that gem of a daddy you had."

"Don't get smug with me, Michael." She slammed her purse on the desk. "I will smack that smile off your face."

"These word games only exhaust me, Kimberly. Out with it."

"How dare you put limits on what I can withdraw from our accounts?" She watched as he opened his mouth to respond, but stopped. "And if you say they are yours, not ours, I'll jump across this desk and strangle you to death."

"To death?" he asked. "Then everything that was . . . ours would be . . . yours. You'd like that, wouldn't you?"

"I'd like some fucking respect, Michael."

"Then you'd better start showing some." His voice held no hint of humor. "Starting with not slamming my office door. Now, what is your problem with . . . our accounts?"

Kimberly took a deep breath to calm herself. "Why am I being restricted?"

"From which account?" Michael asked suspiciously.

"Take your pick," Kimberly said. "What is this supposed to be? More punishment?"

"Why do you want so much money?" Michael asked.

"Why do I?" Kimberly acted amazed. "How do you think shit gets done around that house?"

"What shit are we talking about?"

"The pool for one thing." Kimberly had already rehearsed the lies she would come up with for needing money, and as she listed them one by one, she only hoped Michael wouldn't ask too many questions.

Michael was getting more and more suspicious as every suddenly life-and-death need was presented to him. "Nothing you're saying costs more than what you're allowed to take out. If you don't want to do it, then give it to me and I'll do it."

"Because you don't have any limits, do you?" she asked sarcastically.

"As a matter of fact, I do. I put these limits on both of us while we recoup our resources after buying the house. Even wealthy people have to take it easy when they buy a new home, Kimberly."

"We aren't wealthy," Kimberly argued. "We're filthy, stinkin' rich and I won't be put on an allowance like some upper-middle-class housewife."

"What about your own money?" he asked. "I know you haven't spent every penny you've withdrawn from the accounts. I know you stash some of that away. All you women do it."

"Now we're going to get into a sexism debate?" Kimberly asked. "If I stashed the money away, it means I don't want to use it. Michael, I want to get a summer wardrobe for the boys and I need some new outfits for our trip to Martinique in August. That alone will top one hundred. Also, I want to make additional changes to the pool and get started on the media room in—"

"Enough," Michael interrupted. "Use your card and I'll sort it out later."

Kimberly was afraid he'd say that. They had an American Express Centurion Card, which actually required them to charge two hundred and fifty thousand dollars a year to maintain. Michael had the bill sent directly to Chase Beauty, so a cash advance on that wasn't going to work. "So you can monitor me? No, thanks."

"I'm not asking you, Kimberly." He saw her frown deepening. "Don't piss me off. There's nothing that you want, that you should have, that you can't put on that card."

"That I should have?" Kimberly asked. "What the fuck does that mean?"

"You know damn well what it means," he countered. She was determined to start a fight.

"Why do I get the feeling it has something to do with that vindictive bitch of a mother you . . ."

"You better watch your mouth, woman," he ordered. She was really pissing him off. "The limits are there and they aren't going anywhere."

"Is this where I say yes, master, turn my tail, and go home?" Kimberly asked. "Am I supposed to let you punish me forever?"

"Here we go." Michael pushed away from the desk and got up from his chair. He went to the dresser against the wall and reached in for his scotch. "Cue the violin music all you want. You put yourself in this position, Kimberly."

"No, I think I'm right this time."

"I'm not going to let you use my money to hurt my mother again." There, he said it. His back was to her of course, making it much easier. "No more P.I. trips to Paris to dig up secrets. No more quarter-of-a-million-dollar payments to piece-of-shit designers who want to fuck my mother!"

"Do you think I would be so stupid as to try something like that again?" Kimberly almost laughed at how tame that would all seem if David didn't get what he wanted.

Michael turned back to her. "No, I don't. But that doesn't

make a difference. That happened because I took my eyes off the ball and I'm not going to do that again."

"And you think reining me in financially will control me?"

"I don't need to rein you in financially to control you." Michael took a sip of the scotch and let it burn his throat. "Because no matter how much you bitch and complain, like you said before, I'm the daddy here and I said the limits stay."

Kimberly didn't have a comeback for that one. The look on Michael's face was just about as serious as she'd ever seen, including the months following the incident when he'd threatened to leave her. She wanted to pummel him into the ground, but she didn't have the energy. It was all over. She was totally screwed.

In that second, she thought of taking for herself all the money she had put together for David. She would need it when Michael dumped her after the truth came out. But then she thought about it. The child custody case would cost her millions. She'd get nothing.

No, she wasn't willing to give up on her life yet. As much as she hated Michael right now, she would die without him. It was settled. Murder was her only choice.

"Is there something you want to tell me?" Michael was curious as to why she hadn't attacked him yet.

Kimberly wasn't sure what took over, but she began laughing uncontrollably. Her head fell back and her hand went to her stomach as she laughed until she started crying. Michael was looking at her as if she were crazy, and she was glad he was. Someday she would make him pay for this little conversation. He would also pay for not getting rid of David as he promised. He would pay for making her beg for money. He would pay for laying the cards on the table the way he had. But now she had other things to deal with.

When she heard all the activity down the hallway from the clinic office, Leigh assumed it was one of two things. Something was going wrong as usual or Lyndon had shown up again. Leigh thought she must be crazy for wishing for the former. The last time Lyndon showed up to apologize, they'd gotten into a huge fight when she accused him of being on something and he stormed out. Yesterday he'd sent six dozen bouquets of various-colored roses to the clinic and left several messages on her cell.

Leigh hated arguing with him because she had no facts to back up what she felt. It was all accusation based on brief inter-actions, and even though she had every right to be angry about the car, she knew it was wrong for her to accuse him of being on drugs without any proof. But she was a doctor and had come to recognize drug-induced behavior from just a brief moment.

But it wasn't as if she had never been wrong. Could she be wrong now?

When she heard the knock on the door, she knew it was Lyn-don. As always, he didn't wait for permission before opening the door. When he stepped inside, Leigh was hooked all over again at the sight of him. What was it? She'd lived in L.A. her entire life and seen hundreds of male stars. Being a Chase, she had met some of the most incredible people all over the world. This made her reluctant to believe she was being blinded from the fire by the smoke.

So maybe she really felt something for Lyndon. She thought she'd caught herself before falling for him, but the way her senses came to life proved otherwise.

"I'm busy, Lyndon." *Stay cool, stay calm,* she told herself. *Pretend he's just any other guy and not a hot movie star any woman would give her left breast to have.*

Lyndon didn't seem to bother with the million-dollar box-office smile, giving Leigh the impression he might actually be serious this time and not try to movie-star flirt his way out of this. It was the only way he had a chance.

"I'm busy too," he said, "but I can't get anything done with this thing between us. Can you?"

"What is this thing?" Leigh asked. "Because I know what I think this thing is, but you don't seem to think it's anything."

Lyndon sighed exhaustively. "You are hell-bent on making me a drug addict, aren't you?"

"I'm only hell-bent on the truth," Leigh explained.

Lyndon angrily grabbed a chair and sat down hard. His eyes

were searing into Leigh's. "I wasn't on drugs. I don't do drugs, Leigh. That's the last time I'm going to tell you that."

Leigh tried to remain rational in the face of a man who was not used to being questioned and forced to explain himself. "I'm not doing this out of some sense of superiority or to judge you."

"I know that. You're a doctor. You don't judge people. And I may be rushing this, but I think of you as my girlfriend. That's why I know if there is anyone I can trust to tell this to, it's you."

Leigh was taken aback by that declaration. "I know that you want me to believe you."

"No, I don't want you to believe me," Lyndon said. "I need you to believe me. You're too important. I haven't been famous that long, but I'd still forgotten what a real relationship could be like. A relationship where there isn't an angle or some professional advantage. Where it's just a guy and a girl who enjoy being with each other and want to be closer. We were making that happen."

Leigh cursed herself for falling for this. He seemed so sincere, but she knew this was what he did for a living: acting a part. "Make your friends get help."

Lyndon didn't look as if he was expecting any more demands, and that was why she made this one. He had to know that she wasn't a groupie. She was a doctor and all his bankable looks wouldn't cloud her head.

"Nick and Jack are either alcoholics, drug addicts, or both," she said. "Make them get help and I'll believe you."

Leigh waited as Lyndon appeared reluctant to agree and it bothered her that she was scared he would say no. After all, who was she? She was one woman out of any he could have whenever he wanted. Why would he risk his career, go against the advice of his highly compensated agent, and possibly lose his friends just to please her? Had she placed too high a price on her affection? If he said no, that would be it and she really didn't want this to be it.

"I'll do it," Lyndon finally answered.

Leigh didn't realize how tight she was wound waiting for his response until she felt her shoulders relax. "What if they say no?"

"They will." Lyndon frowned as if he thought that was a silly question. "But they won't have a choice. Right now I'm holding the cards and they'll do whatever I tell them to."

"They might hate you for it," she said. "For a while. Maybe a long while."

"I can deal with them hating me." Lyndon shrugged, but then got very serious. "But I can't deal with you hating me."

Leigh pushed away from the desk and stood up. As she walked around the desk toward him, she noticed the victorious smile wrapping around his lips. He stood up, waiting, ready to receive her kiss, her adulation. When she reached him, she looked adoringly at him and he leaned in for the kiss.

Leigh pressed her finger against his mouth and pushed. His head went back and he frowned. "Get over yourself, Mr. Prior. There are patients to see. Let's go."

Kimberly felt the ulcer forming in her stomach as she knocked on the door to the shady motel room. Over one shoulder was a Louis Vuitton canvas bag with seven hundred and fifty thousand dollars. Over the other was her pink Prada carrying a handgun. It was her intention to leave this place with everything she had come here with.

When David opened the door, he frowned, looking confused at first, but quickly smiled. "What happened to the rich bitch? You look . . . you look like yourself, Paige."

Kimberly cringed at the sound of that name, but she hoped it would be for the last time. She had purposefully disguised herself so she wouldn't be recognizable. She was wearing some rags she found in Marisol's room, a raven-black bob wig and thick glasses. If things went down the way she intended them to, no one could say they recognized a woman that looked anything like Kimberly Chase. She had even removed the plates from the cheap Toyota she had rented with cash for the day, a car no Chase would be caught dead in.

"Can I come in already?" she asked, looking around nervously. She hadn't spotted anyone since driving into the parking lot or walking up the stairs to David's front door.

David stepped aside as she hurried in. He took his sweet time closing the door behind her.

"Let's get this over with." Kimberly tried to breathe slower to calm her heartbeat down, but she was only getting more nervous.

David, dressed in jeans and a Tigers T-shirt, was laughing as he leaned against the door. "What, you don't want to hang out a little while for a tearful good-bye?"

Kimberly dropped the bag of money on the bed with cheap paisley hotel sheets. "There's your money. Now I need your guarantee you'll leave and never come back."

"Now, Paige." David walked over to the bed and grabbed the bag. He opened it up and turned it over. The cash fell onto the bed and he tossed the bag away. "I'm starting to get the feeling that you don't trust me."

"For the last time," she answered, "my name is—"

"There's a million bucks here, right? You wouldn't be shortchanging me." He ran his fingers over the money with an ear-to-ear smile on his face.

"Why would I do . . . ?" Kimberly was halted by the menacing look he gave her. "Are we done here?"

David's eyes squinted as he walked to within inches of her. Kimberly reached for the purse on her right shoulder with her left hand, but he grabbed her arm and she screamed. He pushed her back twice before she slammed against the wall.

"I taught you to lie better than that, Paige." David let go of her arm, but only to take hold of her neck.

Kimberly winced when she felt his rough, dry hand wrapped around her neck. He pushed his body up against hers.

"Stop."

"How much money is on that bed, Paige?"

When she didn't respond, his hand squeezed. Kimberly's hands grabbed at his arm, trying to pull his hand away, but she wasn't strong enough. "David."

"How much, Paige?"

"Okay!" she yelled.

He let go of her neck and Kimberly fell to the floor. The gun was in the purse. If she could only just get the gun, this could all be over.

"How much?" he asked, looking down at her.

"Seven hundred and fifty thousand," she answered. Kimberly yelled as he kicked the wall next to her.

"You disappoint me," David said, "but you were always a troublesome little bitch, weren't you?"

"I can get you the rest, but not now."

"Get up!"

Slowly, as her knees allowed, Kimberly stood up from the floor. When she looked at him, he was smiling and she knew from experience that meant the worst was yet to come. She would have no more chances.

As she reached into her purse, she shuffled around for the gun and in that moment, David started for her. She looked up, grabbing the gun just in time. She was screaming as she pulled it out. Just as she got her hand on the trigger, David grabbed the gun and turned it around, twisting her arm. The pain was excruciating.

"David, you're hurting me."

"You think this is hurting you?" He twisted more until she screamed and had to let go. "You've forgotten what my hurt can really be, bitch."

Kimberly backed away. She was going to die. He was certainly going to kill her now.

"You always were a simple bitch," David muttered as he studied the gun in his hand.

"David, I have children. I can't—"

"This is a sweet piece. How much did it cost?"

Kimberly remembered how he loved to play this game. He would act as if hurting her were the furthest thing from his mind. He would talk about anything else until she let her guard down, let her fear subside. Then he would knock her across the room. Kimberly cursed herself for being unable to kill him. She had the chance, but she'd waited too long. Now she was going to die because she was too chicken to do what could only be seen as justice.

David disarmed the gun, looking in admiration at the car-
tridges.

"You can have it," she exclaimed. "It's worth five grand. You
can sell it."

"What in the hell am I going to do with a gun registered to
Michael Chase?" He tossed the cartridge in the garbage. "No,
you're going to pay off that last two-fifty a different way."

He was handing her the unloaded gun, still playing his game.
Kimberly backed away, ready for him. "I can get you the money."

"No, you can't." He smiled, looking her up and down. "It ap-
pears your husband does know what you are. He's holding the
purse strings and you've gotten all you could. There's no more
without telling him."

"I have two children, David."

"I'm not going to kill you," he said. "So spare me the mommy
guilt trip."

"No, I mean they have trust funds, the boys. I can . . ." She
stopped as David slowly shook his head. "What? You want more
now?"

"I think I'm entitled considering you tried to kill me."

"Enough with the games." Kimberly wiped the tears from her
face. "How much?"

"You pay in trade." He pressed his nose against her and made
a sniffing sound. "Damn, you smell like . . . money."

Disgusted, Kimberly cringed and pushed him away. "No,
David. Just stop it. How much money do you want?"

"Money isn't going to cut it." He used his body to slam hers
against the wall.

When he started grinding against her, Kimberly thought she
was going to be sick. "David, get off of—"

"You've lost your touch." He was trying to kiss her now, but
Kimberly kept moving her face to avoid his mouth. "Paige would
have fought harder."

David stopped and leaned back, studying her. "You're a completely different person than my little Paige. And I want a taste
of this new woman."

"I'm over fifteen," Kimberly noted. "Isn't that a little too old
for you?"

David laughed and quickly slammed his hand against the wall right next to her head, making her jump with a scream. "You're a little long in the tooth, but I still want a taste and I'm going to get it."

"Not on your life." Kimberly punched him hard enough in the stomach to make him back off her. "I'd die first."

David took a second to recover, but didn't seem angry. He looked more bored than anything. He turned his back to her and returned to the bed. "I can understand why you'd feel that way. You can give me some and I'll go away forever or I can call NBC, CBS, and FOX right now. The local affiliates will pay me plenty more than the two-fifty you owe. That damn Chase family is, like, serious celebrity."

"You can't."

"I will." He picked up one stack of bills and flipped through it. "I'll give you one day to think it over. Meanwhile, I'm upgrading to a nicer hotel."

"I can bring the money in one day," she promised. "That's all I need. If you—"

She stopped as he turned and threw a stack bills at her. She ducked away just before it hit her in the head.

"We can hit it now or tomorrow," he yelled. "You tell me what works best for you."

Kimberly rushed out of the hotel room as fast as she could. Neil had been right. She couldn't kill David. Despite hating him with every fiber of her being, there was some hold he had on her that kept her from doing it.

But it still had to be done and Kimberly didn't have time to shed tears over her pitiful weakness. She had to hire someone to kill David, and they had to do it by tomorrow.

10

Avery was flattered at Anthony's attempt to ease her mind with a romantic night out. She was a little concerned that the prices at Al Angelo's Italian Restaurant in L.A. were a bit steep, but she was enjoying herself too much to care. The doctors said Charlie's recovery, because of the love and support of his family, was miraculous. Only two and a half months after being shot, Charlie had been making incredible progress. He would be home soon. Nikki was hopeful again and her optimism affected that of all her children.

Despite her joy over this, Avery found it hard to concentrate on the positives. Her last encounter with Carter was still with her; the taste of his lips on hers was still with her too, distracting her from everything else. She could still feel the strength of his hands when he grabbed her. Avery used to complain about his being so physical, but she really loved it. His aggressiveness excited her. She loved knowing he cared about her enough that she could make him lose his cool, but he never let it go too far. He was always in tune with her response, knowing when to take it easy or when to go harder.

But that was when she was his woman and he was her man. Now she had no right to think about his hands on her; no right to imagine her body rubbing against his lean, muscled physique; no right to see his face when she closed her eyes. Here she was sitting across from a man who loved her and understood her. He was a man who listened to her, soothed her pain and had been her shining light at probably the most difficult time in her young life so far. He was a man who wanted to protect her from what she feared the most.

No, Anthony never took her in a way that made her dizzy with passion. She did want him, desire him. He was good in bed, thoughtful and caring. He was intelligent and sophisticated. His passion for teaching inspired her and his dry, geeky sense of humor made her laugh even when she didn't want to. Avery always felt loved and safe in his arms, but never overwhelmed. She never felt lust that threatened her sanity when she was making love to him, but the one time she had felt that, where had it gotten her?

Anthony was a good man, a man most women would love to marry. And here she was lying to him, sitting across the table from him, lying by forcing a smile on her face.

If she was honest she would tell him that she didn't want to go out for a romantic evening because she was too exhausted physically and emotionally. Her guilt made her a liar. She hadn't slept with Carter, but in her heart she knew she'd already committed adultery. In her heart, she knew that he was still there and he took up more room there than her own husband did.

Anthony didn't deserve this. He deserved the exclusive love every man deserves from his wife, her complete devotion. It was easy to give in Florida, but now it seemed like the hardest thing to do. She had to work harder, be better.

"Baby?" Anthony snapped his fingers in the air to get his wife's attention.

Avery was jolted out of her haze and images of Carter faded away, replaced by an image of Anthony laughing at her.

"What?"

"You're kind of spacey tonight, huh?" He nodded to the waiter standing eagerly between them.

"Sorry." Laughing embarrassedly, she looked up at him. "Uh . . . I'm sorry. What?"

"Dessert, baby," Anthony said.

"Our dusky flourless chocolate torte is world class," the waiter offered. "Or the lemon polenta pudding with—"

"No." Avery pushed the desert menu away. "Thanks, but I'm full."

"We'll take the check." Anthony patted his full stomach before reaching across the table and placing his hand tenderly over hers. "I thought you were having a good time. I'm afraid to ask why not."

"I am." She smiled at the comfort of his touch although she wished she felt more than comfort. "This is nice, honey. I'm sorry. I'm just thinking about Dad coming home and how Mom is going to try to do too much."

Anthony sighed in relief. "I thought you were going to say Carter was still bothering you. I won't let him—"

"No," she said. "Carter isn't going to be a problem for us anymore."

"You seem so sure, but from the way he's behaved since you left, that isn't logical."

"He told me he was—"

"When did you talk to him?" Anthony sat back, a discomforted frown on his face.

Avery hadn't told him about the country club incident. She was too afraid of showing herself and hurting him if she got too emotional. "It's not important."

"I consider the man trying to take my wife from me important."

Avery paused while the waiter brought the check. "He's not trying to do anything. You were right when you came up with this plan. Once he found out the baby isn't his, he lost interest."

Anthony looked skeptical. "Just tell me when you saw him."

"Why does it matter?" she asked. "Everything is a game with him. Once he realized there was nothing left to win, he didn't want to play. He's not going to bother me again. You should be happy."

"I'd be happy if you seemed happy," Anthony said.

Avery didn't know how to respond to this. She could only do, feel so much. Anthony's gaze was making her more uncomfortable by the second. If she spoke it would be a lie.

"What?" she asked in response to his constant stare.

"When was the last time we had sex?"

Avery blinked, completely taken off guard. "I . . . It's been . . ."

"Not since we came here," he answered. "That was over two months ago, Avery."

"I can't believe you're . . ." Avery checked herself, lowering her voice. "I can't believe you're saying that. Things have been insane with my family and—"

"I'm still your husband," Anthony said, "and I have needs."

Avery couldn't tell him that she hadn't wanted him, really wanted him since seeing Carter the first time outside her parents' home.

"You have needs? Well, I have a twenty-five-pound stomach, Anthony. I have a mother at her wits' end and I have a father in the hospital suffering from a gunshot wound. But let me make sure your libido is at the top of the list at all times."

Anthony didn't respond. He turned his attention to the bill, slipping the cash inside the leather check presenter.

"I want to stay here." This was not at all how Avery intended telling him she didn't want to go back to Coral Gables, but she was angry now.

Anthony's head shot up, his face a look of pure surprise. "What do you . . . what do you mean? Until your father is better, right?"

"I went to see my ob-gyn, the one I went to a couple of days before I left. I had all my records forwarded to her office."

"You didn't think to share this with me?"

"I'm doing it now," Avery said. "Dr. Channing said—"

"Avery, what's the matter with you?" He shook his head, looking around. "She'll find out the records are false once she examines you."

"She's already examined me." Avery reached for her purse and riffled through it just for something to look at besides Anthony's injured expression. "And she won't tell anyone."

"Keep the change," he said as he handed the waiter the check presenter. Once he left, he started in again. "Have you forgotten? We're talking about the Chase family here. The family you told me can get access to any information they want. It doesn't matter if she'll tell them."

"They aren't looking anymore," she stressed.

"How do you know that?" Anthony asked. "Nikki said they never give up."

"They do if there's nothing more to find out. Your idea worked."

Anthony was shaking his head, his lips pressed together in frustration. "For now, but when that baby comes a month early, Carter will—"

"You don't know that," Avery said. "And who knows if the baby will even come on time? Mama says first babies almost always come late."

"When did your mother get her medical degree?" He rolled his eyes to match his sarcastic tone.

"I was the first and I came late," Avery answered. "And I remember you saying the same."

"You and me." Anthony huffed his annoyance. "That's a convincing focus group. I'm sure *Scientific American* magazine is awaiting your mother's call."

Avery wasn't going to feed into that. "Dr. Channing said I shouldn't fly anymore now. It's not safe."

"Fine," he said. "Then we'll drive."

"From L.A. to Coral Gables?" Avery asked. "I'll give birth somewhere in East Texas."

Anthony wasn't giving up. "What about the train?"

"Mom needs me," Avery added. "With Dad coming home, he'll need care around the clock. Between that and the gallery, she needs all the help she can get. Sean isn't around and Taylor is still in school."

"You can't help her," he argued. "You're going to be having a baby."

Avery had to agree that she wasn't going to be much use to her mother once the baby was born. "I was thinking. If we could move in with them, I can take care of my baby and help take care of Dad. You can help too."

"I have a job, Avery. I'm already living out of a suitcase. Now I can't even have the privacy of being alone with my wife."

"School is over in May. Dean Roth already promised you're free to do whatever you want after the school year ends."

"I wanted to be home with my wife and baby."

She smiled tenderly at the sound of those words. They reminded her of how good a man this was. From the beginning, he always acted as if this baby was his and he intended to love it as if it was. "I want to be with you and the baby too. But we all have to compromise."

"Don't you think I've compromised enough?"

Avery's smile vanished. "What in the hell is that supposed to mean?"

"I'm sorry, babe. I didn't mean . . ."

"I know what you meant," she said. "Look, Anthony. I don't want to fight with you. I know this has been hard on you, but my family is in the middle of a serious crisis and—"

"I . . . I understand why we're here," he interrupted. "I just don't want to stay."

"Well, I do," she replied. "And I need to. My family needs me and I need my family."

Anthony appeared hurt by her words. "I'm your family, Avery. I'm your husband."

"And that's why I need you to help me do this," she pleaded. "You saw Mother last night. She's completely exhausted. Even with a new baby, every little thing I can do is going to mean so much. And don't you think a baby would bring joy to the house? That would be good for Dad. I think it would be good for all of us."

Anthony stood up, seeming unconvinced. "Let's just go back to the hotel. I'm tired."

He reached out to help her up. Just the act alone brought home his point that she wasn't much of a help. She could barely stand up on her own these days. Avery was beginning to think her staying might even add to her mother's burden. But for some reason, ever since Carter walked away from her at the country club, Avery needed her mother to be near. She felt lost without her.

They made their way to the front of the restaurant and Anthony tossed the keys to the valet. When he looked at Avery, she could tell he was unhappy. He didn't deserve this, but what else could she do?

"I'm worried." Anthony's tone embodied his frustration. "I don't like being separated from you. I don't like leaving you here thinking you have to help everyone. I don't like leaving you here with . . . Jesus Christ!"

Avery turned to see what was upsetting Anthony and she couldn't believe it. Carter had already stepped out of the driver's seat and was tossing his keys to the valet. He was talking to him intently, pointing to the sleek black car. He hadn't noticed them yet.

"You've got to be kidding me," Anthony exclaimed. "So he's stalking you now?"

"Don't be silly." Avery stepped aside as another valet came to the passenger's door. "Carter will eat out every night unless someone cooks for him."

"Where is our damn car?" Anthony asked. "Do you want to go inside?"

"Maybe we . . ." The first thing Avery saw was the golden stiletto heels of Carter's companion as she stepped out of the car.

The woman was beautiful in a greenish gold silk-embellished dress that stopped midway down the thighs of long, mocha-brown legs. She had long, shiny, wavy hair and a soft, full face with very little makeup. Her features were perfectly sculpted. But it wasn't the way she looked that kept Avery from being able to turn away from her. She couldn't turn away because the woman was with Carter and she was just his type. He liked them beautiful, but not too flashy. He liked them sexy, but not too explicit. Just perfect.

"Avery?"

She turned back to Anthony, who was looking at her with a very concerned, almost frightened, look on his face.

"Breathe," was all he said.

Avery exhaled not even realizing she was holding her breath until just then. She was consumed with shame as Anthony's eyes softened in pain.

"Anthony, I . . ." She reached out and touched his arm. "I was just . . ."

"Jealous?" he asked.

"No, of course not," she lied. "I just get anxious whenever he's around."

After feeling he had sufficiently warned the valet about caring for the Maybach, Carter turned toward the restaurant, but was halted by what he saw: Avery and Anthony standing close to each other right under the canopy. They were looking into each other's eyes and she was touching him.

For a second, Carter's hands clenched into fists before he regained his composure. With a smile, he walked toward his date, who had been waiting with an eager smile on her pretty face.

Carter straightened his tie with one hand and reached out for Julia with the other. "I want you to meet someone."

He led her a few steps toward Avery and Anthony, irritated by their closeness. However, when he noticed what Avery was staring at, he felt a kick in his step. She couldn't take her eyes off his hand, the one holding Julia's hand.

"Hello, Avery." Carter smiled as if she were just a casual friend. He had to control himself so his enjoyment of her jealously wouldn't show. She looked so damn cute in the spaghetti-strapped flowered dress with her belly button sticking out.

Avery smiled at him, aware that Carter intended to ignore Anthony. She wondered what he was up to. That smile meant it was no good.

"Julia Hall," Carter said, leaning into his beautiful date, "this is Avery Jackson. She's Chief Jackson's daughter."

"I know who she is." Julia's voice held a hint of a Texas drawl and her expression said she wasn't very pleased.

"Do I know you?" Avery asked.

"No." Julia clung to Carter's arm. "But you were engaged to Carter once, right?"

Avery swallowed, feeling too uncomfortable to do anything but smile. "Once."

"That's all water under the bridge." Carter's tone was purposefully dismissive and he could tell it irked Avery. "Avery is starting her own family now."

"That's good." Julia's tone made Avery think she was a Janet Chase in the making.

Avery ignored her he's-my-man-now tone. "This is my husband, Anthony."

"Anthony's a teacher," Carter offered. He saw the angry glare on Anthony's face as he reached out to shake hands with Julia.

"A teacher?" Julia pressed her lips together to keep a smile from forming. "That's nice."

Avery wanted to slap that smirk off her face. "Anthony is actually a college professor at the University of Miami."

"Gotta love those state schools, huh?" As Carter rubbed Julia's arm, he could almost feel Avery's temperature rising. "I'm surprised you got a seat at this place. They're usually very exclusive."

Before Avery could retort, she felt Anthony take her arm and begin leading her away.

"The car is here," he said. "Let's go."

"Give my best to your father!" Carter yelled back as he and Julia headed for the restaurant.

When Anthony got in the car, he was looking straight ahead. "I'm not going to keep going through this."

"Anthony, it was just a coincidence." Avery watched as Carter and Julia disappeared behind the restaurant doors. "We won't run in the same circles, so I don't expect to encounter Carter often."

"I don't care if we run into Carter." Anthony put the car in drive and looked at her. "I'm not going to keep watching you get jealous every time you see him with another woman."

Anthony stepped on the gas and sped off so fast that Avery had to hold on to the door. She looked at him, seeing that familiar profile take on an unfamiliar form. Anthony was an affable man, which she liked about him. She had never seen him this angry. She wanted to protest, but she had lied enough that night. She was jealous and had no right to be. Carter being with another woman could only work in her favor, but she couldn't stand the image of him making love to that woman tonight.

Standing at the sliding glass doors of the great room, Janet turned away from the pool with a heavy sigh. There was nothing she could do, so she had to just wait and see. Wait and see and keep Steven as far from . . .

"I was looking for you." Steven was pleased to see his wife already standing near the bar. She looked sexy in a violet stretch silk wrap blouse and white pants. After all this time, her curves still excited him. But first things first.

He held up the package in his hands. "Look what finally came."

"You actually ordered something in the mail?" Janet asked, grateful that he went straight to the bar and didn't bother to look out at the pool.

"This baby was in Norway. I didn't have time to fly out there. This is the only way I could get it." He tore the box open.

When Janet saw what was in the box, she rolled her eyes. "Ah yes, the expensive whiskey you went on and on about."

"You're being a smart-ass." Steven cut the seal on the lid, unscrewed the cap, and brought his nose to the glass decanter. He closed his eyes. "This is a rare treasure. Johnnie Walker Blue Label's Best of Blue."

"If you say so," Janet replied. "Nice jar, but it's still liquor."

"This is a luxury item, baby." He grabbed a glass. "This liquor is made from a mixture of fifteen of the best whiskies in the world and a very rare malt, Royal Lochnagar."

"There are more than fifteen different types of whiskeys?" Janet asked not because she cared, but to keep his attention on her and the bottle instead of the pool. "And what is a Lochnagar?"

"There are only four thousand of these in the whole world." Steven slowly poured the whiskey into his glass. "Less than a thousand are in the United States."

"Is that what they told you?" she asked sarcastically. "Just because something is rare doesn't make it quality. And you paid what for the privilege?"

As he lifted the glass to his lips, Steven stopped. Sometimes he forgot that Janet no longer drank. She had gone to rehab for a prescription drug habit, but learned that she would have to stay away from any controlled substance, including liquor. "I'm sorry, babe. Does this bother you?"

"Because I can't drink?" She laughed. "No. You know I was never a big drinker and certainly didn't like whiskey. Besides, I've lost eight pounds since South Africa. So, how much?"

"You don't want to know," Steven said about the price. "And cost doesn't matter. This is special."

Just as he brought the glass back to his lips, Steven heard giggling behind him. He stepped around the bar to get a good view of the pool, and when he saw Leigh and Lyndon kissing in the pool, his blood began to boil.

"What the fuck is he doing here?" Steven slammed his glass on the smoothed granite bar counter. Whiskey went flying everywhere.

"Steven, calm down," Janet urged. "Look, you're ruining your drink."

Steven was already tugging at the glass door. "The nerve of that son of a bitch coming into my house after what he's done."

Steven's first reaction to hearing about Leigh's car accident was to find Lyndon Prior and teach him a lesson, but Janet calmed him down. And Leigh said she wasn't going to see him ever again. Since she wasn't hurt, Steven was willing to let it go. But now that Leigh was going back on her word, he was going to have his say.

"You can't, Steven." Janet reached for him, tugging at his arm. "You can't do anything about it."

"The hell I can't." He turned to her. "This is my house."

"It's her house too," Janet said, "and I couldn't bear it if she left."

Steven slid the glass door open and yelled Leigh's name. When both Leigh and Lyndon saw him, the smiles on their faces vanished. Steven waved for Leigh to come inside.

"Steven," Janet pleaded. "You have to be careful now."

"I can understand that you don't want to get involved in this." Steven had seen the way Leigh's rejection had hurt Janet. She blamed her for everything that led to Richard Powell's death. But after the incident last year, all was forgiven although maybe not forgotten. "I'll take care of it. You can leave if you—"

"I'm not going anywhere."

After wrapping a blanket around her waist, Leigh stepped inside and closed the sliding doors behind her. She expected yelling and even though Lyndon expected it, she didn't want him to hear it. "Dad, I know what you're going to say, but things are different."

"That boy almost killed you!" Steven would have expected something like this out of Haley, but not Leigh. She was soft-hearted, but she was smart.

"It was an accident," Leigh stated. "And he wasn't on drugs. I was wrong."

"Based on what?" Steven asked. "He told you? Because you're the doctor, Leigh. He's an idiot actor. They lie and they do drugs."

"I believe him," Leigh said stubbornly. "I care about him very much, Daddy. I wish you would try and—"

"I'm not going to watch you get taken in by this . . . boy."

"Steven." Janet squeezed his arm. "Leigh, we're just concerned. We're not trying to tell you what to do."

"The hell I'm not," Steven argued. "He's not welcome in this house."

"You can't do that!" Leigh yelled.

"I can't?" Steven asked. "Let me go look at the lease to this place. If your name is on it, then I'll apologize."

"You're making jokes out of this?" Leigh asked. "The car accident was just that, an accident. I don't want to talk about it anymore."

"Still," he said, "he can't come—"

"Is this about his being white?" Leigh asked.

"No," Janet assured her. "We wouldn't want you with any actor or entertainer regardless of his race. That's not good enough for you."

"But you would be more understanding if he was black, right?"

"Race doesn't mean anything to us," Janet said. "But it does to other people."

Leigh had heard this before. "Please spare me the 'we're different' speech. It's dead and tired."

"That doesn't mean it isn't true." Janet's lips thinned with displeasure at Leigh's upsettingly consistent attitude toward her heritage. "If you or your sister or brothers dated a white person publicly, it wouldn't look good. We already fight a battle with the image that we use our wealth and position to run away from our own people."

Leigh was all too aware of this. "I don't pick my dates to prove my blackness. Not to the public or either of you."

Steven was done with this conversation. "You can ask him to leave or I will."

"I'll leave with him," Leigh said.

Steven frowned, looking dead into her eyes. "Only two months with the boy and he's already got you acting like your sister."

Leigh felt guilty making a threat, but what choice did she have if they refused to understand? Lyndon excited her and intrigued her. She felt alive for the first time in a long while.

"I'm not throwing a tantrum, but Lyndon is my boyfriend. I won't get rid of him. You want to throw us out, then do it."

"Leigh," Steven called after her as she opened the door and headed back to Lyndon, who was now sitting on a lounge chair looking very pensive.

"What?" Janet asked as she surveyed Steven's eyes veering away. "What are you thinking?"

Steven cursed a couple of times before returning to the bar and retrieving his drink. "That boy is trouble for her and you know it."

"I don't and neither do you," Janet admonished. "I suspect he is but . . . maybe it was just a careless accident."

Steven took a sip, savoring the challenging taste of the whiskey. "It wasn't. And I'm not going to wait around for it to get worse."

As her driver pulled up to the modest Baldwin Hills home, Janet was already dialing Carter's cell phone. Where was he and what was he up to? Having caught his voice mail so often, she was actually surprised when he picked up.

"Mom." Carter sat up on the edge of his bed.

"Carter, I've been trying to call you since yesterday. What's going on? You had me worried."

As Julia's hands came around his waist, he could feel her bare, ample breasts travel up his back. "I've been busy. Why do you keep calling me?"

"I wanted to tell you that the chief came home yesterday and I'm stopping by there today."

"What for?" Carter smiled as Julia's hand slid down to his penis.

"Just out of common courtesy," Janet said. It was more like insurance for the future.

"They won't want you there." Carter reached behind, grabbed Julia's hair, and pulled her around. She slid off the bed, got on her knees, and moved between his legs.

"That's because of the way you've been acting," Janet said. "Which is why I have to score as many points with this family as possible. Between what you and Haley have done—"

"Well, that's all over," Carter said, "so don't bother."

"You don't sound like yourself. Have you been drinking?"

"I'm hanging up now." Carter guided Julia's head as her mouth came down on him. He pushed her farther every time.

"Wait!" Janet pleaded. "What about Avery?"

"What about her?"

"Is there something you want me to say to her?" Janet stepped out of the car, whispering to her driver, "I'll just be a minute."

"No," Carter proclaimed. "That's all over, Mom. There's nothing to say."

"Is it really?" she asked. Hadn't she heard this before?

"Yes, and for good this time." Carter hadn't noticed how angry his mother's questioning made him until he heard Julia make a whimpering sound and push against his thighs. He loosened his grip.

He didn't say good-bye, only hung up and tossed his phone on the bed. He looked down at Julia and wondered if he would ever care about her. She was so eager to please him; most women were. But it didn't seem to matter. Nothing mattered.

Fuck Avery and her whole family.

Just as she stepped inside the Jackson home, Janet came face-to-face with Nikki and Avery standing in the front hallway. "Hello, ladies."

Both women were a little shocked to see her, but Avery adjusted and approached. She wanted to slap herself for wondering if Carter wasn't close behind. "Janet, what are you doing here?"

Janet held out the bouquet of Casablanca lilies, orchids, and hydrangeas. "This is for the chief's homecoming."

"Thank you." Avery accepted the gift. "They're beautiful. He's resting now, so . . ."

"That's okay." Janet turned to Nikki, who finally approached. "Hello, Nikki. My family's prayers are with you."

"Why are you really here?" Nikki asked.

"Mom." Avery was surprised. It was unlike her mother to be rude to any guest in her home even when someone deserved it.

"It's okay." Janet was smooth and unaffected in her delivery. "It's a mother's prerogative to be overprotective. I'm the same way. And no, this isn't about Carter. As a matter of fact, I just spoke with him and he made it clear to me that there will be no more . . ."

"Stalking?" Nikki asked.

"I wouldn't call it stalking," Janet said.

"No more what?" Avery forgot to check her eagerness.

Janet felt that the look on Avery's face, matched by the broken, heightened tone of her voice, meant something. Maybe it was her desire for the baby to truly be Carter's fooling her or maybe Avery still cared very much.

"No more anything," she answered. "I'm sorry for the way he behaved at the country club, but I guess in the end it was good."

"What happened at the club?" Nikki asked.

"I'll tell you later." Avery had hoped to never have to tell anyone about that horrible moment.

"What's important," Janet continued, "is that he has said it's all over. He's moved on and he won't be bothering you anymore for anything."

Avery gripped the stems tightly in her hand. "That's good."

When she turned to her mother, Nikki's suspicious stare made her lower her head ashamedly.

Janet felt sufficiently pleased with her visit. Avery certainly did care. She looked down at her belly and said, "I wish you and your family well, including the ones yet to come."

"Thank you." Nikki's tone made it clear that she actually meant "please leave now."

Closing the door behind Janet, Avery didn't wait for her

mother to start in on her. "It's not important, Mama. I was having lunch with Janet, and Carter followed her. We talked and—"

"Why were you having lunch with that woman?"

"Was that Janet Chase?" Taylor asked as she entered the hallway. "I saw someone getting out of a smooth black car."

"Go put these in some water." Avery handed the flowers to
Taylor.

"Did you kiss him again?" Nikki asked, even though she wasn't
in any condition to deal with her daughter's drama today.

Feeling the baby kick, Avery moved her hand to her belly.
"This is good news, Mama. Carter has made it clear he doesn't
want anything to do with me anymore."

"Until he does again," Nikki said.

"No." Avery awkwardly cleared her throat. "This was different.
His pride and ego have been too damaged to keep this up. He's
done with me."

Nikki reached out and gently touched her daughter's chin.
With her index finger, she lifted Avery's face so their eyes met.
"He's done with you, but I only wish you felt the same."

"Where are you going?" Kimberly asked as she rushed after
her husband headed for the door.

"Out with Carter." Michael stepped aside as Marisol, who was
already at the door, picked up the mail that had fallen through
the mail slot and onto the floor. "I'll be home late."

"Is that all you have to say?" Kimberly was completely on edge
and suspicious of everything.

It had been almost five days since David gave her his twenty-
four-hour ultimatum, and Kimberly knew she was chancing luck
with every second. She hoped she could work up the nerve to do
what she had to do, but it didn't happen. She hadn't been able
to bring herself to hire someone to kill David even though there
was nothing more she wanted in this world than his death.

It was too much. She was already risking enough by doing any
of this. To bring another person in, who could link the family to
a murder, would be suicide.

So Kimberly did what she never thought she'd do. She took
money from the children's trust fund. It was the one thing left

that Michael hadn't put a limit on or required prior notice. This was because he would never have suspected that Kimberly would even consider putting her hands on that money in a million years.

"*Quiére usted el correo?*" Marisol asked Michael as she offered the mail.

"Sure." Michael took the mail, skimming for anything interesting.

Kimberly's heart jumped when she saw the exchange. Ever since those first pictures came, Kimberly made a point of getting the mail or making sure that Marisol gave it to her instead of Michael. She had to run interference unless David thought to pull another mail stunt. Nothing had happened since the first time, but she was still nervous. And that large white envelope, larger than any other piece of mail, really frightened her.

Feeling his wife's eyes on him, Michael looked up and saw the most pensive look on her face ever. "What?"

Kimberly swallowed hard, trying to pretend the mail wasn't what she was worried about. "You could at least pretend to care what I think and tell me where you're going."

"I just did." He ignored her judgmental tapping of her shoe on the hardwood floor and tossed the mail on the console table.

"It doesn't count when I have to ask you first." Kimberly was able to breathe now that the mail was out of his hands. She noticed he was wearing his favorite navy blue Salvatore Ferragamo blazer over the sky-blue D&G twill shirt she had brought him last Christmas. "And I assume from the way you're dressed, you're going to a club again."

"You can assume whatever you want," Michael said. "I always come home, baby. It's Carter that whores it up. I'm just there to keep him from doing more damage."

"Yeah," she said with a smirk. "I'm sure it's a painful job for you."

"I'd tell you not to wait up," Michael said as he opened the door. "But you always do anyway."

"You're damn right." Kimberly gave him the finger in response to that mischievous wink of the eye he offered her before heading out.

As soon as the door was closed, Kimberly rushed to the mail. The second she could see the large white envelope was from the stationery of the Millennium Biltmore Hotel in Los Angeles and addressed to Michael, she ripped it apart. What she saw made her scream so loud, Marisol came running as if someone were being murdered.

"Where you at, boy?" Michael made haste down the hallway of Carter's condo. Swinging his keys around his fingers, he was ready to get downtown and start the night. "Let's hit the . . ."

When he stepped into the dining room, where he'd thought he'd heard something, Michael came face-to-face with a petite Asian woman dressed only in black panties and a matching bra.

"Well, hello." Michael took his time to look her up and down. Fake tits, but otherwise, she was pretty nice.

"Hi." She just stood in the archway looking clueless and not at all concerned about her state of dress.

"Where's Carter?"

She nodded in the direction behind Michael, who turned around to see Carter, also only wearing underwear.

"Hey, bro." Carter rubbed his hand over Michael's head as he passed him.

Michael could tell Carter was either drunk or high. "What's going on?"

Carter turned around. "What?"

"We still going out?"

"Oh yeah." Carter waved the woman over. "Emily Kim, this is my brother Michael. You've met Michael before, haven't you?"

"Actually I haven't," she answered. "Surprising, but no. Nice to meet you, Michael."

"Yeah." Michael was confused. "Why would he think we've met?"

"At the office," she says. "At Chase Law."

Michael was speechless as he looked from Emily to Carter. In the air, he thought he smelled weed, but Carter had to be smoking crack to be sleeping with an employee.

"Emily, can I get a second to speak to my brother, please?"

"Go on and get dressed." Carter patted Emily on her butt.

"Are you crazy?" Michael pushed Carter backward.

"Take it easy." Carter was looking around for his glass of scotch. "Where did I put that—"

"You're a fucking lawyer, Carter! You should know better than to sleep with one of your underlings. You might as well just write that big check out to her now. Save the court fees."

Carter waved a dismissing hand. "She's just temporary help. I hired some freelance lawyers to help with the Keltech deal."

"Is your name on her paycheck?" Michael asked.

Carter laughed, nodding at his little brother. "You have a point there."

"What happened to Julia?"

Carter had to think for a minute. "Oh yeah, Julia. Nothing. She's cool. I like her."

"Do you know who she is?"

"I know her better than you," he said. "Jealous?"

"Look, man." Michael took a step closer, lowering his voice. "You want to mess around, that's your choice, but not with women like Julia Hall. Our families know each other and her father is very influential. Upsetting her could hurt a lot more than her feelings."

"Who is upsetting who?" Carter asked. "I said I liked her. What do you want?"

"I want this to stop." Michael pointed in the direction Emily had gone.

Carter wasn't laughing anymore. Michael was starting to piss him off. "So now you're telling me who I can fuck?"

"No," Michael said, "I'm telling you who you can't fuck, specifically family connections and employees. Stick with the models, actresses, and assorted buppies you come in contact with."

"Look, little brother. You don't have to worry about Julia, Emily, or anyone else. I'm handling these women. Matter fact, watch me go get rid of Emily without any drama. You'll see what I mean and then we'll go out, okay? Make yourself a drink."

Michael jerked away as Carter tried to guide him toward the living room. "I don't want a drink. I'm sick of this."

Carter threw his hands in the air with an exhaustive sigh. "Sick of what? You sound like a woman, Mikey. It's my life. If you don't like it, then why don't you just leave me the hell alone?"

"You don't have to tell me twice." Michael turned to leave, stopping at the hallway to look again at the brother he had always looked up to. "I knew that bitch coming back would mess you up again."

"Don't call her that." Carter's words seethed between his teeth. "And this isn't about her. I'm single, I'm hot, and I'm rich. What the fuck else should I be doing?"

"Keep saying it," Michael advised, "and maybe you'll convince yourself, but not me. Avery was the worst thing to ever happen to you and she still is."

Carter rushed over to him, standing only a few inches away. As he pointed his finger into his brother's chest, he said, "This is all your fault, so you don't get to say another word."

"My fault?" Michael laughed, slapping Carter's finger away. "I didn't make you do anything you didn't want to, big brother. I never have."

"I let you talk me into using Lisette to get Alex out of the way." Carter poked again at Michael's chest. "You said it was better with someone we knew because she would understand how powerful our family was and we could control her."

Michael pushed back. "If you had bucked up and handled your shit, you wouldn't have needed any help convincing Avery to leave Alex for you."

Carter's fist hit Michael's jaw hard and before he could react, Carter hit him again. Michael stumbled to his left, hitting the wall. He pushed against it like a springboard and lunged at Carter. He wrapped his arms around him and slammed him against the ebony wood dresser, sending an expensive antique vase crashing onto the wood floor.

Michael let out a grunt when Carter's right fist hit him in his side two times.

"You mother—"

When Carter came in for a third blow, Michael swerved out of the way and came back at Carter with a slam to his gut. Carter doubled over and in a tenth of a second, Michael's fist connected with his chin and he went flying back.

Emily's sudden screaming as she entered from the hallway took Michael off guard, and Carter took advantage. He grabbed

Michael by the neck and used all the strength he had to pin him against the wall.

Is he fucking trying to strangle me? Michael asked himself as he grabbed Carter's pressing arm. "Get off me, you—"

"Don't push me!" Carter let go, pushing Michael away. He backed up, a fierce expression setting on his little brother's face. "Don't fuckin' push me!"

Michael was rubbing his neck and shaking his head at the same time. "You're crazy."

"You're all making me crazy," Carter shouted. "Get off my back!"

Michael looked at his brother, his disgust showing all over his face. "You know what your problem is? You want to be the good guy and the bad guy at the same time, but neither of you can deal with the consequences of the other's choices."

"Stick to finance, asshole." Carter was trying to shake away the pain in his right hand. You sound like an idiot when you try psychology."

"Decide, Carter! Are you gonna be the guy who does what he should do or the one who does whatever he has to?"

Michael turned to leave and saw Emily still standing on the top step from the hallway, her mouth wide open in surprise. It was the same look most people had on their faces when they found out the perfect Chase family was full of nothing but nuts.

Looking back at Carter, who was leaning against the dining room table, Michael said, "And do whatever . . . or whoever you have to to get Avery out of your system once and for all. This shit is beneath you."

When Michael slammed the door behind him, Emily rushed over to Carter, but he held his hand out. "Don't."

"You look hurt," she said. "I . . ."

"You want to help me?" he asked.

"Yes," she said eagerly.

"Then leave." He was unaffected by the hurt, dejected look on her face. It had become so easy to hurt a woman's feelings.

Alone in his home, Carter felt the silence all around him. He turned on the plasma television in the living room and attached his iPod to the stereo in the living room, but the silence wouldn't leave. No matter what or who he filled this apartment with, he would still be alone if Avery wasn't there.

He should let her go for everyone's sake, but he wasn't going to. Michael's words rang in his ears. *Are you gonna be the guy who does what he should do or the one who does whatever he has to?*

Carter knew what he had to do. He went to the phone and dialed the number. It picked up after two rings.

"Hey, son," Steven said. "What's up?"

As soon as David opened the door to his suite at the Millennium Biltmore Hotel, he got a fist to the face. He fell back a few steps and Kimberly pushed her way inside before anyone in the hallway could see her.

"You bitch!" David was rubbing his chin, checking to see if there was any blood on his lips.

"How dare you do this?" Kimberly tossed the illicit photos at him.

David reached for them, but only caught one before they all fell to the floor. "I was being kind, Paige. I have much worse."

"How did you get those?" She couldn't bear to look down at the pictures showing her naked on all fours giving a blow job to some bloated, middle-aged white man.

"How do you think?" He tossed the picture on the floor. "I took them."

"You didn't tell me?"

David looked at her as if she were crazy. "Why the hell would I tell you? You're the ho, I'm the pimp. I don't tell you shit."

She looked around the suite, but couldn't find anyone. "Michael had those in his hands!"

"They were addressed to him," David said.

"Well, it didn't work," Kimberly said. "He never saw them."

"I gave you twenty-four hours," David said. "It's been almost a week. Those pictures were my way of saying 'fuck you' right back."

"I have the rest of the money." Kimberly tossed a backpack at him. "It took a while, but—"

Kimberly jumped as he leaped toward her. She pushed away,

but this time he wasn't caught off guard. He grabbed her arm and twisted it behind her back until she yelled in pain.

"I told you," he whispered into her ear, "I don't want any more money."

Kimberly cringed as she felt his dry tongue lick the side of her face. She felt like throwing up.

He let her go and she fell backward. He was shaking his head as he looked her up and down. "No deal, baby. I want to see what a high-class ho tastes like. I want a piece of what Michael Chase made you into. It's ass or nothing. Now you decide. I won't force you."

He took one step and then another closer to her. Kimberly turned her head, and her eyes glazed over as David ground his body against hers. His mouth slobbered on her neck as his hands pushed against the wall behind her. She let out a whimper before David grabbed her hair and pulled her head back hard.

"You about to cry, Paige?" He laughed as if he was aroused by her fear. "Go ahead and cry. Just like you did the first night I dug you out. You sentimental bitch."

Kimberly's body went rigid as she felt his hand grab at her crotch. He was pulling at her panties and suddenly he ripped them apart, the fabric burning against her skin.

Kimberly did the only thing she could do. She went back into that world, the world that there seemed to be no escaping from. It was only in that world that she would be able to do this and not feel anything. She channeled her mind and in a second, she was gone. She would return some time after it was over.

11

Kimberly had still not yet found herself as she sat on the edge of the bed, putting her clothes back on. That fifteen-year-old girl that learned to channel the world out was still a part of her, seeming to be so now more than ever.

"I gotta tell you, Paige." David stuck his head out the bathroom door. "I was a little disappointed. I mean, you're getting a little long in the tooth, but I know you have better stuff than that. You were stiff as a board."

Kimberly stood up slowly, feeling light-headed. She had done what she had to do.

"You had to put it on Prince Charming," David continued as he made his way to the closet. "Otherwise, there is no way he'd settle for you."

"This is over, David." She reached for her purse.

"Well, I don't know about that." David was rummaging through the closet.

Kimberly turned to face him, certain she was hearing things. "This was the deal. You get nothing more."

"You know those pictures?" he asked. "I lied. The ones I sent you were the only ones I had. I didn't even have negatives."

Kimberly remembered the pictures were on the floor in the

next room. She would get them and burn them. "So you've got nothing to corroborate you even knew me."

"No." David turned around, still dressed only in cheap silk shorts. "There is no way for me to prove that I knew you ten years ago. But I have something better than that."

From behind his back, David pulled out a tiny object and held it up for Kimberly to see.

"What is that?" she asked, taking a step closer.

"It's a video card." David laughed as her face went stark white. "The only better thing than proving I knew you ten years ago is proving I know you now, in a biblical sort of way. Yeah, I taped us."

"You son of a bitch!" Kimberly lunged at David.

He pushed her away, but not before she left a deep scratch on his chest.

"Look what you did." David looked down at his bleeding chest. "Is that any way to treat your daddy?"

"Give it to me," she demanded. If he had taped them just then, this was the only copy. All she had to do was get it. "Give it to me or I'll kill you."

"We've been through that before, Paige. You can't do it. You're too chickenshit."

Kimberly could barely breathe. She was shaking all over. "I have nothing more to give you!"

"I agree." David casually walked to the bed and sat down. "But I don't want anything from you anymore."

"What do you want?"

"You're not the reason I lost the last seven years of my life." David leaned back on the bed. "Well, you are the cause, but not the reason. Now I get back at Michael Chase."

"You can't!" Kimberly rushed to the bed, pleading. "You can't do it. You don't know who you're dealing with."

"When the world sees a tape of his wife in bed with another man spread all over the Internet, he'll be humiliated beyond words." David sneered. "No matter what happens to me, once it gets on the World Wide Web, all the money and power in the world can't stop it. He'll know then who the real man is."

"You're willing to risk your life just to embarrass him?"

David's smile faded. "If you could catch a glimpse of my seven years in that prison, you wouldn't bother to ask me that."

He moved the video card between the fingers of his left hand. "You'll have a lot of explaining to do to the in-laws. And what are your little boy's school friends going to say when—"

Kimberly snapped. The mention of her sons sent her into a rage she didn't even know she was capable of. When she jumped on David, he seemed surprised enough to yell out in fear. He tried to push her away, but her will was stronger than his might. She grabbed his head and pounded it against the headboard. She was screaming something, but she couldn't comprehend her own words. She could only feel her anger.

David finally pushed her away and onto the floor, but just as he got off the bed, Kimberly was up again and this time with a kick to his groin. As he doubled over, she looked around. All she could find was the nightstand lamp. She grabbed it and pulled until the extension cord ripped out of the socket. He was still holding himself with one hand, trying to straighten up.

"Paige!" David held his hand up to stop her.

Kimberly saw real fear in his eyes, something she had never seen before. He suddenly looked like a pitiful excuse for nothing, what he really was. She felt no intimidation, no misplaced paternal longing. She felt no fear.

"My name is Kimberly," she said just before she flattened the lamp on his head.

The lamp broke into several pieces. David fell back, the front of his head gushing blood. What happened in a second seemed like a minute or more to Kimberly as she watched him hit the back of his head against the bedpost, knocking himself forward again. He fell facedown onto the plush cream carpet.

Kimberly was frozen in place as she looked down at him. Blood was streaming out like a water fountain so fast that it seemed fake. Slowly, she reached down and placed two fingers against his neck. She could hear her heartbeat as loud as a jet engine, but felt nothing against her fingers.

She gasped, pulling her hands away. She pushed at his back once, then twice. Grabbing his right hand, she checked for a pulse at his wrist. Nothing.

Looking at his lifeless body, Kimberly stood up and took a deep breath. She knew then that she had wanted to kill him since that first night he'd taken her to the motel more than ten years ago. She thought she should feel panicked but she didn't. She was calmer than she could remember being in a long, long time.

It was over.

Turning to the bed, she saw the video card nestled against the pillow as if it had been put there just waiting for her. She reached for it, but that was when she saw the blood on her hand and arm. David's blood.

Kimberly rushed to the bathroom and was relieved to see the blood hadn't gotten on her clothes. She reached for a towel and quickly wiped her arm and hand down. She tossed the towel in the hamper and returned to the sink. Running the water until it was freezing, she knelt down and splashed it on her face. It felt . . .

Thump.

Kimberly's head shot up, her eyes as wide as saucers. She turned toward the half closed bathroom door. Was it all in her mind or had she heard . . .

Slam!

Kimberly freaked at the sound of a door slamming. That wasn't in her mind at all.

She searched the bathroom and saw nothing but a glass tissue holder. She grabbed it and with weak legs stumbled out of the bathroom. She would just have to kill him again.

The first thing Kimberly did was go around the bed and look at the floor. David was still there, lying lifeless in a pool of blood. Confused, she looked around the room and what she saw made her scream. No, it was more like what she didn't see.

The video card wasn't on the pillow. It wasn't anywhere! Kimberly tossed the tissue holder to the floor and rushed for the door. She got outside just in time to look down the hallway and see the girl, wearing that same pink shirt she had on the first day Kimberly saw her in the café, step into the elevator.

Kimberly ran toward the elevator as the girl pressed a button over and over again. The doors closed just as she reached them.

Kimberly pressed the Open button again and again, but it only lit up. Nothing happened.

The girl was gone.

As soon as she reached the front door to Lyndon's mansion, Leigh noticed it was already open and that was odd to her. *Stay positive*, she said to herself. Lyndon answered the call box when she drove up to the gates and his voice sounded a little weird to Leigh. It was high pitched and he was laughing; no, almost giggling. She wanted to stop being a doctor all the time, but she couldn't help it. In the few seconds it took her to drive from the gate up to the house, her stomach wound tighter and tighter.

As she walked inside, she told herself that she was being paranoid because of what her parents said. She really let them get to her too easily. Wanting to please them both, above all else, had led her down the wrong path so many times, yet she couldn't stop.

So maybe that was it. Her subconscious was trying to make Lyndon into everything she didn't want him to be, so she could say she stopped seeing him for reasons of her own and not just to please her parents.

"Lyndon?" Passing through the foyer, Leigh stopped for a second. She didn't hear a response, but heard noises coming from behind the winding staircase, in the media room.

When she entered the room, designed to look just like a movie theater right down to the cup holders on the side of each lush, velvet chair, Lyndon was lain out in the front row of seats with all the armrests pushed up. He was watching one of his movies, an action film. Or rather it was on, but he didn't appear to be paying attention to it. The room held the pungent odor of marijuana and beer.

"Lyndon." Her tone was harsher this time. This wasn't at all what she wanted to see.

Lyndon turned and tried to lift himself up, but he couldn't control his own body and fell to the floor. He was still laughing when Leigh walked around to the front of the seats. As he stumbled to his feet, she felt her heart fall into her stomach.

"So I guess we aren't going out tonight," she said.

His eyes were bloodshot, what little she could see of them considering they were half closed.

"Yeah, yeah . . ." When he reached her, he leaned in for a kiss, but she pulled away.

"Not a chance," she said. "I'm not taking you anywhere near that art gallery like this."

Lyndon rolled his eyes. "Come on, Leigh. Don't be so uptight. I'll just go wash up a little bit and we can go. I'm looking forward to it."

She doubted that was true. The look on his face had been anything but excitement when she suggested they go to an African art exhibit instead of their usual dinner and a party. But if they were going to be serious, he had to learn about her world.

"You're already going to stand out, Lyndon. I don't want—"

"Because I'm white?" he asked.

"No," she answered, already annoyed with him. "Because you're Lyndon Prior. And these people know who I am. Those two things combined mean we're already guaranteed to make the press. I can't have you—"

"You can't have me what?" Lyndon seemed to try to appear angry, but didn't have the wits to pull it off. "Embarrass you?"

"Embarrass yourself. And how do you think you can convince your friends to get help if this is how you behave?"

"It's just a little weed," Lyndon claimed. "You said yourself you've smoked it from time to—"

"You're a mess, Lyndon." She looked around the room, counting the bottles and cans she saw. "There has to be . . . you've been drinking all day?"

"No." He held up a pointed finger as if he was going to say something important, but apparently forgot it and lowered the finger. "Look, I'm going to clean up real quick and I'll be fine."

"Lyndon," she called after him, but he was already running out of the room and headed for the stairs.

"Stop it. Stop it. Stop it." She repeated the words in a whisper to herself. So he got drunk and smoked a little weed. What guy didn't do that? Well, the kind of guy she wanted didn't do that, but most guys did. That didn't make him a bad person and it certainly didn't make him an addict.

But something was wrong. Leigh counted at least ten bottles of beer and even more cans. There were also two glasses half filled with something that looked like straight liquor. If Lyndon had been drinking all this, he would've passed out by now. There must have been . . .

"Hello, Doctor."

Leigh jumped with a start as she turned around to face Nick only a foot away from her. "Nick . . . where did you come from?"

"I was in the bathroom," he answered in a slur.

He looked worse off than Lyndon, and Leigh felt a cold chill run down her spine at the way his eyes set on her. "I didn't hear you."

"I guess not." He reached out as if he wanted to touch her hair, his fingers coming only inches from her face before she stepped back. "What's wrong? I just wanted to touch your pretty curly hair."

"No, thanks." Leigh tried to step around him, but Nick moved to block her way. Her female intuition told her to run, but her ladylike upbringing told her to stay where she was and not be rude. "What are you doing?"

"I'm just giving you a compliment." His tone held a hint of anger. "I like your hair. It's pretty and . . . it's not a weave, right? I know black girls like to wear those weaves."

"Excuse me?" Leigh looked him up and down. "What would you know about black girls? No, don't answer that. Just get out of my face."

This time he not only blocked her, but he grabbed both her arms. "In my experience—"

"Let me go." Leigh struggled against him, fear spreading through her.

"In my experience," he repeated, jerking her once very hard. "Black rich bitches are even more stuck-up than white rich bitches."

"Get off me!" Leigh was trying to push away with all her might now, but the more she tried, the tighter his grip seemed to get.

"And you're the ones who should be the most appreciative." He slipped his foot against her legs, tripping her up.

Leigh felt her legs go out from under her and she fell against him. His hand went to the base of her head as he pulled her face to his. He was trying to kiss her and Leigh felt panic take over. She was pushing harder and harder while still trying to stand up straight.

"Stop it!" She turned her face to the left to avoid his mouth. "Lyndon!"

"No need to include him." Nick's hand groped her butt. "He's already had his taste. It's my turn."

She kept screaming no as she pushed away. His smell was making her sick and she felt as if she was losing control at any minute.

"Stop fighting," a frustrated Nick mumbled.

That was when it hit her. She wasn't fighting. She was trying to get away and that was the wrong move. Everything she'd learned about self-defense told her she needed to fight first and then break free.

Nick seemed stunned by her sudden change in attack. Instead of pulling away, she was leaning into him, hitting him with her hands, her legs, and even butting his head with her own. He stumbled back, loosening his grip on her to just one arm. Leigh turned inward and kicked as high as she could. She hit his thigh with the sharp point of her Denueve pumps.

She was finally free and was ready to run when Lyndon suddenly appeared in the doorway.

"I was calling you!"

"I didn't hear . . ." He looked at Nick on the floor. "Was he . . . What was he doing?"

"He was trying to rape me!" Leigh screamed.

"She's lying!" Nick used the wall to stand up. "She pretended like she wanted to kiss me and then when I—"

Nick was completely taken off guard when Lyndon punched him flat in the face, sending him spinning into the row of seats, where he fell to the floor unconscious.

Leigh ran to Lyndon and he wrapped his arms around her. She felt like crying, but she also felt like screaming out loud. She pushed away from him in anger. "Where were you?"

"I'm sorry," he said. "I thought it was the film. I didn't realize you were . . . I came as soon as I could."

Leigh rushed over to her purse, which had fallen to the floor in the struggle. She grabbed her phone and flipped it open. She only pressed 9 before Lyndon ripped the phone out of her hand.

"What are you doing?" he asked.

"I'm calling the police." She reached for the phone, but Lyndon held it away. "Lyndon, I have to—"

"You can't do that." He immediately began pacing in front of her. "Just wait a second. I have to call James first."

"Your agent?" Leigh couldn't believe what she was hearing. "Why would you . . . Give me the phone, Lyndon."

"Do you know what this could do to me?"

"To you? He didn't try to rape you, Lyndon."

"You don't know that was what he was going to do," Lyndon said. "Nick is a jerk. He's always kissing women and playing games. He's never raped anyone."

"That you know of."

"Okay, look." Lyndon ran his fingers through his hair and grumbled. "Having an attempted rape happen in my home, by one of my friends, would be one hundred times worse than sending a friend to rehab. Jesus, Leigh. It could ruin me."

Leigh was speechless. She was looking at Lyndon and seeing something she had never seen before, and it hurt her more than she could even explain to herself. "You want me to let him get away with—"

"No," he proclaimed. "I just think we should talk to James first. He'll know what to do."

"Give me my phone," Leigh ordered.

"Just wait, and—"

"Give me my phone now or I will find the nearest phone I can and call every news station in L.A."

Lyndon appeared shocked by Leigh's threat. She sensed he doubted her, but she held his eyes with her own until his doubt was gone. He offered her the phone and she snatched it back. She heard him call her name once as she ran out of the house, but she wouldn't, couldn't look back.

Once she was safe in her car, Leigh locked the doors. She put the key in the ignition, but she couldn't turn it. Suddenly, her hands were shaking. Then her arms, her legs, and finally her entire body. She slammed her fist against the dashboard a few times before gripping the steering wheel and leaning forward as her face streamed with tears.

As Carter stood at the glass doors to Hue Gallery watching Avery discuss a painting with a tall man dressed in all white linen, he thought about his conversation with his father last night. For all the bad blood between him and Steven, Carter didn't doubt his dad would do anything for him. They were Chases and that meant so much more than a name. He hadn't wanted to hear what his father told him; not really. He wanted something easier and quicker, but Steven hadn't achieved all he wanted to by satisfying a need for instant gratification.

Avery was worth it all. Carter smiled when she turned and her profile showed her belly. She looked ready to bust open and in another month she would. It killed him that the child wasn't his, but that was life. You mess up and you pay for it. But like Steven told him, he was going to love that kid so much that it would seem as if it was his to everyone, especially to Avery.

No, it wasn't right, but he had to do what he had to do. It was in his blood and in his last name. He always got what he wanted and he wasn't about to give up just when he found what he wanted most. He would try his best to do it his father's way, but God, how he wanted her in his arms, in his bed again now.

By habit, Avery glanced at the front door when the chimes sounded. Seeing Carter walk inside made her unable to turn away even though the customer standing right next to her was still talking. She wondered if there would ever be a day when seeing him wouldn't take her breath away. He was more handsome than any man had a right to be.

"Morning, Avery." He used that cool, calm, collected voice that usually got him anything he wanted from anyone.

"Carter." Avery clenched her teeth together to keep her mouth from smiling in response to his I-can't-lose smile.

That he still had this effect on her made his day. He gestured to the man behind her. "Your customer?"

"Oh." Avery shook herself free from her trance and turned

back to the customer, who seemed amused by her desertion. "I'm so sorry. You were saying?"

The man looked Carter up and down with an expression that meant one thing and one thing only. "Don't apologize. I would drop anything I was doing if a man that fine walked over to me."

Avery felt her face flush with embarrassment. "I . . . I don't . . ."

"Thank you," Carter said with an enunciated smile.

"You're welcome and then some." The man winked at Avery. "I'll just look around a little bit and come back to you."

Avery wanted to protest, but the man was already walking away. She turned back to Carter, who looked so smugly pleased with himself. She couldn't help but smile. "Stop it."

"What?" Carter asked.

"You're enjoying this. The world has to stop when you enter the room, right? You're so arrogant."

"Among other things," he said with a smirk. "I see you haven't taken Haley's advice on the banana clips?"

Avery touched the back of her head, reminding her that she was holding her hair together with a banana clip. "Yes, that was Haley who said I needed to come out of the nineties and get a real hair accessory, wasn't it?"

"It doesn't sound nearly as rude when you leave the swearing out."

"That girl and her mouth." Thinking of all her encounters with Haley, none of them pleasant, Avery suddenly remembered the first time she and Haley met and it saddened her.

"What's wrong?" Carter asked, seeing her expression change. He thought he was doing well.

Avery shook her head. "It's nothing."

"It certainly changed your mood. Or are those just hormones?"

"Maybe they are," she answered. "Do you remember that night I came to your parents' house for the first time? When your mom invited me."

"Yes, I remember. She wanted to keep you from blaming us for the explosion at your shop and making more trouble for us in the press."

"I just told the truth."

"Daddy loved you for it."

"Is that where I went wrong with Steven?" She laughed. "He never really warmed to me."

"You say that as if he warms to anyone? Dad and Haley are the same in that way. They only have enough energy to show affection for my mother, and the rest of us have to settle for fumes."

"That's not funny." Avery remembered seeing the anger and pain Carter felt over his run-ins with his father and hated that she was often the source of their fights.

Carter took a step closer to her and to his delight, she didn't step away. "Remember, that was the night you tossed a glass of very expensive wine in my face."

"You deserved it," she said.

Carter nodded, remembering fondly those few moments they had alone by the pool before all hell broke loose at the dinner table.

"After you left to change your shirt," Avery continued, "Haley came outside."

"You never told me that."

"I didn't want to." She remembered how silly she thought the girl was at the time. "She was upset that Sean wasn't protecting her anymore. He was spending more time with me because of what happened."

"So there was an explosion that almost killed you. I was almost killed too and I didn't need any cuddling."

"Don't make light of it." Avery slapped him on the arm. "I would've been killed if you hadn't come banging on that back door like a wild man. You saved my life."

She looked into his eyes and for a moment, Avery could absorb the memory of their connection. She had never been closer to a man and she feared she never would be again.

Carter spoke softly. "That was when I first realized that I was falling in love with you. I knew that I wanted you before that, but when I walked into that hospital room and saw you . . . I felt something that surprised the hell out of me."

Avery wasn't sure how long the silence lasted as they stared at each other. A few seconds or a few hours; it was too dangerous. He was entirely too dangerous.

"My point was," she said, averting his glance, "that night when Haley came out she told me that you wanted me. I laughed it off, but she said that you get whatever you want."

Carter spoke without hesitation. "I do."

He slowly reached up and touched her arm. Avery couldn't hide the shiver as her body reacted to his touch. Too, too dangerous. "But she said I wouldn't last six months and she was right. Give or take a month."

Carter's hand lowered to his side. "She said that?"

Avery nodded. "I was too soft and weak. She said your family would break me down."

"Well, she was wrong there," Carter stated. "My family was harmless. I ran you away all on my own."

"Why are you here?" she asked. "Don't you have a law firm to run? If I remember, you were at that office sunup to sundown almost every day of the week."

"I do whatever I want, remember?" Carter shoved his hands into his jean pockets, unsure of what else to do with them. This only happened with Avery. "I came to tell you I'm happy that your father is home."

"You didn't have to come here for that." She headed for the front counter, hoping she could use it as a barrier between the two of them. Unfortunately, he came right behind the counter with her.

She wasn't getting away from him that easily. "I also wanted to apologize."

"For what?"

"Take your pick," he answered. "The way I treated you, your family, your husband . . . anyone."

"I appreciate that." Avery didn't believe it, but wished she could. "We all do. We just want to move on with . . ." She paused, with her hand on her belly.

"What's wrong?" Carter asked, alarmed.

"Nothing." She took a deep breath. "Baby's been acting up a lot."

"Maybe you should sit down." Carter looked around for a chair, but didn't see any that he could move behind the counter.

"No. If I sit down, it will take about ten minutes to get back up again. I have too much to do here today."

"Okay." He didn't sound very convinced because he wasn't. "You do have help, right?"

"Nina is in the back." She pressed the button to ring the back room. "I'm fine, Carter. This happens a lot. It's normal."

"If you say so." He couldn't shake his concern and wished he could really show it. "I just wanted to say about the other night when we ran into each other at the restaurant—"

"And you insulted my husband's profession?"

"Did I do that?" he asked with a grin. "I don't remember that, but—"

"You think you're so funny." Avery pointed to the other side of the counter. "This area is for employees only."

"Then what are you doing back here?"

Avery sighed, wishing that he would stop being witty. He was such an ass, knowing exactly what effect it had on her. "I'm very busy, Carter."

"The woman I was with," he said, walking around the counter, "was Julia Hall."

"Why are you telling me?" Avery tried to busy herself, her attention anywhere but where Carter could see her reaction.

"I thought you'd want to know," he answered.

"You thought wrong." The truth was that she did want to know, so badly that she was almost tempted to call Kimberly and ask. "I'm glad you at least know her name."

Carter sent her a suspicious frown. "Who have you been talking to?"

"Take your pick." She repeated his words with a smart grin on her face.

Carter nodded. "Okay, I have been a little bit of a ho of late, but that's over. Julia is a very special woman and I want to explore a relationship . . . a real relationship with her."

Avery swallowed hard. "I'm happy for you."

"I hope so." Carter knew she wasn't and that was all he needed to know. "So, you can be reassured that I will be on my best behavior from now on. We'll probably be running into each other and I don't want that to be awkward."

How could it ever not be awkward? "That won't be a problem once we go back to Miami."

Carter was taken off guard. "Why would you go back?"

"It's our home."

"This is your home, Avery. You don't have to run away from me or my family anymore. You can't say that you don't want to be with your mother. She's your best friend."

"No, Carter." Avery's resolve was weakened by the emotion that slipped through his voice. "My husband is my best friend now."

Ouch. Carter didn't have a snappy comeback for that and he wasn't interested in pretending that it didn't hurt. "How nice for him."

Carter remembered what his father had said he would do to take care of Anthony. Carter opposed the idea at first, remembering what scheming in the background had cost him before, but Steven told him not to worry because he would take care of it all.

"I think that's good," Carter lied. "If I really want a chance to get on with my life and build something with Julia, I think it's best if you're not around. No offense."

"None taken." That was a lie. She felt a hole in the pit of her stomach thinking of how much it would hurt to see him in love with someone else. She had to get over it. His heart no longer belonged to her.

"I wish you all the best with that." He pointed to her belly.

"Thank yo—" She placed both hands on her stomach and hunched over with a moan.

Carter was behind the counter in a tenth of a second, his arms around her. "This isn't normal, Avery. You're in pain."

"This is the worst it's gotten since . . ." When she reached to push the button for the back room again, the pain ripped through her like a lightning bolt. She let out a loud groan this time.

"Come here." He guided her around the counter toward the closest bench. "You're sitting down. Who is your doctor? I'll call him."

"Her, and no, Carter." She sat down gingerly. She had never

felt this pain before and she was getting very scared. "I can do that myself."

"Stop being so damn stubborn," he ordered.

"What's going on?" Nina asked as she rushed over to the two of them. The look on her face was sheer panic. "Oh my God! You're going into labor?"

"No," Avery said. She couldn't do it. Not now. Anthony was in Miami. "I'm sure it's just false labor."

"You can take over here, right?" Carter asked Nina, who nodded in response without taking her eyes off Avery. "Fine, then let's go, Avery."

"Carter, I don't need you. If you can just get me my phone, I'll call my moth—"

This time she yelled loud enough to be heard throughout the entire gallery, and the two customers inside rushed to the front in alarm.

"Yeah, right." Carter lifted her up from the bench. "Let's go."

"It's a month early." Nina followed as Carter led Avery out the front door. "What's wrong?"

"Nothing's wrong," Carter snapped back at her. "Just handle the store."

"Nina," Avery called back to her. "Please call my mother now! Tell her to call my husband."

"It is early, Avery." Carter led her a few feet from the store where his Maybach was parked. "Maybe there is something wrong."

"I don't know." Nothing was wrong, she thought. The baby was really due in one week.

He opened the passenger door, thinking of how crazy he would be if anything happened to her. He looked into her eyes and said, "It's going to be okay. I won't ever let anything happen to you or this baby."

Avery's eyes never left his as he sat her in the seat of the car. He was speaking as if he knew the baby was his. If she wasn't in so much pain and scared to death that her secret would be found out, she would be able to appreciate his concern. It was fate that Carter would be around when she went into labor. This was a sign from God. She wasn't going to get away with this.

When Carter got in the car, he was worried about the look of anguish on Avery's face. "I only ask one thing."

"What?"

"This is a four-hundred-thousand-dollar car, so please do not let your water break until we get to the hospital."

"Just drive!" she ordered, trying not to laugh because it would hurt.

At least he made her smile. Carter was satisfied with that.

12

"I don't want this!" Evan pushed away the glass of juice Marisol placed in front of him at the kitchen table.

Marisol grabbed it just before it tipped over.

"Hey." Michael put his copy of the *Wall Street Journal* down just in time to see this. "You almost spilled that, Evan. Stop acting up and drink your juice."

"I want apple juice!" Evan raised his little arm in the air as if he were protesting some type of injustice. "I will only drink apple juice."

"Just shut up and drink it," Daniel said without even looking up from his cereal.

"Don't say shut up," Michael scolded Daniel.

Maybe it was the fight last night, but this morning looking at his two boys eating breakfast, Michael saw so much of himself and Carter in them. Evan was always starting something and Daniel was always the calm and collected one. They fought constantly but would act as if you were trying to kill them if you separated them for even a minute.

Boy, how things changed. Now Michael felt like the older brother, the only one with a sane head on his shoulders, and

Carter was the impulsive one. Michael didn't like this change one bit. He wanted his brother back and he'd wanted him back since Avery took him away.

"Apple juice is too sweet." Michael refused Marisol's offer of another croissant. "It's not good for your teeth. Marisol squeezed the oranges for the orange juice herself."

Evan rolled his eyes as Marisol slid the juice back toward him and patted him on the head. "This sucks."

"Hey." Michael gave him the sternest look he could without laughing. To be safe, he hid his face behind the paper.

"Fine!" Evan exaggerated his sigh. "But this is messed up, Daddy. Can we at least watch cartoons?"

"No," Michael answered. "We'll leave the news on until I hear the traffic."

"Where's Mommy?" Daniel asked.

Michael put his paper down. He never got any reading done around these kids when Kimberly wasn't there to deflect their attention. "She's asleep."

"She's sick?"

"Stop that," Michael ordered as Daniel tried to undo his tie. He hated wearing those stuffy private school uniforms. "She's not sick. Why would you say that?"

Michael didn't know what was wrong with Kimberly. He hadn't been happy to come home last night to find his wife gone, but after a few drinks it didn't matter anymore.

"When I went by the room"—Daniel popped a piece of fresh melon in his mouth—"you were in the shower and she was in bed looking sick."

"She's not sick."

"Cartoons!" Evan slammed his fist on the table.

"Do that one more time," Michael warned.

"If you make my glass spill I'm gonna punch you," Daniel warned.

Evan looked furious at the threat. "See if I don't punch . . . Hi, Mommy!"

Michael turned around to see Kimberly standing in the archway to the kitchen. She looked awful and he guessed maybe she was sick. "Hey, baby."

Kimberly grumbled something as she dragged herself to the counter where Marisol was already pouring her a cup of coffee. Seeing the three of her men sitting at the table together only brought last night's disaster back to her. She could hope it was a horrible nightmare, but it wasn't. Her life was over and the worst part was that she wasn't dead.

"Mommy." Evan spoke in a baby's voice. "Can you pour me some apple juice?"

"That's it." Michael pretended to push away from the table and it was enough to make Evan put his head down and start eating quietly.

Something was wrong. Michael knew Kimberly too well, and as he waited for her to turn around, he studied her composure. Ever since the incident, she had gone through short bouts of depression and he sensed another one was coming on. He would have his assistant get two tickets for a weekend at that resort she loved so much in Playa Del Carmen.

"Honey, what's . . ." Michael was stopped midsentence when Kimberly dropped the coffee cup just as it reached her mouth. He jumped up from his seat and rushed over to her.

"*Dios Mio!*" Marisol was rushing around as both boys just stared at Kimberly, who was focused on the radio.

When Michael reached out to her, she pushed away. He turned to the television and his body stiffened in shock at what he saw.

A mug shot of David Harris filled half the screen as the reporter told the story.

"The victim, David Harris, has a long rap sheet in Detroit, Michigan, for drugs and has spent time in prison for running a prostitution ring. Why he was in Los Angeles, police don't know. He was registered at the hotel under the name Roger Willis and paid in cash."

"Jesus!" Michael's hands went to his head as his heart beat so hard it felt as if it would break through his chest bone.

"This murder is unusual for the Biltmore." The television showed the outside of the high-end hotel. "Police can only say they believe they're looking for a woman."

"Marisol," Michael said calmly.

"I'm cleaning it up." Marisol pushed Kimberly away from the broken pieces as she placed a towel on the floor.

"Mommy wants apple juice too!" Evan screamed victoriously.

"Marisol!" Michael yelled loud enough to make both boys jump. "Take the kids out now."

"But I—"

"Now!"

As the news moved on to another story, Michael turned to his wife and was confused by the still, grim expression on her face. He waited until Marisol and the kids were out of the kitchen before speaking.

"Kimberly, did you . . ." He grabbed her by the arms and turned her to him. Her eyes were blank and she felt as cold as ice. "What's going on? Did you know about this?"

Kimberly was struck by a sudden urge to reach out and touch his face. She loved him so much. She loved her life so much. "You taught me how to really love, you know."

Michael leaned back. "Kimberly, you're scaring me."

"I did it."

Michael blinked, certain he had heard her wrong. "What?"

"You were supposed to handle this, Michael. You said we would never hear from him again."

"We weren't supposed to." Michael let her go and rushed to the table where his phone was. "I was supposed to be told if he ever left, died, or—"

"You trusted someone who works at a Mexican prison?" Kimberly asked.

"How did you know he was . . ." He suddenly realized what she had said and the phone dropped out of his hand onto the table. "What did you do?"

"What I had to," she answered. "I got the pictures and the money back. I took it. The money was in the closet and I—"

"Kimberly!" Michael was completely freaked out at this moment. "Concentrate, baby. Tell me what you did!"

"He was threatening to destroy everything—our life, our family. I couldn't let that happen after what I'd already done to Janet. He had pictures. He . . . he wanted money."

Without thinking, she turned and headed out of the kitchen,

but Michael grabbed her and turned her around. "I want my boys."

"The boys are fine." Michael took her face in his hands to make her focus. "Are you listening to me?"

Kimberly nodded.

He spoke slowly. "Tell me what happened."

Kimberly began telling him everything, but couldn't bring herself to divulge the whole truth. The more she told him, the more he freaked out. By the time she got to the point just before when he demanded she sleep with him, Michael was hunched over the kitchen table. She couldn't go any further.

Michael was livid and still in half disbelief. "Why didn't you tell me? Kimberly, I could have handled this."

"Like you did before?" she asked, even though she was aware her attitude would only make things worse. Could things get any worse?

"I would have taken care of him for good this time." Michael began pacing all over the kitchen in no direction. "Okay, tell me what happened at the hotel."

"I went there to give him the money and he told me there weren't any more pictures."

"So he lied?" Michael thought that was good. "So the cops won't find any pictures of you there?"

Kimberly shook her head. "But he wanted more money and I refused. We struggled and . . . I swear, baby, it was an accident. I just wanted to get away."

Michael wrapped his arms around her as she sobbed uncontrollably. His mind was racing a mile a minute. "I'll fix this, baby. If there isn't any trace of you in that room, I can fix this. Think. Did you leave anything that could be traced back to the family?"

Kimberly tried to remember everything she had done when she returned to the room, but she had been practically catatonic and her memory was a haze. "I took the money and there was a towel in the bathroom where I washed my hands."

"Please tell me you took that."

"I tossed it in a garbage can ten miles away. They won't find it."

"No, they won't. Anything else?"

"My fingerprints, Michael. They're all over that place."

Michael knew what this meant and it wasn't good. Her fingerprints were in the system from when she was arrested in Detroit. The cops knew David was from there.

"You were fifteen when you were arrested, right?"

"Sixteen."

When Michael tried to get Kimberly's file erased from the Detroit Police Department, he was only successful in getting the hard copy. He couldn't erase it from the computer. The hacker he hired said it was impossible for him to get to juvenile records.

"Your file is probably sealed. I don't know. I'll have to ask Carter." Michael felt sick to his stomach at the thought of what he had to do next. "I have to call Dad."

Kimberly began crying again. "No. No. No. No."

"He's the only one who can fix something like this," Michael told her.

"What can he do?" Kimberly saw from the expression on Michael's face that he didn't really know, but that didn't matter.

Steven Chase had contacts at the highest levels of every arena. He was a billionaire, but it wasn't just his money. Steven was a very powerful man who had done favors for other powerful people. They owed him and he always used his IOUs cautiously. He could impose his will on anyone.

But he wasn't a magician, Kimberly thought. He could erase fingerprints, but not DNA. How would she tell him that her DNA was all over that bed?

"Dad can do anything," Michael said quietly as he reached for the phone.

As a child and basically his entire life he'd believed his father was Superman, God of the Universe, and as perfect as a person could be. But it wasn't until now, at the age of thirty, that he needed desperately for that to be true.

All hell was about to break loose in the Chase family . . . again.

Janet could only stand one Haley. If Leigh intended on turning into another version of her younger sister, Janet didn't think she could take it. It was so unlike Leigh to be unreliable, and the fact that she hadn't even come to her with the bad news made Janet even angrier.

Janet's full-time job was as head of the Chase Foundation, and she had an office both in downtown Los Angeles and in Chase Mansion. She spent about half of her time in either, but preferred her home office, which was just across the hallway from Steven's home office. She'd expected to spend a relaxing day at home before leaving for lunch with the wife of L.A. General Hospital's first black chief surgeon when she got a call from Jeannine, her assistant, asking her if she had found a replacement for Leigh's now-canceled piano performance at the musical benefit only one week away. Janet had thought she was kidding at first and was furious to find out she wasn't.

Immediately calling the clinic, she found out Leigh had called in sick that day and Janet was worried. Leigh had to be dragging on the floor before she wouldn't go into the clinic. Janet's maternal instincts shifted into high gear.

Walking through the house in search of her daughter for an explanation, Janet's suspicions were further raised by what she saw at the front door when she entered the foyer. She watched in silence as Maya refused Lyndon Prior entry into the house, repeating over and over again that Leigh wasn't in. He was pleading with Maya to take the flowers he had brought, but she refused. Janet smirked at the cheap display of affection. Flowers. This boy was way beneath her daughter.

Janet waited until Maya shut the door to ask what was going on. "Leigh's car is right in the driveway. I know she's here somewhere."

Maya shrugged. "She said if he came by to say she wasn't here. I don't have to explain anything to him. If he comes back I'm not even going to answer the door."

"Did she say why?" Janet asked.

"You won' know," Maya said with a slip of her Caribbean accent, "then ask her."

"Where is she?"

"Working out like a maniac."

It took her a few minutes to reach the exercise room in the

basement of the house. The room, housing more than three hundred and fifty thousand dollars of exercise equipment and weights, had recently been updated with a mirror wall, a water rower, and a new elliptical machine. When Janet finally arrived, she stood in the doorway for a minute watching Leigh run on the treadmill at a fierce, almost dangerous pace with her back to her. Yes, her mother's intuition said something was definitely wrong.

Leigh jumped, almost falling over herself when, out of nowhere, her mother appeared in front of the treadmill. She extended her legs to the edge of the machine and took the iPod headphones out of her ears. "What is it?"

Janet noticed right away that Leigh had been crying. Her eyes were red and swollen. "Why didn't you see fit to tell me you were canceling your performance at the benefit?"

"Why do you think?" Leigh asked. She just couldn't deal with her mother today.

"That's a very mature response." Janet eyed Leigh's hand as she seemed tempted to put the headphones back in. "Answer me."

Leigh sighed. "Mom, I can't do it, okay? I'm just too busy and too tired."

"You made a commitment and people are spending a lot of money to—"

"They spend the money so they can dress up and be seen by other rich people." Leigh stopped the machine. "No one will give a damn whether I'm there or not."

"I will."

"Well, that's too bad, then." Leigh stepped down and reached for her towel.

Janet wasn't sure how to respond to that reaction. Her perfect angel never spoke like this. "What has gotten into you?"

"I'm not doing it, okay? And stop trying to guilt me. I'm sick of you trying to impose your life on me. Everyone thinks they can push me around and I'm not taking it anymore. Not from you or anyone."

"Or Lyndon?" Janet noticed the expression on Leigh's face

went from frustration to pure anger. "He tried to get in just now but Maya ran defense as you instructed her to. What did he do?"

"I don't want to talk about that." Just the mention of Lyndon's name made her angry. She was just so damn angry.

After she had left Lyndon's house, Leigh drove around for hours. She hated herself for being such a gullible idiot. How had she been such a fool as to believe Lyndon could really care for her? Hollywood stars don't care about anything other than their image. They don't have relationships; they have opportunities. How had she allowed herself to ignore all the warning signs and be seduced by his lifestyle? She had red flags the second she saw Nick, yet she tried to be positive because she wanted to be with Lyndon. She wanted his friends to like her. This was what her positive, weak-willed thinking had gotten her, and she was sick of being taken advantage of and deceived.

She couldn't close her eyes because all she saw was Nick coming at her. She knew she wouldn't call the police because Lyndon and Nick would deny everything. She didn't even want to think of the racial implications. No, her family had been through enough. What had happened was over. There was no use in making it worse.

"Leigh." Janet reached out to her baby, seeing pain that she hadn't seen since that day in the hospital when Richard died and Leigh blamed her for it. "I don't care about the benefit. Just tell me what's upsetting you."

Leigh slapped her mother's hand away. "Just leave me alone!"

Janet was too shocked to respond as Leigh ran out of the room. Yes, she wanted her to leave her alone, but she was genetically incapable of doing so.

Janet reached in her pocket for her cell phone, intending to call her husband, but thought twice about it. Whatever was going on was very serious and she needed to know more before Stephen was involved. She didn't want a repeat of Richard. She would have to handle this one by herself for now.

Although he tried to hide it, Carter's eyes squinted when Avery squeezed his hand. She was killing him, but there wasn't anywhere he'd rather be than with her right now in this hospital room.

"Why don't you get some drugs?" Carter asked, standing on the left side of the hospital bed. Avery was sweating and breathing hard. She looked as if she was in terrible pain and he didn't like seeing it.

"Not yet." Avery tried to concentrate on her breathing exercises, but it was hard to concentrate with Carter right next to her.

She knew she should have made him leave, but she didn't want to. Not just because she didn't want to be alone, but because in her heart she knew she wanted him here. She just didn't have the time to feel ashamed about it because of the pain. With every growing contraction, she cared less and less about what was right.

"It's too soon." Avery's head fell back on the pillow. "I need more water."

"Give me that thing." He grabbed the call button and pressed hard. "Where is that damn nurse? I'm gonna go—"

"Carter!" She snatched the button away from him. "Do not have one of your elitist tantrums with the people delivering my baby."

"Me?" Carter asked. "You've yelled at everyone since we showed up at this hospital."

"I'm having a baby! I get a free pass to scream at everyone. They're already pissed at you for insulting the room."

"Screw them," Carter said. "This hospital has a whole wing of suites two floors up. I can get you a room in five—"

"Enough!" Avery leaned forward as soon as she heard the front door opening. She needed her mother, but it was Dr. Channing.

"Mrs. Harper, how are we doing?" The young Dr. Channing was five-eleven with blond hair and a perky disposition. She stood at the end of the bed looking as if she was having the best day of her life.

Avery wanted to lunge across the bed and strangle her. "What do you think?"

"Sounds about right." She looked down at the chart in her hand. "Your water broke?"

"As soon as I got to the emergency room." Avery was glad that happened when Carter had gone to park the car. It wasn't pretty.

"Thank God," Carter added.

"And you're five minutes apart still?" she asked.

Avery nodded. "How much longer?"

"This is your first." Dr. Channing leaned forward with an excited smile. "On average, about six hours."

"Six hours?" Avery felt like crying. "I can't go through this for another six hours."

"Shouldn't she be in a special room getting special attention or something?" Carter asked.

Dr. Channing looked Carter up and down. "You must be the one who called our maternity wing a dump."

"Not because of that," Carter said. "She's preterm. Isn't that dangerous?"

When Dr. Channing looked from Carter to Avery, Avery's panicked expression must have given the right message. She turned back to Carter. "And you are?"

"He's no one." Nikki tossed her purse in the chair and rushed to the side of the bed, taking Avery's hand away from Carter's and into her own. She kissed it. "Baby, are you okay?"

"Oh my God, Mom." Avery couldn't remember ever being so happy to see someone. "She said it could be another six hours."

Nikki kissed Avery on the forehead and smiled. "You took ten, sweety. Hello, Dr. Channing."

"It's nice to see you again, Mrs. Jackson. How is your husband?"

"He's doing much better," Nikki said. "He was so happy to hear Avery had gone into labor. He would be here if he could."

"Did you call Anthony?" Avery asked.

"He should already be in the air, hon. But don't worry." She pushed against Carter with her body, moving him farther out of the way. "I'm here and I'll take care of you."

"If you had let me send my father's jet," Carter offered, "he would be here in a couple of hours."

"You're not helping, Carter," Avery warned.

"Hello, Nikki." Carter smiled even though he knew any gesture with Nikki was fruitless at this point.

"He's not family." Nikki ignored him, talking to Dr. Channing. "He should leave."

"I agree," Dr. Channing said.

Carter looked at the doctor with disdain. Who did these women think they were? "If Avery wants me to—"

"Actually," Dr. Channing interrupted, "it really doesn't matter what she wants. She can only have one person in here at a time. It's either you or Mama. I vote for Mom."

Carter turned to Avery, but her eyes were shut. Another contraction was coming and when it set in, Avery leaned into her mother, calling out to her. He knew he was doomed, but he didn't want to leave.

"Sir." Dr. Channing motioned her head toward the door.

"Fine." Carter took steps away, but turned back to look at Avery just as she looked up. In her eyes, he could swear she wanted him to be there.

Avery couldn't help but stare into his earnest eyes. He seemed so sincere and she was lying to him in a way that was unforgivable. This wasn't just about whether or not it would work. It was about right and wrong.

Besides, she didn't want him to go. And that fact forced her to turn away.

Outside the room, Carter caught the attention of a young, blond nurse passing by. As she smiled with him flirtatiously, he checked her name tag. "Natalie?"

"Yes?" She flipped her hair back and showed her perfect white teeth. "Can I help you?"

"I hope so," Carter said with a charming smile. It was just so easy. "Can you take me to the family-only waiting room?"

Anthony wasn't going to be here any time soon. Carter's luck couldn't get any better.

Michael had never seen this look on his father's face. Steven almost fell back against the front of his desk as Michael laid it all out for him. Nothing astounded Steven Chase and he was clearly speechless. This was not encouraging.

It had taken everything Michael had to come over to his father's office with Kimberly. His entire life he had wanted to please this man, relishing his position in Steven's heart and Chase Beauty. He intended on having everything, taking over the company and becoming even more powerful than his father was one day. But after the incident, Michael felt a distance from his father, furthered by his moving out of the house. He had done all he could to get back in Steven's graces, but he hadn't been willing to give up Kimberly. She was his wife, and although he wasn't a perfect husband, he loved her. And it seemed that Steven was letting him inside again. But now, after all this, Michael could only pray his father would even speak o him.

Michael looked over at Kimberly, sitting in the chair next to him. She hadn't looked up from her hands, set on her lap, since he began talking. And as his father stared at them both in silence, Michael couldn't hide his fear.

"I . . ." Steven hesitated, measuring for a moment what exactly he had heard. "I . . . How could you keep this from me?"

"I did what I thought was best," Michael answered in a shaky voice.

Steven let out an anguished moan. "My God, Michael."

"He was trying to protect me," Kimberly offered without looking up. She was shaking all over. Just hearing Michael tell their secret to Steven dropped her even deeper into despair than she already was.

"I don't want to hear one word out of you," Steven responded. "Is there no end to the problems you've caused this family?"

"Dad." Michael sat forward. "It was my choice to hide the truth about Kimberly's past from you. It was my choice to frame David Harris and send him to Mexico. Kimberly didn't even know about it."

"Trust me." Steven's tone was ruthlessly hardened. "I'm angrier at you, Michael. But at least you didn't kill anyone."

"It was an accident," Michael said.

"That's what she told you." Steven sent Kimberly a hostile stare.

"She wouldn't lie to me about that," Michael said.

Kimberly let out a weak whimper as she died a little more inside. Michael was defending her because he loved her, but she was lying to him. She was lying to everyone.

"Do you know what position you have put this family in?" Steven slammed his fist on the desk behind him. "This could ruin everything we have built!"

"Nothing can ruin you," Michael said. "That's why I came to you. That's why I'm telling you. As soon they run those prints, it will lead to Kimberly, and it's only a matter of time before they trace her to—"

"The prints will lead them to a sixteen-year-old prostitute from Detroit." Steven's jaw tightened as he gritted his teeth. "That's ten miles from a member of the Chase family."

"The cops aren't going to bend over backward to solve the murder of a pimp from Detroit," Michael added. "That will give us . . . you time to do something."

Steven wanted to smack that look of expectation off Michael's face. He had spoiled these kids too much; let them know they could have anything, everything they wanted and not suffer consequences. He had been the one to teach Michael that a few million and some ingenuity could get you out of even the worst situations.

"I'll take care of it." Steven was shaking his head, still in disbelief of the situation. "Neither of you deserves this, so understand that I'm not doing it for you. I'm doing it for your mother and for the other members of this family that shouldn't have to suffer for your selfishness."

Kimberly finally looked up. "You don't have to—"

"Don't." Steven sneered at her. "Don't you dare make a request of me. I will tell my wife and you'll deal with the consequences."

Kimberly turned to Michael, her eyes screaming desperation.

"Why does she have to know?" Michael asked. "You've done . . . we've done plenty of stuff without letting Mom know."

"I'm actually going to need her help for this," Steven said. "I'll need to use some of her contacts."

"She won't give them to you," Kimberly proclaimed. "Janet won't do anything to help me."

"No," Steven answered. "She won't do it for you, but she'll do it for this family. To protect her children, her grandchildren, and our family's name from what you two have done."

Kimberly turned away from his icy stare.

"Is there anything else?" Steven asked. "As if there could be."

"No." Michael turned to Kimberly. "Right?"

Steven watched as a shaky Kimberly clutched the armrests of her chair tighter and tighter, and a sense of dread swept over him. "What is it?"

Kimberly's head shot up as she looked into his fierce gaze. She turned to Michael, who looked confused at both of them.

"What is it?" Steven repeated. "Tell me now or I will feed your worthless ass to the wolves."

"Hey!" Michael yelled.

"There's a tape." Kimberly covered her mouth as if the words had escaped against her will. Her chest felt tighter and tighter.

"What?" Michael's expression was clouded in anger. "What tape?"

"He was . . . going to . . ." Kimberly couldn't breathe. She tried to slow down, but it only got worse. "Send it . . . to the news and . . . put it on the . . . Internet."

"Fuck!" Steven pushed against the desk, looking at Michael. "She wouldn't lie to you, right?"

Michael was halted by his own confusion. "Kimberly?"

She wiped the tears from her cheeks, feeling nauseated. "It was a tape of me and him and he was going to do it. He didn't want money and . . . he wanted to get back at Michael."

"Oh my God." Michael fell back in the chair, his hands covering his face. This was his worst nightmare.

Steven took a second to compose himself. "Where is the tape?"

"Someone took it," Kimberly said. "She was hiding in the closet when we fought and when I . . . I was in the bathroom and she—"

"You saw her?" Steven asked. "She saw you?"

"No, no, no," Michael repeated to himself.

Kimberly nodded. "I didn't know she was there."

Steven threw his hands in the air in defeat. There was a witness to this. He couldn't fix a witness to murder. "She saw you kill him."

Kimberly shook her head. "She saw me fight him and he fell. He was going to kill me."

"We have to find her," Michael said. "I'll find her. We'll pay her whatever . . . we'll fuckin' kill her if we have to."

"There's been enough of that." Steven's resolve was bothered by his belief that Michael meant everything he'd just said. "No one needs to die. She's probably one of his whores. She'll take money."

"The tape," Michael said.

"It's too hot right now," Steven said. "David is a murder victim. It isn't in her interest to send that tape to anyone but us. Besides, the news stations won't give her money for it."

"Do you think she's smart enough to figure that out?" Michael asked. "I'm not taking that chance."

"We won't," Steven assured. "We'll find her first. If she left anything in that hotel room, we'll find her. Kimberly, are you sure of this tape? Did you see it?"

Kimberly shook her head. "I didn't have to. He wasn't lying."

"He would have been exposing himself as a statutory rapist," Steven said.

Kimberly gasped as she realized what Steven thought and realized that Michael thought the same.

"He doesn't care," Michael argued. "The statute of limitations is way over."

"Michael." Kimberly reached her hand out to him and he took it. "It's not from when I was a kid. It's from yesterday. I slept—"

Kimberly screamed as Michael whipped her hand away and shot up from the chair. His eyes darkened and his face transformed into a fury she had never seen before. The man that had been defending her just minutes ago was gone.

Steven jumped in between them just in time. "Michael, no."

"You whore!" Michael's mind was gone now. It had left the second he realized what she was saying. "You slept with that asshole?"

"He said I had to." Kimberly clumsily stood up, holding on to the chair to stay upright. His face was a glowering mask of rage and she knew he would kill her if Steven hadn't been there. "He promised it would be over if I did it. I needed it to be over. It didn't mean anything."

"I'm gonna kill you!" Michael was pushing against his father, whose grip only got tighter. "Get off me."

"No!" Steven had to use his entire body against Michael and he was barely containing him. "Michael, stop it."

"You're a fucking liar!" Michael yelled, pointing his finger at Kimberly. He felt unable to comprehend his own insanity. Him? How could she do this and with him? "Did you think you could keep this from me? After everything you've done and what I've done for you, you still lie to me. You sleep with that . . ."

Sheer, black fright swept over Kimberly. Michael was completely unhinged. "I did it for you and our boys, Michael. I did it—"

"My boys!" Michael raised a fist at her. "They are not our boys! They're mine."

All sense having left her, Kimberly walked toward Michael. "Don't say that. You can't take my—"

"I will take everything!" Michael pushed against his father and got enough room to move to just within a few inches of her.

"Son!" With both hands, Steven gripped Michael's face and turned it to his. Looking into his eyes, he called on all the power he had over this boy. "You'll only make this worse. Think of the boys."

"It can't be worse." Michael's eyes gave away his torture.

"It can," Steven asserted. "Come with me and calm down."

"Michael!" Kimberly reached out to him, but pulled her arm back when she saw the hateful look on Steven's face as he turned to her.

"Shut up!" he roared. "You dig your grave further every time you open your mouth."

Exhausted from his own emotion, Michael didn't fight his father as he pushed him toward the door.

Once outside his office, Steven was grateful neither his assistant nor her assistant was at their desk. The area was secluded from the hallway, so there was no one to witness or overhear this disaster.

"Michael, I know how you feel."

"How can you say that?" Michael asked.

"Fine," Steven said. "I don't know how you feel, but this is a disaster, the worst our family has had to face. I need you to be strong. No matter what you think, I can't fix this without you."

Michael took a deep breath and stood up straight. "Nothing can fix what she's done."

"That's between you and her. Everything else, we have to solve as a family. You want to break down? Fine, but do it later. Do it after we've gotten this under control."

Vivian, Steven's executive assistant, appeared from around the corner and immediately sensed there was a problem.

"Not now, Vivian." Steven approached her to usher her away. "This is not a good time to—"

Steven swung around when he heard the door to his office slam shut. Just as he reached it, he heard Michael turn the lock. Steven grabbed the handle, but the door wouldn't budge.

"He's going to kill her." Steven turned to Vivian. "Get your key, now! Open this door!"

Kimberly's eyes had been set on the door, so the second she saw Michael reenter, she knew she was in trouble. She screamed, rushing for the only place she could go—Steven's private bathroom.

"Michael, I'm sorry," she pleaded as she locked the door.

Thump!

Kimberly jumped back at the sound of the kick. A stark and vivid fear ripped through at the second kick. Where was Steven?

"Michael!" she shrieked. "Please!"

When the door burst open, Kimberly backed against the wall, bracing herself for his wrath. There was nothing else she could do. "Our children, Michael."

Michael grabbed her by the shoulders and pressed her against the wall. The hate in his heart was spurred on by the fear in her eyes. "They're my children. And just like them, everything you have I gave you."

"Michael!" Steven rushed into the bathroom expecting to see the worst.

"And just like them." Michael leaned in until his face was only an inch from hers. "I'm going to take it all away from you."

Michael let her go and leaned back with a wicked smile on his face. After everything he had done for her, after all he had forgiven, she would pay for making him the weak link in this family.

Steven pushed Michael aside and looked at his daughter-in-law. "Leave."

Kimberly was too petrified to even move. "You can't take my babies."

"Leave!" Steven roared.

Once she was gone, Steven turned to his son and was very worried by the look on his face. He was almost smiling. "Pull yourself together, boy. We have a lot of work to do."

13

Ladera Heights was a mostly black, middle-class western sub-urb of Los Angeles near View Park and Baldwin Hills. Al-though there were plenty of beautiful homes, the town had a great deal of landscape issues because of its plant problem: too many weeds and snails. It was the perfect place for the first Chase Botanical Conservatory, Janet's latest Chase Foundation environmental effort. The building of the lavish domed glass and metal structure was in process and the solarium, which would house the French restaurant, lounge, and coffee shop, was almost complete.

Today, the workers were concentrating on the Show House, which would display plants indigenous to the Ladera Heights area. So the café was empty, the perfect place for a secretive meeting.

Lyndon didn't hide the disappointment on his face when he entered the café and saw Janet sitting at the only table in the room.

"Sit down, Lyndon." Janet gestured toward the chair across the table. "Leigh isn't coming. I was the one who sent the text message from her phone."

Lyndon cautiously sat down. "I thought Leigh said you knew better than to get involved in her love life."

Janet's pasted-on smile faded. "You need to remember who you're talking to before you open your mouth. I'm not one of your little groupies."

"I'm aware of that," Lyndon said. "I didn't mean any disrespect."

"I know what happened." Janet's impatience was obvious. "I know why you were at the house this morning and I can't believe you think flowers can fix this."

Lyndon looked around the café and this made Janet very nervous. Of course she didn't know what had happened but intended to call his bluff. The anxious expression on his face made Janet feel as if she needed to brace herself.

"Look, Mrs. Chase." Lyndon took a deep breath. "I wasn't bringing flowers to fix it. I was bringing flowers so she would give me a chance to tell her how I fixed it."

"Why should she?"

Lyndon's brow furrowed as he seemed to contemplate his response. "I really think this is between me and Leigh. I know you're concerned, but I have taken care of everything."

"If you ever want to see my daughter again," Janet warned, "I'm you're only chance. You're right. For me to meddle in Leigh's affairs would have gotten me in trouble before. But she came to me this time. So I think you know this is different."

Lyndon nodded. "It was horrible, but if you could just tell Leigh that I sent Nick to Marigolds, that rehab that she told me about. I didn't ask him. I made him go. I drove him there and checked him in. He agreed to it. He felt awful."

Janet slid her hands under the table so Lyndon couldn't see her grip the straps of the purse on her lap. "And you think rehab is all he needs?"

"I couldn't involve the police," Lyndon said. "I'm sorry I wouldn't let her call the cops, but everything has worked out. It would have only—"

"Made things worse." Janet swallowed hard. "That's one thing you and I can agree on, Lyndon. The last thing high-profile people need is the press that inevitably comes when police get involved."

Lyndon nodded, seeming grateful that she understood. "Besides, he would never have done it, really. I mean, he's not like that."

"People do a lot of things under the influence of drugs." Janet wasn't sure how long she could hold her composure. With every word, she moved closer to panic, but she couldn't give herself up.

"No matter what he might have done, I would never have let him rape her. And I stopped it anyway, so—"

Lyndon stopped as Janet gasped and jumped to her feet. "Rape!"

Lyndon looked around nervously. "Keep your voice down, Mrs. Chase. These paps follow me every—"

"He tried to rape her?" The horrified look on her face gave her away.

Lyndon's anxiety quickly turned to anger. "You . . . you don't know anything, do you? You were just playing me."

Janet sneered. "I know everything now."

Lyndon stood up and rushed across the table. "Look, lady. I don't know what you're—"

Janet slapped him in the face so hard that he fell back at least a foot. "I knew you were no good when I laid eyes on you. You are going to be so sorry for what you allowed to happen."

"Nothing happened," Lyndon said. "That's what I'm trying to say."

"Tell that to my daughter." Janet moved toward him, pointing her finger in his face. "You thought you could protect your flimsy image at my daughter's expense?"

"My image is not flimsy." Lyndon's body tensed up. "There are millions of dollars at risk and it wasn't fair to me if—"

"To you?" Janet laughed. "Oh, Mr. Prior. You have no idea what unfair is, but you will. You think you're special, but you're nothing. You can be made into nothing."

As Janet began walking away, Lyndon said, "I'm not afraid of you, Mrs. Chase."

Janet turned back to him. "You should be."

"Why are you still here?"

Carter looked up from his BlackBerry to see Sean standing in the doorway with Taylor right behind him. They had both been at the hospital for hours, but kept an eerie distance from him.

Carter felt as if they were afraid to be near him and he wasn't sure why. Yes, he had made himself an eternal enemy for the way he'd been acting since Avery left, but they'd beat him. They won. So why would they be afraid of him?

"So the Boy Scout does speak." Carter leaned back in the uncomfortable chair he had spent the last five hours in. "I was beginning to think I was invisible."

"We could only wish," Sean said. "You've been on that damn BlackBerry or your phone the whole time. If you want to work, why not just go to your office? You're not needed here."

Carter eyed Taylor as she walked by her brother. He got the sense that she was doing everything she could to avoid looking at him, and Carter was getting a little suspicious.

"That's the joy of being the boss," Carter said. "You can work anywhere you want to."

"That should be on your tombstone when you die." Sean laughed. "Harvard lawyer Carter Chase. He did whatever he wanted."

Carter wanted to put Sean in his place, but he restrained himself. He had made a promise to his father last night. Somehow, he would get on the good side of this family. It was necessary if his strategy was going to work.

"No matter what you think of me, Sean, I care about Avery."

"Her husband is coming," Taylor warned.

Carter looked at Taylor, sitting on the sofa near the vending machine. He could see Avery in her face, but not in any way he could define. She would be the easiest of them all to win over. "I know. I'm not here because of any of that stuff."

Sean huffed and Carter had to bite his tongue to avoid making this worse.

Everyone turned to the archway when Nikki appeared. She was in tears and Carter felt a panic like he had never known before. "What is it? Is Avery okay?"

"She's fine." Nikki forced a smile for her children, who looked worried. "They're both fine. It's a girl."

Carter watched as the three of them celebrated, acting as if he wasn't even there. This was going to be a hard egg to crack, he thought. Especially when Nikki turned to him with an expression that seemed as if she was in pain just from looking at him.

"Can we go and see her?" Taylor asked.

"No," Nikki answered. "Not yet. She wants to see you first."

Carter blinked, completely shocked. He looked at Sean and Taylor, who seemed less so. "What is going on here?"

"She wants to talk to you," Nikki said. "I suggest you hurry up. Her husband is on his way here."

Carter's instinct wanted to say that he didn't care where Anthony was, but he was too eager to see Avery to bother. He raced to her room, still confused as to why she wanted to see him but not interested in questioning anything. He would be there and he would be there before Anthony.

He felt an ache in his stomach at the sight of Avery lying on the bed with the baby in her arms. She looked like she'd been through the ringer, but she would never be anything but beautiful to him.

"Avery?"

Avery looked up and smiled when she saw Carter. "It's a girl, Carter. Look."

Carter came to the edge of the bed looking down at the wrinkled little baby. "I'm glad you're both okay."

"She's beautiful, isn't she?" Avery gently moved the blanket away so he could see her whole face. She was the most beautiful thing Avery had ever seen, and the love she felt in her heart was more overwhelming than she could ever have imagined.

Carter thought she looked like any other baby he'd ever seen. "She's very tiny."

Avery laughed. "This is exactly what I expected from you. Don't be afraid of her."

"I'm not afraid," he lied. "What's her name?"

Avery looked down at her angel. "Connor."

Carter's eyes widened in surprise. "That's—"

"The name you wanted," Avery said. "I know. When we were engaged, you said whether we had a boy or a girl, you wanted to name it Connor."

Carter looked at Avery, unable to hide his pain. "Why would you—"

"No, Carter." Avery could see how upset she'd made him. She reached out and touched his arm. "You have it wrong."

"What do I have wrong?" Carter asked in a terse tone.

"I named her Connor because she's yours." Avery withdrew her hand, scared and hopeful at the same time. She watched as Carter stared at her in disbelief.

She had no choice but this. The joy she'd felt the second she held Connor in her arms told her there was no worse crime than to withhold this love from someone. It would be the worst thing she could do, not just to Carter, but to her baby.

"Avery?" Carter's voice caught in his throat. "Are you saying . . ."

"Whatever price I have to pay for deceiving you," she said, "I'm willing to pay. I'm so sorry, Carter. I was so scared."

Carter's hands went to his head as he stepped back. He stood blank, amazed and shaken.

"I never intended to do it this way." Avery wiped the tears from her cheeks. She could see the anger mixed in with his astonishment. "Things just got so out of hand. The way you searched for me. I just felt like . . ."

"She's mine," Carter whispered. "The medical report said—"

"We expected you to search for the records. Anthony knew a gynecologist who owed him a favor. He agreed to—"

"He did this," Carter pronounced. "I knew he—"

"Carter, please." Avery slowly held Connor up. "Do you want to hold her?"

Carter took a step forward, wiping his hands on his pants. The baby was holding her little arms in the air and making a sweet little sound. "She's really small."

"Put your arms out," Avery instructed. "It's going to be okay."

Avery helped tenderly place Connor in Carter's arms and positioned them to hold her properly. "Keep your hand behind her head."

Carter felt a bottomless well of emotion looking down at this tiny little creature. Everything inside him softened as he held her close. He took in every inch of her face and gloried in the connection he had once thought he'd never feel.

"She has your little button nose."

Avery basked briefly in the moment before her. Watching the

gleam in Carter's eyes as he looked at their daughter was a
dream she'd had since even before he'd asked her to marry him.

Carter was in love and had never been filled with such deter-
mination and fear at the same time. Everything was different
now. Everything.

"She's our chance," he said to Avery. "She's our miracle and
we can—"

"Carter." Avery paused, praying to avoid the worst. "I'm married to Anthony because I love him, not because I was pregnant.
That hasn't changed."

Carter didn't want to hear this, but nothing could deter his
resoluteness. "He took advantage of you."

"Let's not go back to that," Avery pleaded. "All I can ask is that
we start over from this moment on. If you can learn to forgive
me, I think we can be great parents to our baby."

"I should be angry with you." He looked down at Connor as
she uttered tiny cooing sounds. "And I am, but . . . I'm just so
fuckin' happy."

Seeing him laugh, filled with pure and complete joy, made
Avery so happy it frightened her. She didn't deserve his forgiveness so easily, but maybe he did understand. Maybe looking at
Connor had the same effect on him it had on her. He could see
why she would do anything for her baby.

"But parents are all we can be, Carter. I hope you know that."

He shrugged, keeping his eyes on his baby. "I thought we already resolved that."

"Well, yes." Avery wasn't sure what to make of his careless demeanor. "I just thought you were suggesting something else."

"It's all good, Avery." He looked at her and smiled. "When I
said she's our chance, I meant to make peace with each other. If
you want to stay married to Anthony, that's your choice. All I
care about is this little miracle and being her daddy."

Avery wasn't sure if it was just because she wanted to, but she
decided to believe him for now. Connor made her only want to
believe good things.

When Anthony entered the room the look of amazement on
his face was understandable considering Carter was holding the
baby, his face only inches away from kissing her.

"What's going on?" Anthony asked. "Avery?"

"Anthony." Avery felt relief more than anything as she recognized the love she felt for him upon seeing him again. She was afraid she'd forgotten why she loved him, but she hadn't. None of that had changed. "It's a girl."

"What is he doing here?" Anthony took a step toward Carter, who hadn't looked away from Connor.

"I told him," Avery said, confused as to why Carter was ignoring Anthony.

Anthony's eyes widened in fear and she understood why. She was the one who told him how dangerous the Chase family was. "It's okay, honey. Everything is going to be okay."

Anthony came around the other side of the bed just as a nurse entered the room with Nikki right behind her.

Avery felt compassion for Anthony's situation. He had been willing to love this baby, raise it as his own. It had to hurt that she had decided to tell Carter after all.

She reached up to take his face in her hands and brought it down to hers. When she kissed him tenderly on the lips, she hoped he could understand the words she couldn't say in front of Carter.

Stealing a quick glance at Carter, Nikki noticed he looked up for just a second. He seemed to only have eyes for the baby, but Nikki didn't believe that. "The nurse needs to take the baby again."

Avery and Anthony separated and she looked deeply into his eyes, so steady and reliably there for her. "I love you."

As his uncertain frown slowly turned into an uncertain smile, Avery knew it would have to be enough for now. When they were alone, she would explain everything. He would understand. Anthony always understood.

"Please, sir." The nurse held her arms out to Carter, but he didn't budge.

"She needs the baby," Nikki said.

"It's all right," Avery said. "She's fine, Carter."

Reluctantly, Carter handed the baby to the nurse, who put him in the moveable glass bassinet. As he watched her roll Connor away, Carter and Nikki exchanged a glance. He wanted to show her up for thinking she could get away with this, but he wouldn't. He had more important concerns now.

He turned back to Avery and swallowed the pain of seeing her so intimate with Anthony. They were acting as if no one else was in the room but the two of them. He almost felt sorry for Anthony. The poor guy didn't know what was coming.

When Dr. Channing entered the room the look on her face was not at all happy. "There are too many people in this room. She gave birth a half hour ago. Please, one person at a time."

"I'll leave," Carter offered. He saw the look of surprise on everyone's face. Yes, this was unlike him, but things were changing and he would have them all eating out of his hand soon.

As soon as he stepped outside the hospital room, Carter came face-to-face with Sean and Taylor. He couldn't ignore how pissed he was that they all knew this; all this time they knew it was his baby and they were all willing to lie to keep him from his God-given right. His nature urged him to seek revenge, but he had no choice. At least not right now.

He was grateful that his phone rang because it gave him an excuse to ignore them. Besides, when he saw his father's number on the I.D., all he could think of was sharing the good news. His mother had wished it would be a girl.

"Dad, you're not going to believe—"

"Where are you?" Steven asked abruptly.

"No, listen to me. I have great news."

"Get over to the house now."

"What's wrong?"

"Now!"

"I knew it," Janet asserted. "I knew it!"

"Don't start with me, Mom." Michael had just been ushered into his father's office after Steven had time alone with Janet to tell her everything.

She'd started in on her son the second he showed up and was led into his father's office.

"I don't need this right now, Mom."

"This is a nightmare." Janet was fanning herself, trying to control her breathing. "Steven, I told you we would regret that girl coming into our family."

"Janet." Steven thought she was acting surprisingly calm for how much she hated Kimberly and how serious this was. "No looking backward. There's too much to do."

"That little whore is going to destroy our family!" Janet had known Kimberly was from the gutter even before meeting her, but she could never have imagined any of this. And now everything she had spent more than half of her life working to build was about to be torn to pieces.

"I warned you all." Janet's hand went to her uneasy stomach. She looked at the glass of whiskey sitting on Steven's desk. Her sobriety had never been tested and now it was being tested beyond belief. "If you'd gotten rid of her last September when she tried to kill me, we wouldn't be here."

"How do you figure that?" Michael asked. "This was set in motion ten years ago. I'm glad that motherfucker is dead. I only wish I'd done it."

"Great." Janet saw the fabric of her entire family unraveling with every second. "We've raised wannabe murderers, Steven."

Steven watched as Janet, who had been circling the chaise Michael was sitting on, moved closer to the desk he was sitting behind. He saw her glance at the glass once again.

"Janet." He placed his hand over the glass. "No. You don't need this."

"Don't tell me what I need," she snapped. "I'm the only one who knows what I need. I need a family that isn't completely insane. If you can't give me that, Steven, at least you can give me a drink."

Thinking he was going to send his mother back to her addiction did nothing to worsen Michael's situation. He knew that even on the slight chance they could fix this, he had ruined everything. There would be no coming back from this. And he would make Kimberly pay for putting him in this position.

"I won't let you," Steven said. "I need you, Janet. Our family needs you now. You have to be stronger."

"I'm as strong as I can be right now." Janet paused, feeling on the verge of a breakdown. "My God, Steven."

Steven got up and went over to her, wrapping his arms around her. "Sweetheart, this is not beyond our control. If we all work together, we can fix this."

"There's something else." She held on to her husband for support. "It's Leigh."

"What about her?" Steven asked.

"It's bad."

Steven nodded. "Okay, but right now we have to deal with this. Then we'll deal with Leigh's problem."

"But we have to deal with it." Janet's tone was as definitive as she could muster under the circumstances. "And as soon as possible."

Steven was too afraid to ask after hearing that. "Just tell me she's safe and sound right now."

"She's safe," Janet answered, "but not sound."

The second Carter stepped inside the house, he saw his baby sister rushing out from the family's library.

She moved swiftly to meet him. "What are you so happy about?"

Carter couldn't conceal his joy. "Come here and give me a kiss, princess."

Haley pushed against him as he grabbed her and tried to kiss her on the cheek. "Stop it, Carter."

"What's wrong?" he asked, letting her go. "Has someone upset the baby?"

"Don't call me that." Haley glanced down the hallway. "What's going on down there?"

Carter shrugged. "It's an empty hallway, so I'm assuming nothing's going on."

Haley socked him in the arm. "Are you high or something?"

"Something." He laughed.

"Well, you better wipe that grin off your face. Mom, Dad, and Michael are in Dad's office and shit is going down."

"What shit?" He started down the hallway.

"You tell me." Haley stayed right where she was.

Carter looked back at her. "Let's go and see."

"I can't. Dad threatened me if I came any step beyond this

damn library. I've been trying to listen into the walls, but I can't hear anything."

"He used the old trust fund trick again, huh?"

"Yeah, right," Haley said. "Try something more violent. Whatever they're talking about, Mom has been screaming for the last ten minutes."

"If Mom's screaming, it's probably about you." Carter smiled. "Don't worry, Lil' Bit. I'll let you know what you've done as soon as I find out."

"What's wrong with Leigh?" Michael asked.

"Don't you worry about it," Janet replied. "I'll handle Leigh. You go get my grandchildren and bring them here. I don't want them to spend one more second with that little slut."

"They're in school," Michael said. "I'll pick them up and bring them here tonight."

"They're never to see her again," Janet ordered.

"I know that!" Michael assured her.

And that was only the beginning. Kimberly would be lucky to have the clothes on her back and five dollars when he was done with her.

When Carter opened the door and stepped inside, everyone's eyes were on him and he knew something was horribly wrong. "What's going on?"

"What are you smiling for?" Janet asked.

"I—" Carter began.

"You're to blame for this too," she said.

"For what?" Carter sensed a Chase family crisis was at hand.

"Close the door behind you," Steven ordered. "I don't want your sister to hear."

"What did I do now?"

"You kept this secret from us." Janet walked over to him and pointed her finger in his face. "You knew that Kimberly was a whore from the beginning and you let him keep this lie from us?"

Carter's mouth fell open, but no words came out. He turned to Michael, who was sitting on the chaise looking completely broken. "What the fuck is going on?"

"They know," Michael said. "Something's happened."

"Why would you help him keep this secret?" Steven asked.

"Because he's my brother and he loves her. And that wouldn't have mattered to either of you."

"Encouraging his infatuation with some whore was more important than protecting this family?" Steven didn't believe that either of his sons was on his side anymore.

Janet turned away, shaking her head. "Steven, we have no chance of fixing this if our own sons work against us."

"What happened?" Carter asked, knowing already this was not the time to share his good news.

As Steven and Michael told Carter of everything that had happened since David had come to L.A., Janet sobbed and moaned her way through it. Carter was blown away.

"Why didn't you tell me?" Carter asked. "Since when do you keep things like this from me?"

"Are you serious?" Michael asked. "First, I didn't fucking know. Second, when I did, I was a little sore from when you tried to choke me to death to pick up a phone and call you."

"What?" Janet fell onto the leather sofa next to the bookcase of Steven's first editions. "When did . . . You know what, never mind. I can't take any more."

That fight seemed like a year ago to Carter. "I'm sorry."

"We don't have time for that," Steven said. "You need to get on your phone now and call the district attorney's office. Use your connections to find out where the case stands."

Carter took his phone out of his pocket. "Dad, I—"

"Don't worry," Steven said. "I know you're a lawyer. If anything illegal has to be done, you won't know about it. But I need you to make that call."

As Carter made the call, Steven took one last sip of the whiskey and let it burn his throat. "Any talk of revenge or anything like that needs to stop now. We have to focus on the only thing that matters. First, getting that tape. Second, making sure nothing leads to Kimberly. Michael, you have to put together an airtight alibi for her just in case."

"We have to protect her?" Michael asked.

"No," Janet said. "We have to protect the family. As much as I would like to abandon her and let her go to jail, if she is exposed we are exposed."

"Third," Steven continued, "we have to find that witness."

Carter hung the phone up. "She's at the station now."

"Oh my God." Janet felt a heat flash coming on.

"This is good news," Steven said.

"She was picked up trying to get back in the room."

"The tape?" Michael asked.

Carter shrugged. "She had nothing but the clothes on her back."

"Is that good or bad?" Janet asked.

"One thing I know is bad," Carter added. "The assistant D.A. said the lead detective is Sean Jackson."

"Just perfect." Steven wondered if they would ever be free of that damn Jackson family. He looked again at his phone. "Now it's time for me to make some calls."

Leigh had locked up her office at Hope Clinic and was on her way toward the lobby when she heard raised voices. Just a few minutes from being able to go back home and get under the covers, and now there was foolishness to deal with. She wasn't in the mood already, but when she got out front and realized it was Lyndon making the fuss, Leigh was livid.

"What are you doing here?" she asked as she approached him trying to negotiate with Carlos.

Lyndon appeared relieved to see Leigh although she was giving him anything but a welcoming expression.

"We need to talk," he said.

"We're closed," Carlos said. "Let's go, buddy."

"I've got nothing to say to you." Leigh nodded to Carlos.

"Let's go, movie star!"

"Fine." Lyndon jerked his arm out of Carlos's grasp. "But you listen to me. I don't know what your mother is up to, but you better not fuck with me."

"Oh, you must be crazy." Carlos grabbed Lyndon by the collar of his polo.

"This isn't one of your movies." Leigh smiled vindictively as

Lyndon struggled like a little boy. "You can't win a fight when the other guy isn't paid to take a dive."

He was nothing but what others had made him up to be. Everything about him was only enough to maintain a surface. Once that surface was chinked a bit, it all went to rust.

"I know your family is asking around about me," Lyndon said. "About Nick."

Carlos pushed him out the door.

"It's not just me, Leigh." Lyndon grabbed the door before Carlos could pull it shut. "There are a lot of people who need me, live off of me. They're not going to put up with this."

Leigh tossed the clipboard in her hand on the floor and darted for the door. She grabbed the handle, looking Lyndon in the face. "It doesn't matter. They can't help you. They can't save you."

She slammed the door in his face so hard the building shook.

"Damn," Carlos said. "I didn't know you had it in you."

Leigh felt a rush of energy invigorate her. "You know what, Carlos? You're the last person that is ever gonna say that."

She was done being the angel.

Sean Jackson rang the bell at Booking for a third time. "For Christ's sake, where is everyone?"

He slammed his hand on the counter until Jerry Carlson wobbled into the area behind the security gate.

"Where the hell were you, Jerry? I've been here for about five minutes."

"And the whole world was gonna fall apart?" Jerry stuffed the last piece of his hoagie sandwich in his mouth and licked his fingers.

"Really nice," Sean said. "Can you take five seconds away from getting fatter to tell me where my suspect is?"

"Look at you." Jerry feigned impression. "The chief gives you your first homicide case and you think you're in charge of the joint."

Sean might have been a little too anxious, but this case could be what got him his promotion to Homicide. He had to do this perfectly. "I don't want to fuck this up."

"It looks like you already have." Jerry slid the sign-in sheet under the partition. "The FBI already stepped in."

"The FBI?" Sean smirked. "Yeah, right. Like they'd be interested in a dead pimp."

"They said it was some interstate crap. I don't know. Look, their signatures are right there. Special Agent Allen and Special Agent Booker."

Sean read the names but didn't recognize anyone. "I would know if the FBI was coming in on my case, Jerry. Did you see ID?"

"What do I look like, an idiot? Of course I saw ID."

Sean knew something fishy was going on. "Fine, where are these jokers at?"

"They're gone." Jerry pointed to the sheet. "Can't you read? They left about ten minutes ago."

"What the . . ." Sean grabbed the sheet, ripping it off the board.

"Hey," Jerry yelled. "That's official—"

"They stole my suspect? Did Chief Mills approve this?"

Jerry furrowed his brows. "Have you been listening, Junior? They're the FBI. He has to do what they say. They took the girl and her stuff."

"Stuff?" Sean's fingers reached through the bar between him and Jerry. "Jerry, please do not tell me they took all the evidence."

"They took all the evidence." Jerry appeared pleased to share the news.

Sean realized his textbook hooker-kills-pimp case might not be textbook after all. He couldn't say why, not yet, but he had a bad feeling he wasn't going to see that suspect or the evidence again. And he was probably not going to see a promotion to Homicide.

Reluctantly, he dialed the number for his FBI contact. He got a sinking feeling in his stomach when his buddy told him there were no such cops named Allen and Booker, and the FBI wasn't at all interested in a pimp murder case.

14

When Carter stepped out of the kitchen and onto the back patio, he didn't see his parents anywhere. Maya said for certain they were out there.

"Maya!" he called back. "Where are . . ."

Just then he saw the front door to the Caribbean-style guest house about fifty yards from the pool open and both of his parents stepped out of the rarely used but fully and luxuriously furnished two-thousand-square-foot residence.

"What's wrong?" were the first words to exit Janet's mouth at the sight of Carter.

"You hiding someone in there?" Carter asked. He made his way to the bar alongside the pool.

"We were thinking it might be nice to turn it into a sporty playhouse for the twins," Janet said. "We never use it for anything else."

Carter offered Steven a drink. "Haley will put a contract out on anyone who lives in that house. You know she wants to live there."

"Not a chance," Steven said. "The last time she lived in there, she thought it meant she could throw a pool party every day. There was at least one near drowning."

"That happens a lot around here." Carter offered his mother a glass of tonic water.

"And a small fire," Steven added.

"So there are no bodies in there?" Carter asked.

Steven could see he was smiling, but knew he wasn't kidding. "You're a lawyer, Carter. There are things you just don't need to know."

"Stop it," Janet said. "No one is in there. As usual, money did the trick."

Carter knew he couldn't know more than that. "Michael wants the tape."

"Ugh." Janet put the glass down.

"I destroyed it," Steven admitted. "And no, I didn't watch it."

"Now that that's taken care of," Janet said, "it's time to get on with business."

"Before you start planning Kimberly's demise . . ." Carter put his drink down. "I have some good news for once."

"I'll believe that when I hear it," Steven said.

"Avery gave birth two days ago."

Steven nodded. "Isn't that a little—"

"Early!" Janet inhaled sharply as she saw the smile curving on the edge of Carter's lips. "Carter, no!"

"Yes." He was beaming with endless pride. "I was right the first time. It's mine."

Steven was shocked. "How do you—"

"She told me," Carter said. "She felt guilty and confessed."

"I knew it!" Janet felt her heart leap with joy, much needed joy. "What is it?"

"Who in the hell does she think she is?" Steven asked. "How dare she think she can keep this from us? That whole family. They were in on it too, weren't they?"

"Yes." Carter's smile faded for only a second, returning for his mother. "You got what you wanted, Mom."

"A girl!" Janet was around the bar in a second. She wrapped her arms around Carter and leaned up to kiss him again and again.

"Those sons of bitches," Steven ranted.

"Steven!" Janet huffed. "It's wrong how they went about it, but you're kind of missing what's important here."

"Of course," he said. "I'm sorry. I'm happy for you, son. I know this is what you wanted."

Carter could only partially hug his father because his mother hadn't let go. "I haven't forgotten what we talked about, Dad."

"You've seen her?" Janet asked.

Carter was beaming. "She's beautiful, Mom. Perfect."

"Things are a little different now, right?" Steven asked. "You can't still want her after finding out she's lied to you."

Janet looked suspiciously at the two of them. "What are you talking about? What are you up to?"

"Nothing, Mother." Carter kissed her on the forehead as he reached for his ringing cell phone. "You're wrong, Dad."

"We have to go over there now," Janet said. "Michael is supposed to be here with the boys and the rest of their stuff, but I can't wait another second."

"Here's our boy now." Carter brought the phone to his ear. "Where are you? I have some news that's going to blow your fuc . . ."

Janet finally let Carter go when he slammed his drink on the bar. Looking up at him, she could see his brows turn down and his eyes get smaller and smaller. She couldn't take any more. She honestly couldn't.

"Just calm down." He looked at Steven and rolled his eyes. "Michael, listen. It's gonna be all right. Just get over here now. This won't be hard."

Steven braced himself as Carter hung up. He would be dead in a year because of these kids. "What now?"

"It's Kimberly," Carter said. "She picked the boys up from school and they're gone. Michael went home and Marisol said that she's packed some stuff, taken some money and her jewelry. They're gone."

So much for enjoying the good news.

Haley made her way to the piano at a brisk pace and slammed her iBook right on top of it. Leigh stopped playing and looked up.

"My ears are bleeding," Haley exclaimed. "I'll pay you to stop."

"Careful," Leigh said. "This is a Macassar ebony Steinway."

Haley made a smacking sound with her lips. "I'll chop it up and put it in the fireplace right now."

"Yeah, right." Leigh gently placed the cover down. "That would actually require you to exert yourself and work. We all know that's not happening."

"I know why you did it." Haley turned the Mac around to face Leigh.

"Did what?" Leigh grabbed the laptop to take a closer look.

"Dumped Lyndon." Haley laughed. "This is so juicy. I swear."

It was the most popular celebrity blog on the Internet, one that broke more big news than the gossip magazines combined. BREAKING NEWS was flashing at the top of the page, just above a picture of Lyndon Prior being led to a police car in handcuffs.

"This has actually made you kind of interesting," Haley said.

"Lyndon Prior has been arrested and charged with the assault of his friend and . . ." Leigh paused as she read the next word. "Lover?"

"Did you know this guy, Nick?" Haley asked. "Please, please tell me you walked in on them. You should've taken a picture. You would have made millions."

"Don't be gross." Leigh read on.

Nick Gagan was in the hospital in critical condition. He had accused Lyndon of beating him up after threatening to come clean about their love affair and mutual drug addiction.

"Those twelve steps are a bitch, huh?" Haley laughed. "And to think I had him on my he-can-get-it list. Good thing I took him off the second he showed interest in you. I knew something was wrong with him then. Your flat chest probably reminded him of a boy."

"Shut up!"

Haley blinked, shocked by Leigh's reaction. "What's your problem? There's no mention of you in there. Only that Lyndon's reputation is shit now. He won't even get a commercial in Japan."

Leigh stood up, handing the Mac back to Haley. "Where's Mom?"

"In the castle room." This was what all the Chase children

called their parents' bedroom, which took almost the entire west wing on the second floor of the house. "Why?"

"Nothing."

"Hey," Haley called after Leigh turned to walk away. "What's going on?"

"Nothing." Leigh turned around. "Mind your own business."

"Oh . . . My . . . God!" Haley yelled. "Did Dad do this?"

"Seriously, Haley. You need to stay out of it."

"Of course he did." A bemused smile traced Haley's lips. "His perfect little angel got into some trouble or something. It had to be serious for Mom and Dad to interfere with you again."

"Don't you have a class to fail?" Leigh asked.

"At least no one got killed this time." Haley didn't back down from Leigh's glare. "What? That's good news, right? You only caused Dad to ruin a guy's life instead of end it."

"Go to hell, you little brat." Leigh turned and headed upstairs.

Haley slammed the Mac down on the piano again and then kicked the shiny bench over. She didn't care if it was a Steinway. Maybe if she chopped it up, she'd get a little attention for once. Between Leigh and whatever was going on with Michael, Haley was sick of being left out of the loop. It wasn't that she cared. It was the principle of the matter. She didn't like being sidelined in her own family.

So, she decided, it was time to do something about that. It was time for her to do something that would turn the attention back where it belonged: on the baby. But what would she do to shake this family back up to her satisfaction?

"So many choices," she said to herself. "So little time."

Leigh lightly knocked on the door to her parents' bedroom before opening it. The massive room included a bedroom and a sitting area facing the front of the house that was the size of an average living room. Janet wasn't in either, but Leigh could hear her voice. She poked her head in the six-hundred-square-foot master bath and found no one. There was only one other place Janet could be.

The master closet was the size of Leigh's entire bedroom with closets, cabinets, drawers, and retractable levels. Haley passed through it into the dressing room, a small room with a wall of mirrors. Her mother was sitting, partially dressed, on the rose-colored cashmere bench talking on her cell phone.

"They have to be somewhere!" Janet let out an exasperated sigh. "I don't know, but how far could she have . . . What money?"

Janet looked up as soon as she noticed Leigh walking toward her. Leigh had enough problems to deal with. She didn't need to know that Kimberly was missing with the boys and one million dollars that she stole back from the pimp she killed.

"Steven, call me back as soon as you can." Janet hung up without waiting for a response. "What is it, dear?"

"Is something wrong?" Leigh asked, joining her on the bench.

Janet felt like laughing. "Silly stuff. How are you feeling, baby?"

"Haley showed me a gossip blog." She paused. "About Lyndon."

Janet leaned back against the wall, studying her daughter's face. "It's a hard choice, Leigh, but I decided I'd rather be your mother than your friend. So if you're—"

"I'm not mad at you." Leigh leaned against her mother.

Janet ran her fingers through her baby's hair. "I'll tell you whatever you want to know."

"I don't want to know anything. I just know I'm done being the naive fool."

"You were never a naive fool, baby. You're an incredibly intelligent, accomplished, and strong woman. And you have the biggest heart I've ever known."

"So why am I always losing?"

Janet knew that no matter how old your kids got, a parent would always pray to take their pain for them. But it just wasn't possible. "You bring light into this world. If you let Nick and Lyndon stop you from being who God meant you to be . . . that's when you lose. Besides, you're the only sane person in this family. We need you."

Leigh laughed a little bit, snuggling up closer to her mother. "If I'm the only sane person here, this family is in a lot more trouble than I thought."

Janet wanted to protect Leigh and Haley from the inevitable mess that would be this summer because of Kimberly. "Your baby sister wants to go to Australia and New Zealand for a couple of months after school is over in one week."

"You want me to go with her so I can keep an eye on her?"

"Just to keep the damage down to a minimum," Janet said. "You could use the break from working like a slave at that clinic."

"That clinic allows me to escape the world."

"So would a luxury presidential suite overlooking the harbor at the Four Seasons."

"I can't argue with that," Leigh said. "I can promise to think about it."

"Feel better?" Janet kissed Leigh's forehead.

"I will." Leigh didn't expect to say that and really mean it, but she thought she might.

"I have more good news," Janet said. "It's about Carter."

"I need those passports today, Neil." Kimberly was leaning over the desk against the wall in the small Santa Barbara hotel room talking into a prepaid cell phone she had purchased at a convenience store a few hours ago.

"Mrs. Chase, I can't . . ."

Kimberly heard him sigh or breathe or something, but he wasn't talking anymore. "Neil? Are you there? What about my passports?"

"Your husband contacted me an hour ago, Mrs. Chase."

Kimberly shivered in fear. "Did you tell him . . ."

"No, I didn't tell him where you were, but I can't help you anymore. They'll know."

Through the reflection in the mirror, Kimberly could see her boys playing on the bed completely oblivious of her hell. How was she ever going to get them out of this country and away from Michael? After she ran out of the bathroom in Steven's office, Kimberly went straight home. She grabbed some clothes and the money she had taken back from David. In the fervor of everything, Michael had not yet put it back in the bank. Staying the night at a hotel, she thought of how she could get the boys and get away from Michael.

She picked them up from school and drove them as far as Santa Barbara before she realized she wasn't getting anywhere as

Kimberly Chase. She decided to call Neil for fake IDs, which she needed quick before the furor of the Chase family came down on her full force. Now that was falling through.

"Is he on to me?" she asked nervously. She was trying her best to keep her wits about her, but it was hard. She was scared to death.

"I don't know, but I think you should hang up now."

"Neil, I need someone in Santa Barbara who can—"

"Don't say that over the . . . I can't tell you. Good-bye, Mrs. Chase, and good luck."

As soon as he hung up the phone, Kimberly realized he was saying that the phone was bugged and now Michael knew she was in Santa Barbara.

Kimberly knew they had to go, but where?

She heard a noise and thought it was the television until the hotel door opened.

She jumped up from her chair. It felt like her chest caved in when Michael entered the room. It was as if he moved in slow motion with an intense anger defining every inch of him.

"Daddy! Daddy!"

The boys hurtled off the bed and stumbled over each other to jump all over their father, and Michael smiled and laughed as if nothing were wrong. While they were each hugging a leg, he took a quick glance at Kimberly and his eyes darkened and bored into her.

Kimberly was shaking so badly her teeth were chattering. He wouldn't kill her in front of their children, would he?

"Daddy, are you coming with us?" Daniel asked, looking up.

"Where?" Michael asked, smiling gently. They'd only been missing for a day, but he felt as if they'd been gone a year.

"Mommy said we're going on a trip," Evan squealed. "And we don't have to go to school, which I really liked about this whole thing."

"And you can't come 'cause of work," Daniel added. "But Mommy said you'd come later."

"Did she say that?" Michael looked at Kimberly, feeling crazy over the fact that he felt something at seeing her too, something along with wanting to slit her throat. "Well, there has been a change of plans. We're going back home for now."

"No!" Evan stomped his foot on the floor. "I wanna go!"

Daniel turned to his mother. "Mommy, tell him."

"We'll . . . have to see," she answered with a noticeable tremor in her voice.

Daniel frowned. "What's wrong, Mommy?"

"Nothing is wrong with Mommy." Michael put his hand on Daniel's chin and turned his face to him, away from Kimberly. "We'll go on the trip after school lets out."

Kimberly gasped when she noticed a tall, burly raisin-brown man enter the room, his attention on both boys.

"Go ahead." Michael stood up.

"No!" As soon as Kimberly saw the man move toward Evan, she ran at them. No one was going to take her babies!

Michael grabbed her by the arm just as she passed him and pushed her back. His dark face was set in a vicious expression. "This can be easy or hard."

"Mommy?" Daniel looked back at her.

Michael turned to the boys, blocking Kimberly from their vision. "This nice man is going to take you two to the car while Mommy and I pack up and bring your stuff down."

The boys mumbled their disapproval, but didn't fight as they were led out.

Kimberly felt her heart breaking into sharp, stabbing pieces. "Please, Michael. Don't . . ."

He wanted to kill her. She had ruined his life. So what was that voice in the back of his head telling him he didn't want to give her up? "You must be the craziest bitch on the planet. Have these last seven years taught you anything?"

"They're my babies," she stammered.

"I guess not." Michael looked around and saw the duffel bag full of money. He went to retrieve it. "Even before this, you should have known there was no escaping me. I guess you thought if Avery could elude Carter, why couldn't you do the same?"

"You said you were going to kill me."

Michael glared at her. "But it isn't really an accurate comparison because you know I'd do things that Carter never would."

"What choice did I have?"

Michael's laugh was laced with bitterness and hate. "Just my point, baby. You had none. You used up all of yours. You have nothing, are nothing now. Avery had a whole family on her side. Who will help you?"

Kimberly tried to keep her fragile control. "I don't need help. I just need my kids."

"My kids!" He lifted the bag up. "My money. It's all mine. The sooner you learn that, the safer you'll be."

"I don't care what happens to me." Kimberly swiftly backed up as Michael took three steps toward her.

He looked her up and down, hating and wanting every piece of her. "I wish I could say the same, but I can't. I do care what happens to you because I want you to suffer."

Kimberly rigidly held her tears in check. "I don't deserve that."

"In that case, I'll only enjoy a little bit instead of a lot."

"Michael!"

Michael was spurred by the fury of his emotion. "You didn't have to fuck him, Kimberly!"

"He wasn't going to stop!"

"I would have stopped him," Michael asserted. "Even if I had to kill him. Mom and Dad never had to know anything."

"But you would," she argued. "I had already lost so much of you since we moved out of that house."

"Which was your fault!"

"And yours!" She met him with a determined stare of her own. "If you had put me ahead of your father's golden approval, none of this would have happened. We both know you haven't been faithful during our marriage. Your hypocritical ass is mad because you're not enough of a man to own up to that."

"Not him!" Michael yelled. "Anyone but him!"

Kimberly placed her hands on her hips and tilted her head to the side. "So that's it, right? It's not me. It's David. You're mad because I slept with the only other man who owned me. You wished you could forget that you married a—"

"You say one more word and I'll—"

"Hit me, then!" she yelled, coming so close she pushed against him. "You think you'd be the first man to do that? You think you're the first man to tell me I'm nothing? I survived all of them and I'll survive you. So go ahead and do it!"

Michael saw her eyes water up, but he fought the urge inside him to feel anything for her. "You may survive, but if you ever try to take my boys from me, you'll wish you hadn't."

"I don't want to take them away," she said. "I just want to be with them."

Michael turned away, cursing himself inside. "Then be with them."

He waited only a second before heading out of the room and he knew she was behind him. She said nothing. He said nothing. She was with him and he still hated her.

Nikki turned away from the window to warn her family. "Here they come."

"Please be nice," Avery pleaded. "Connor is a part of their family too."

Carter had been by every day since Avery returned from the hospital to her parents' house. Each time had been difficult for Avery for reasons she had to keep to herself.

First, he had been on his best behavior, and although her mother and Anthony weren't buying it, Avery was touched. She wanted desperately to believe that Connor would change the way Carter acted around the family.

Second, when visiting, Carter barely paid any attention to Avery except to ask her if she was all right. And that wasn't what she wanted. Watching him with Connor tugged at her heart, but she felt excluded when he was with her as if she'd had a right to be included. She didn't, which was why she never said a thing.

But today would be different. The whole Chase clan was coming to see the baby for the first time, and everyone in the Jackson household knew the drama was just about to begin.

Anthony was sitting next to Avery on the sofa and Connor was in the bassinet right next to her. As soon as the door opened and Carter walked through, Anthony stood up. Avery could see he wasn't okay with this even though he'd said he was after she explained everything.

"Anthony." She tugged at his pants until he looked down at her. "Let's give them a chance."

Anthony leaned down. "Nikki told me how to deal with these people."

"Oh no." Avery stood up. "Just let me handle Carter. I don't want him getting into it with you."

"I'm not afraid," Anthony whispered.

Things started off well. Not everyone was there, only Steven, Janet, Carter, Leigh, and Haley. Avery wondered where Kimberly was.

After quick hellos, they darted for the bassinet. Janet picked Connor up and refused to let anyone else hold her. Avery was touched at the sight of Steven softening to the baby. He smiled and cooed, let her grab his finger with her tiny hand before kissing it. Even Haley, of all people, cracked a smile and leaned in for a quick kiss. Avery felt proud this was because of her baby, her little Connor.

Nikki expected to hear threats over their attempt at deception, wanting them to believe the baby wasn't Carter's. But there weren't any. Avery told her mother that babies change everything and she'd hoped that Connor would change the relationship between the Chases and the Jacksons.

And Carter continued to ignore her. Avery hated that this was what she thought of the most. Janet and Leigh showered her with affection. Even Steven gave her a compliment or two. Carter only smiled and again asked her how she was doing. She said fine and he hadn't even looked at her since. And for some reason, Avery couldn't stop looking at him, waiting for him to acknowledge her. She was insane, but watching him holding Connor standing with Steven away from everyone else, she wanted him to look at her.

It wasn't until Anthony yanked at her blouse that she realized that someone was talking to her. She apologized, but could tell that Anthony had noticed because he so abruptly walked away.

"Is your husband all right?" Janet asked.

"He's fine," Avery answered. "I'm sorry I was distracted."

"I don't blame you," Janet said. "I can't take my eyes off her either. She's beautiful. Where is your mother now?"

"She's in the bedroom checking in on Dad. Leigh went with her to say hello."

"That's fine." Janet scrolled through her BlackBerry. "You can fill her in later. I've already scheduled an appointment with Dr. Moss and Elizabeth Prescott. They'll meet with you and Carter next week."

"Who . . . are they . . . What?"

"Didn't Carter tell you? We have to apply now if we want Connor to get into Post Academy when she turns five."

Avery started laughing until she realized from Janet's expression that she wasn't joking. "How much does that cost?"

"It's only twenty-five thousand dollars a year." Janet made a dismissive gesture. "That's now. Who knows what it will be five years from now? But Carter can take care of that, no problem."

"Janet, I don't—"

"Avery." Janet placed her hand on Avery's shoulder and looked at her intently. "You want what's best for Connor, right?"

"Of course I do."

"You may have tried to avoid this, but she is a Chase."

Avery's eyes gave away her guilt. "I'm sorry about that, Janet."

"I know." Janet gently touched her cheek. "I don't need your apologies, dear. I just need you to understand that your baby is a Chase. That means something and you can't deny her that."

"I don't plan to." Avery nodded her compliance. She would have to pick her battles and she didn't want any today.

"Good." Janet returned her attention to her BlackBerry. "From now on, you will have to see Dr. Lauren Green. She's the best pediatrician in L.A. County. She hasn't taken new patients for a year, but she'll take Connor. I'm still working on the christening. Let me run a few dates by you."

"You see that?" Steven asked, pointing to the flowers on the console table near the front door.

Carter looked up from Connor to where his father was pointing. "People send flowers when a baby is born, Dad."

"Look at the name," Steven ordered.

Written in big, red letters was an aluminum sash that read WELCOME, BABY HARPER. Carter sneered his displeasure.

"You get that changed right away," Steven directed. "It probably says Harper on the birth certificate."

"I'm sure it's just someone who doesn't know yet." Carter leaned down and kissed Connor's tiny mouth. That was his favorite. Her little mouth and the bottom of her tiny feet. "No one knows yet."

"We're going to make sure they do."

"Dad, you know what we talked about the other night."

Steven still couldn't believe this was Carter's reaction to a woman who had been willing to keep his child from him until just a week ago. "You still want her?"

Carter nodded.

"Fine," Steven said. "Nothing changes. It'll just be easier."

The plan, as Steven had described to Carter over the phone that night, was to be the best thing that ever happened to Avery. To do everything he could for her, but not so much that she would suspect his intentions. It would take a while, and it was important he be in a high-profile relationship with someone else. This would take her off her guard.

"Now that you're this baby's father," Steven stated, "you be the best father in the world. You be self-sacrificing and committed a hundred and fifty percent. You give the baby everything Anthony can't, but it's about more than money. You'll become the one who solves Avery's problems before Anthony even gets a chance. You can use the guilt she feels for deceiving you in your favor. Because of it, she won't deny you anything when it comes to the baby. For a while at least."

"What about Coral Gables?" Carter asked.

"He'll be fired by the university as soon as he gets back. I've been assured of that. And unlike you and Michael, I know how to make sure it doesn't get back to this family. He'll be out of a job and living off your child support."

"That won't last long."

"It will be long enough for him to hate you for no good reason. His animosity toward you will come between Avery wanting what is best for the baby."

Carter smiled. "Then what?"

"We'll work it from there. Maybe a job offer in New York. Something . . . anything that, coupled with your interference in his life, will make him want to leave."

"Avery is not the kind of woman you leave," Carter said.

"He won't be leaving Avery," Steven corrected. "He'll be leaving you and by that time, Avery will only remind him of you."

If Carter couldn't get Avery to leave her husband, he would get her husband to leave her. Meanwhile, Carter knew what he did for Connor and for Avery would bring her closer to him. Close enough that when things went bad with Anthony, he would be there for her.

"In the end," Steven said, "she'll want you. She'll want to be with her child's father."

Carter only hoped he could wait that long. He wanted Avery back now, and Connor only made him want that more. "It's hard, what I'm doing now."

"You have to make her believe that your only interest in her is because of Connor. If she thinks you're still in love with her, she'll keep her guard up around you. Even with Connor being yours, she'll still believe she needs to limit her interaction with you for the sake of her marriage."

"This way, she'll catch on early that I'm no longer a threat to her marriage. There's no reason for her to be cautious."

As she made her way toward them, Carter knew it would be difficult to pretend he didn't want her. It seemed so unnatural to him, a man who felt no need to hide how he felt. A man so used to getting everything he wanted right away, especially when it came to a woman, the woman who pushed all his buttons.

"What?" Avery asked, certain from the way they looked at her that they had been talking about her.

"Nothing." Without protest, Carter offered Connor to her outstretched hands.

"I need to feed her." Avery kissed Connor before holding her against her chest.

"There are a lot of things that need to be hammered out," Steven stated.

Avery didn't want to get into that today. She dreaded what that might turn into especially if Steven and Janet were involved.

"There's time for that," Carter said. "When it comes to it, Avery and I will sort that out ourselves. Today is just about Connor."

When she smiled her appreciation Carter thought that this might be a lot easier than he had expected.

Standing on the front porch of the Jacksons' home with his mother, Carter left the third message in the last hour for Michael. When he hung up, he shrugged helplessly.

"I can't do more than that," he said. "As soon as I leave here, I have to go to the office. All hell is breaking loose there because I've been out so long."

Janet gave him a grudging nod. "I understand. I'll take it from here. I just wish I knew where he was."

"I'm telling you, Mom. He's with her."

Janet refused to believe that. "He can't be."

"He can," Carter stated. "He shouldn't be, but I bet he is."

Just as she started inside the house, Anthony was stepping outside. He made eye contact with Carter and Carter could sense his uneasiness. He resisted showing how much that pleased him.

"I was looking for you," Anthony said.

"I'm right here." Carter leaned against the railing. Anthony had no idea how often Carter planned to be right here.

Anthony gripped the railing, choosing to look out onto the street instead of at Carter. "I'm willing to give this a try. I hope you are."

"Of course I am." Carter stared at him, noticing the clenched jaw. Anthony already hated him. The feeling was mutual.

"Avery believes we can all work together for Connor's sake."

"I agree," Carter said. "I'll do anything for Connor. I'm her father."

Anthony looked at him, suspicion on his face. Carter could tell he wasn't sure if Carter meant that innocently or as an affront. He expected that suspicion to grow with everything Carter said and Avery would find Anthony's reactions more and more unreasonable in light of his behavior.

"We'll be going home in a month or two." Anthony's tone was resigned. "But we've already decided to come back as soon as I've secured a job."

"You don't have to wait until then." Carter spoke in a casual, almost lighthearted tone. It would annoy Anthony more this way. "Avery will be able to afford a place here with the money I'll be giving her."

"Carter, I—"

"I mean, we haven't worked it out yet, but—"

"Carter!" Anthony's frustration showed itself sooner than expected. "I can support my family."

"And I can support mine," Carter added. "Connor is my daughter. She's a Chase and I'll be taking care of her in a manner expected of a Chase."

"We've got to work together on this, Carter. You can't just—"

"Don't worry, Anthony. You won't have to take care of anything when it comes to my kid. When Connor needs something, it'll be like you're not even there."

Carter's lips inched into a cocky grin as he saw Anthony try to control his temper.

"Be happy," Carter said. "You'll be living at a much higher standard than you did in Miami."

Anthony was clearly angry now. He turned to face Carter head-on. "How dare you suggest you're going to support me?"

"How dare you think you could keep my child from me?" Carter's eyes narrowed as he leaned in close enough to make Anthony take a step back. "And don't try to put this on Avery. She would never come up with something like this."

Anthony stared, seeming to contemplate whether he wanted to make peace or go on the attack. After a second, he sighed and his shoulders slumped. "I was doing what I thought was best for Avery and the baby."

"And I understand that." Carter smiled at Anthony's confusion. "I just hope you understand that that's exactly what I plan on doing."

Carter left him on the porch to stew in the mess of his own making. The professor's days were numbered and Carter got the distinct feeling he was finally aware of that.

* * *

"Mommy, are you sick?" Evan tried to climb onto his mother's lap as she sat at the kitchen table of their home.

"Mommy has a tummyache." Kimberly took his hand and twirled him around to face his chair. "You sit in your own chair for now, okay? Let Marisol make your lunch."

Evan did as he was told, but was clearly unhappy about it. He continued to take quick, concerned looks in his mother's direction. Daniel was too involved in the cartoon on the television to notice anything.

Kimberly had come home with Michael and the boys yesterday. She tried several times to talk to Michael, but he would only look at her with disgust before walking away. He'd sent Marisol to tell her all her things had been moved to the guest bedroom on the other end of the house from him and the children.

Kimberly had thought she would never go to bed afraid after she married Michael. The promises he made to her, the love he showed her all convinced her that going to bed afraid was over. But last night, she had felt more afraid than ever in her life. Every little noise shook her awake. Even though she had locked the door to her new bedroom, she knew Michael could come in any time he wanted. He'd said he wanted her to suffer and here she was just lying in wait for his torment to be unleashed. But until she figured out how to get her kids, what choice did she have?

Kimberly couldn't hear her sons call her name as she stood up and left the kitchen. She was in a daze, so tired and uncertain. But maybe if she talked to Michael one more time, he would listen. She couldn't afford to give up.

She passed through the dining room and the living room and into the foyer, but before taking the stairs to find Michael, she was halted by the sound of a slow clap and then another. When she turned around, her heart skipped a beat at the sight of Janet Chase standing just in front of the door.

Janet clapped one last time. "I have to applaud your performance, Kimberly. For more than seven years you have only made me suspect you were a worthless piece of trash."

Kimberly didn't have the energy for a fight, but it didn't appear to matter to Janet.

"You've been lucky," Janet said. "Your pimp, your tape, and your murder have all vanished into thin air."

"What do you mean?" Kimberly asked, curious since Michael hadn't given her any update.

"My family has done what was necessary to protect its name. The name you so thoughtlessly tried to destroy."

"If you think I'm going to try and explain myself to you, Janet, you're wasting your time."

"You couldn't if you tried." Janet slowly placed her purse on the antique Roman table. "Because I wanted you to know that even though it is gone, it's never going to be forgotten."

"I'm still here, bitch." Kimberly stood her ground as Janet took a couple of steps toward her.

"A fact I will have to stomach." Why Michael allowed this woman back into this home was beyond Janet. She was livid that he would let her go anywhere near the boys. He had to hate her, so why would he do it? She could only imagine it was part of his plan.

"But you won't be here for long. You see, whatever it is Michael has planned for you is going to take time. That's why he's allowed you to come back."

"You don't know what happens between me and Michael."

"I do now," Janet said bluntly. "I know he's canceled all your credit cards, moved all the bank accounts so you can't find them. If you check your key chain, I'll bet you there isn't even a car key on it anymore."

"Get out of my house!"

"No." Janet smiled. "Nothing is yours anymore. Not this house. Not my son and not my grandchildren. You can call around all you want. With Carter's help, Michael has made it clear to all the divorce lawyers in L.A. that it would be disastrous for them to take your case."

"You know my past now, Janet. You should know that I'm a survivor."

"But you'll never survive this," Janet said. "What person do you know has gone against this family and succeeded? Steven de-

stroyed that tape, but everything else is still in a very safe place. And that witness? She'll stay on our payroll and help us if we ever need her. Call it all insurance in case you lose your mind and think you can fight us for those boys or even one red cent."

"Exposing me hurts your family too." Kimberly's voice was trembling. She couldn't cover it up.

"Don't be mistaken, dear. What was done was to take back control of the situation. Now that we have it, we can manipulate it how we see fit." Janet's mouth twisted into a threatening grin. "It's all I'll be thinking about. You see, Kimberly, you could never understand the advantages of good breeding. One of them is being able to use even what could hurt you in your favor."

"So you're the winner, Janet." Kimberly just wanted to get away from her so she could break down. "Congratulations."

"Oh, honey, I was always the winner. I told you this time would come. You were warned with eyes wide open and you still fell into the trap of your true nature."

"I'm not trapped," Kimberly stressed as she folded her arms across her chest. "And I'm not done."

Janet took an amused note of this defiant gesture. "It's adorable how you try to hold on to hope. I guess that's the street in you, always thinking there's a way out of that gutter, but never getting that there is no way out because the gutter is where you belong."

Janet took her sweet time leaving and when she was finally gone, Kimberly fell to her knees. This was going to be her punishment. She wouldn't leave because she couldn't. There was nowhere to go, no one to go to, and she wouldn't leave the boys either way. Her prison was to never escape this family and be at the mercy of a man who believed she had ruined his life.

But Janet was right. Kimberly's hope was the street in her. The street that helped her survive was going to be the street that helped her take this family down for good. America's black royal family was about to lose its crown in the most disastrous way she could imagine.

NO MORE GOOD

ANGELA WINTERS

ABOUT THIS GUIDE

The questions and discussion topics that follow are
intended to enhance your group's reading of
this book.

DISCUSSION QUESTIONS

1. What does Carter's self-destructive behavior in the six months after Avery left say about him? Do you believe his car accident was just an accident?

2. Is it fair to blame Anthony for concocting the lie about the baby or should Avery take the blame? And after finding out the truth, should Carter have been so forgiving of Avery?

3. Was Carter right when he accused Avery of always playing the victim?

4. Do you think Leigh over-reacted to the incident with Nick? Why or why not?

5. Do you think Lyndon ever really cared about Leigh? Did she ever really care about him?

6. Do you feel that Leigh has changed forever and will no longer be the sweet girl she's always been? Is that a good thing or not?

7. Do you think that Michael was right to isolate Kimberly from his family after Janet's "accident"?

8. Who is to blame for David's death? Kimberly for not telling Michael or Michael for not getting rid of him the first time he had a chance?

9. Was it fair for Michael to forgive Kimberly for killing David but not for sleeping with him? Michael's pain seemed to be worse because of who it was. Why?

10. Do you think Carter's final decision to go after Avery in a sneaky way is a good idea or proof that he'll never change? Should he just give up or keep trying?